orange

ICHIGO TAKANO presents

6

—future—

the sixth
volume

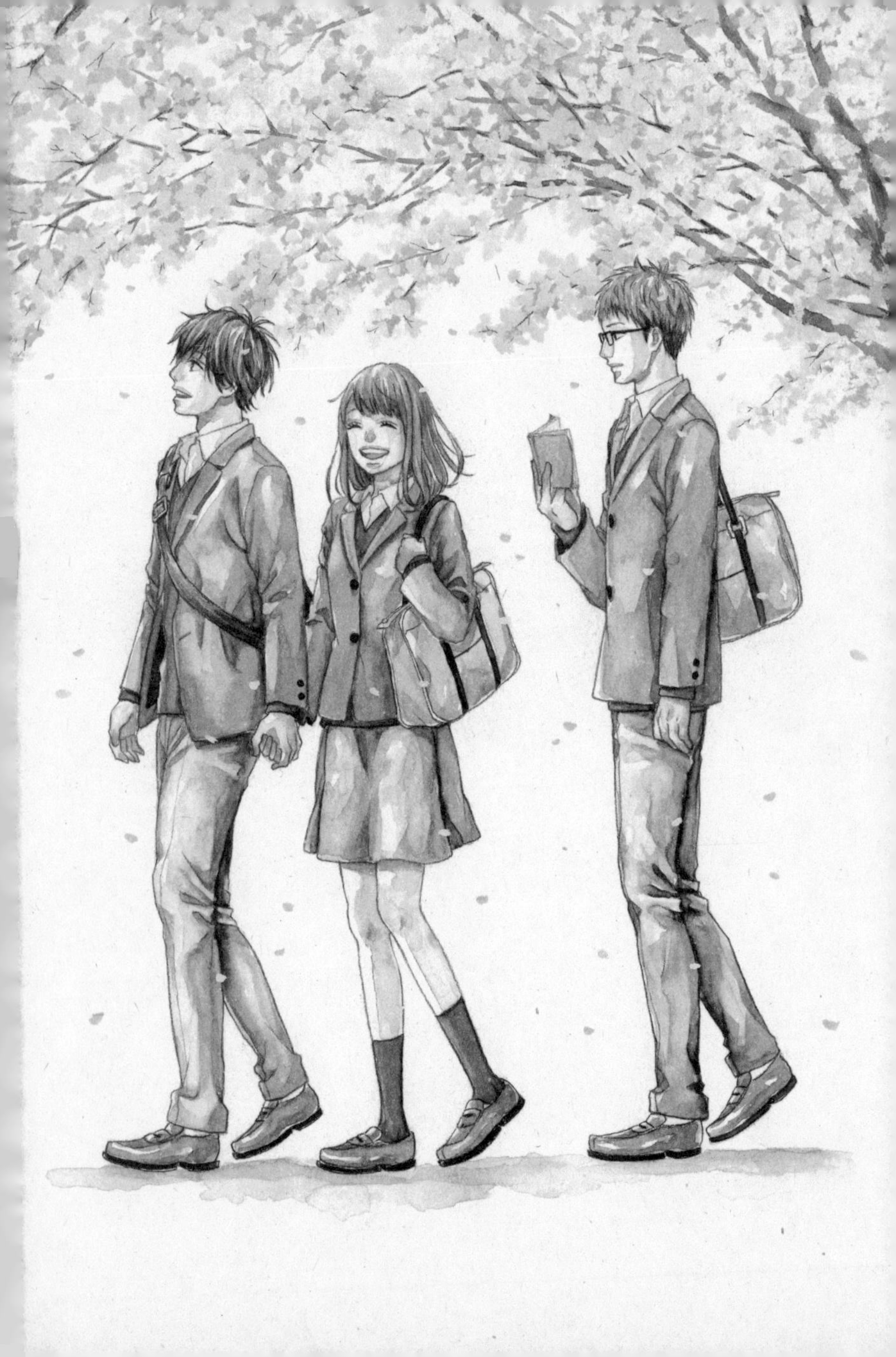

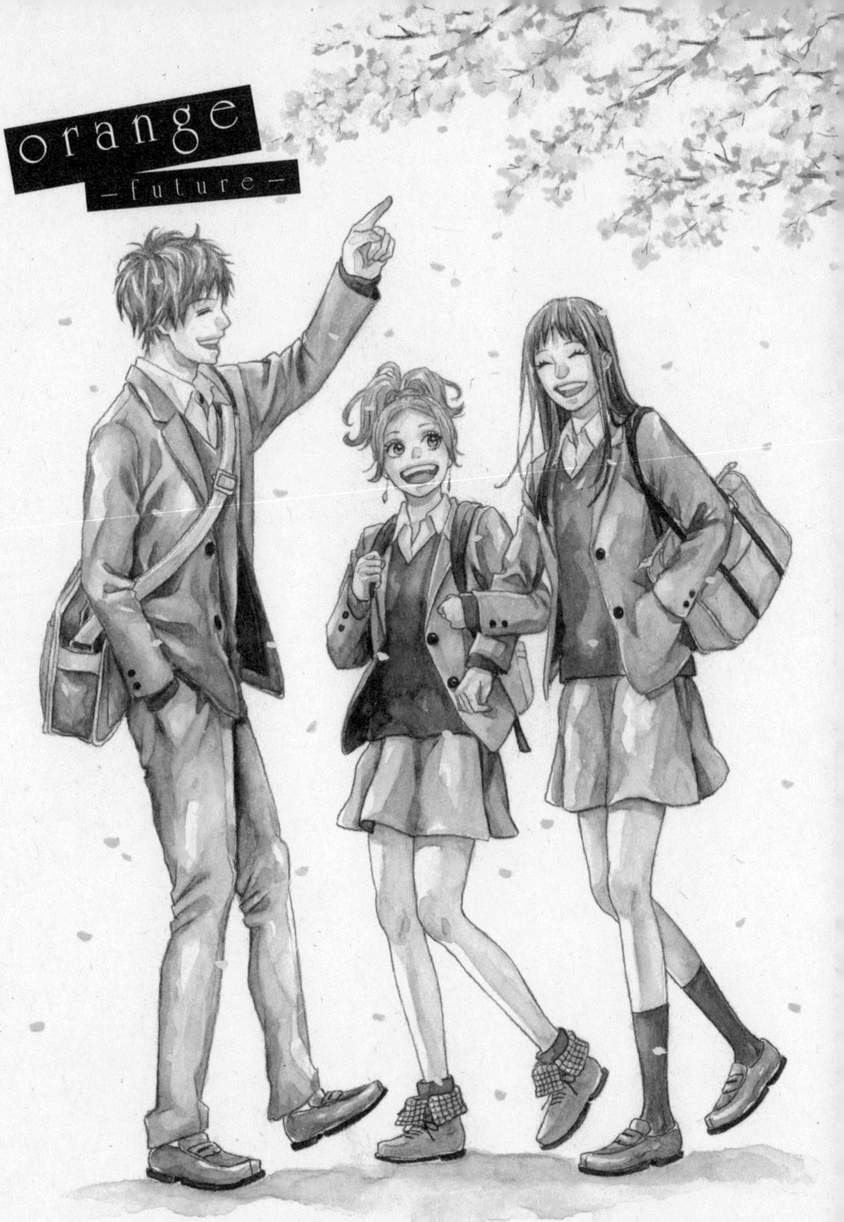
orange
—future—

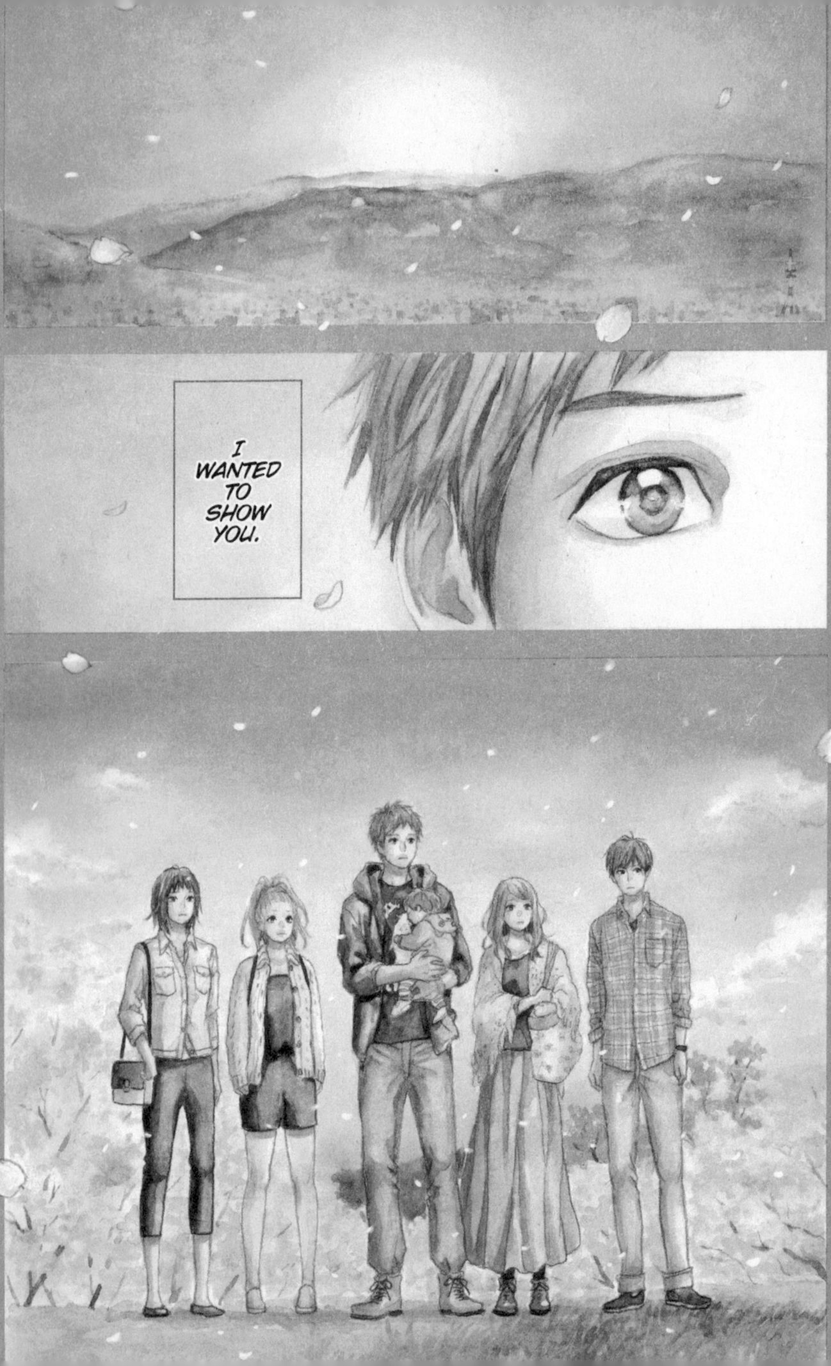
I WANTED TO SHOW YOU.

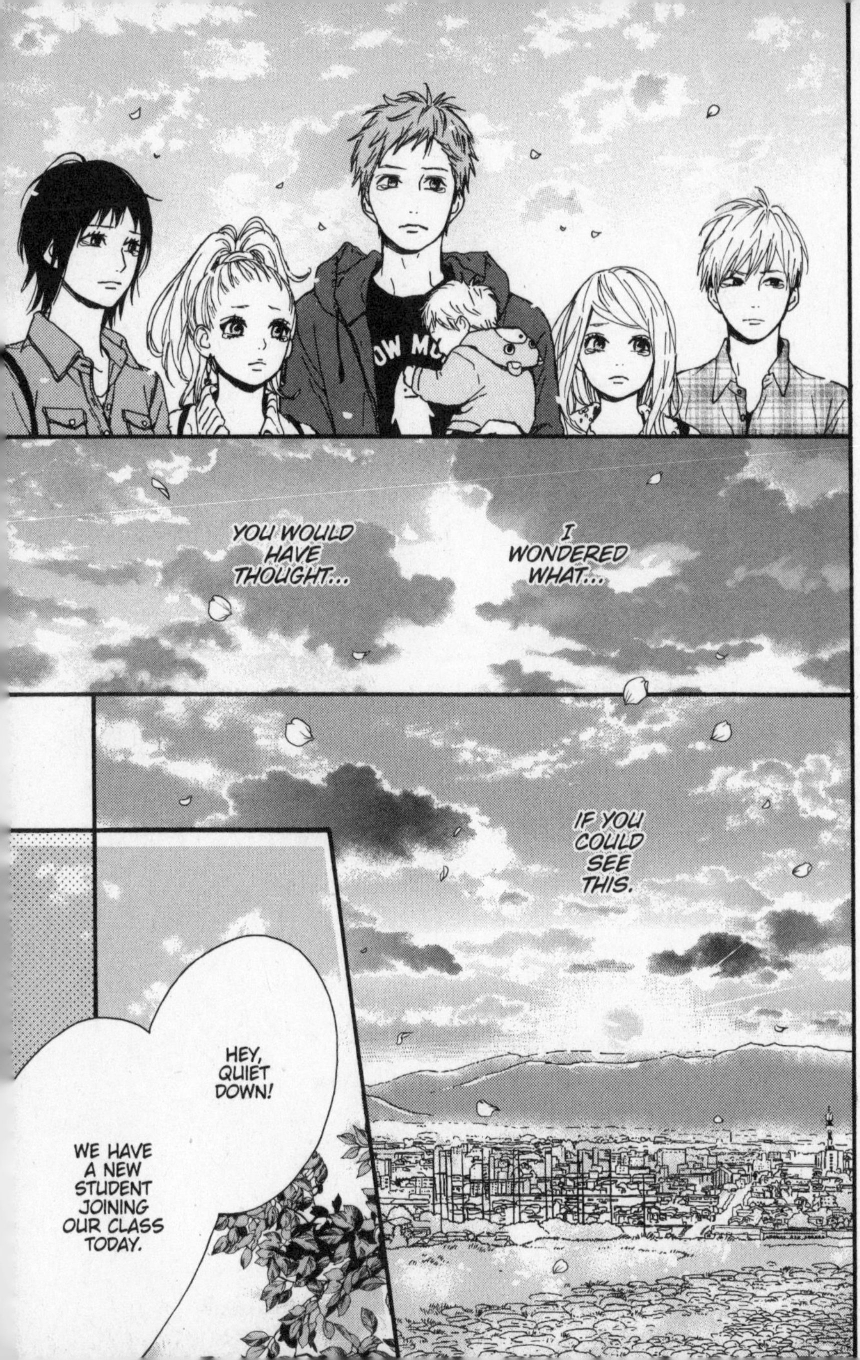

YOU WOULD HAVE THOUGHT...
I WONDERED WHAT...
IF YOU COULD SEE THIS.
HEY, QUIET DOWN!
WE HAVE A NEW STUDENT JOINING OUR CLASS TODAY.

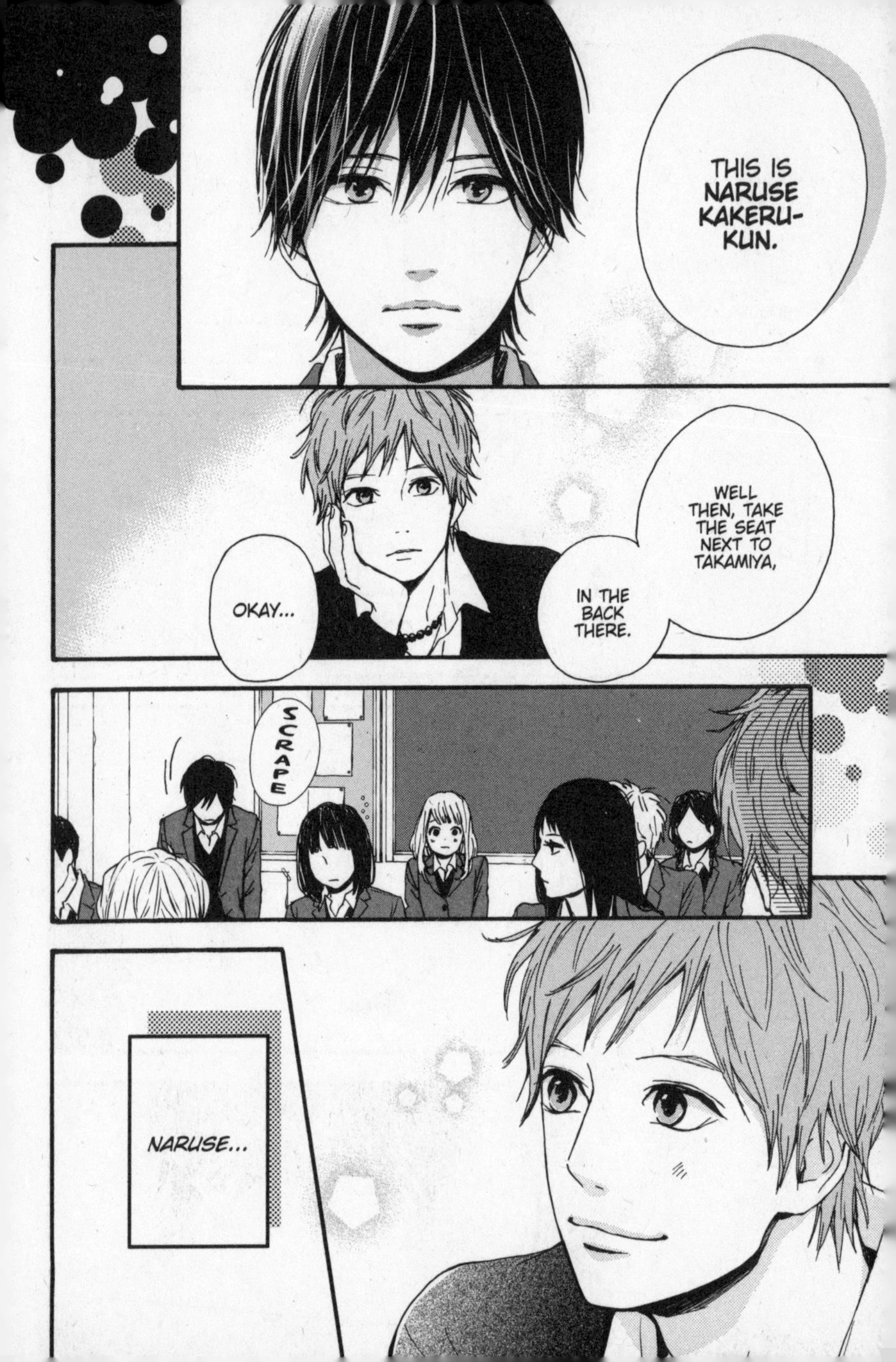
THIS IS NARUSE KAKERU-KUN.
WELL THEN, TAKE THE SEAT NEXT TO TAKAMIYA,
IN THE BACK THERE.
OKAY...
SCRAPE
NARUSE...

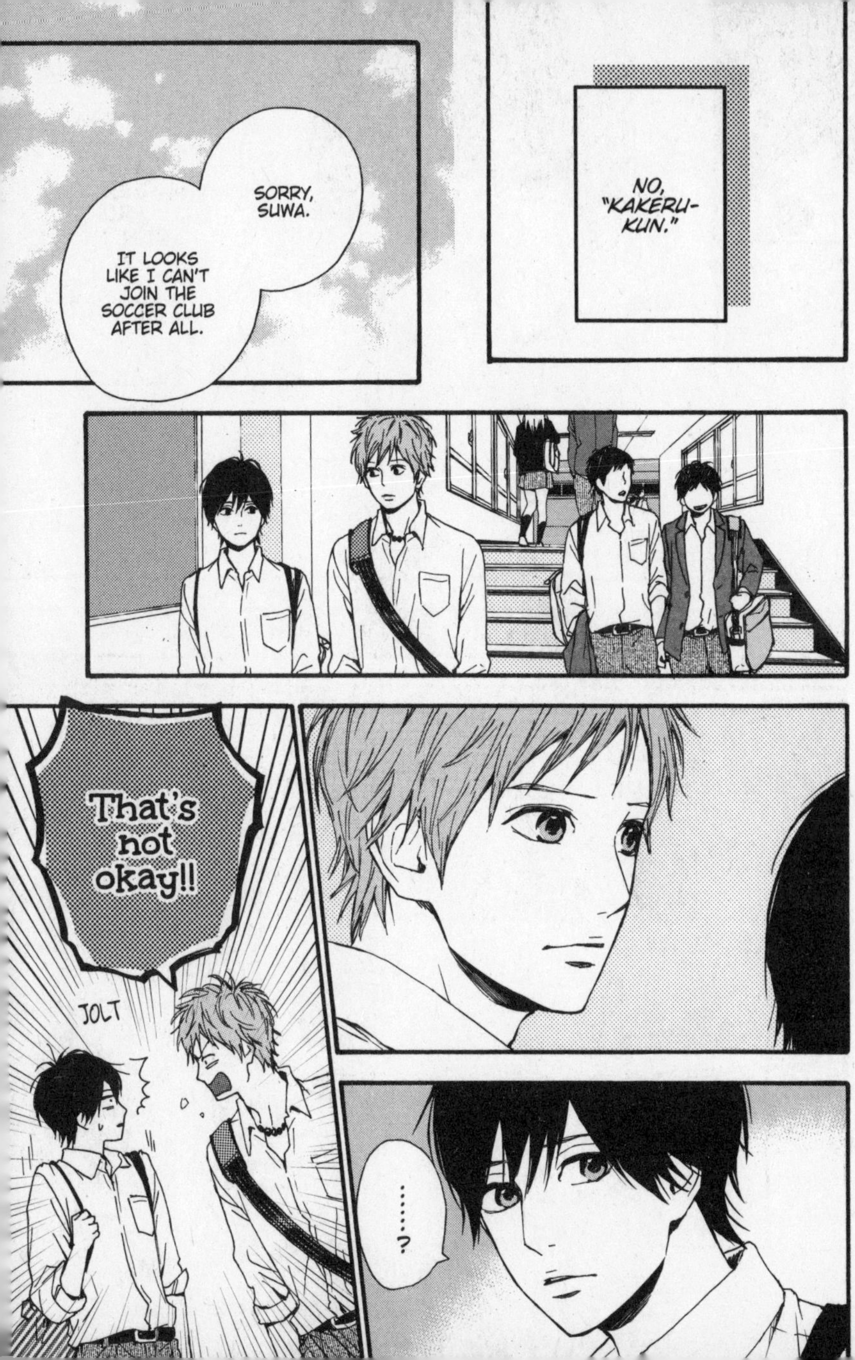
NO, "KAKERU-KUN."
SORRY, SUWA.
IT LOOKS LIKE I CAN'T JOIN THE SOCCER CLUB AFTER ALL.
That's not okay!!
JOLT
......?

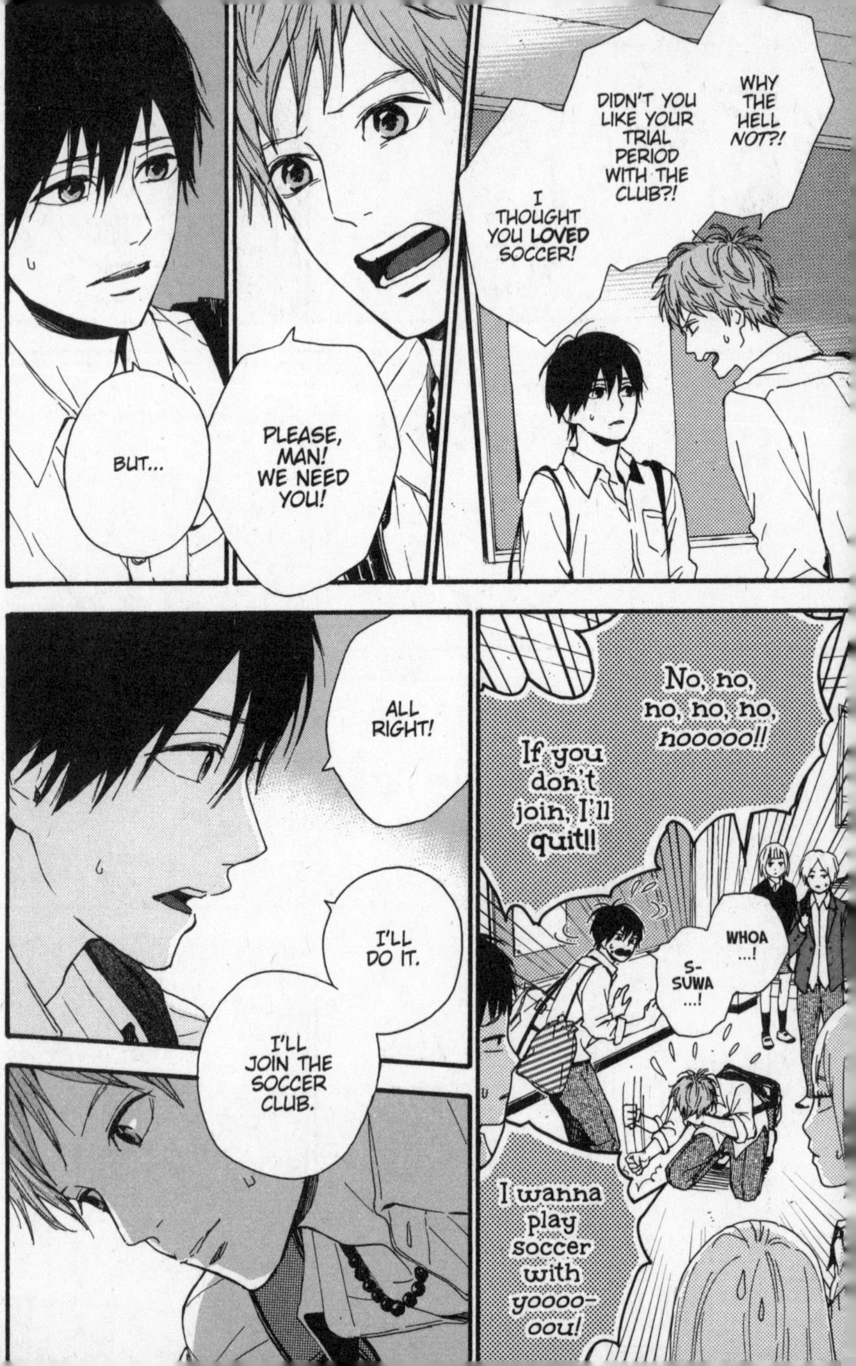
WHY THE HELL NOT?!
DIDN'T YOU LIKE YOUR TRIAL PERIOD WITH THE CLUB?!
I THOUGHT YOU LOVED SOCCER!
PLEASE, MAN! WE NEED YOU!
BUT...
No, no, no, no, no, nooooo!!
If you don't join, I'll quit!!
WHOA ...!
S-SUWA ...!
I wanna play soccer with yoooo-oou!
ALL RIGHT!
I'LL DO IT.
I'LL JOIN THE SOCCER CLUB.

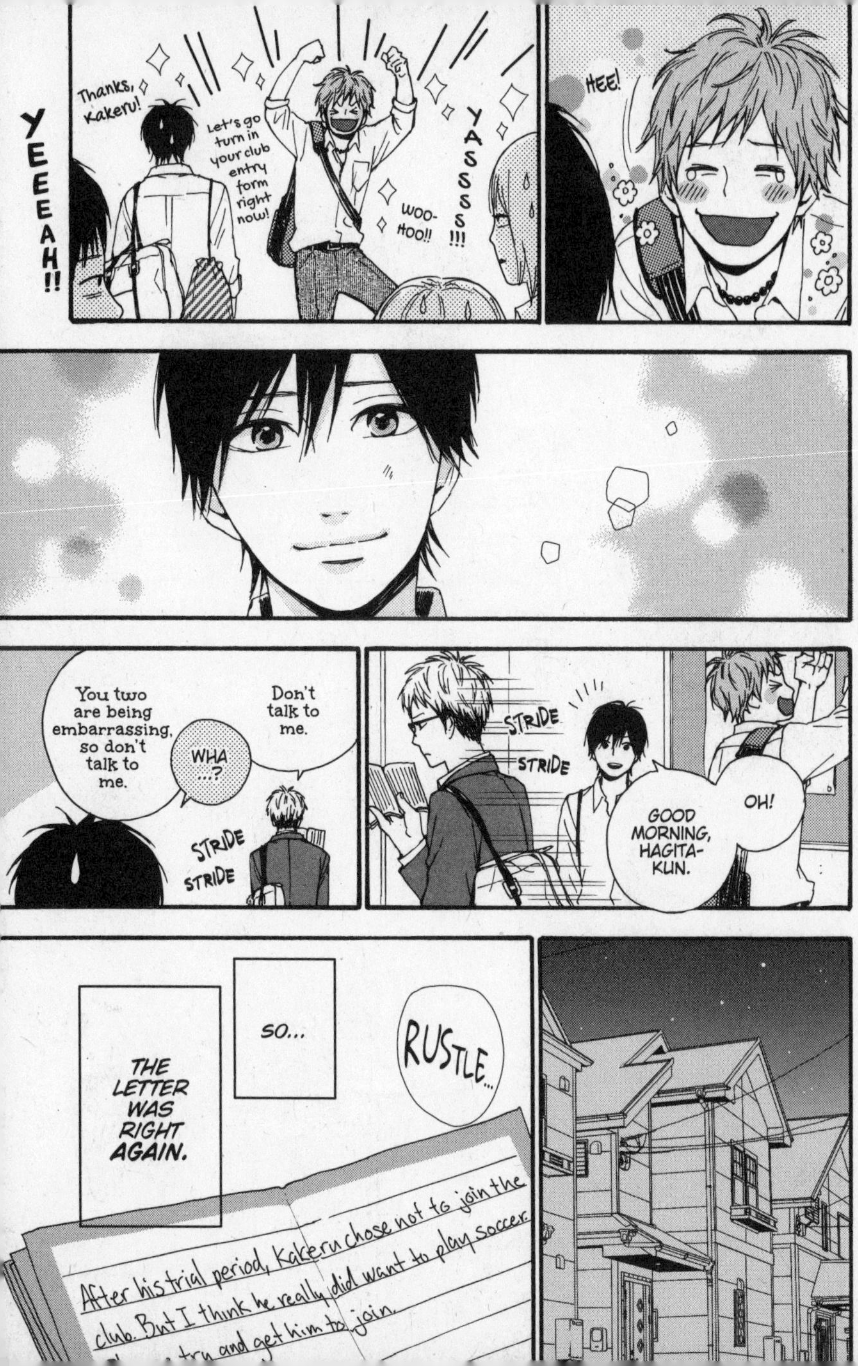
HEE!
YASSSS!!!
WOO-HOO!!
Let's go turn in your club entry form right now!
Thanks, Kakeru!
YEEEAH!!
OH!
GOOD MORNING, HAGITA-KUN.
STRIDE
STRIDE
Don't talk to me.
WHA ...?
You two are being embarrassing, so don't talk to me.
STRIDE
STRIDE
RUSTLE...
SO...
THE LETTER WAS RIGHT AGAIN.
After his trial period, Kakeru chose not to join the club. But I think he really did want to play soccer.
try and get him to join.

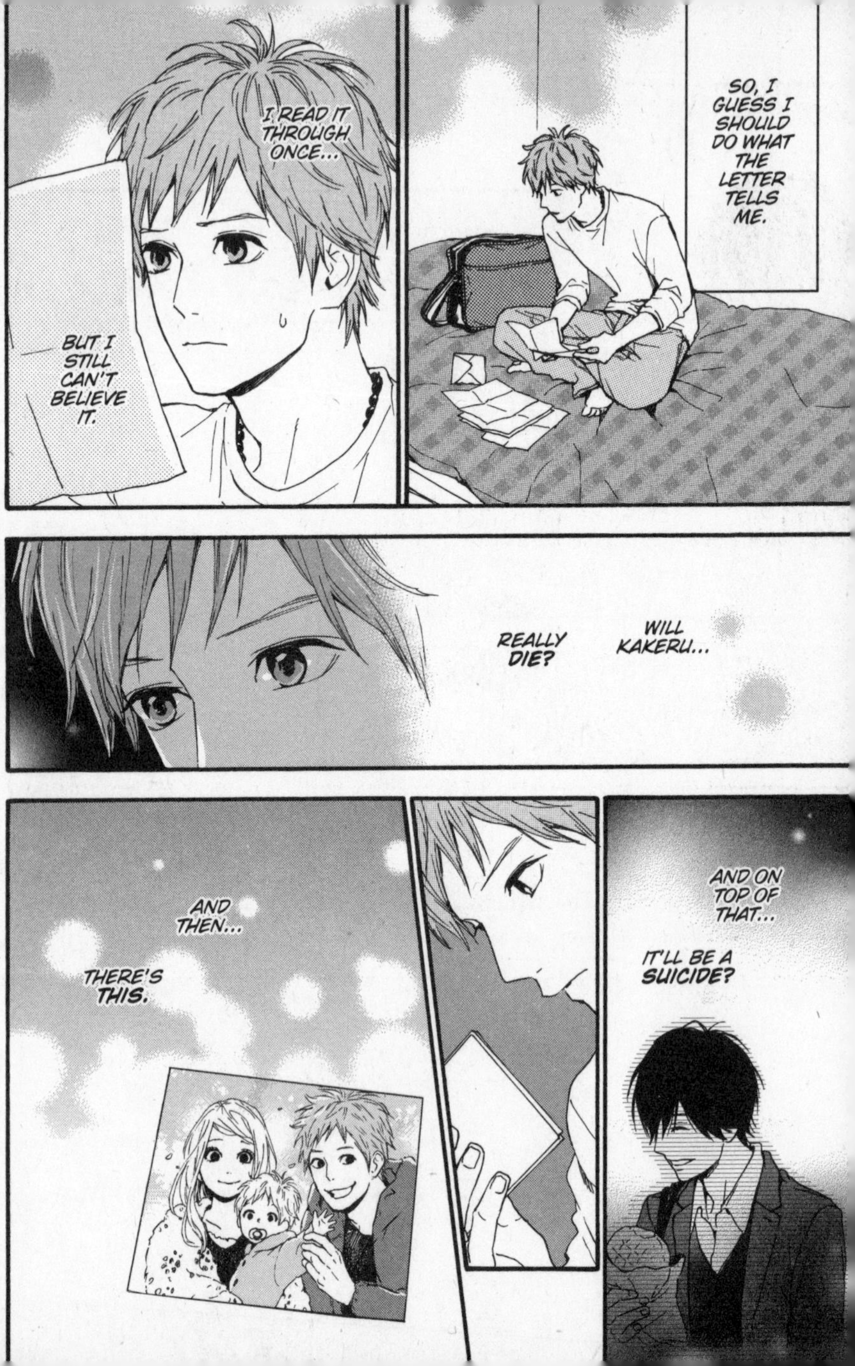
SO, I GUESS I SHOULD DO WHAT THE LETTER TELLS ME.
I READ IT THROUGH ONCE...
BUT I STILL CAN'T BELIEVE IT.
WILL KAKERU...
REALLY DIE?
AND ON TOP OF THAT...
IT'LL BE A SUICIDE?
AND THEN...
THERE'S THIS.

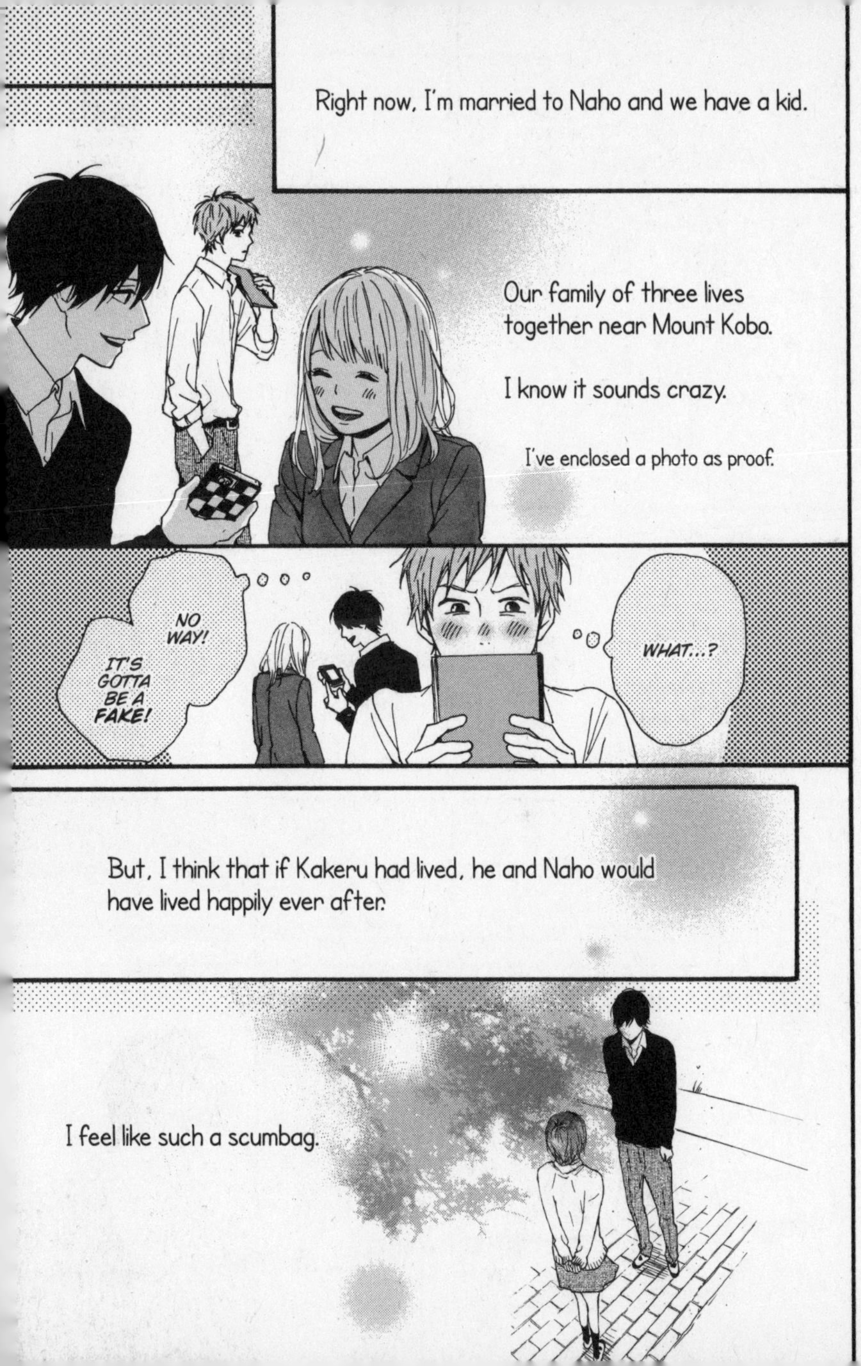
Right now, I'm married to Naho and we have a kid.
Our family of three lives together near Mount Kobo.
I know it sounds crazy.
I've enclosed a photo as proof.
WHAT...?
NO WAY!
IT'S GOTTA BE A FAKE!
But, I think that if Kakeru had lived, he and Naho would have lived happily ever after.
I feel like such a scumbag.

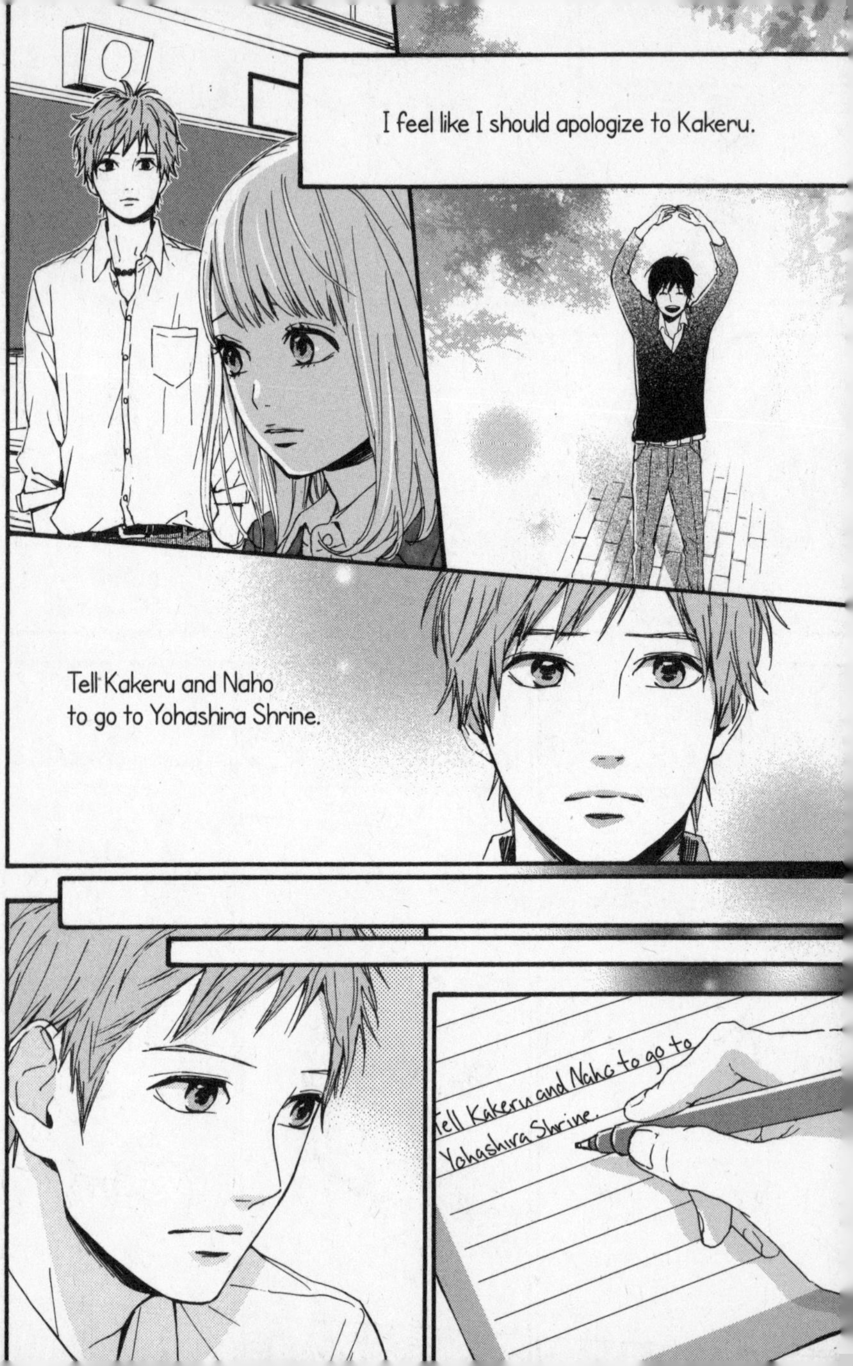
I feel like I should apologize to Kakeru.
Tell Kakeru and Naho to go to Yohashira Shrine.
Tell Kakeru and Naho to go to Yohashira Shrine.

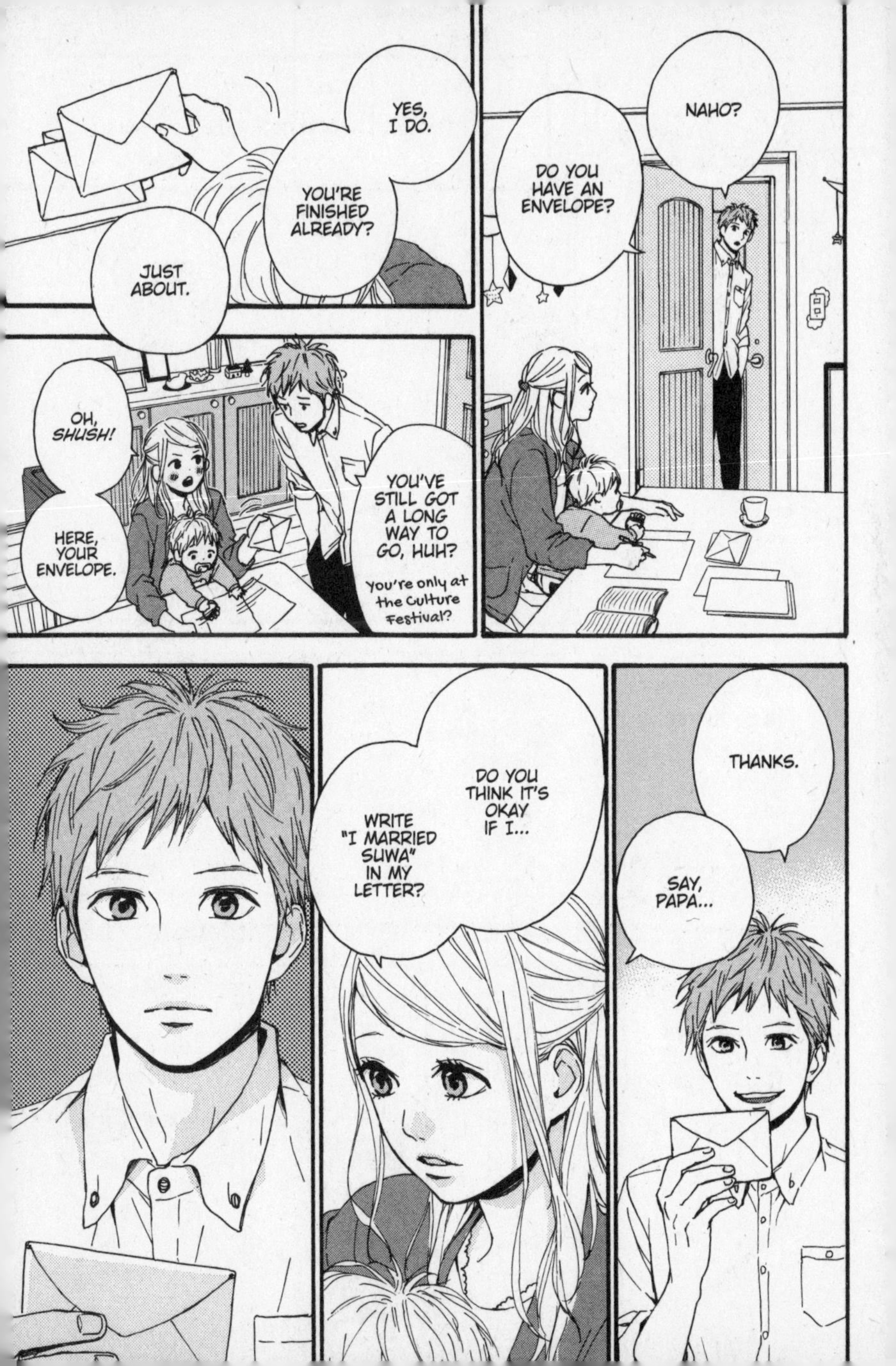
NAHO?
DO YOU HAVE AN ENVELOPE?
YES, I DO.
YOU'RE FINISHED ALREADY?
JUST ABOUT.
YOU'VE STILL GOT A LONG WAY TO GO, HUH?
You're only at the Culture Festival?
OH, SHUSH!
HERE, YOUR ENVELOPE.
THANKS.
SAY, PAPA...
DO YOU THINK IT'S OKAY IF I...
WRITE "I MARRIED SUWA" IN MY LETTER?

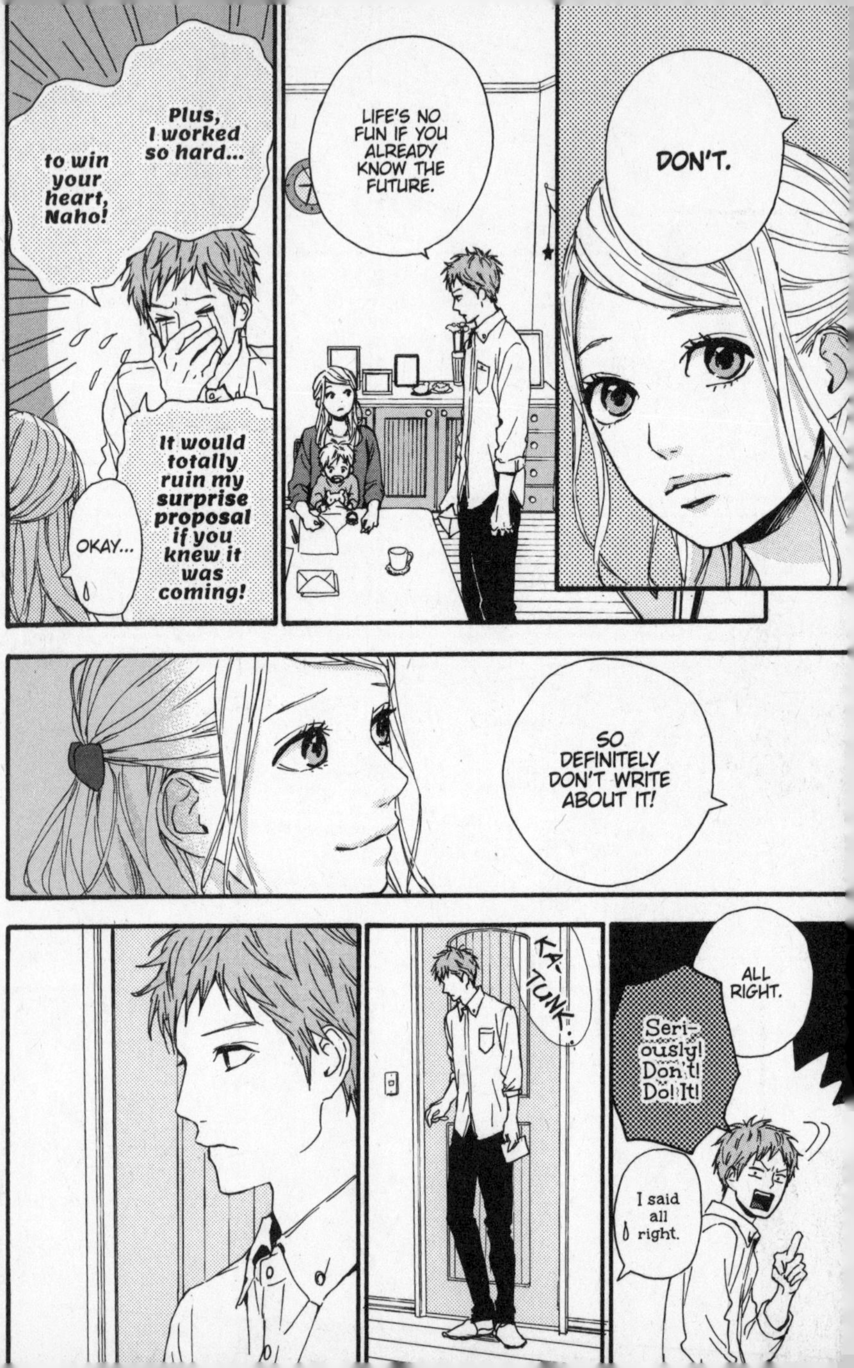
DON'T.
LIFE'S NO FUN IF YOU ALREADY KNOW THE FUTURE.
Plus, I worked so hard...
to win your heart, Naho!
It would totally ruin my surprise proposal if you knew it was coming!
OKAY...
SO DEFINITELY DON'T WRITE ABOUT IT!
ALL RIGHT.
Seri-ously! Don't! Do! It!
I said all right.
KA-TUNK...

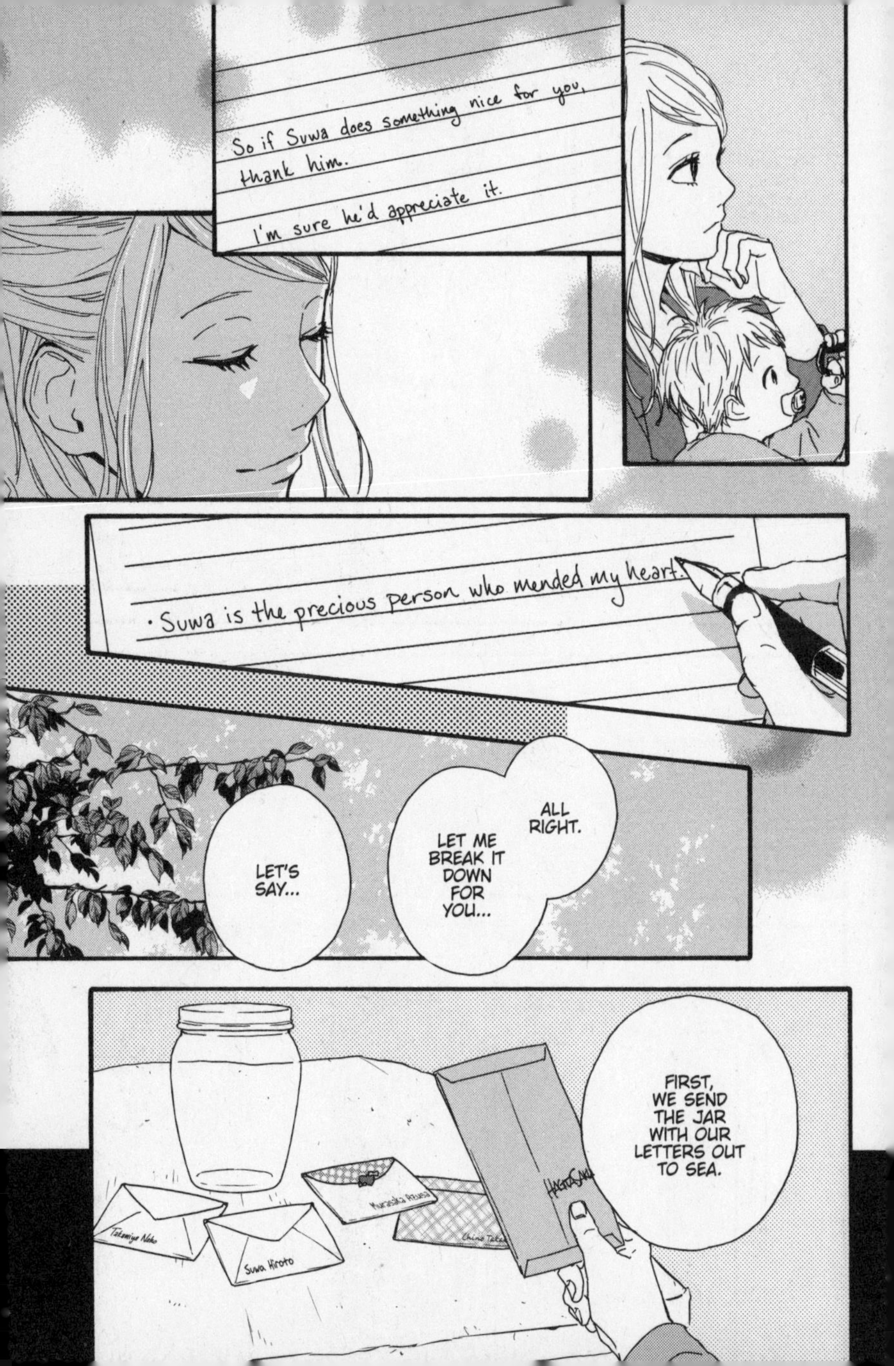

So if Suwa does something nice for you, thank him.
I'm sure he'd appreciate it.
· Suwa is the precious person who mended my heart.
ALL RIGHT.
LET ME BREAK IT DOWN FOR YOU...
LET'S SAY...
FIRST, WE SEND THE JAR WITH OUR LETTERS OUT TO SEA.
Takamiya Naho
Suwa Hiroto

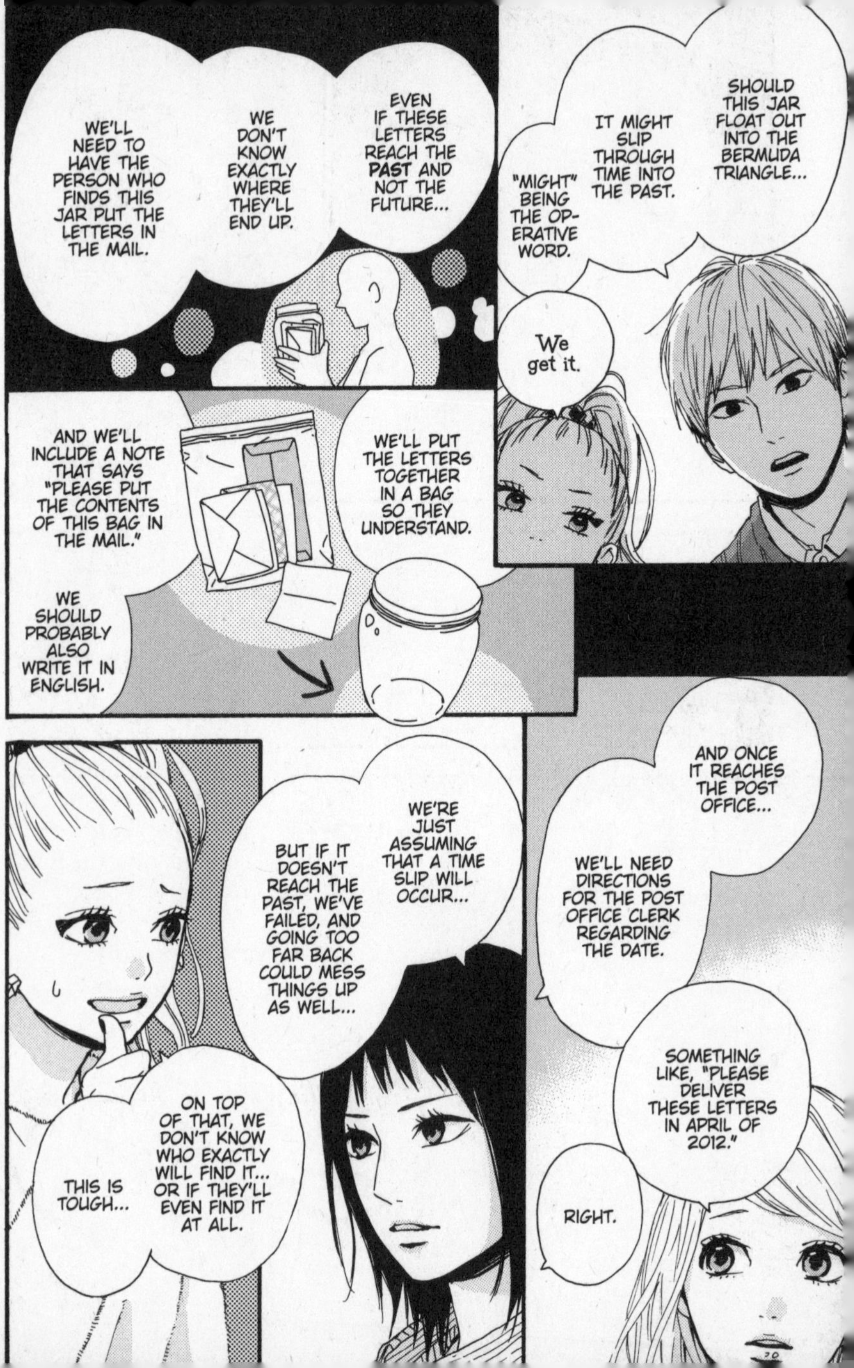
SHOULD THIS JAR FLOAT OUT INTO THE BERMUDA TRIANGLE...
IT MIGHT SLIP THROUGH TIME INTO THE PAST.
"MIGHT" BEING THE OPERATIVE WORD.
We get it.
EVEN IF THESE LETTERS REACH THE **PAST** AND NOT THE FUTURE...
WE DON'T KNOW EXACTLY WHERE THEY'LL END UP.
WE'LL NEED TO HAVE THE PERSON WHO FINDS THIS JAR PUT THE LETTERS IN THE MAIL.
WE'LL PUT THE LETTERS TOGETHER IN A BAG SO THEY UNDERSTAND.
AND WE'LL INCLUDE A NOTE THAT SAYS "PLEASE PUT THE CONTENTS OF THIS BAG IN THE MAIL."
WE SHOULD PROBABLY ALSO WRITE IT IN ENGLISH.
AND ONCE IT REACHES THE POST OFFICE...
WE'LL NEED DIRECTIONS FOR THE POST OFFICE CLERK REGARDING THE DATE.
SOMETHING LIKE, "PLEASE DELIVER THESE LETTERS IN APRIL OF 2012."
RIGHT.
WE'RE JUST ASSUMING THAT A TIME SLIP WILL OCCUR...
BUT IF IT DOESN'T REACH THE PAST, WE'VE FAILED, AND GOING TOO FAR BACK COULD MESS THINGS UP AS WELL...
ON TOP OF THAT, WE DON'T KNOW WHO EXACTLY WILL FIND IT... OR IF THEY'LL EVEN FIND IT AT ALL.
THIS IS TOUGH...

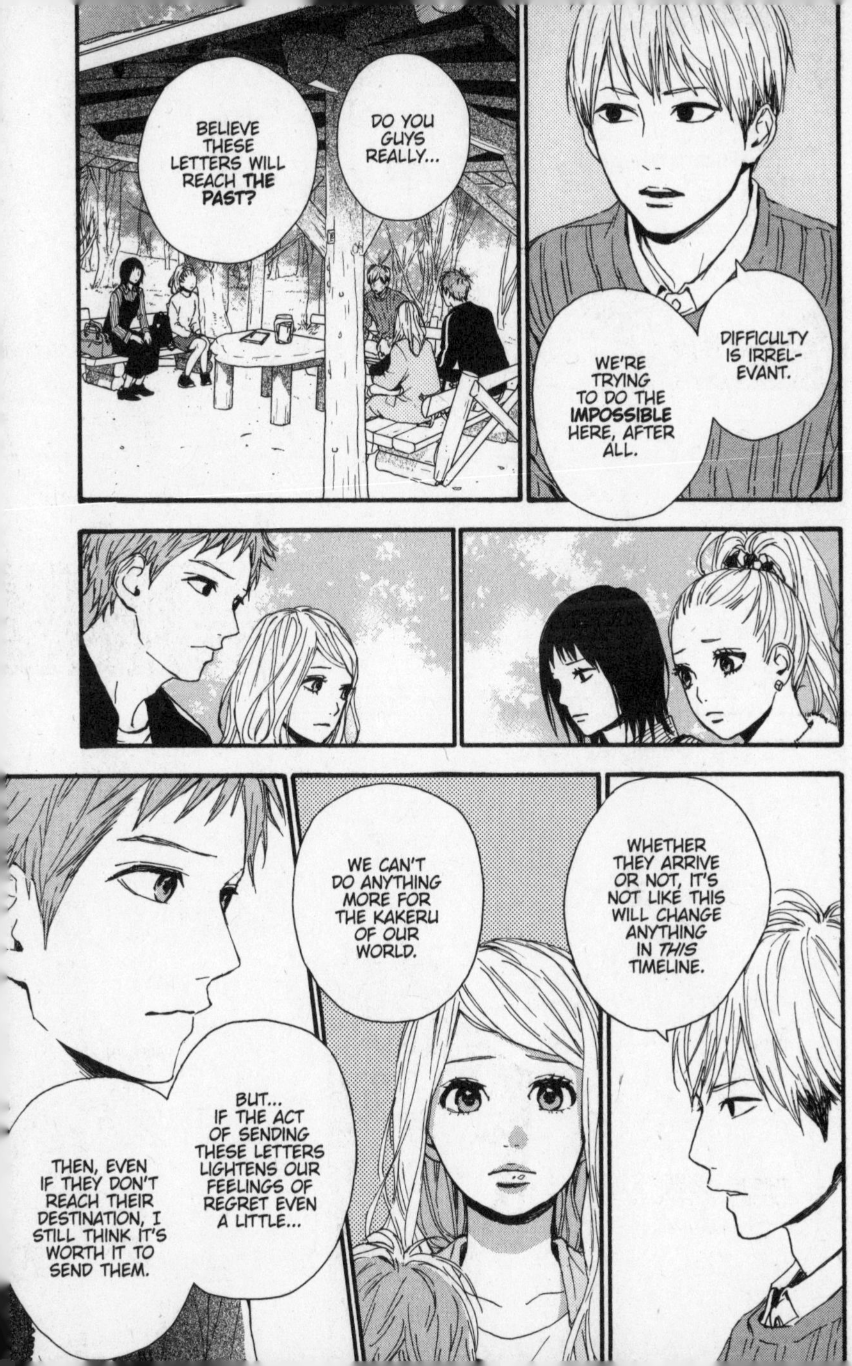
DIFFICULTY IS IRREL-EVANT.
WE'RE TRYING TO DO THE **IMPOSSIBLE** HERE, AFTER ALL.
DO YOU GUYS REALLY...
BELIEVE THESE LETTERS WILL REACH **THE PAST?**
WHETHER THEY ARRIVE OR NOT, IT'S NOT LIKE THIS WILL CHANGE ANYTHING IN *THIS* TIMELINE.
WE CAN'T DO ANYTHING MORE FOR THE KAKERU OF OUR WORLD.
BUT... IF THE ACT OF SENDING THESE LETTERS LIGHTENS OUR FEELINGS OF REGRET EVEN A LITTLE...
THEN, EVEN IF THEY DON'T REACH THEIR DESTINATION, I STILL THINK IT'S WORTH IT TO SEND THEM.

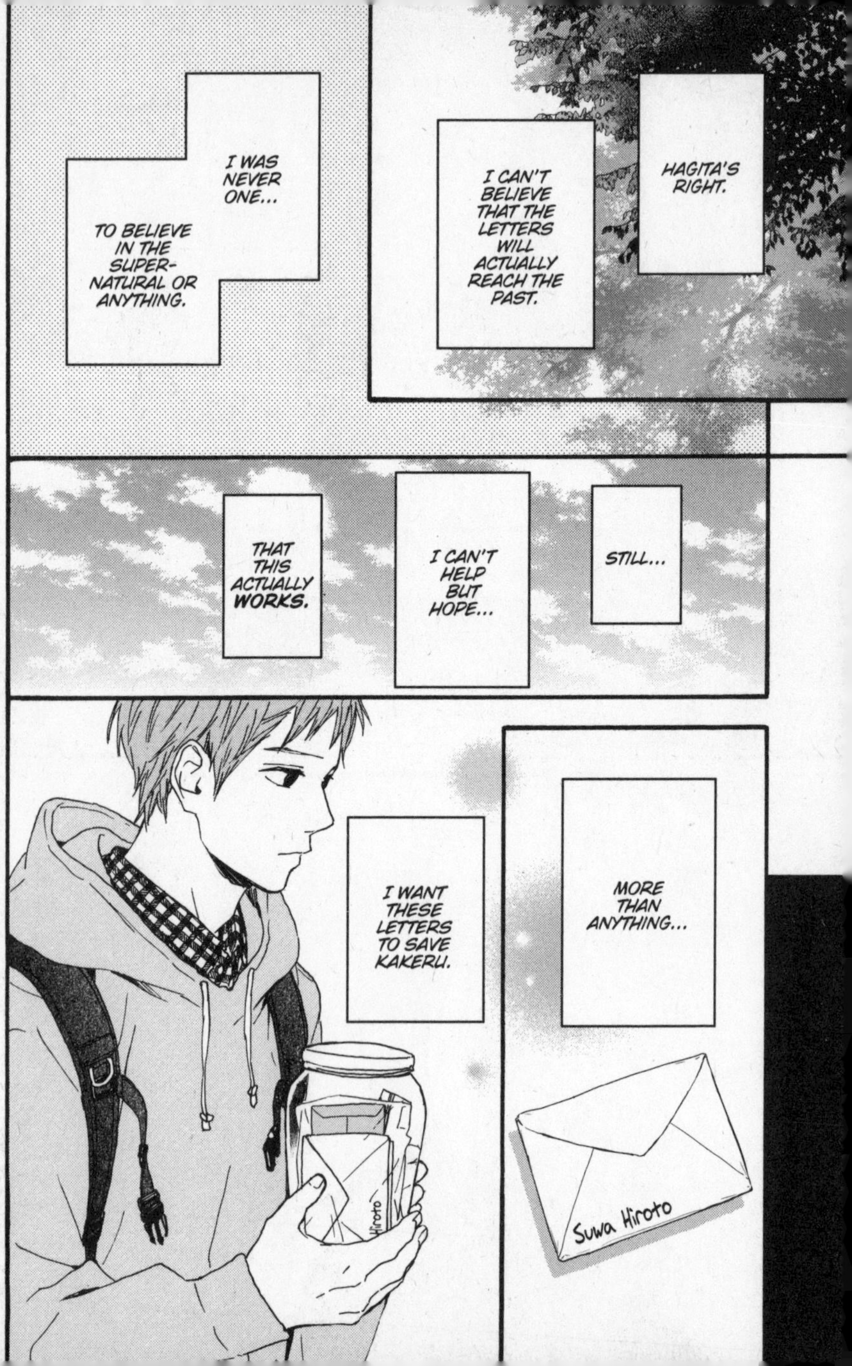
HAGITA'S RIGHT.
I CAN'T BELIEVE THAT THE LETTERS WILL ACTUALLY REACH THE PAST.
I WAS NEVER ONE...
TO BELIEVE IN THE SUPER-NATURAL OR ANYTHING.
STILL...
I CAN'T HELP BUT HOPE...
THAT THIS ACTUALLY **WORKS.**
MORE THAN ANYTHING...
I WANT THESE LETTERS TO SAVE KAKERU.
Suwa Hiroto
Hiroto

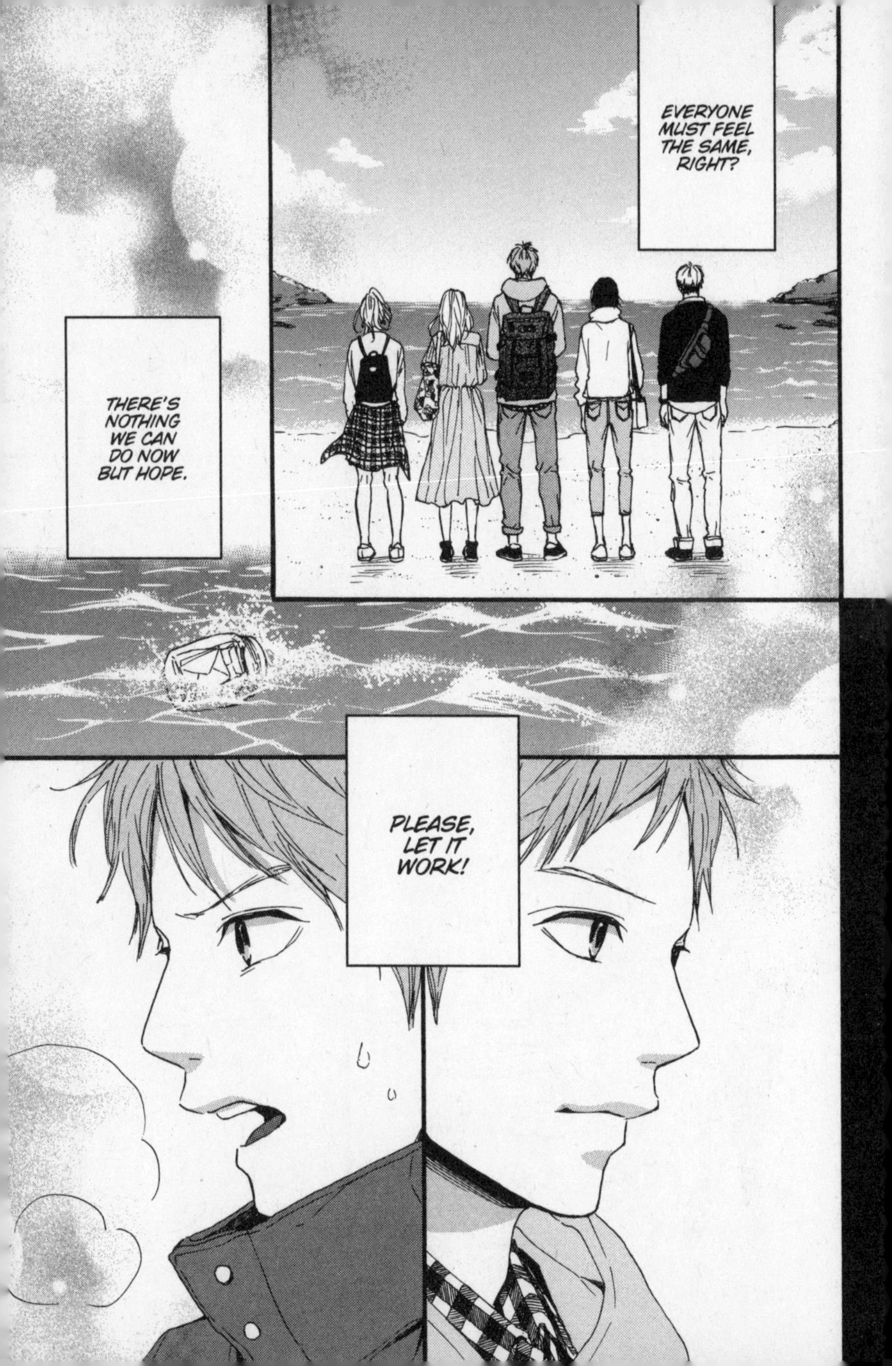
EVERYONE MUST FEEL THE SAME, RIGHT?
THERE'S NOTHING WE CAN DO NOW BUT HOPE.
PLEASE, LET IT WORK!

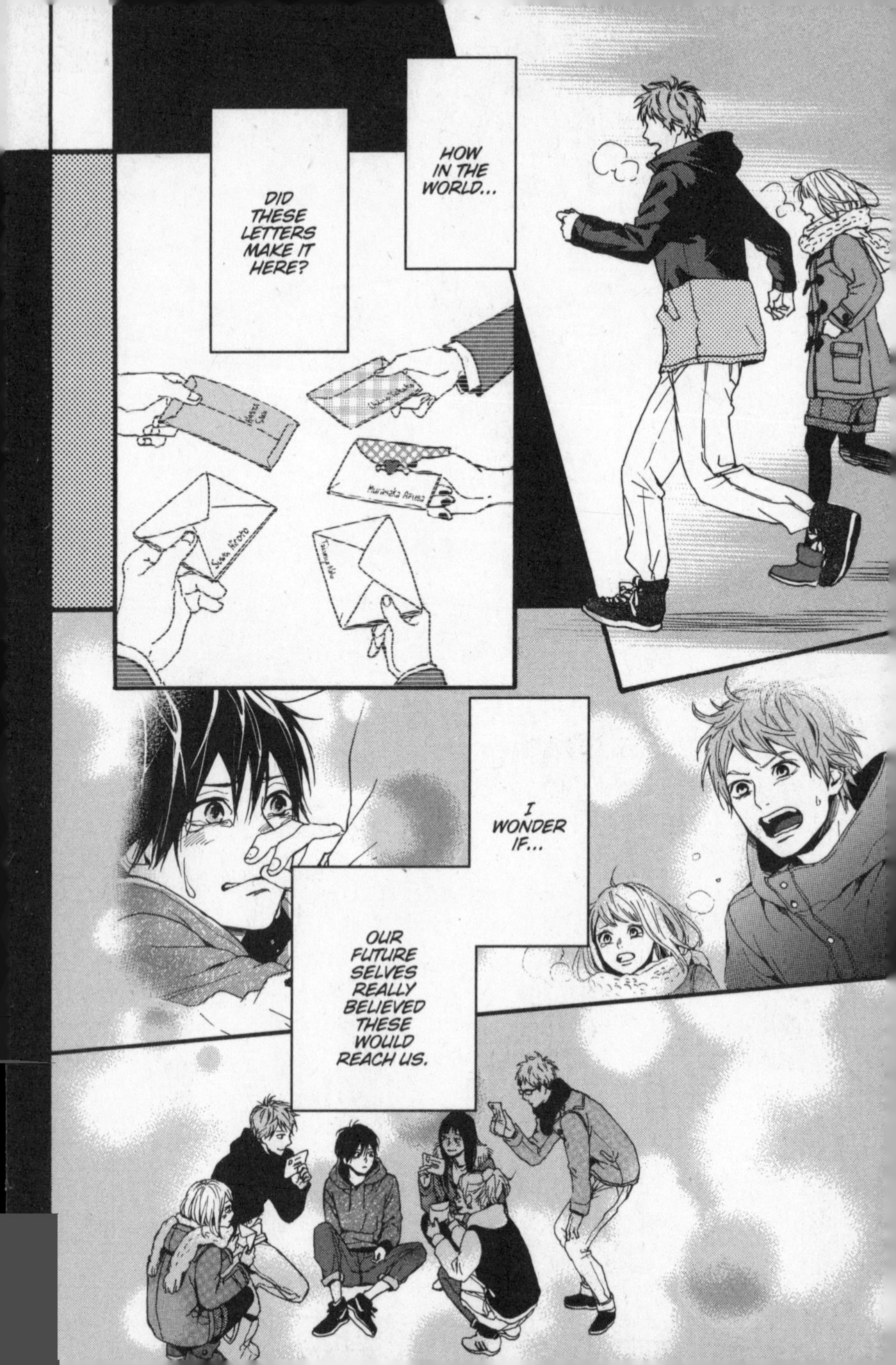
HOW IN THE WORLD...
DID THESE LETTERS MAKE IT HERE?
I WONDER IF...
OUR FUTURE SELVES REALLY BELIEVED THESE WOULD REACH US.

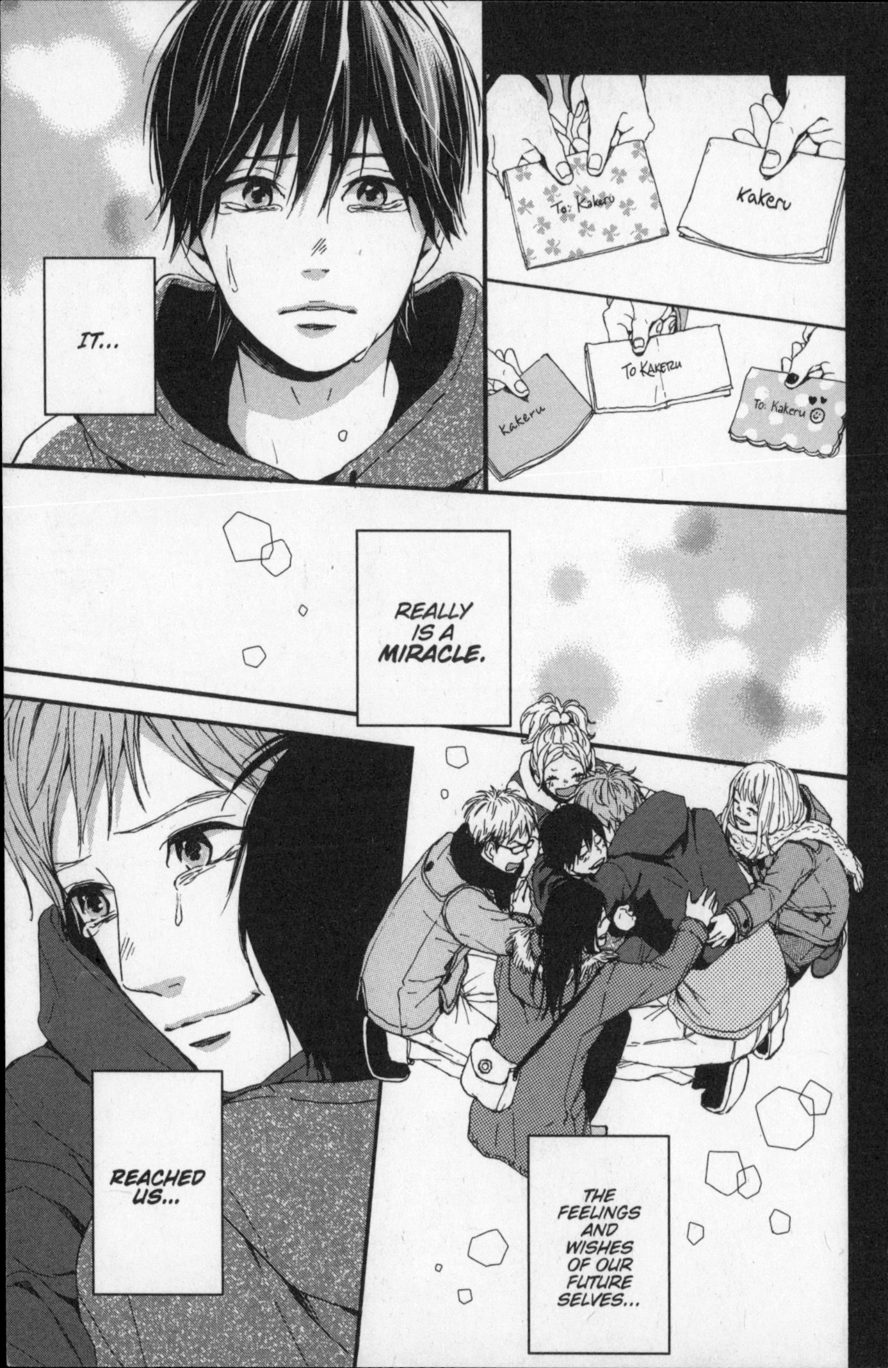
Kakeru
To: Kakeru
To: Kakeru
To Kakeru
Kakeru
IT...
REALLY IS A MIRACLE.
THE FEELINGS AND WISHES OF OUR FUTURE SELVES...
REACHED US...

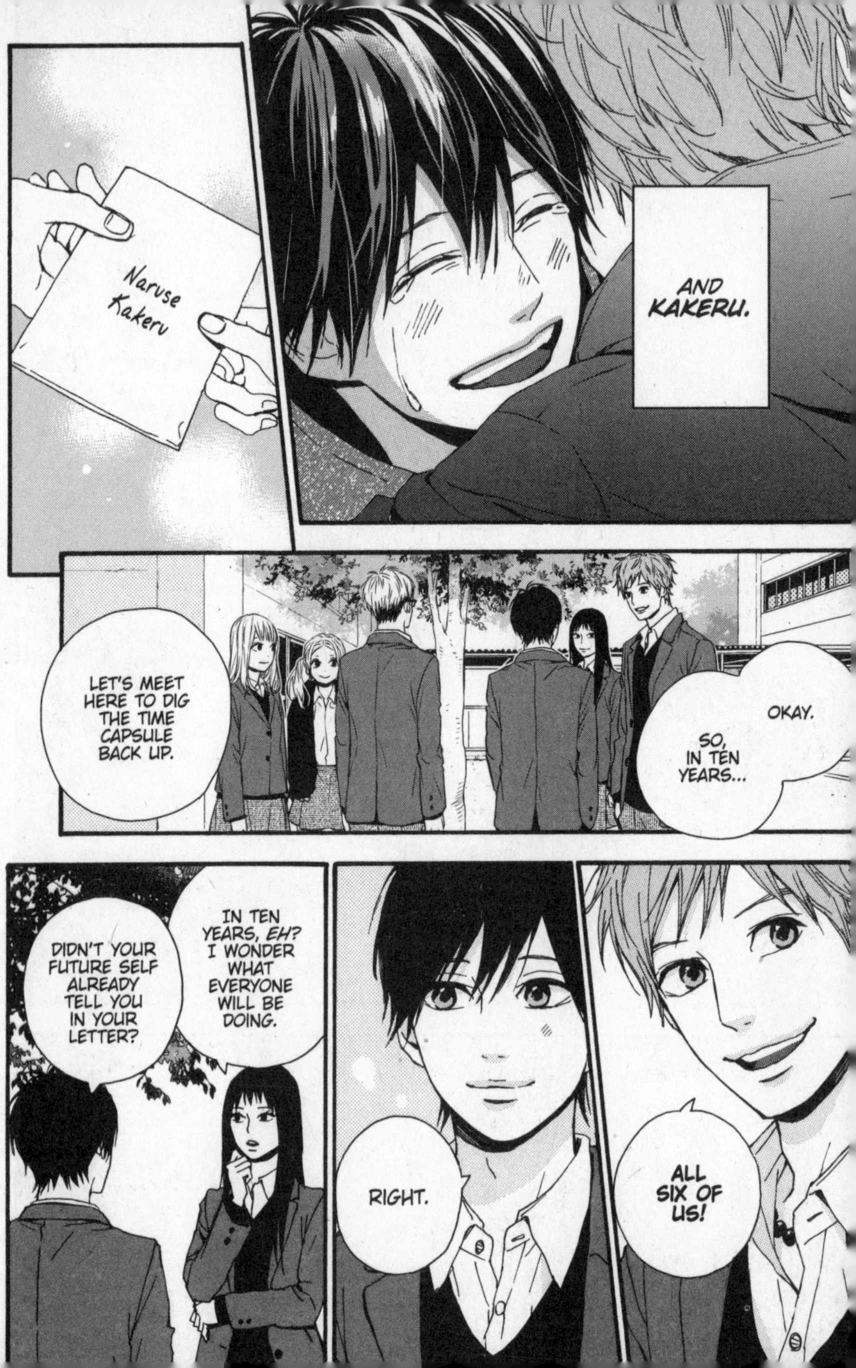
AND KAKERU.
Naruse Kakeru
OKAY.
SO, IN TEN YEARS...
LET'S MEET HERE TO DIG THE TIME CAPSULE BACK UP.
ALL SIX OF US!
RIGHT.
IN TEN YEARS, EH? I WONDER WHAT EVERYONE WILL BE DOING.
DIDN'T YOUR FUTURE SELF ALREADY TELL YOU IN YOUR LETTER?

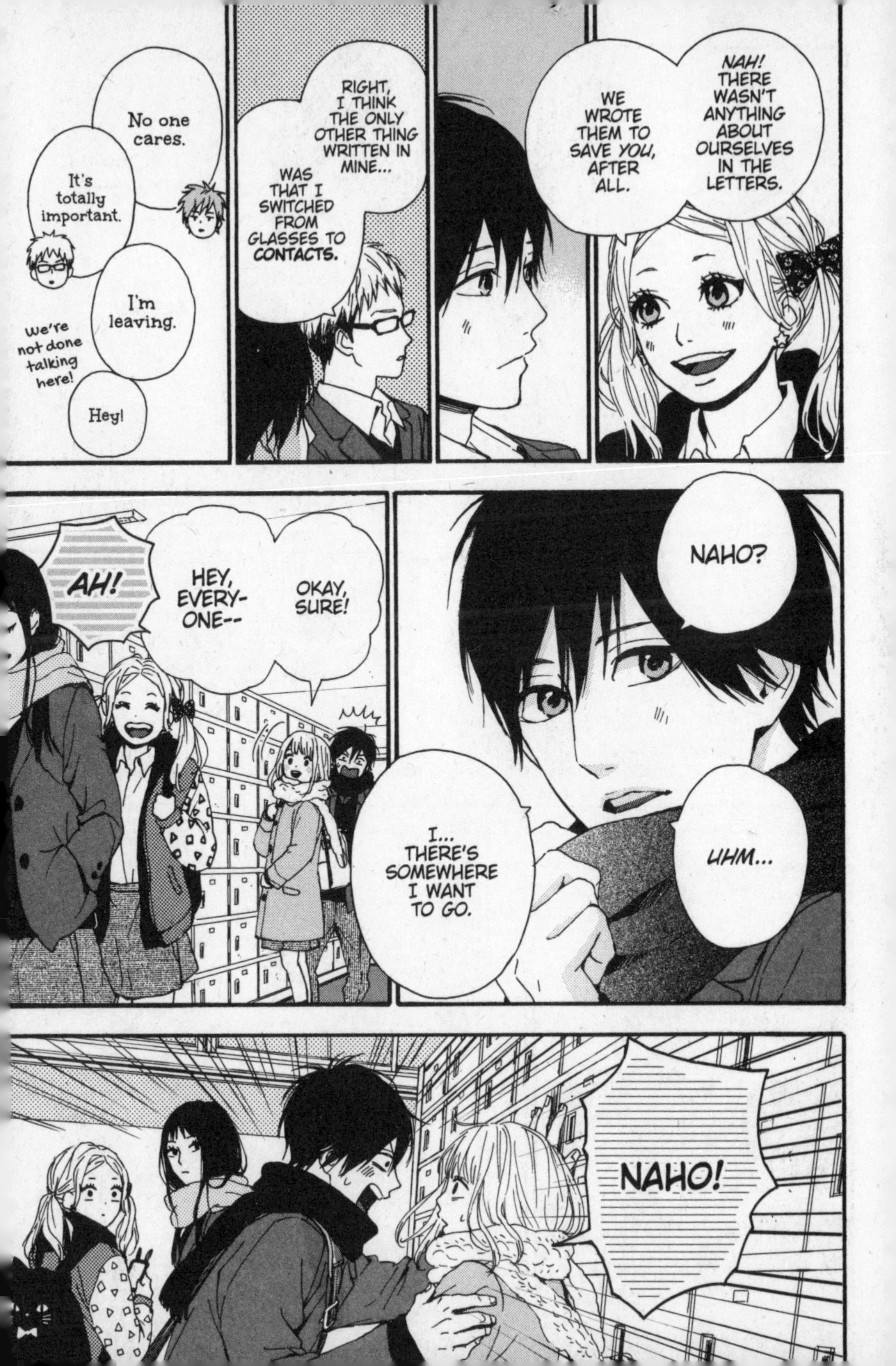
NAH! THERE WASN'T ANYTHING ABOUT OURSELVES IN THE LETTERS.
WE WROTE THEM TO SAVE YOU, AFTER ALL.
RIGHT, I THINK THE ONLY OTHER THING WRITTEN IN MINE...
WAS THAT I SWITCHED FROM GLASSES TO CONTACTS.
No one cares.
It's totally important.
I'm leaving.
We're not done talking here!
Hey!
NAHO?
UHM...
I... THERE'S SOMEWHERE I WANT TO GO.
OKAY, SURE!
HEY, EVERY-ONE--
AH!
NAHO!

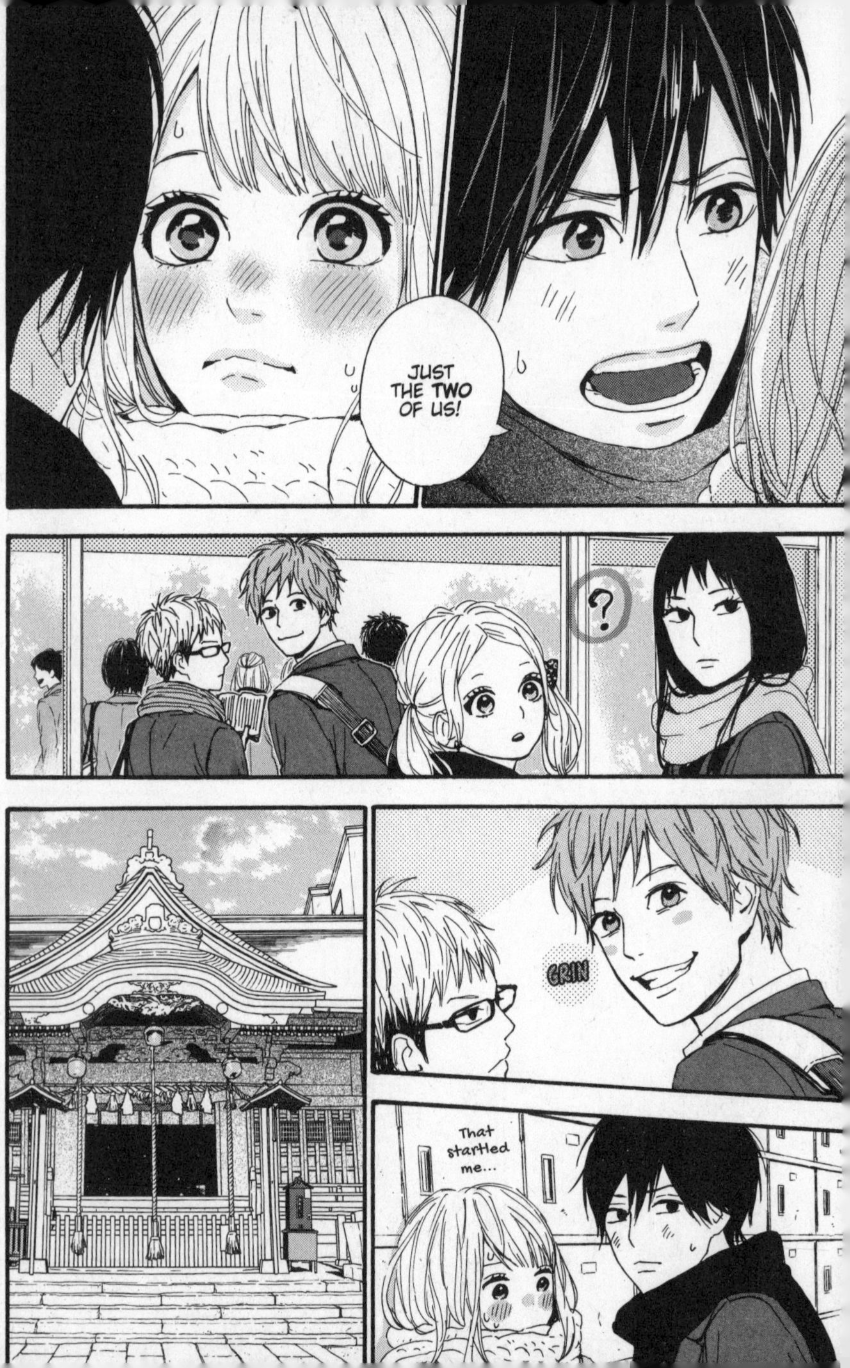
JUST THE TWO OF US!
?
GRIN
That startled me...

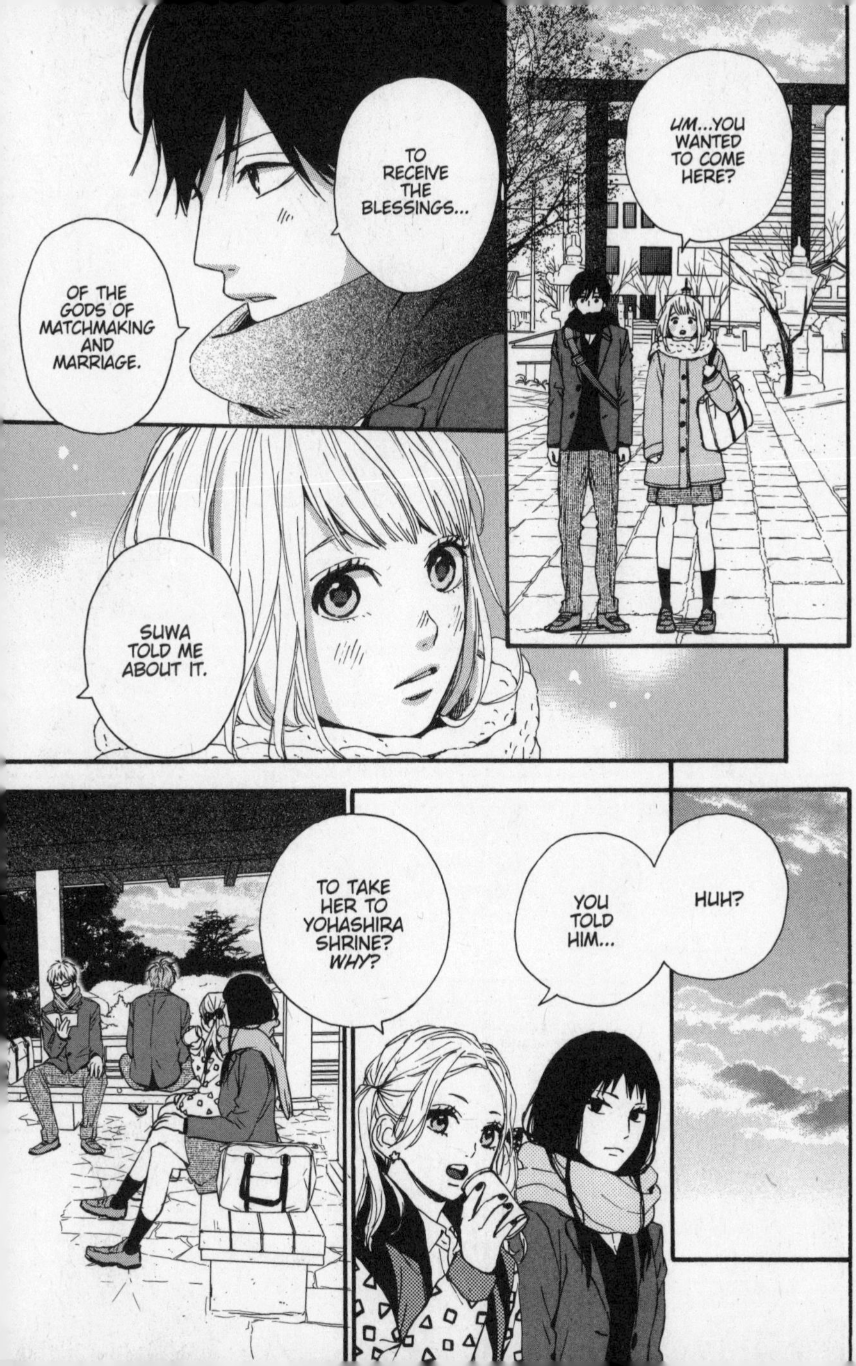
UM...YOU WANTED TO COME HERE?
TO RECEIVE THE BLESSINGS...
OF THE GODS OF MATCHMAKING AND MARRIAGE.
SUWA TOLD ME ABOUT IT.
HUH?
YOU TOLD HIM...
TO TAKE HER TO YOHASHIRA SHRINE? *WHY?*

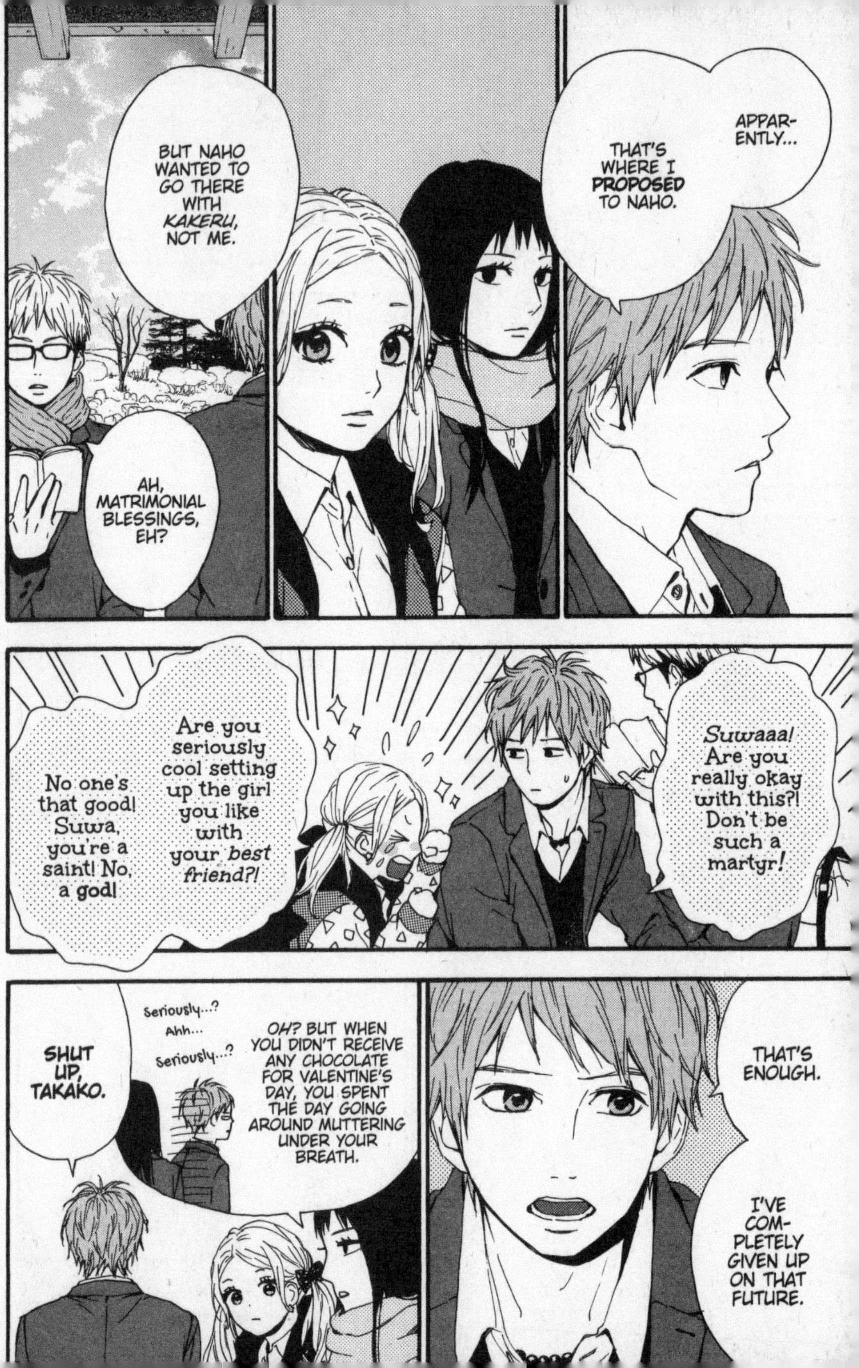
APPARENTLY...
THAT'S WHERE I PROPOSED TO NAHO.
BUT NAHO WANTED TO GO THERE WITH KAKERU, NOT ME.
AH, MATRIMONIAL BLESSINGS, EH?
Suwaaa! Are you really okay with this?! Don't be such a martyr!
Are you seriously cool setting up the girl you like with your best friend?!
No one's that good! Suwa, you're a saint! No, a god!
THAT'S ENOUGH.
I'VE COMPLETELY GIVEN UP ON THAT FUTURE.
OH? BUT WHEN YOU DIDN'T RECEIVE ANY CHOCOLATE FOR VALENTINE'S DAY, YOU SPENT THE DAY GOING AROUND MUTTERING UNDER YOUR BREATH.
Seriously...?
Ahh...
Seriously...?
SHUT UP, TAKAKO.

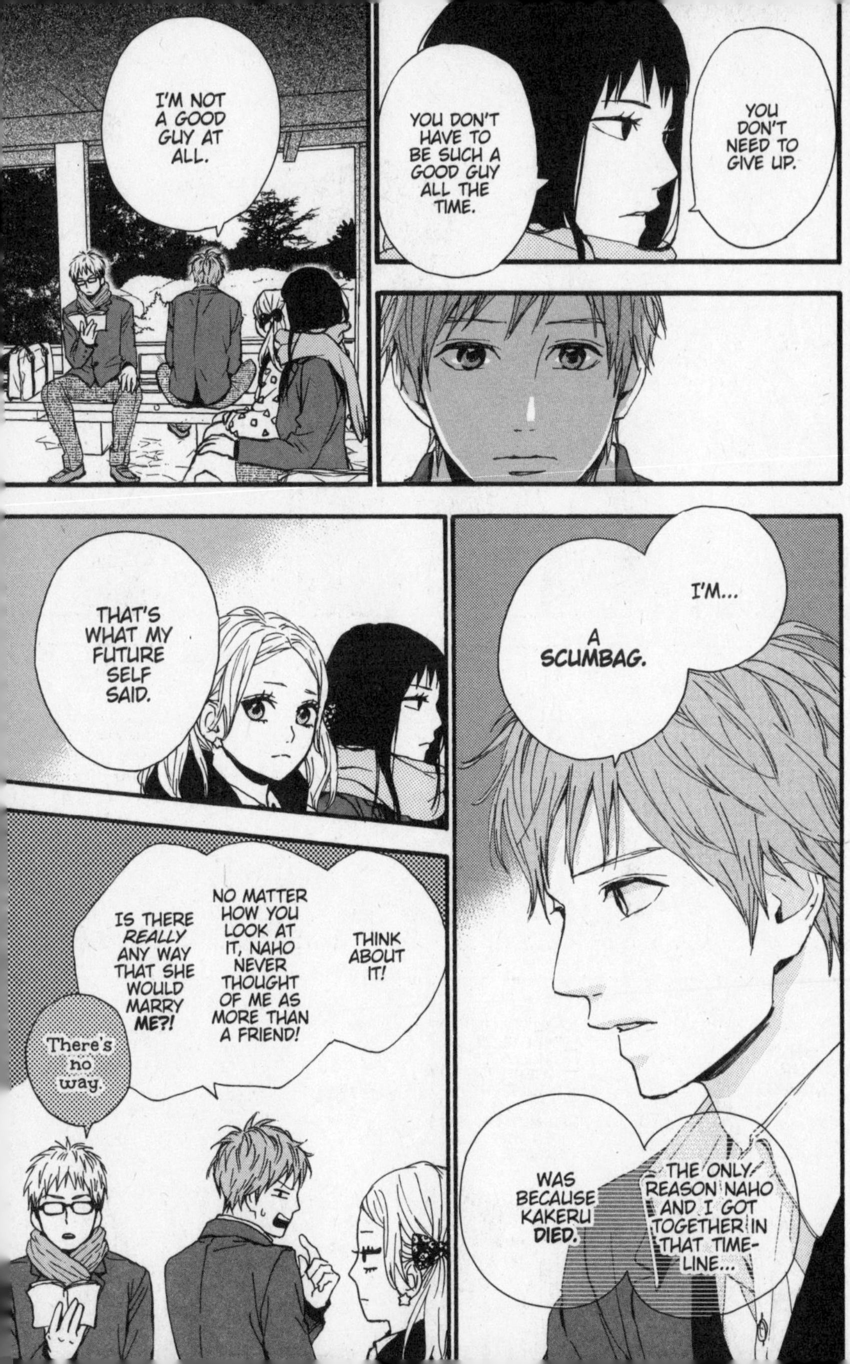
YOU DON'T NEED TO GIVE UP.
YOU DON'T HAVE TO BE SUCH A GOOD GUY ALL THE TIME.
I'M NOT A GOOD GUY AT ALL.
I'M...
A SCUMBAG.
THAT'S WHAT MY FUTURE SELF SAID.
THINK ABOUT IT!
NO MATTER HOW YOU LOOK AT IT, NAHO NEVER THOUGHT OF ME AS MORE THAN A FRIEND!
IS THERE *REALLY* ANY WAY THAT SHE WOULD MARRY ME?!
There's no way.
THE ONLY REASON NAHO AND I GOT TOGETHER IN THAT TIME-LINE...
WAS BECAUSE KAKERU DIED.

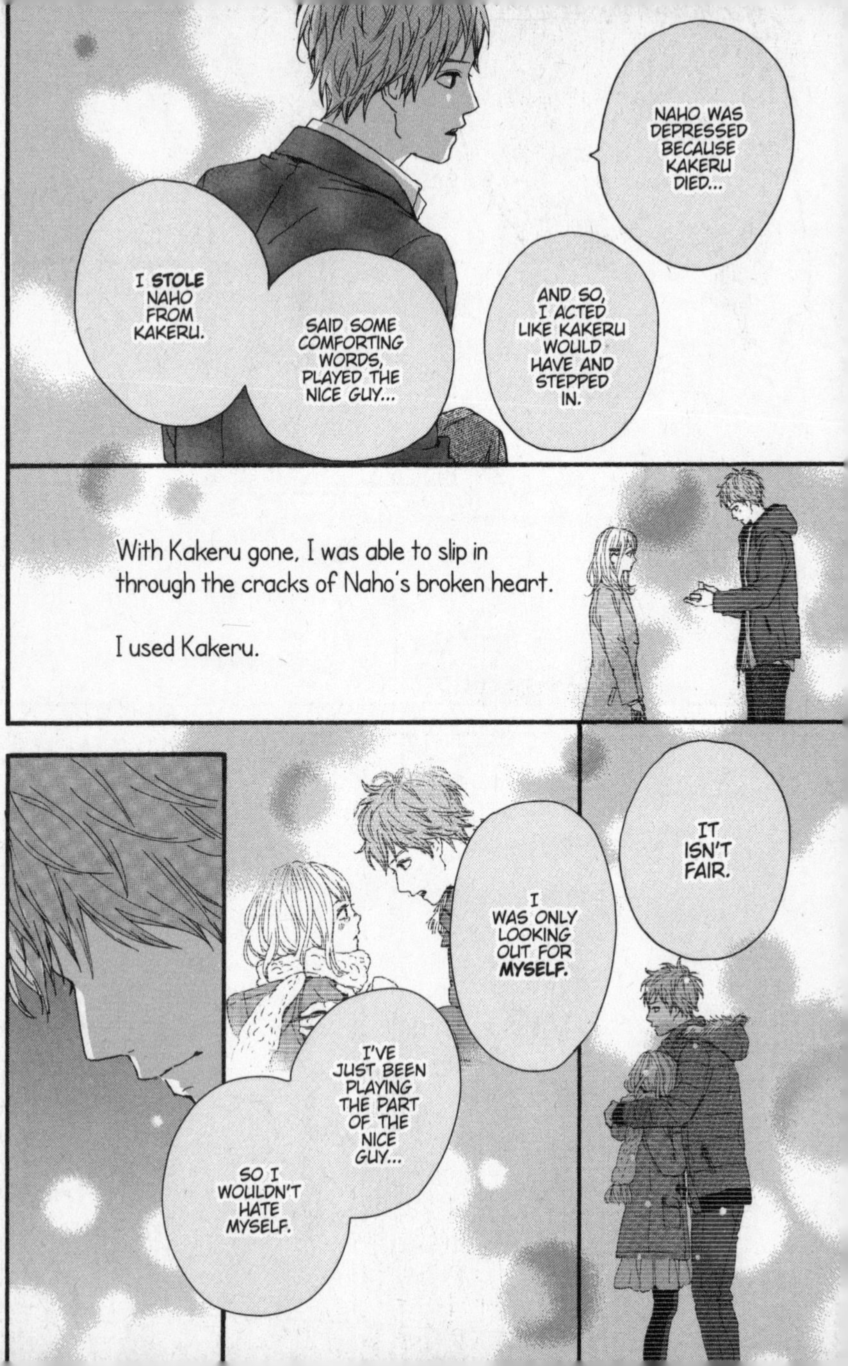
NAHO WAS DEPRESSED BECAUSE KAKERU DIED...
AND SO, I ACTED LIKE KAKERU WOULD HAVE AND STEPPED IN.
SAID SOME COMFORTING WORDS, PLAYED THE NICE GUY...
I **STOLE** NAHO FROM KAKERU.
With Kakeru gone, I was able to slip in through the cracks of Naho's broken heart.
I used Kakeru.
IT ISN'T FAIR.
I WAS ONLY LOOKING OUT FOR **MYSELF.**
I'VE JUST BEEN PLAYING THE PART OF THE NICE GUY...
SO I WOULDN'T HATE MYSELF.

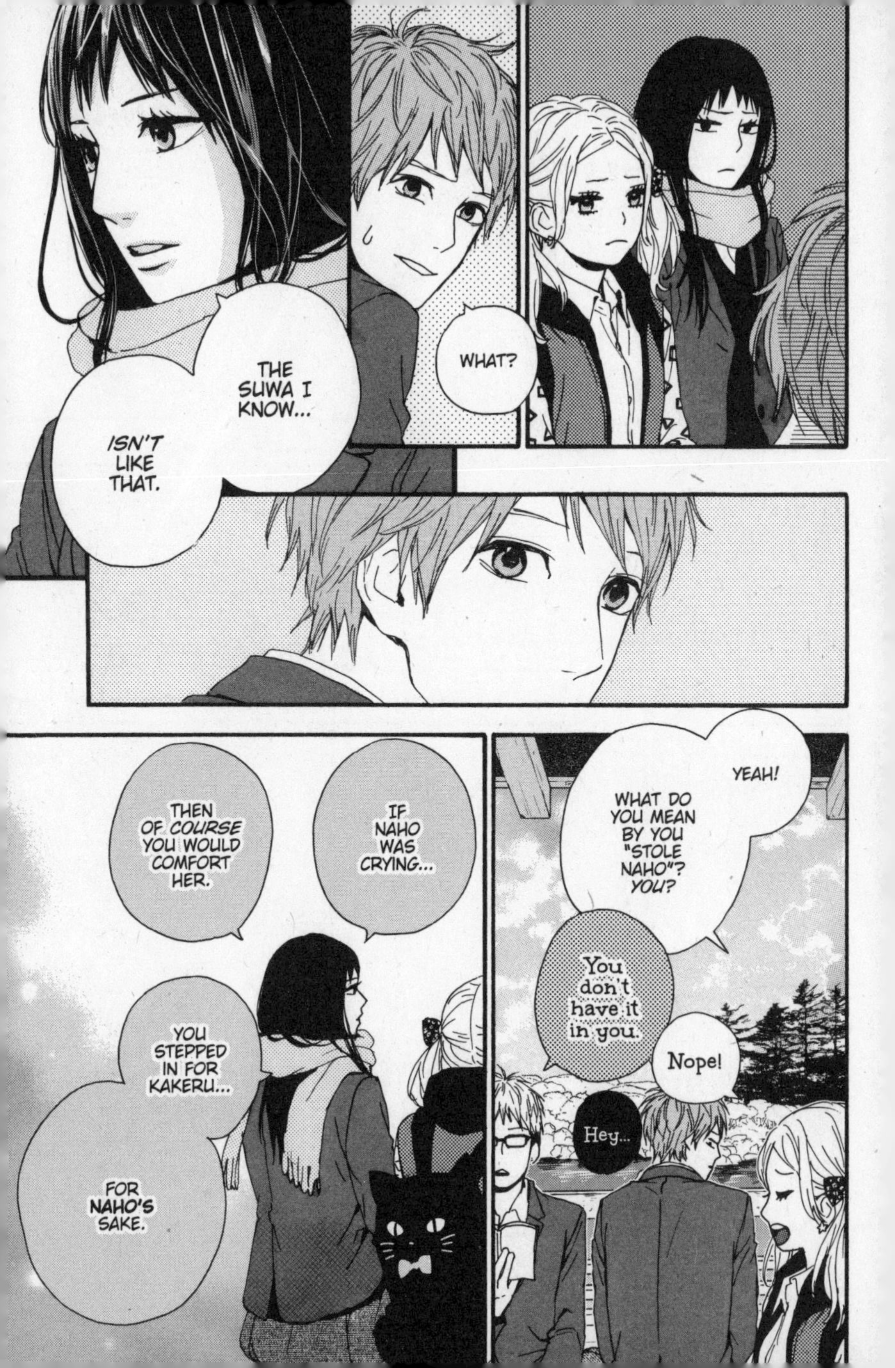
WHAT?
THE SUWA I KNOW...
ISN'T LIKE THAT.
YEAH!
WHAT DO YOU MEAN BY YOU "STOLE NAHO"? YOU?
You don't have it in you.
Nope!
Hey...
IF NAHO WAS CRYING...
THEN OF COURSE YOU WOULD COMFORT HER.
YOU STEPPED IN FOR KAKERU...
FOR NAHO'S SAKE.

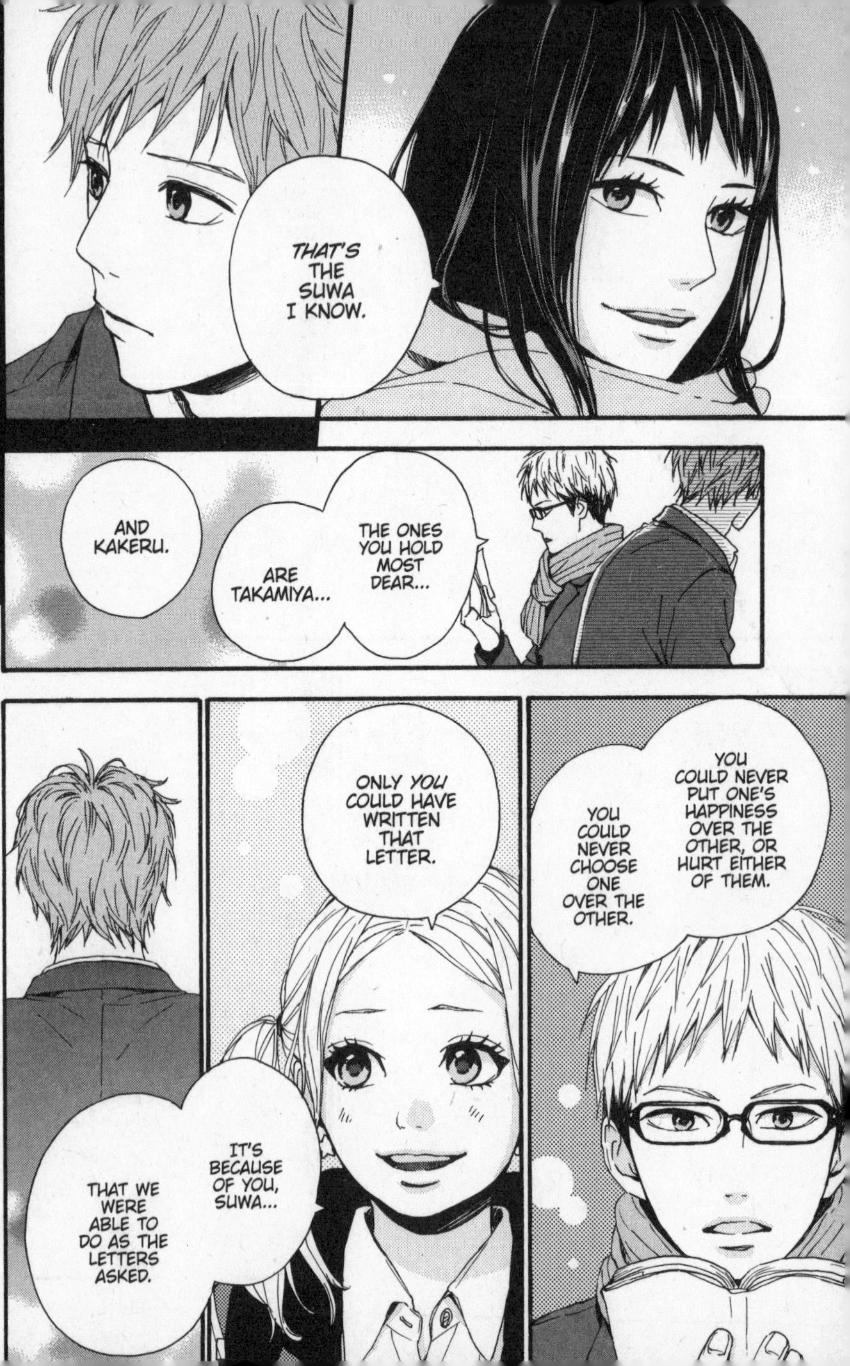
THAT'S THE SUWA I KNOW.
THE ONES YOU HOLD MOST DEAR...
ARE TAKAMIYA...
AND KAKERU.
YOU COULD NEVER PUT ONE'S HAPPINESS OVER THE OTHER, OR HURT EITHER OF THEM.
YOU COULD NEVER CHOOSE ONE OVER THE OTHER.
ONLY *YOU* COULD HAVE WRITTEN THAT LETTER.
IT'S BECAUSE OF YOU, SUWA...
THAT WE WERE ABLE TO DO AS THE LETTERS ASKED.

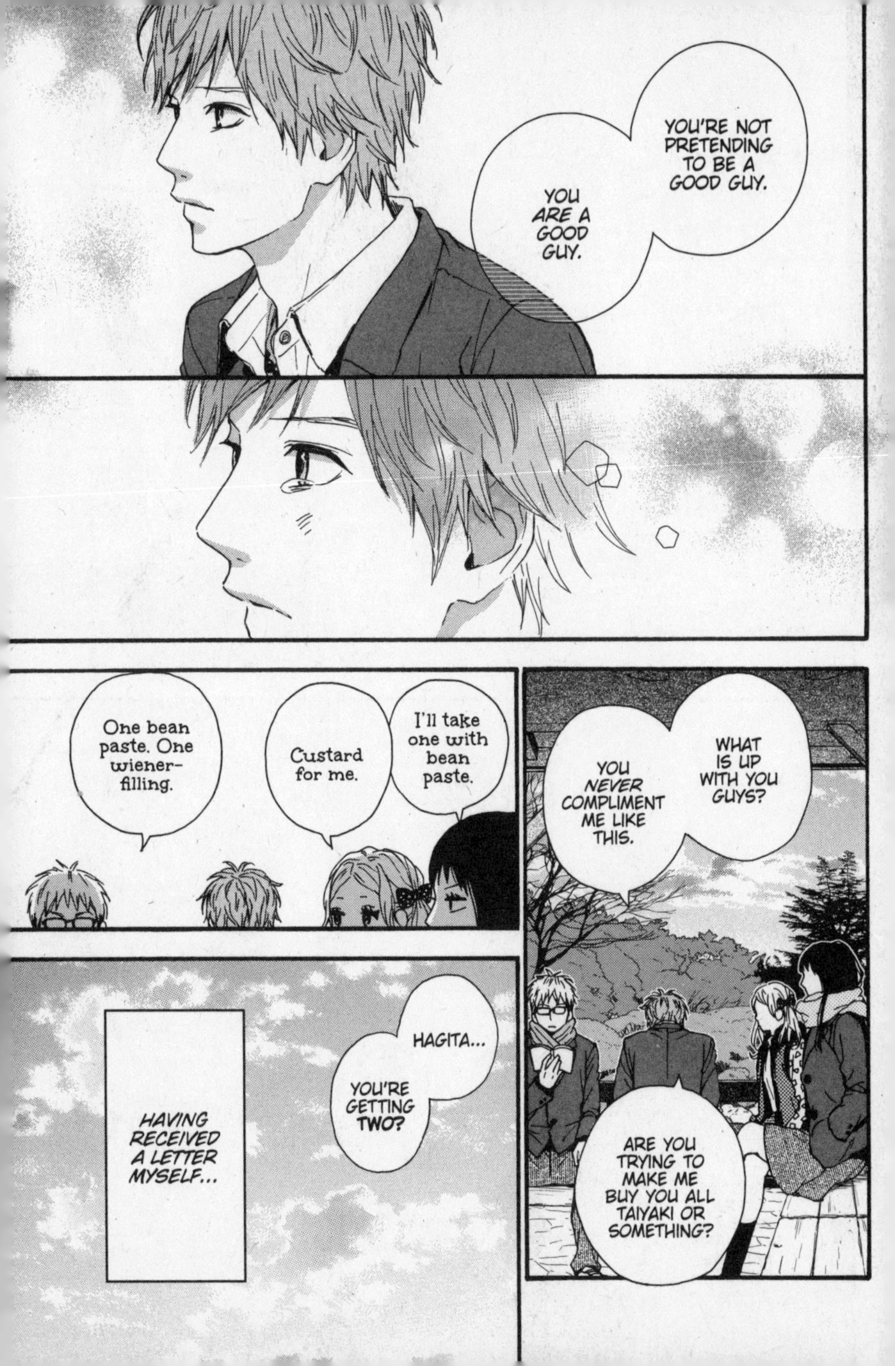

YOU'RE NOT PRETENDING TO BE A GOOD GUY.
YOU ARE A GOOD GUY.
WHAT IS UP WITH YOU GUYS?
YOU NEVER COMPLIMENT ME LIKE THIS.
ARE YOU TRYING TO MAKE ME BUY YOU ALL TAIYAKI OR SOMETHING?
I'll take one with bean paste.
Custard for me.
One bean paste. One wiener-filling.
HAGITA...
YOU'RE GETTING TWO?
HAVING RECEIVED A LETTER MYSELF...

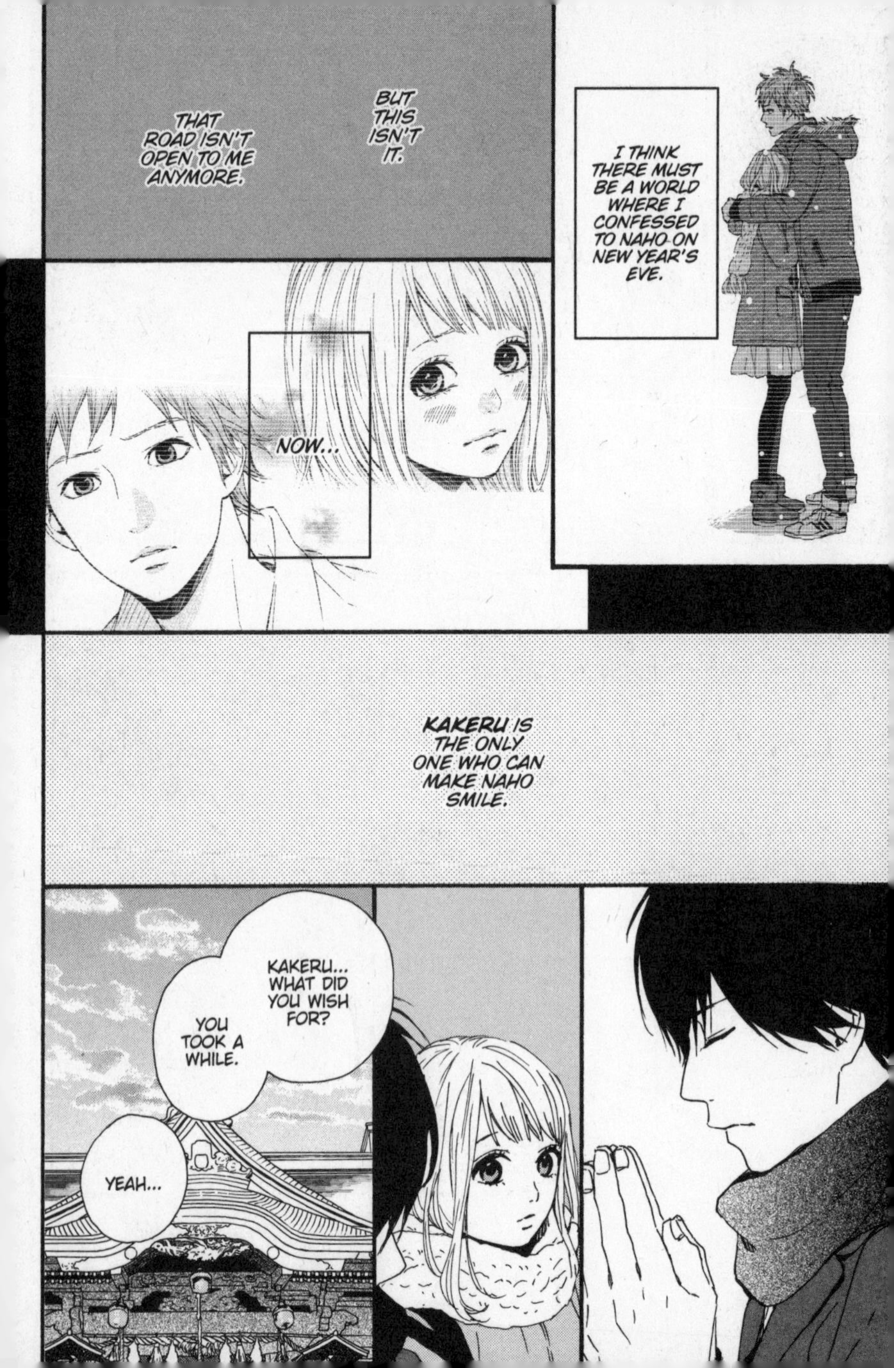
I THINK THERE MUST BE A WORLD WHERE I CONFESSED TO NAHO ON NEW YEAR'S EVE.
BUT THIS ISN'T IT.
THAT ROAD ISN'T OPEN TO ME ANYMORE.
NOW...
KAKERU IS THE ONLY ONE WHO CAN MAKE NAHO SMILE.
KAKERU... WHAT DID YOU WISH FOR?
YOU TOOK A WHILE.
YEAH...

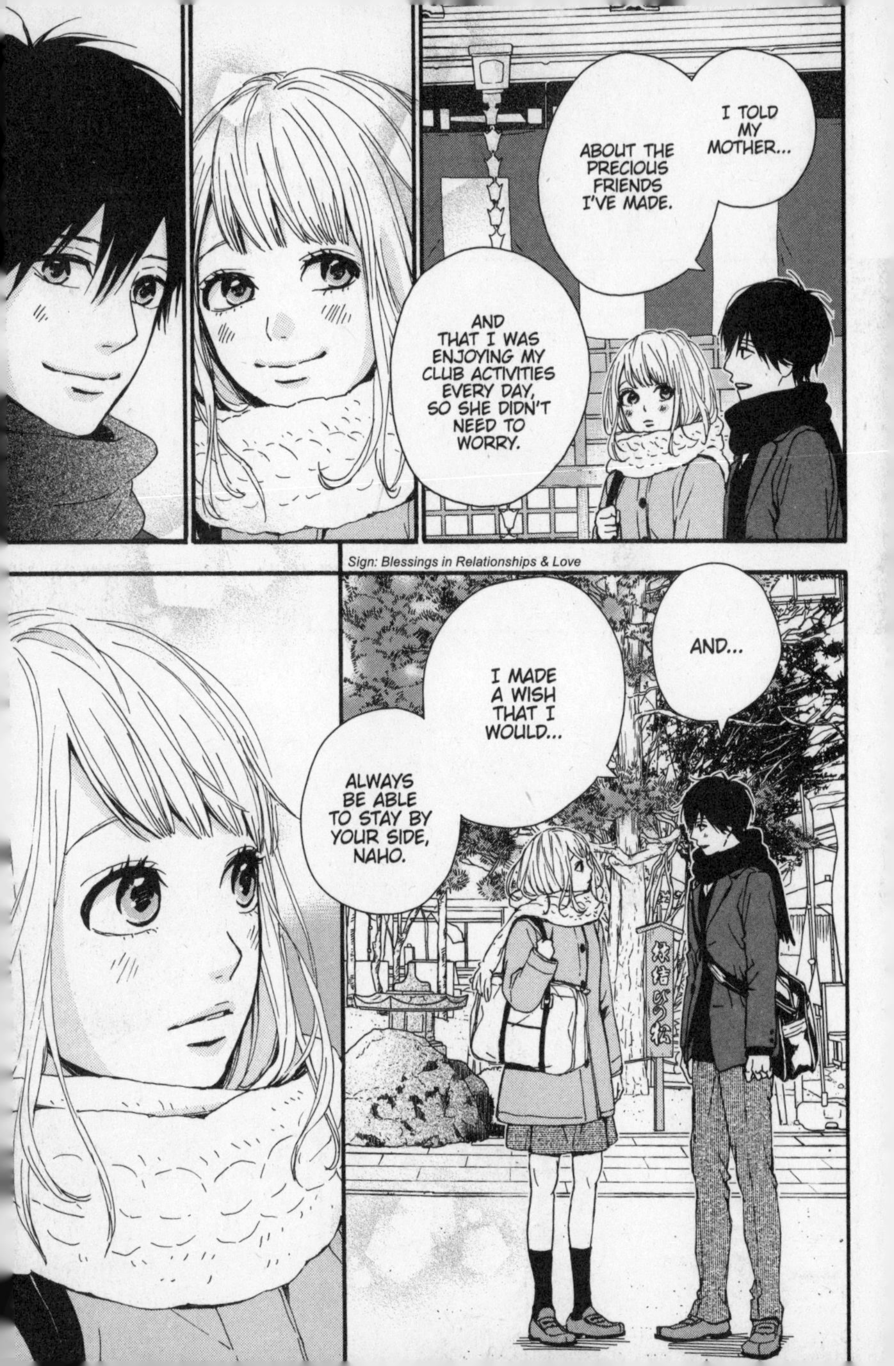
I TOLD MY MOTHER...
ABOUT THE PRECIOUS FRIENDS I'VE MADE.
AND THAT I WAS ENJOYING MY CLUB ACTIVITIES EVERY DAY, SO SHE DIDN'T NEED TO WORRY.
AND...
I MADE A WISH THAT I WOULD...
ALWAYS BE ABLE TO STAY BY YOUR SIDE, NAHO.

Sign: Blessings in Relationships & Love

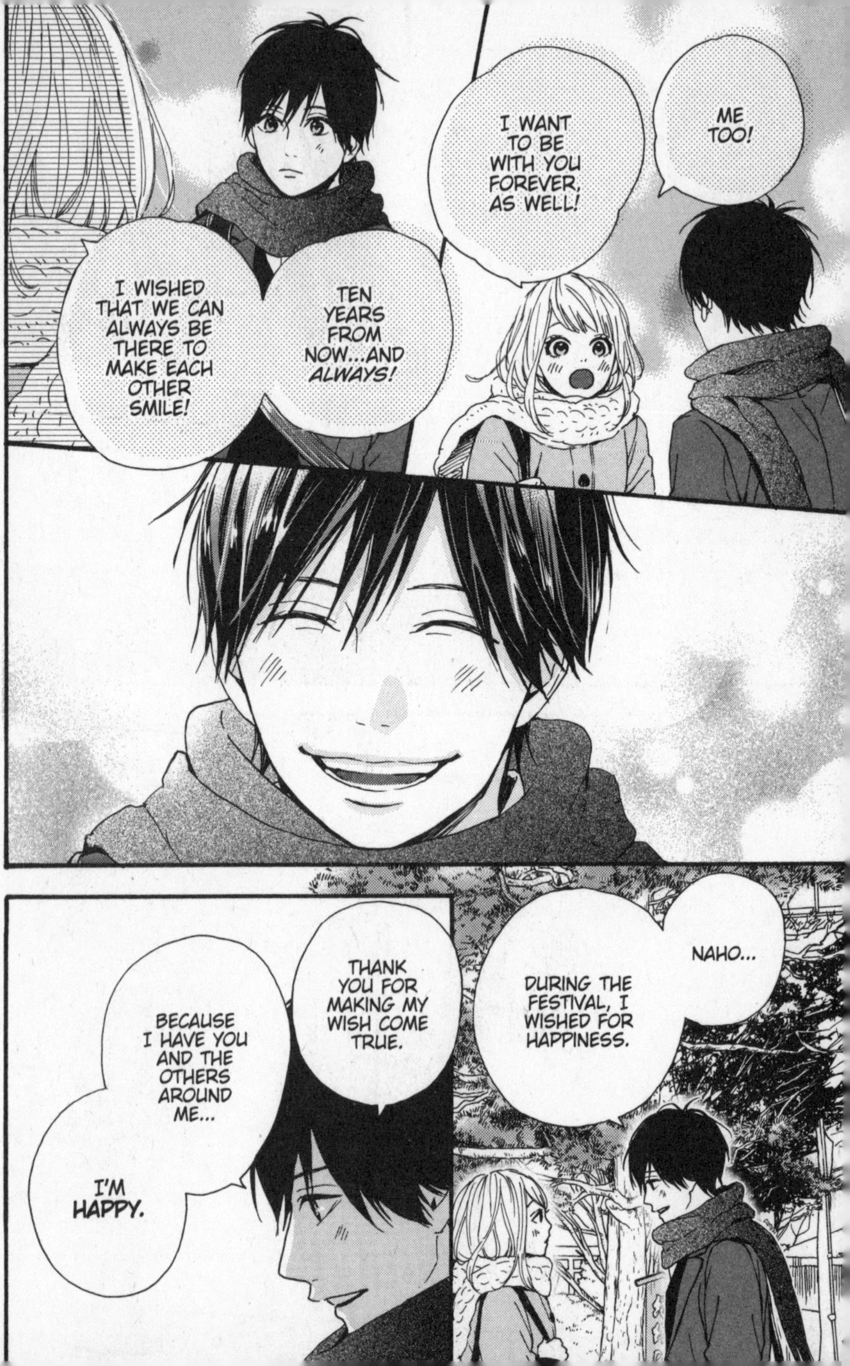
I WISHED THAT WE CAN ALWAYS BE THERE TO MAKE EACH OTHER SMILE!
TEN YEARS FROM NOW...AND *ALWAYS!*
I WANT TO BE WITH YOU FOREVER, AS WELL!
ME TOO!
NAHO...
DURING THE FESTIVAL, I WISHED FOR HAPPINESS.
THANK YOU FOR MAKING MY WISH COME TRUE.
BECAUSE I HAVE YOU AND THE OTHERS AROUND ME...
I'M **HAPPY.**

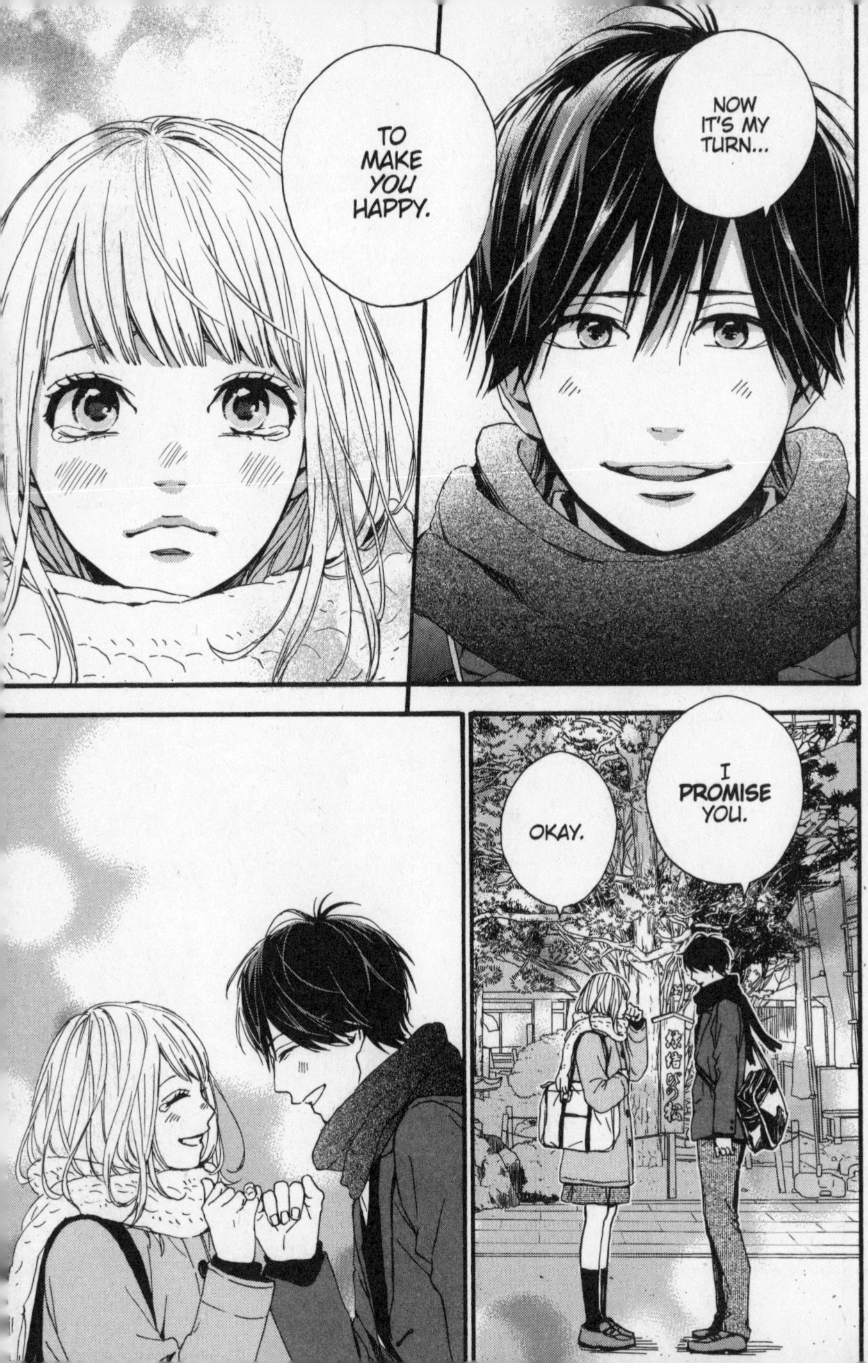
NOW IT'S MY TURN...
TO MAKE YOU HAPPY.
I PROMISE YOU.
OKAY.

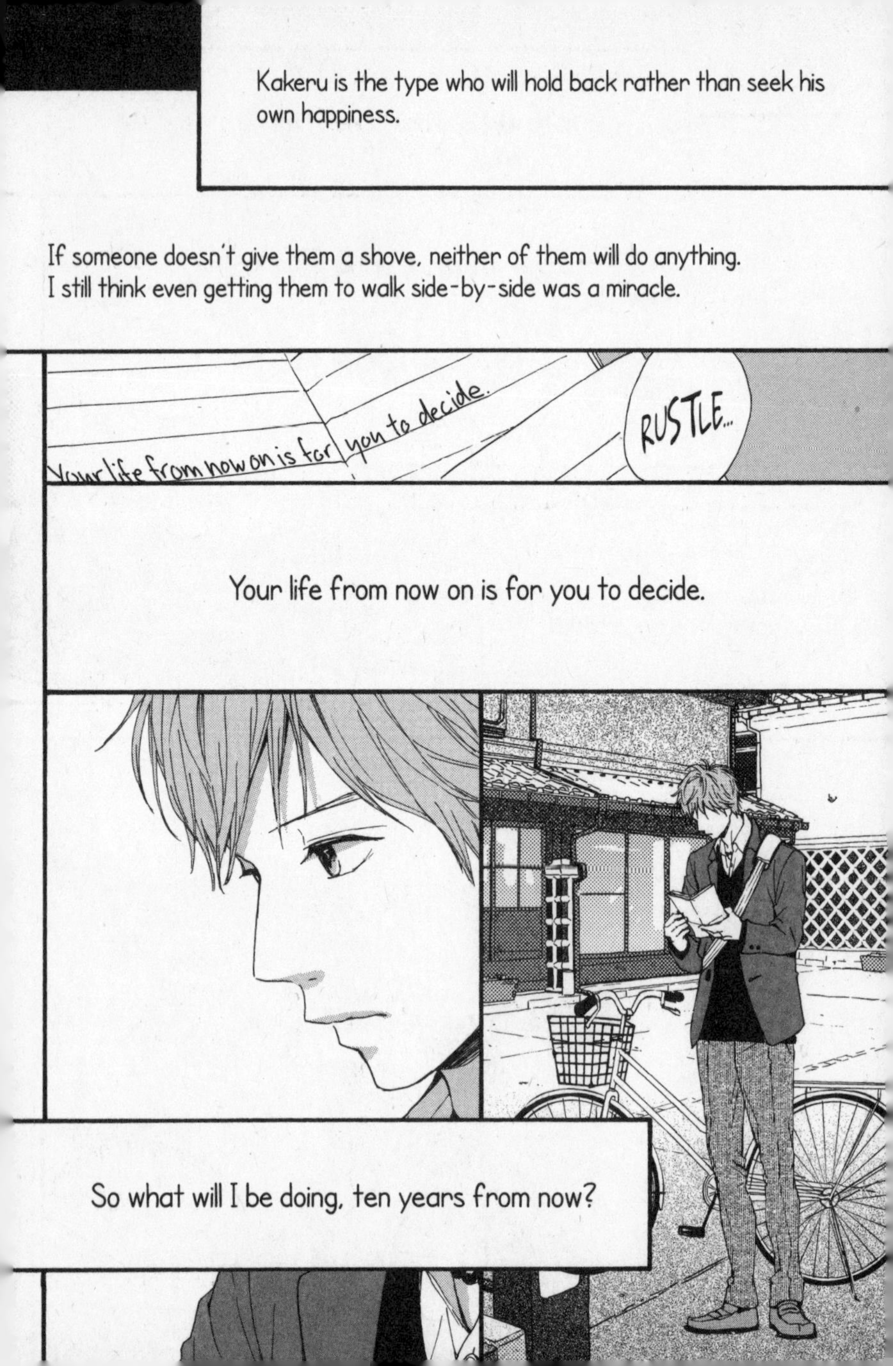
Kakeru is the type who will hold back rather than seek his own happiness.
If someone doesn't give them a shove, neither of them will do anything.
I still think even getting them to walk side-by-side was a miracle.
RUSTLE...
Your life from now on is for you to decide.
Your life from now on is for you to decide.
So what will I be doing, ten years from now?

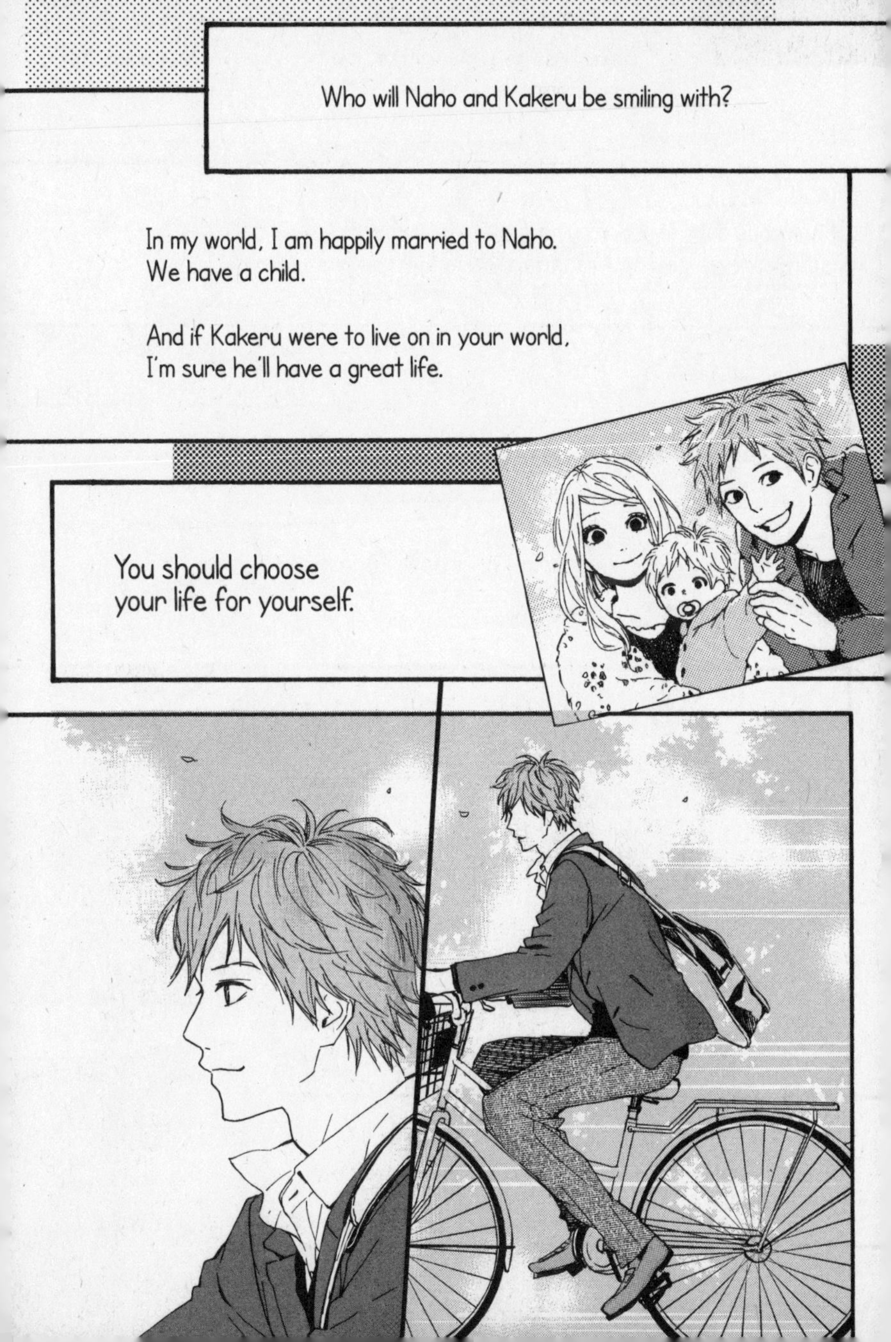
Who will Naho and Kakeru be smiling with?
In my world, I am happily married to Naho. We have a child.
And if Kakeru were to live on in your world, I'm sure he'll have a great life.
You should choose your life for yourself.

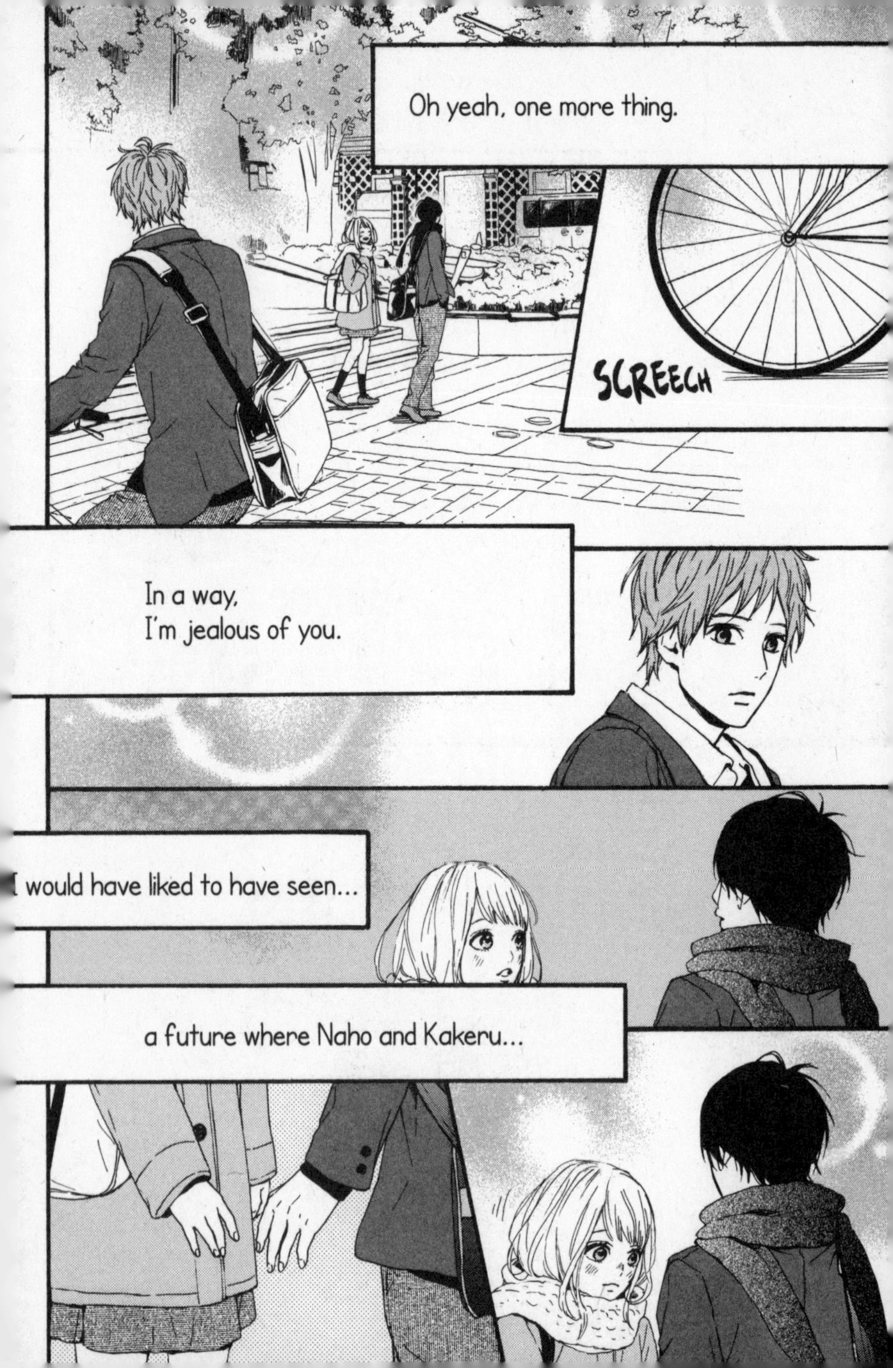
Oh yeah, one more thing.
SCREECH
In a way, I'm jealous of you.
I would have liked to have seen...
a future where Naho and Kakeru...

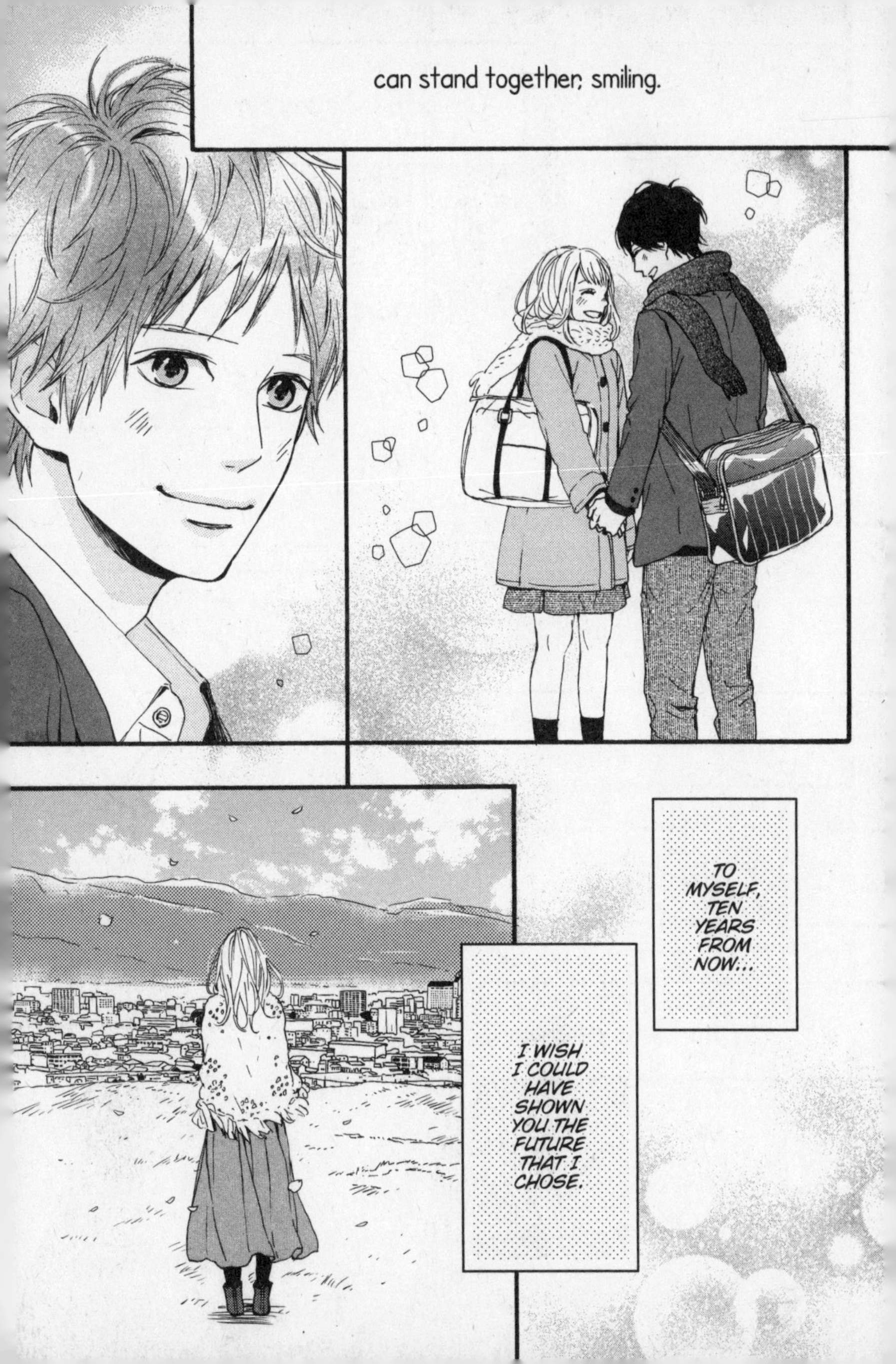
can stand together, smiling.
TO MYSELF, TEN YEARS FROM NOW...
I WISH I COULD HAVE SHOWN YOU THE FUTURE THAT I CHOSE.

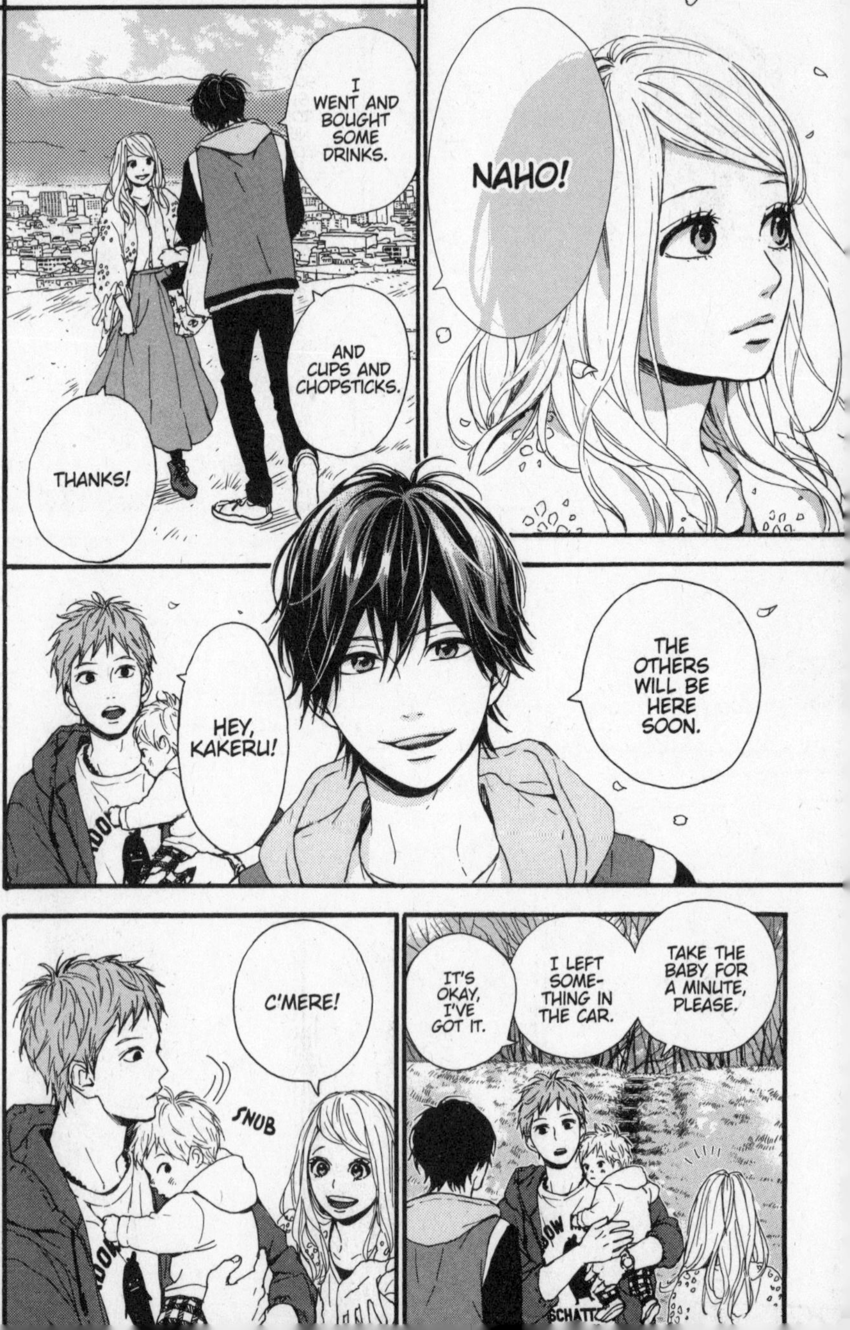
NAHO!
I WENT AND BOUGHT SOME DRINKS.
AND CUPS AND CHOPSTICKS.
THANKS!
THE OTHERS WILL BE HERE SOON.
HEY, KAKERU!
TAKE THE BABY FOR A MINUTE, PLEASE.
I LEFT SOME-THING IN THE CAR.
IT'S OKAY, I'VE GOT IT.
SCHATT
C'MERE!
SNUB

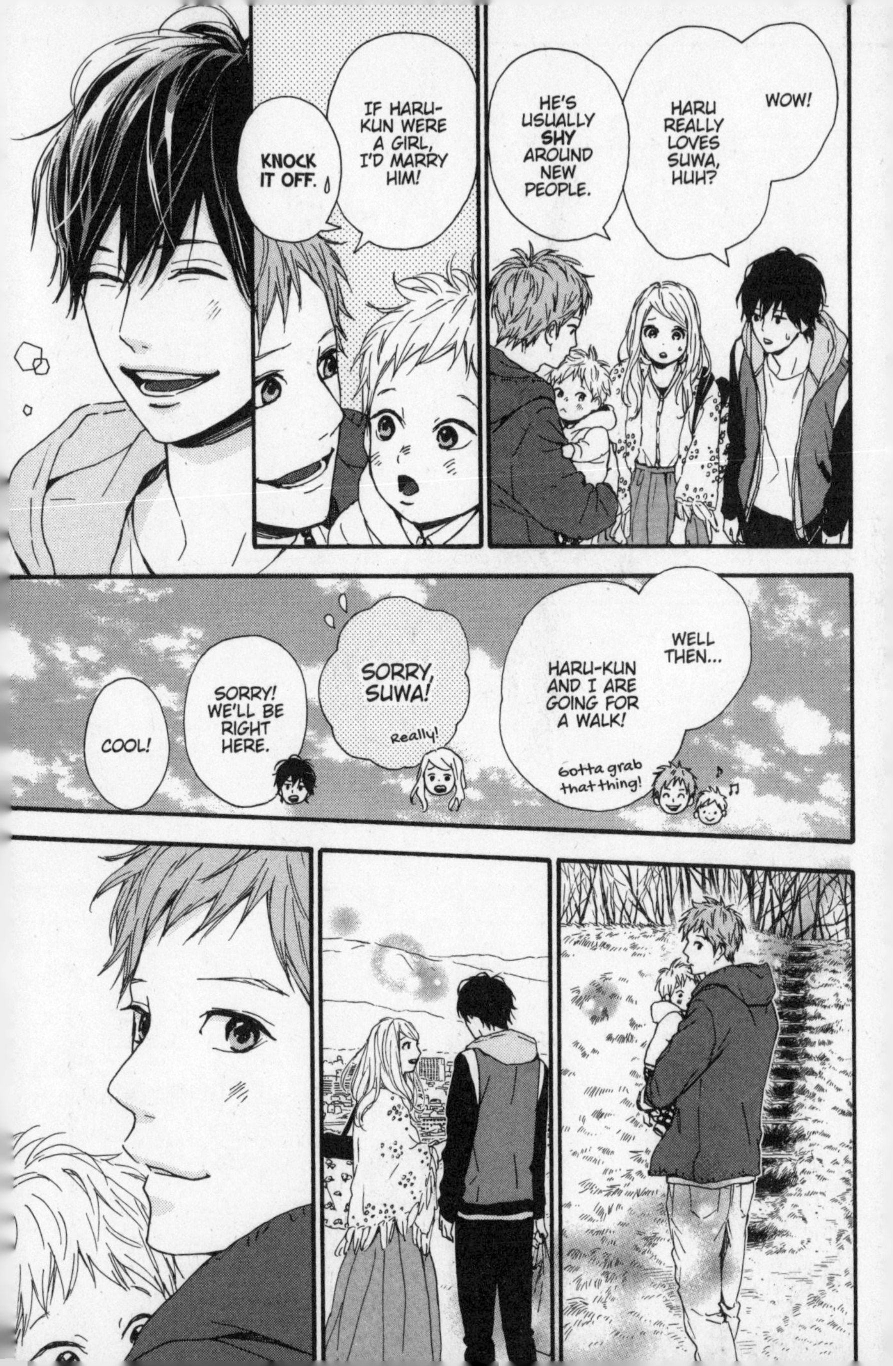
WOW!
HARU REALLY LOVES SUWA, HUH?
HE'S USUALLY SHY AROUND NEW PEOPLE.
IF HARU-KUN WERE A GIRL, I'D MARRY HIM!
KNOCK IT OFF.
WELL THEN... HARU-KUN AND I ARE GOING FOR A WALK!
Gotta grab that thing!
SORRY, SUWA!
Really!
SORRY! WE'LL BE RIGHT HERE.
COOL!

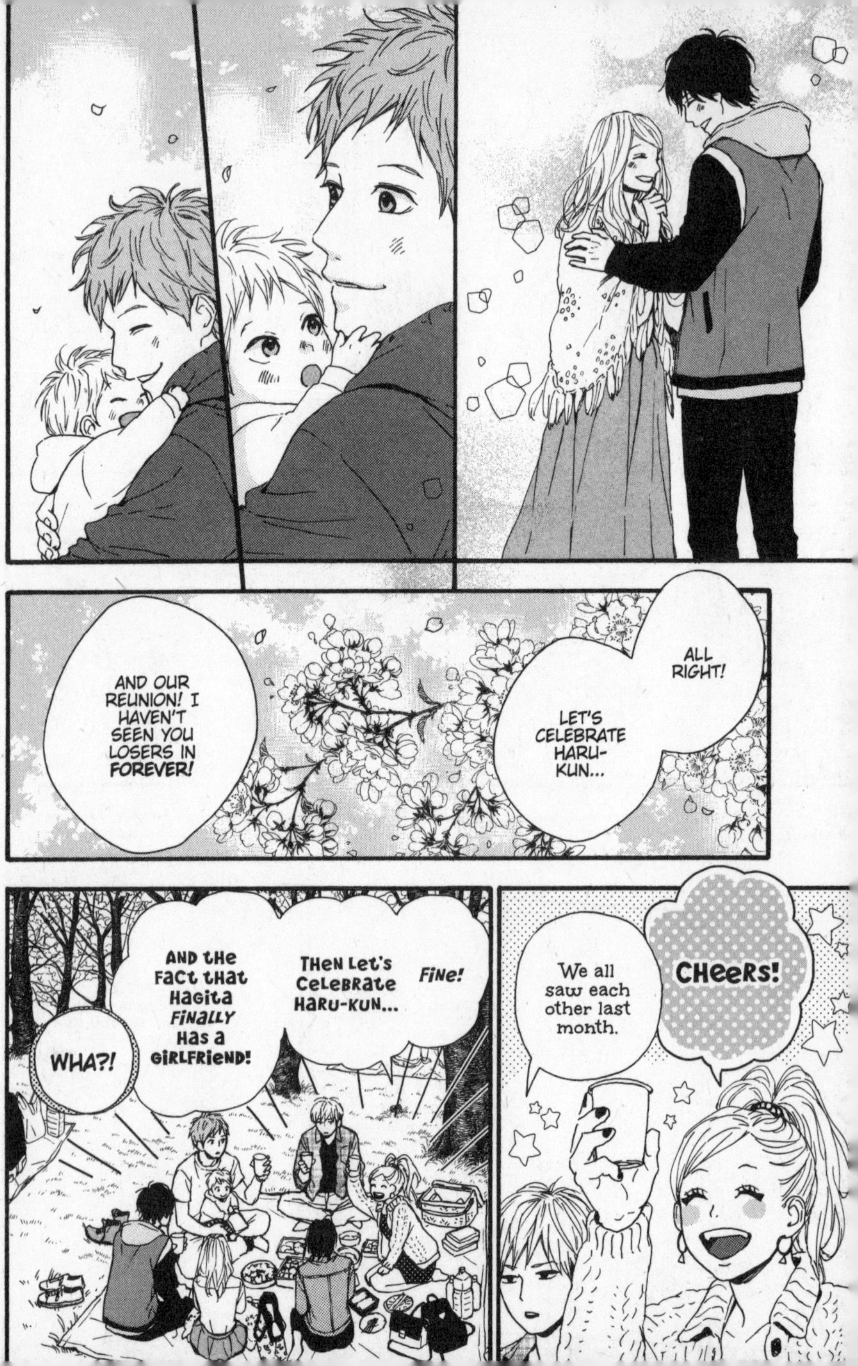
ALL RIGHT!
LET'S CELEBRATE HARU-KUN...
AND OUR REUNION! I HAVEN'T SEEN YOU LOSERS IN FOREVER!
CHEERS!
We all saw each other last month.
FINE!
THEN LET'S CELEBRATE HARU-KUN...
AND THE FACT THAT HAGITA FINALLY HAS A GIRLFRIEND!
WHA?!

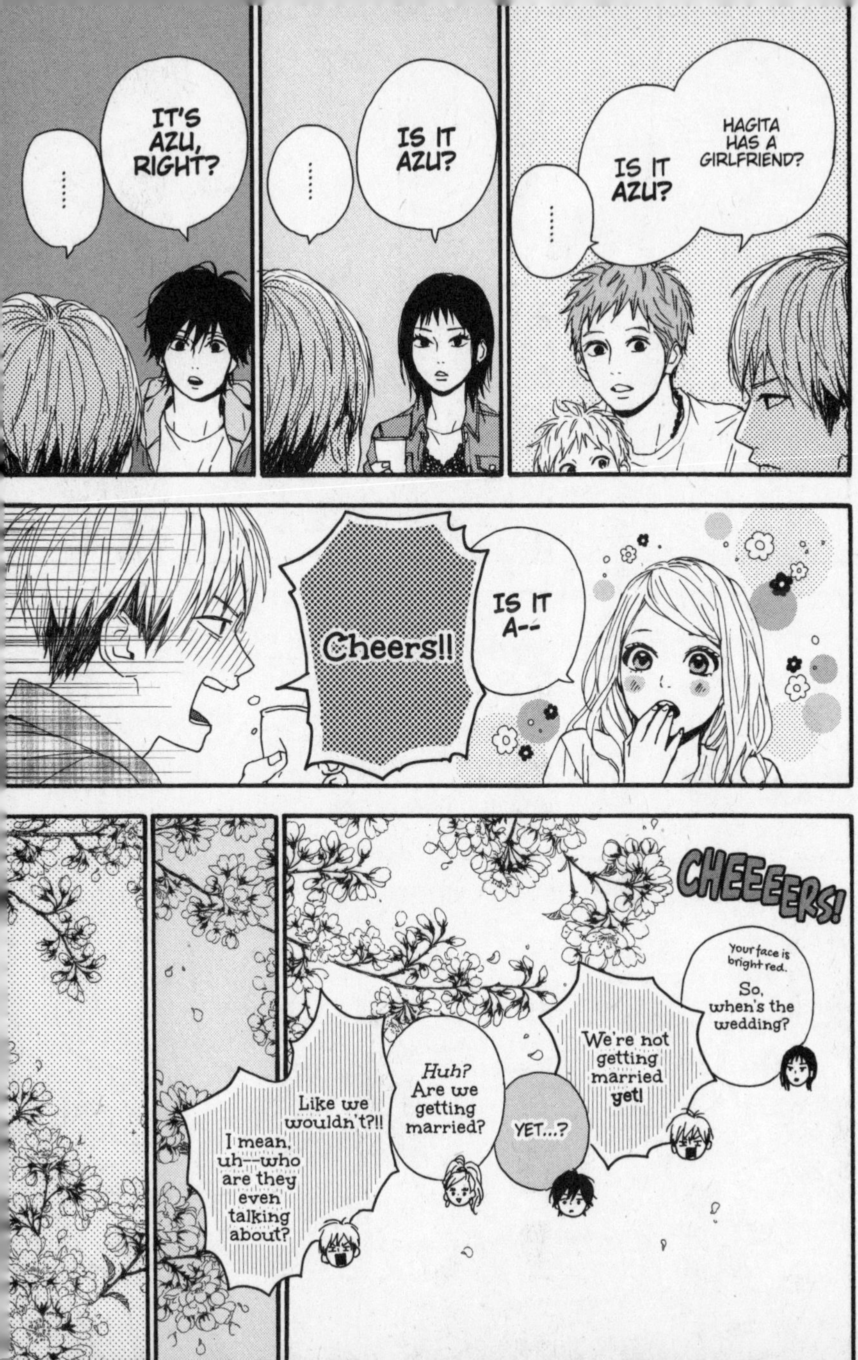
HAGITA HAS A GIRLFRIEND?
IS IT AZU?
......
IS IT AZU?
......
IT'S AZU, RIGHT?
......
IS IT A--
Cheers!!
CHEEEERS!
Your face is bright red.
So, when's the wedding?
We're not getting married yet!
YET...?
Huh? Are we getting married?
Like we wouldn't?!!
I mean, uh--who are they even talking about?

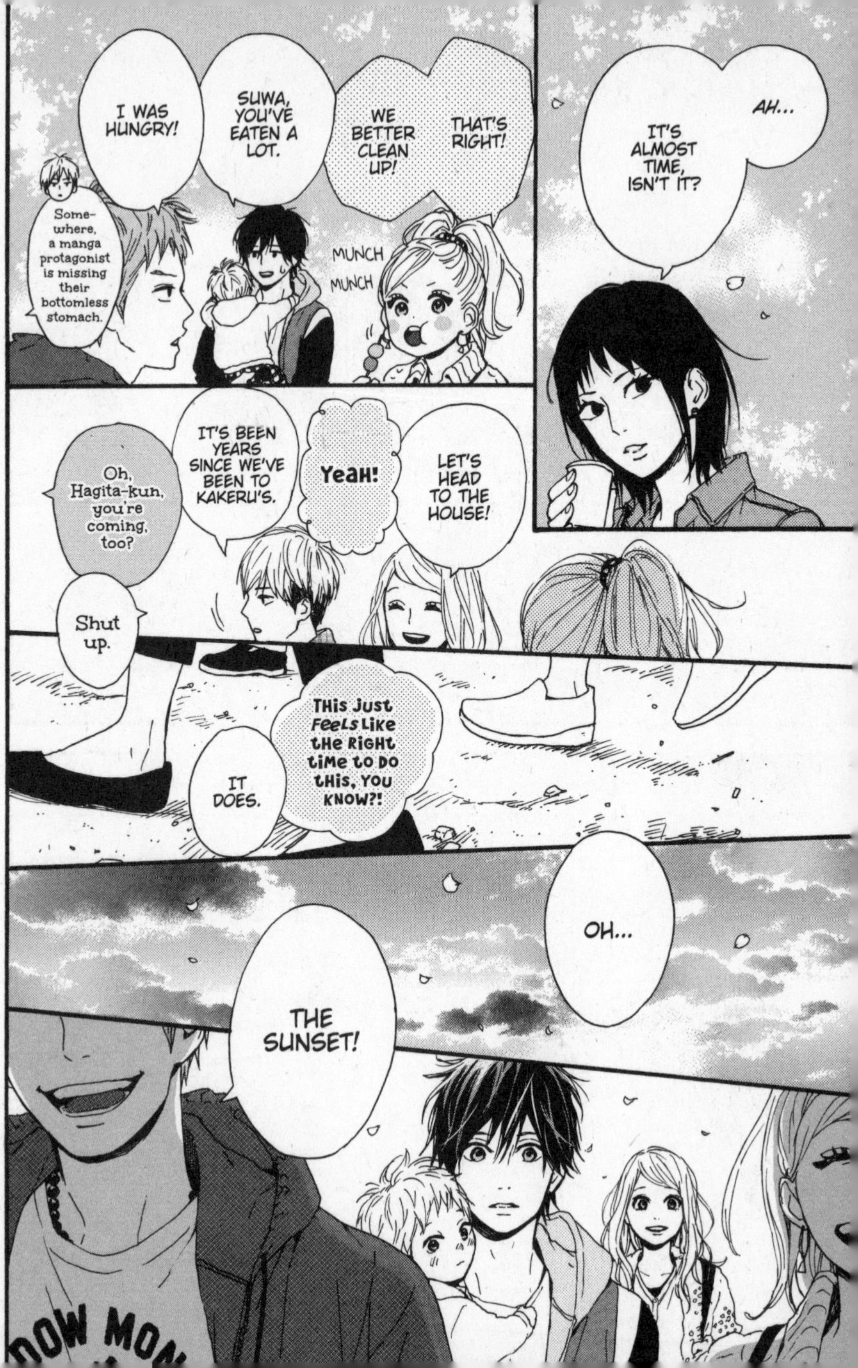
AH...
IT'S ALMOST TIME, ISN'T IT?
THAT'S RIGHT!
WE BETTER CLEAN UP!
SUWA, YOU'VE EATEN A LOT.
I WAS HUNGRY!
MUNCH
MUNCH
Some-where, a manga protagonist is missing their bottomless stomach.
LET'S HEAD TO THE HOUSE!
Yeah!
IT'S BEEN YEARS SINCE WE'VE BEEN TO KAKERU'S.
Oh, Hagita-kun, you're coming, too?
Shut up.
This just feels like the right time to do this, you know?!
IT DOES.
OH...
THE SUNSET!

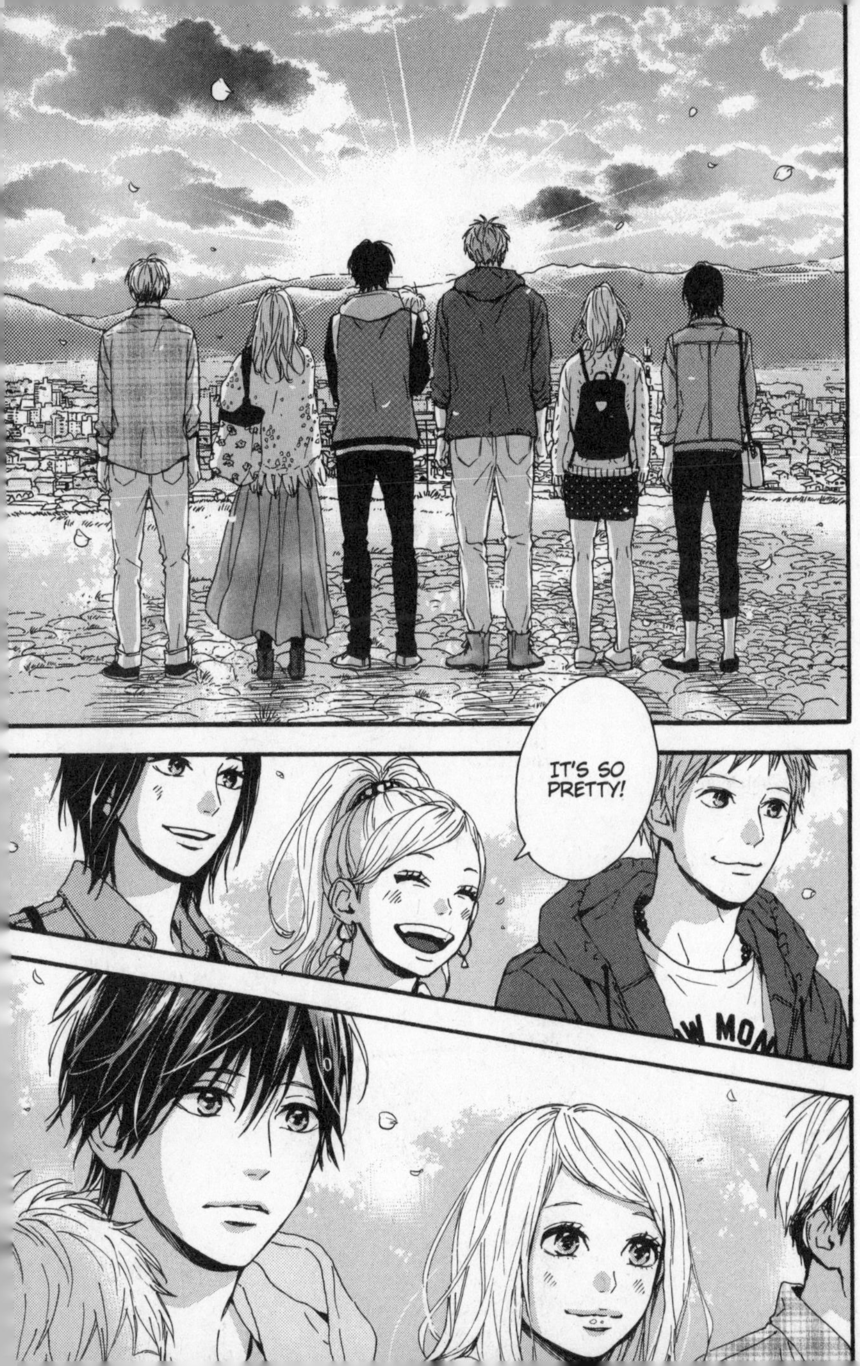
IT'S SO PRETTY!

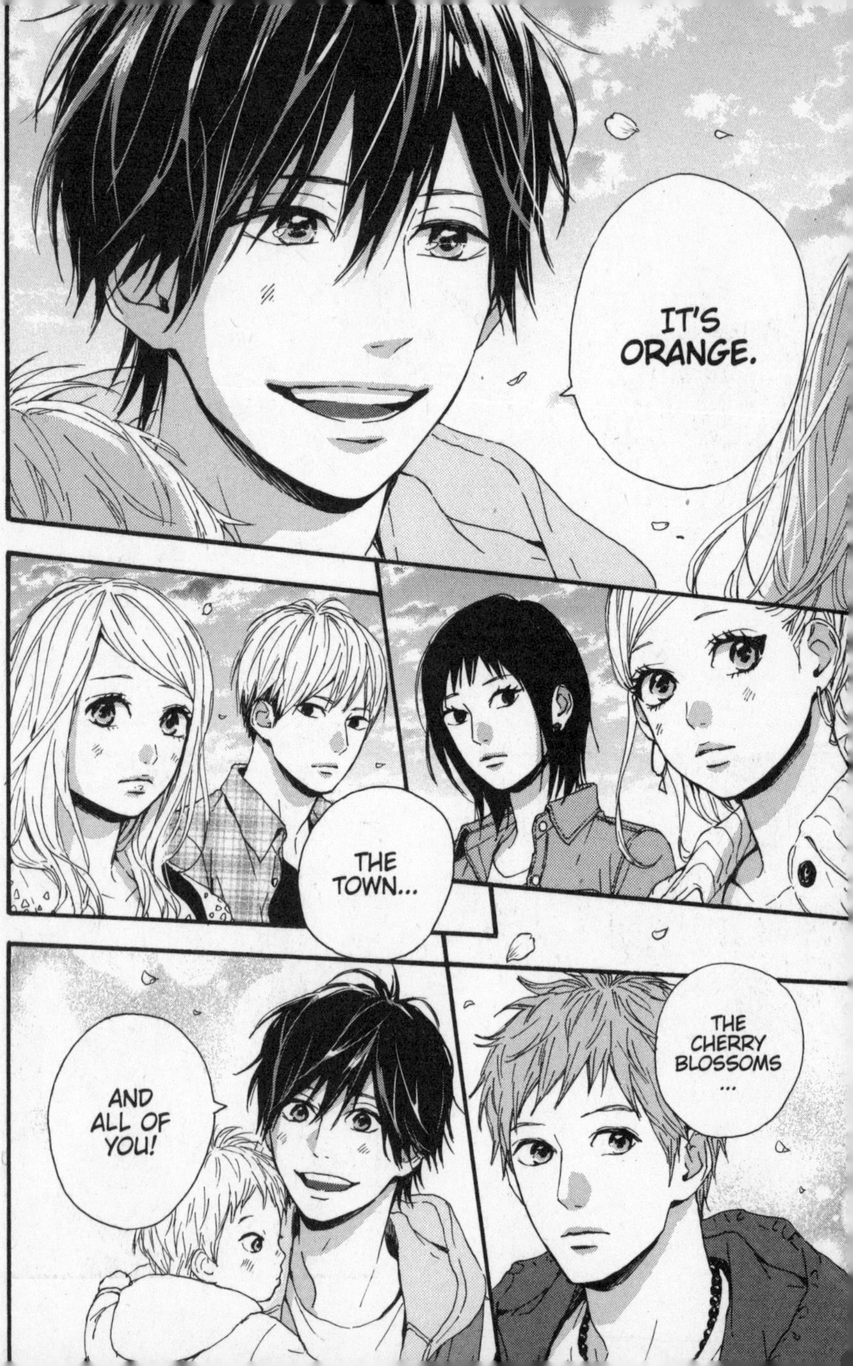

IT'S ORANGE.
THE TOWN...
THE CHERRY BLOSSOMS ...
AND ALL OF YOU!

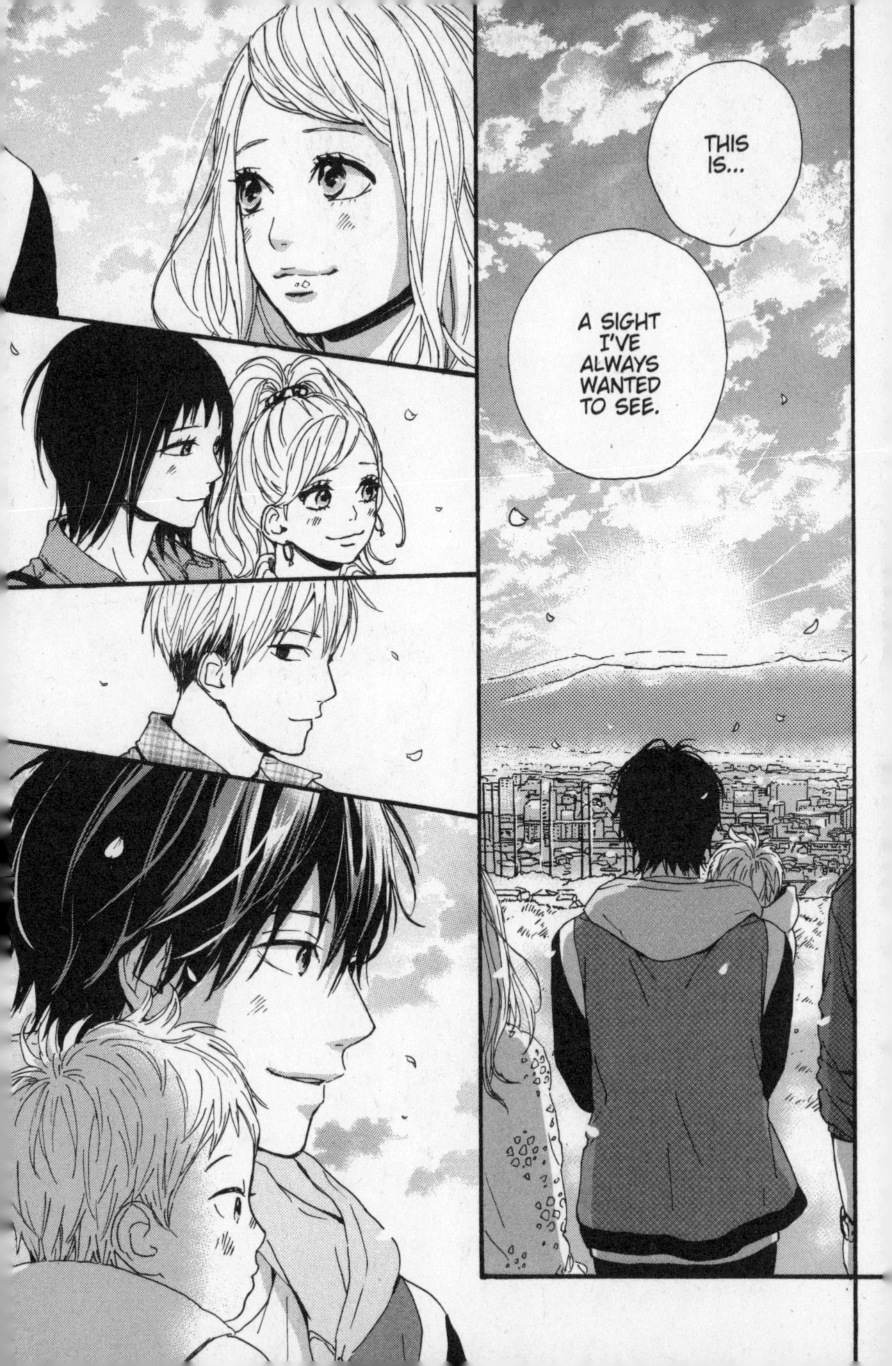
THIS IS...
A SIGHT I'VE ALWAYS WANTED TO SEE.

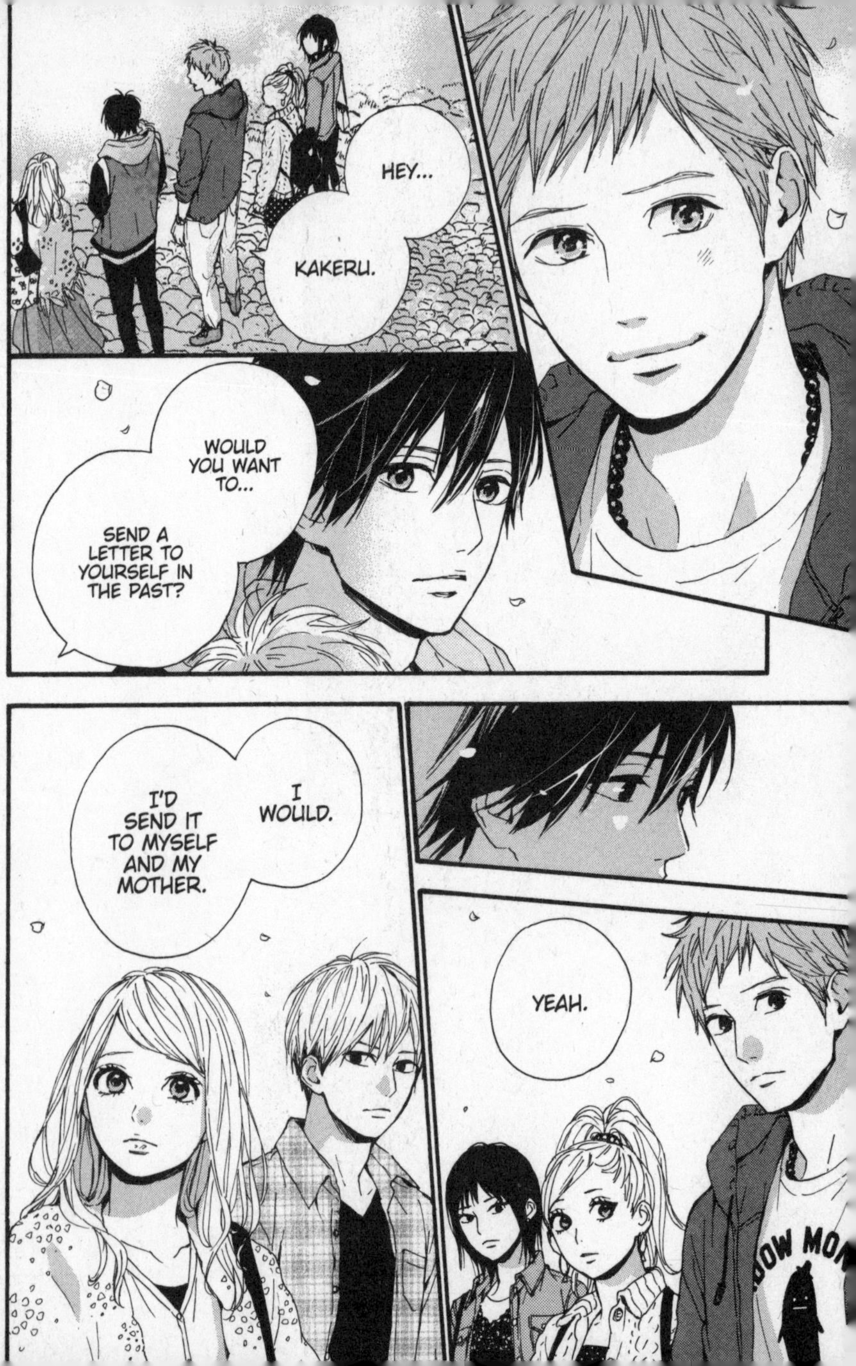
HEY...
KAKERU.
WOULD YOU WANT TO...
SEND A LETTER TO YOURSELF IN THE PAST?
I WOULD.
I'D SEND IT TO MYSELF AND MY MOTHER.
YEAH.

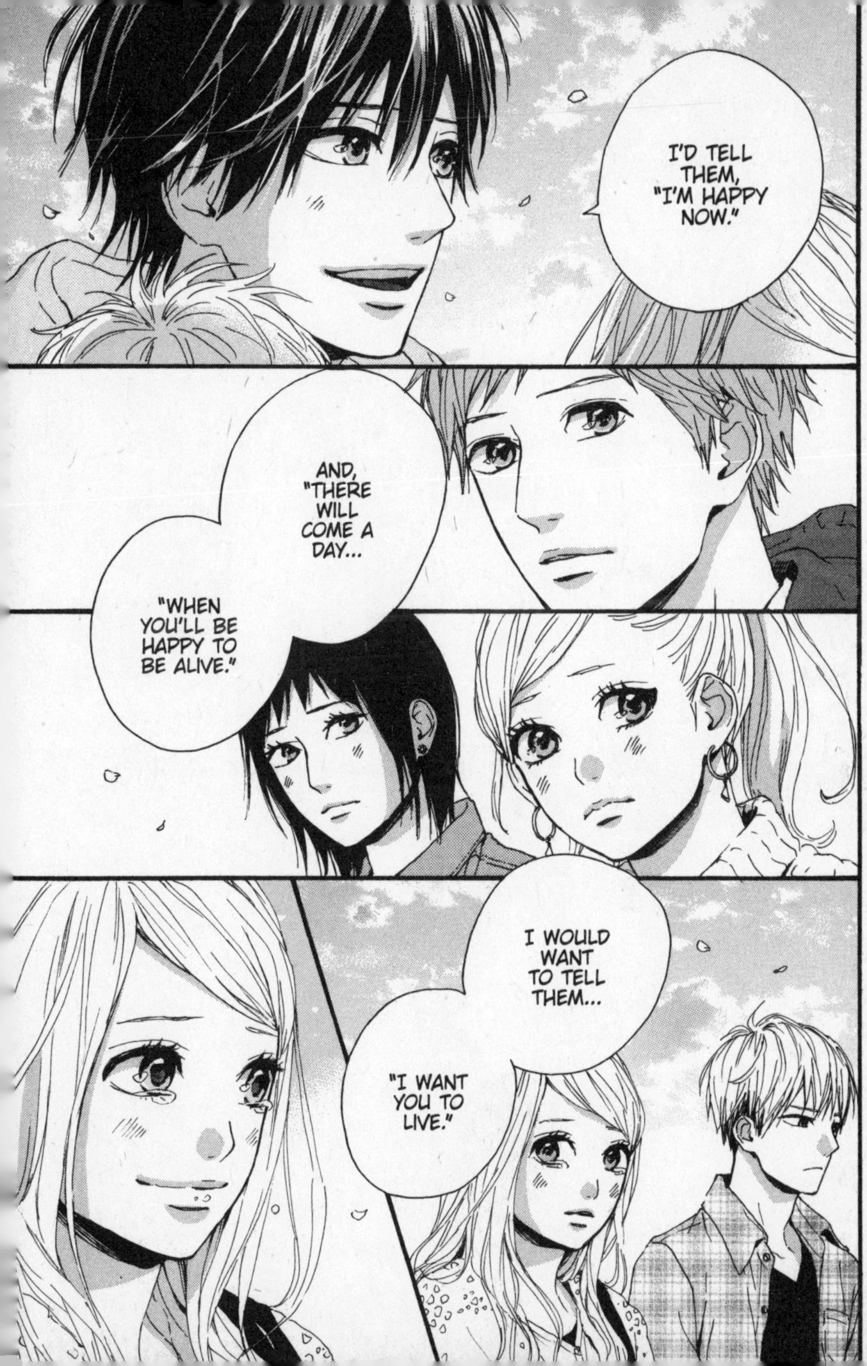
I'D TELL THEM, "I'M HAPPY NOW."
AND, "THERE WILL COME A DAY...
"WHEN YOU'LL BE HAPPY TO BE ALIVE."
I WOULD WANT TO TELL THEM...
"I WANT YOU TO LIVE."

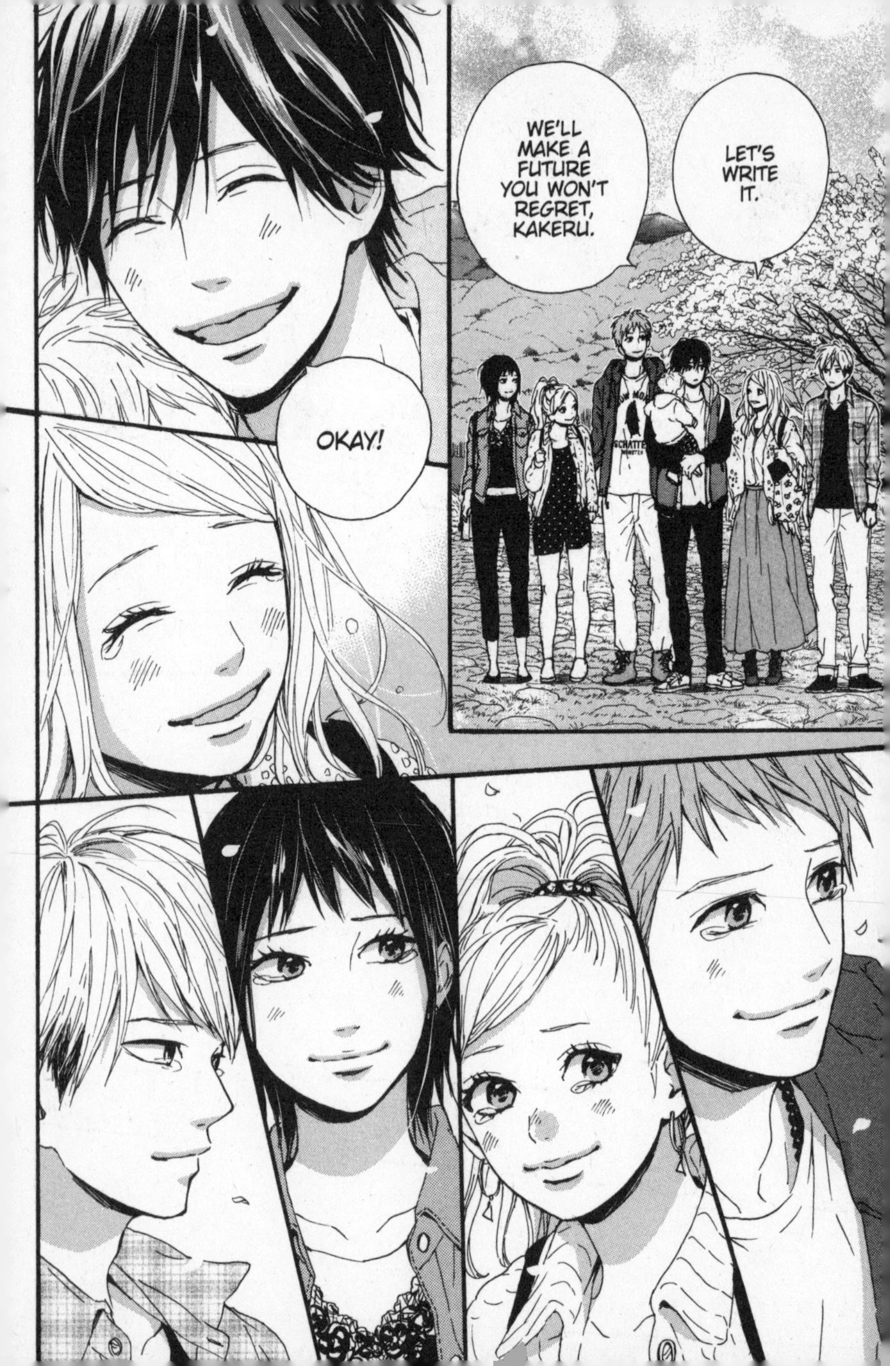
LET'S WRITE IT.
WE'LL MAKE A FUTURE YOU WON'T REGRET, KAKERU.
OKAY!

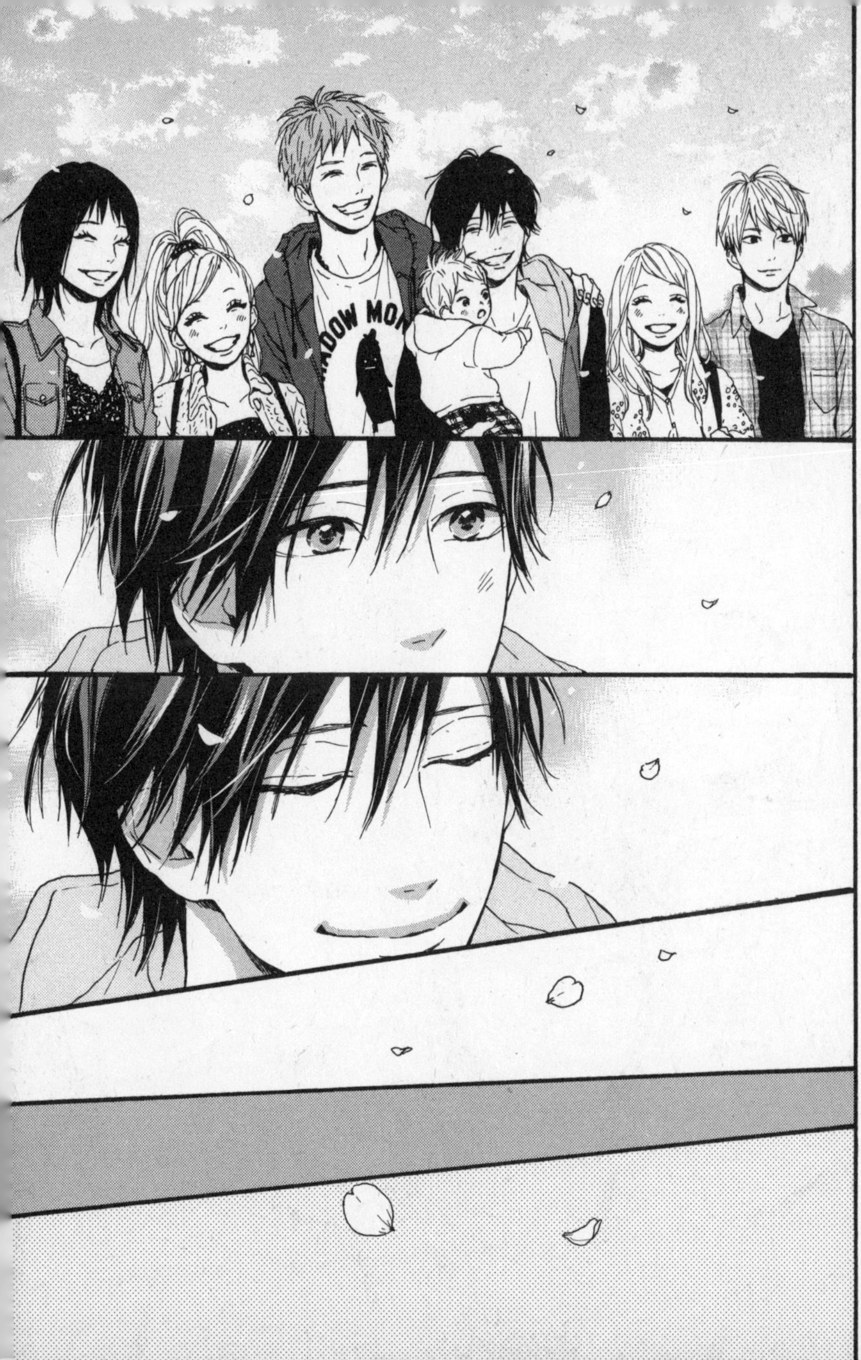
ADOW MON

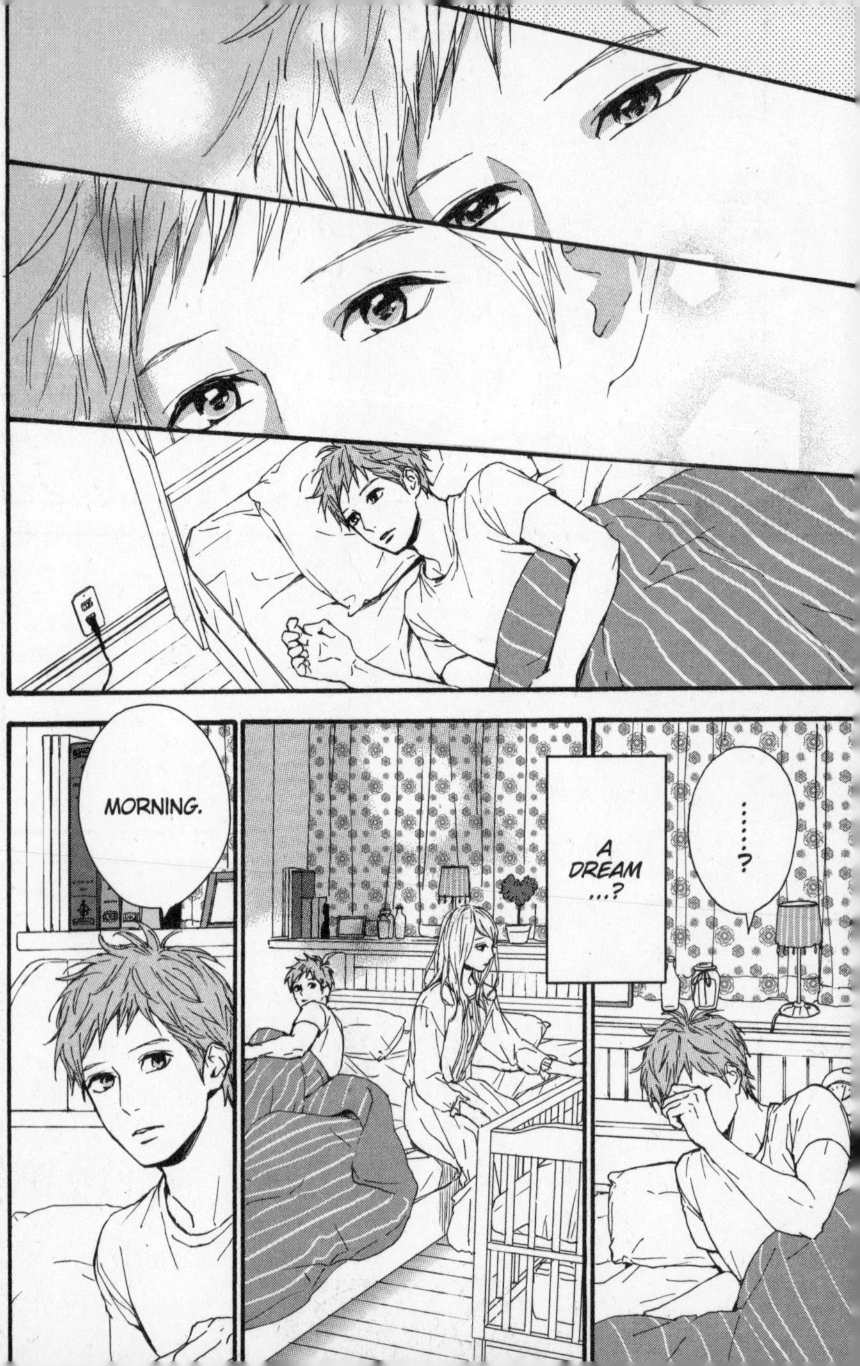
......?
A DREAM ...?
MORNING.

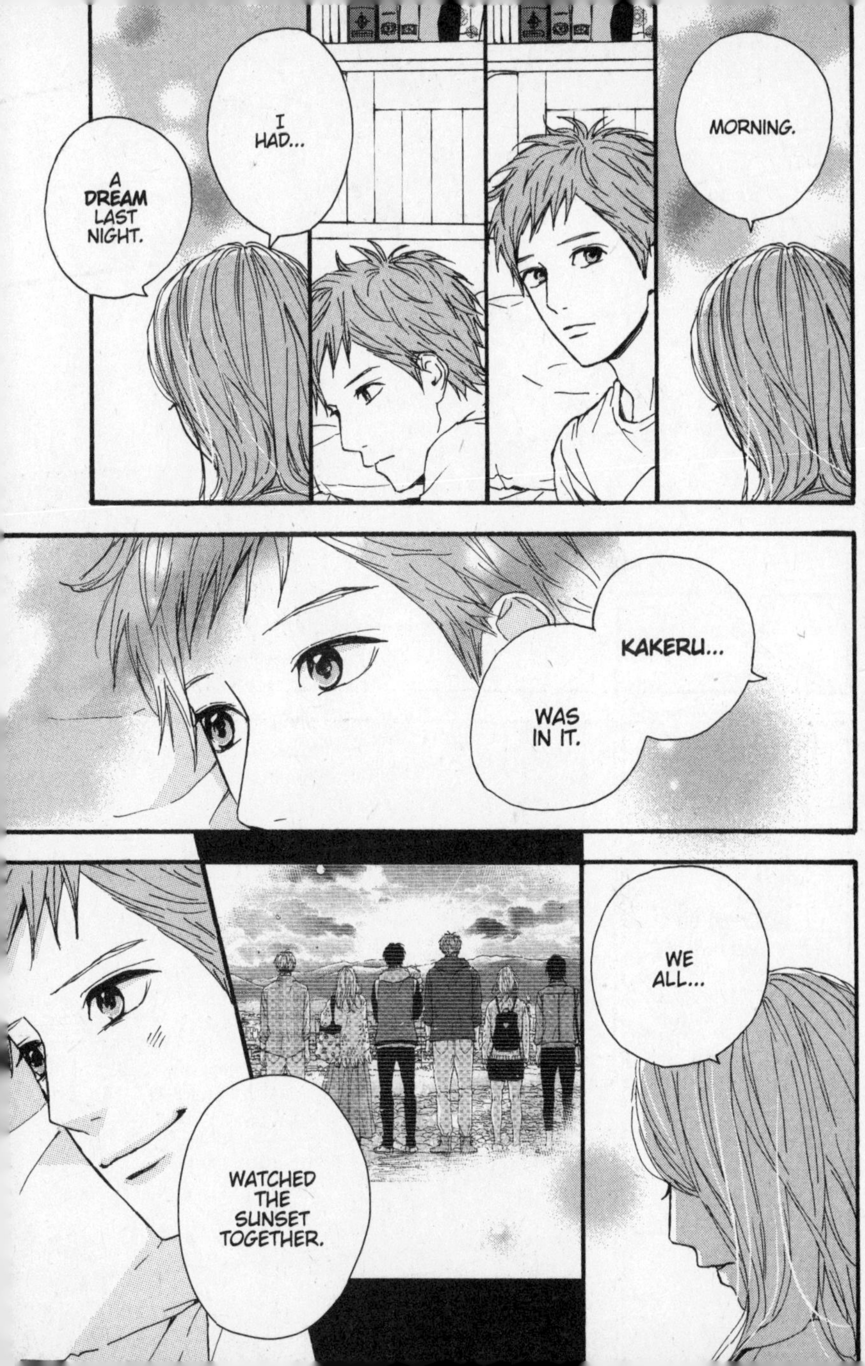
MORNING.
I HAD...
A DREAM LAST NIGHT.
KAKERU...
WAS IN IT.
WE ALL...
WATCHED THE SUNSET TOGETHER.

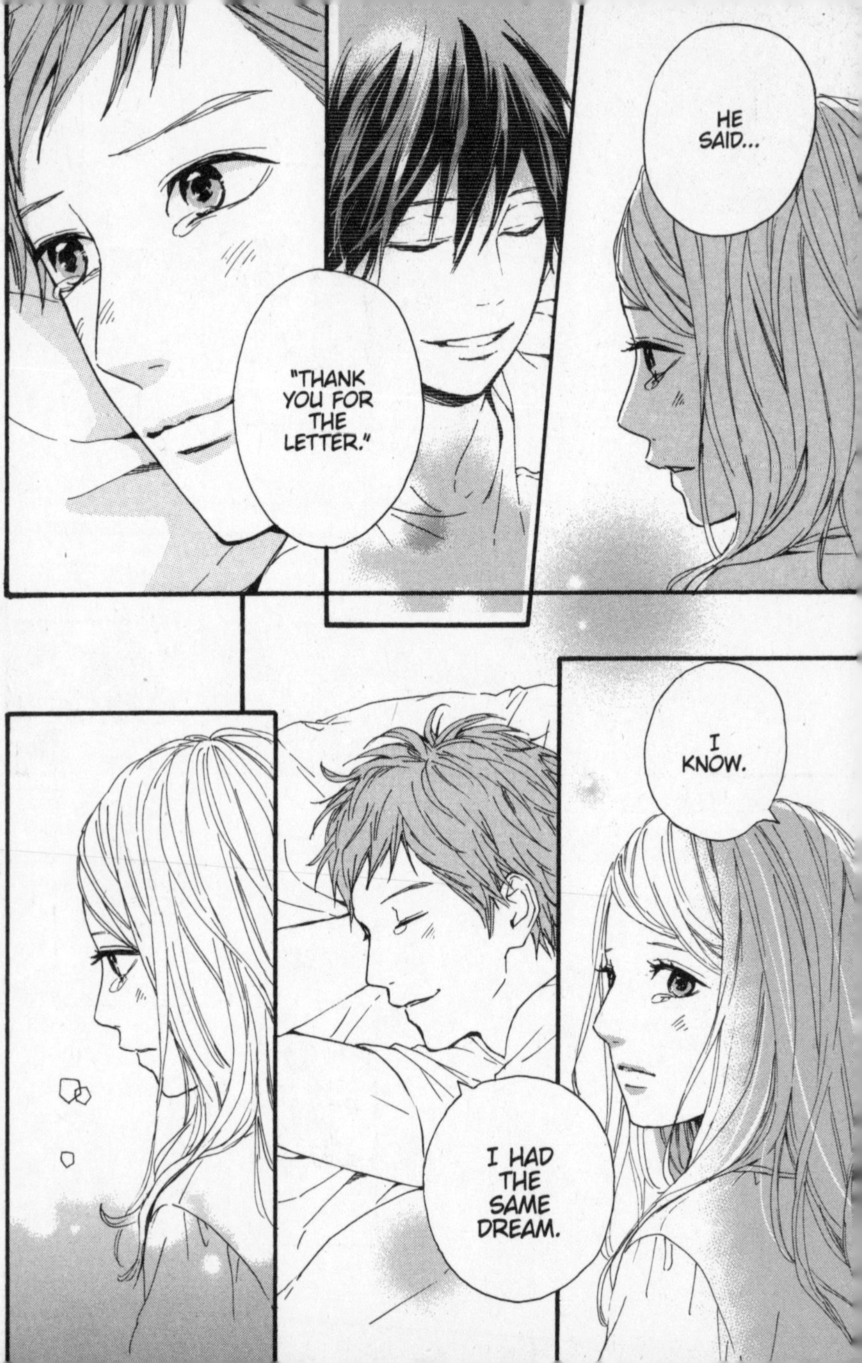
HE SAID...
"THANK YOU FOR THE LETTER."
I KNOW.
I HAD THE SAME DREAM.

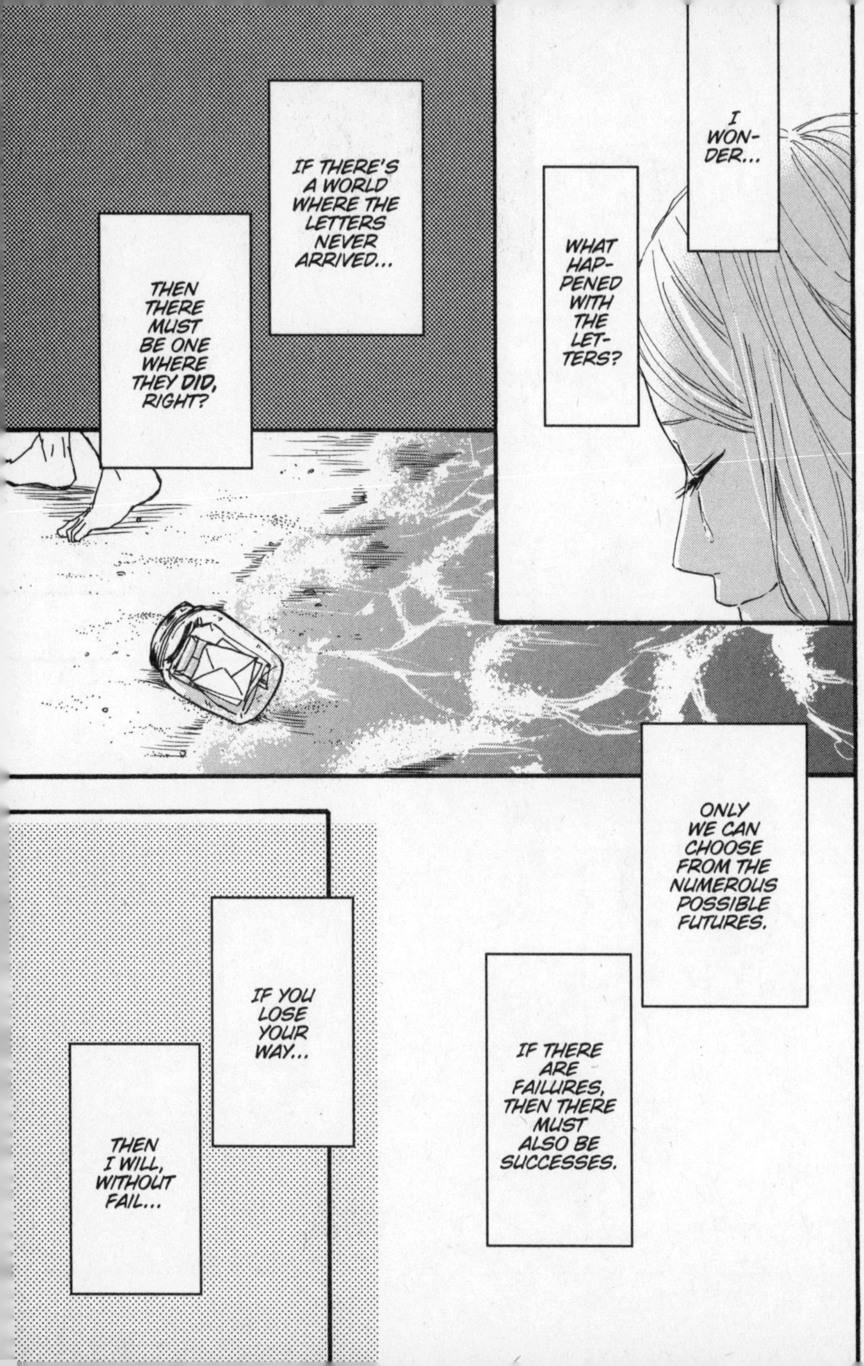
I WONDER...
WHAT HAPPENED WITH THE LETTERS?
IF THERE'S A WORLD WHERE THE LETTERS NEVER ARRIVED...
THEN THERE MUST BE ONE WHERE THEY DID, RIGHT?
ONLY WE CAN CHOOSE FROM THE NUMEROUS POSSIBLE FUTURES.
IF THERE ARE FAILURES, THEN THERE MUST ALSO BE SUCCESSES.
IF YOU LOSE YOUR WAY...
THEN I WILL, WITHOUT FAIL...

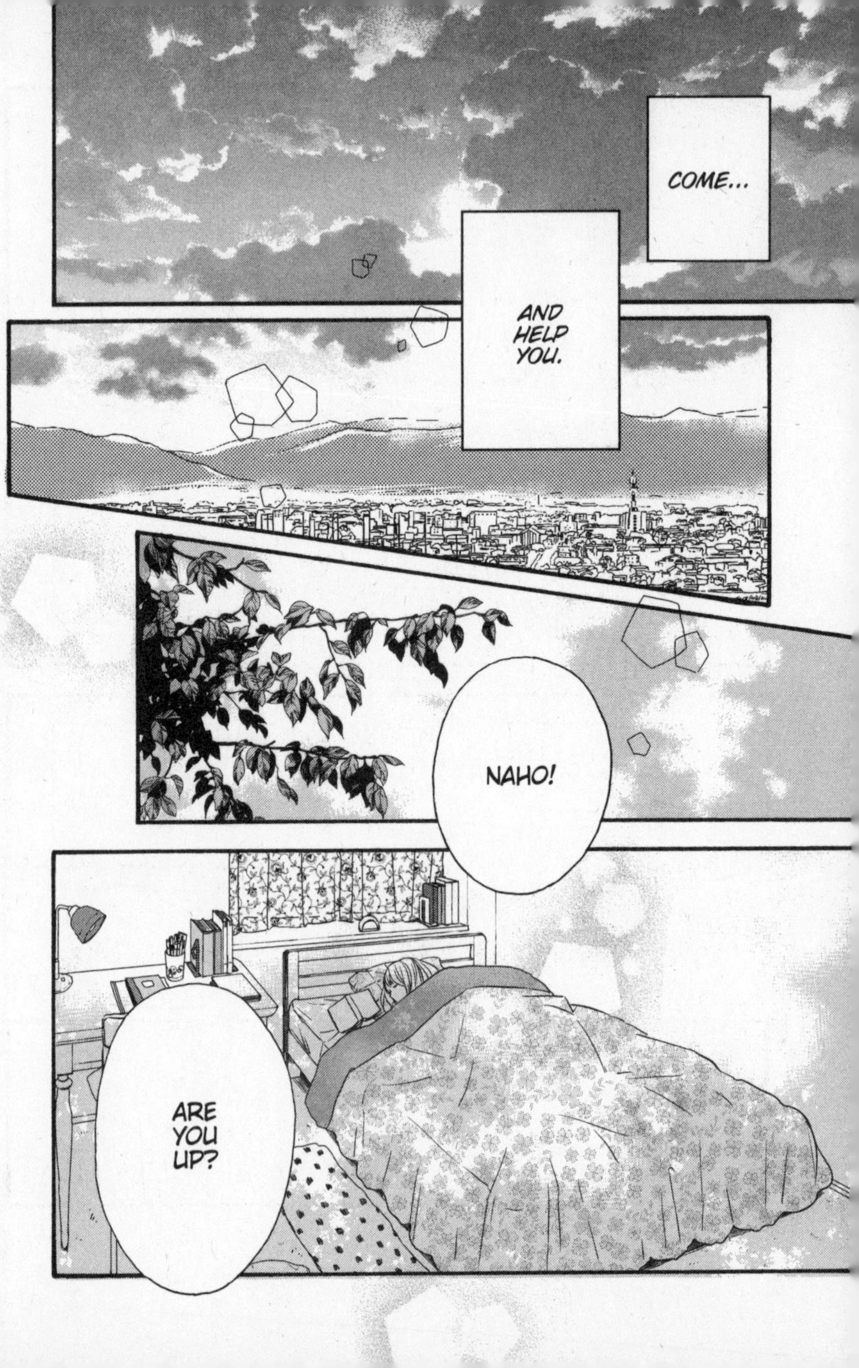
COME...
AND HELP YOU.
NAHO!
ARE YOU UP?

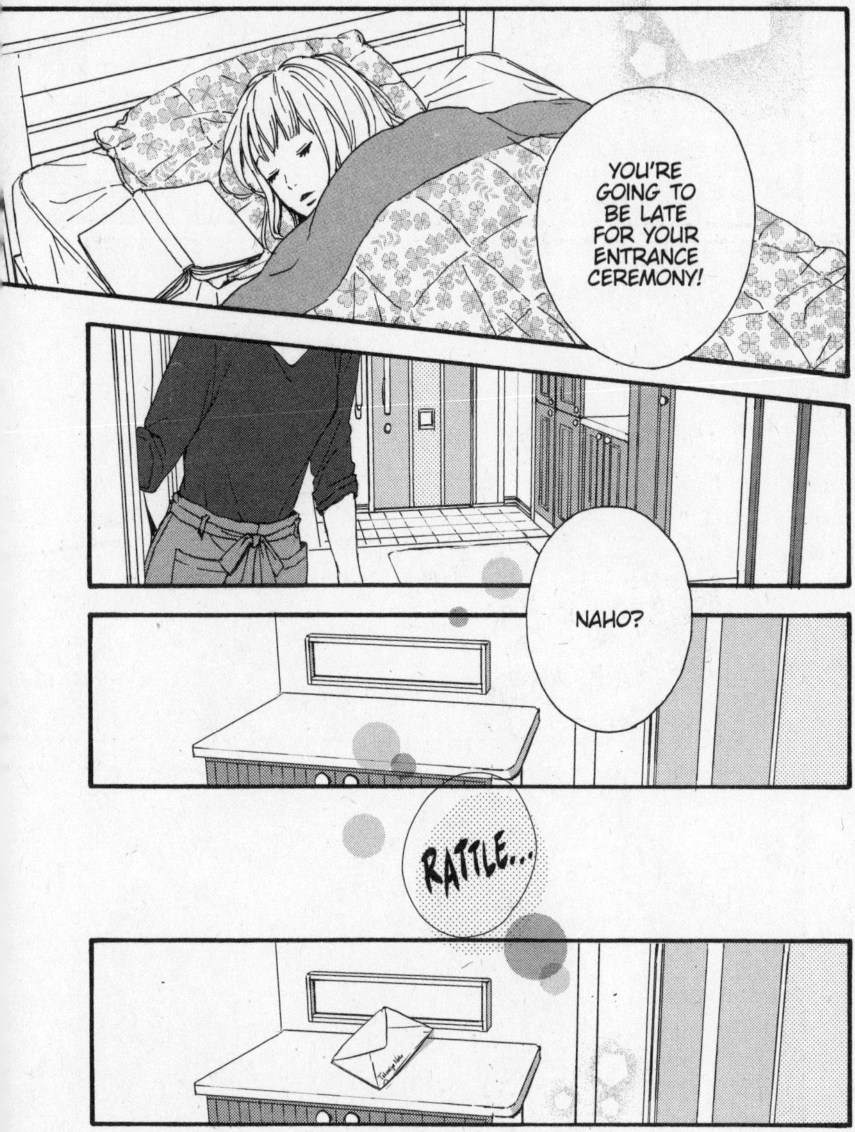
YOU'RE GOING TO BE LATE FOR YOUR ENTRANCE CEREMONY!
NAHO?
RATTLE...

«End»

orange

—Suwa Hiroto— #1

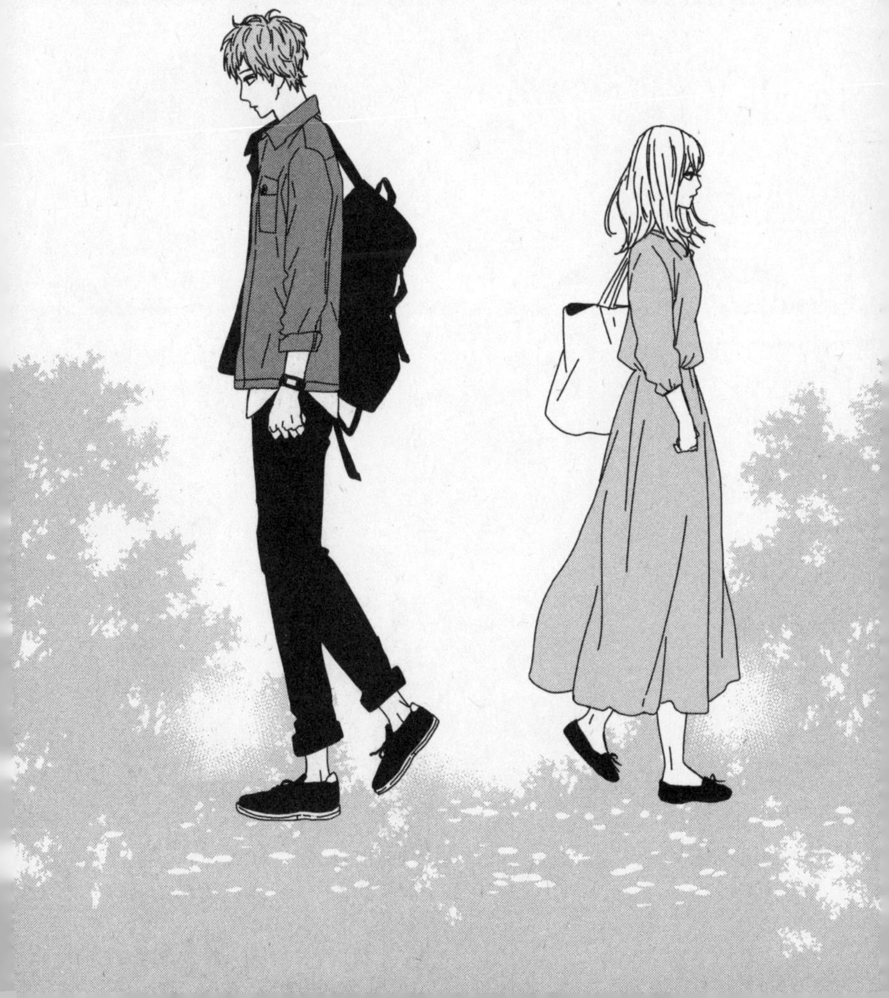

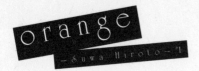

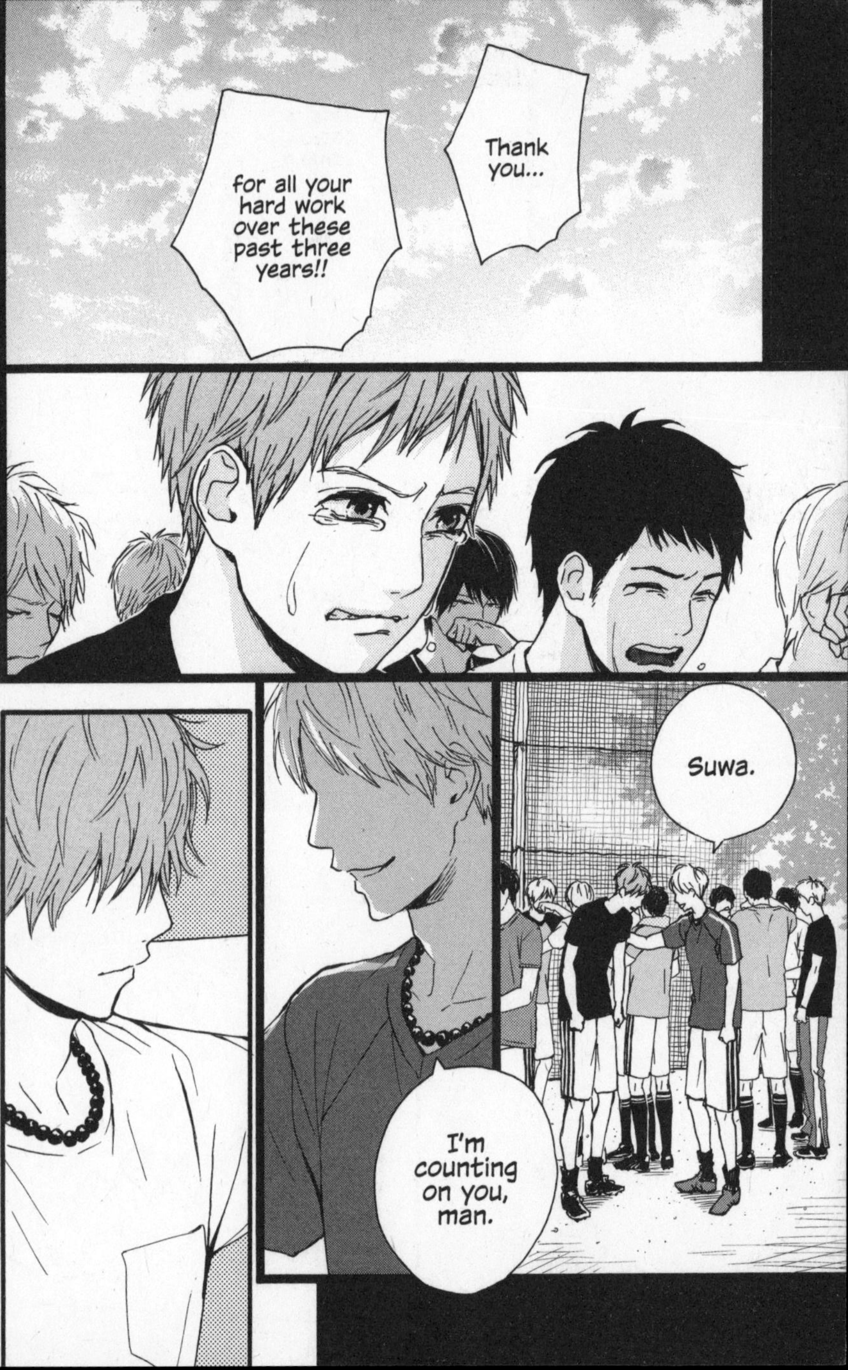
Thank you...
for all your hard work over these past three years!!
Suwa.
I'm counting on you, man.

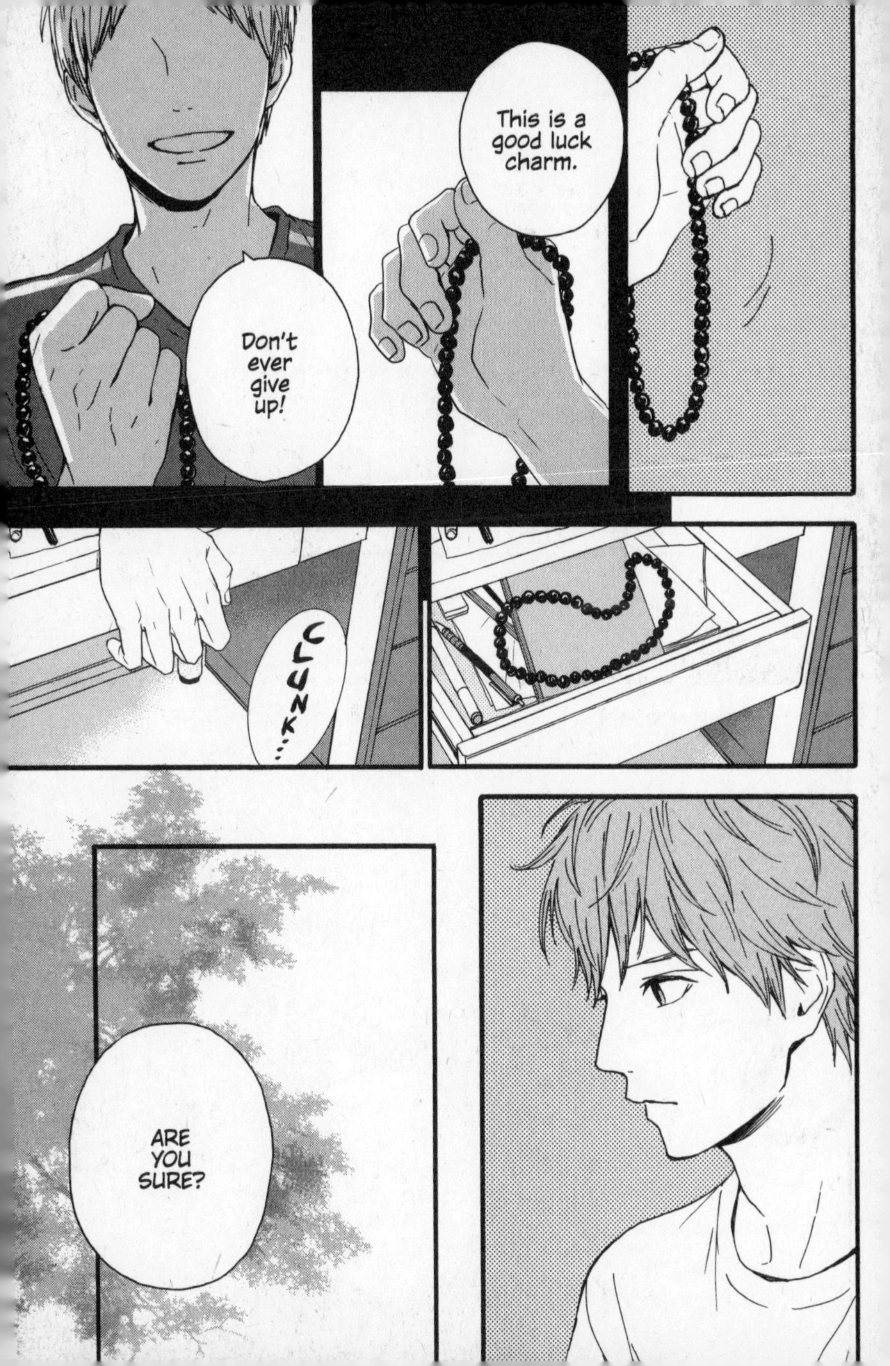
This is a good luck charm.
Don't ever give up!
CLUNK...
ARE YOU SURE?

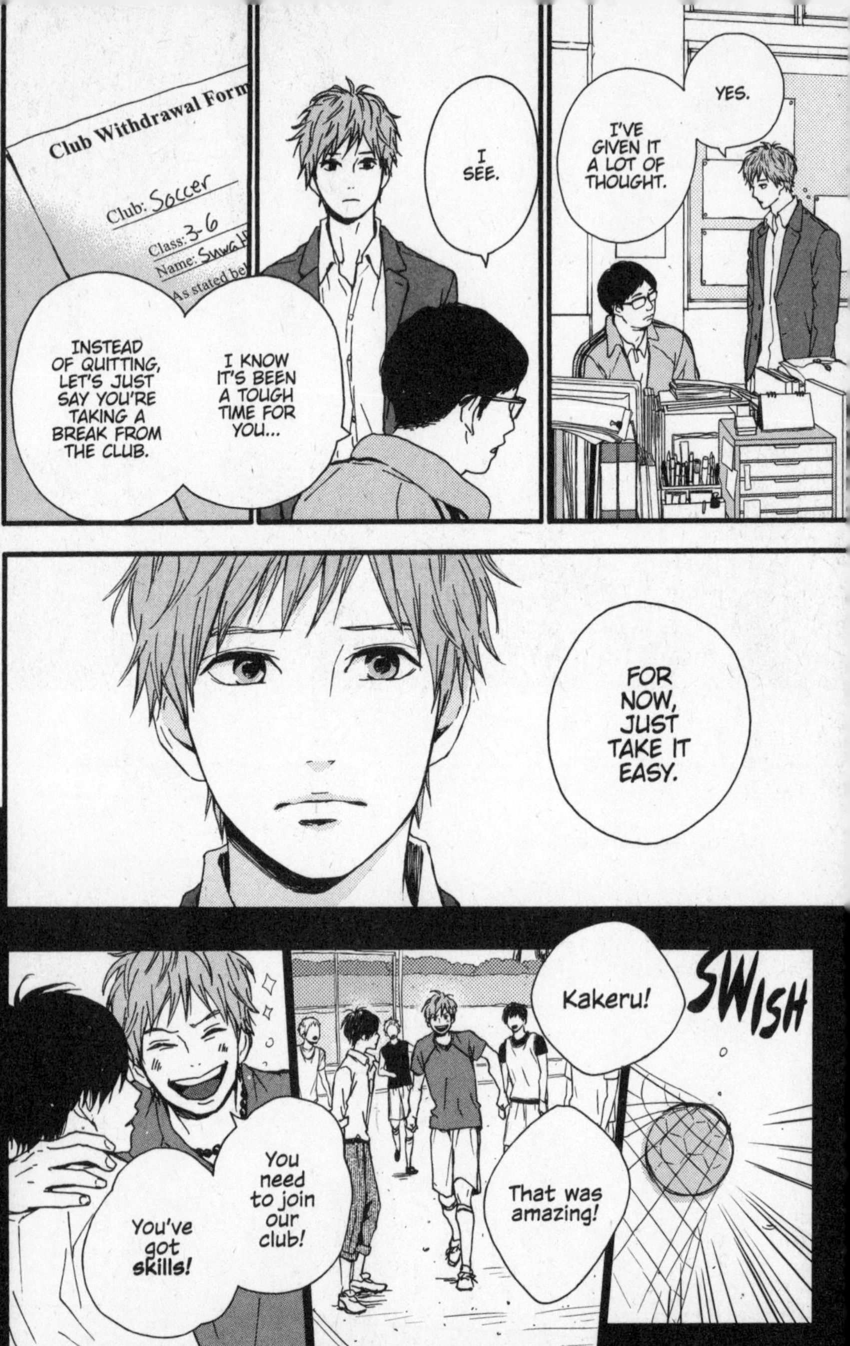
YES.
I'VE GIVEN IT A LOT OF THOUGHT.
I SEE.
Club Withdrawal Form
Club: Soccer
Class: 3-6
Name: Suwa
I KNOW IT'S BEEN A TOUGH TIME FOR YOU...
INSTEAD OF QUITTING, LET'S JUST SAY YOU'RE TAKING A BREAK FROM THE CLUB.
FOR NOW, JUST TAKE IT EASY.
SWISH
Kakeru!
That was amazing!
You need to join our club!
You've got skills!

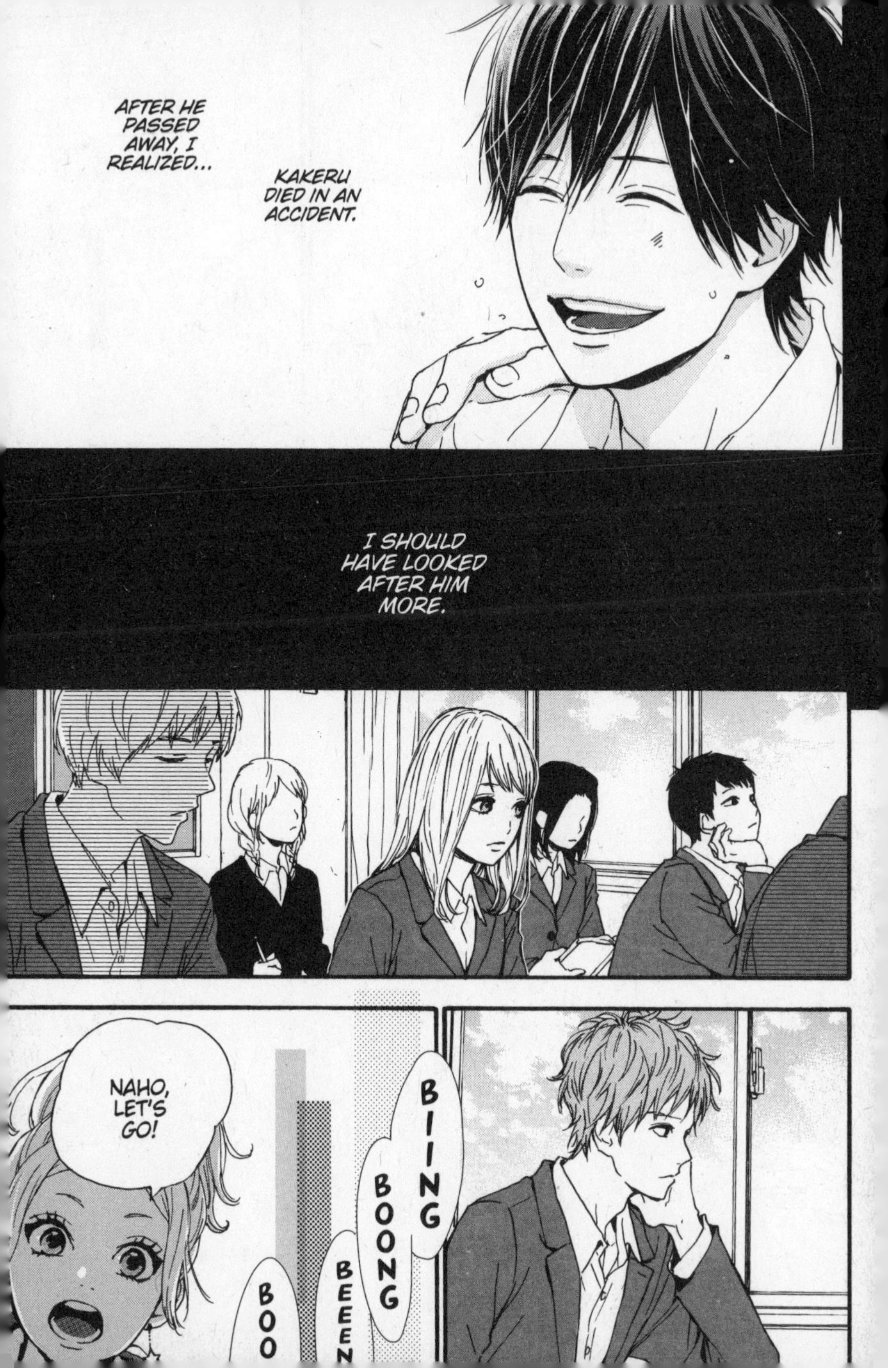
KAKERU DIED IN AN ACCIDENT.
AFTER HE PASSED AWAY, I REALIZED...
I SHOULD HAVE LOOKED AFTER HIM MORE.
BIING
BOONG
BEEEN
BOO
NAHO, LET'S GO!

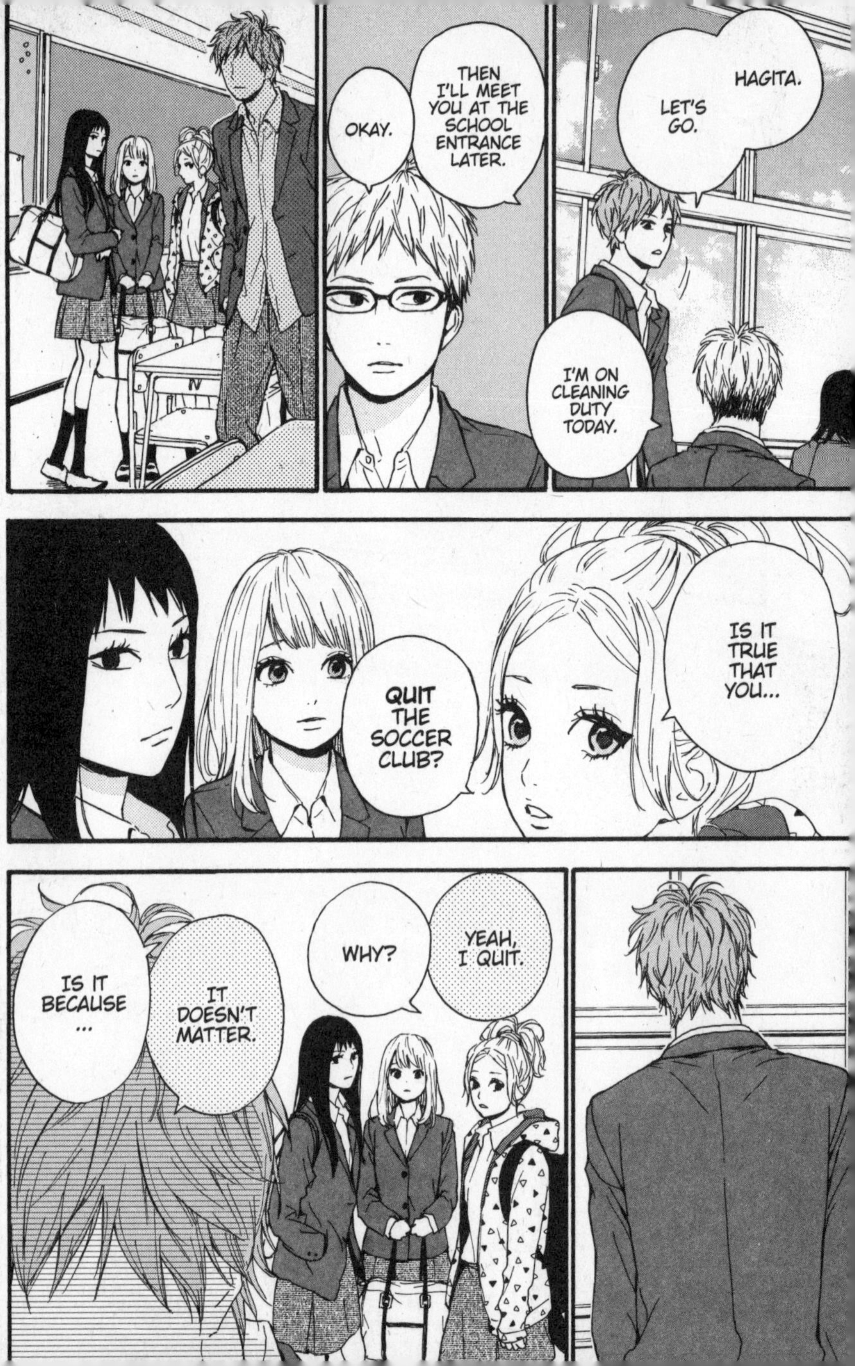
HAGITA.
LET'S GO.
I'M ON CLEANING DUTY TODAY.
THEN I'LL MEET YOU AT THE SCHOOL ENTRANCE LATER.
OKAY.
IS IT TRUE THAT YOU...
QUIT THE SOCCER CLUB?
YEAH, I QUIT.
WHY?
IT DOESN'T MATTER.
IS IT BECAUSE ...

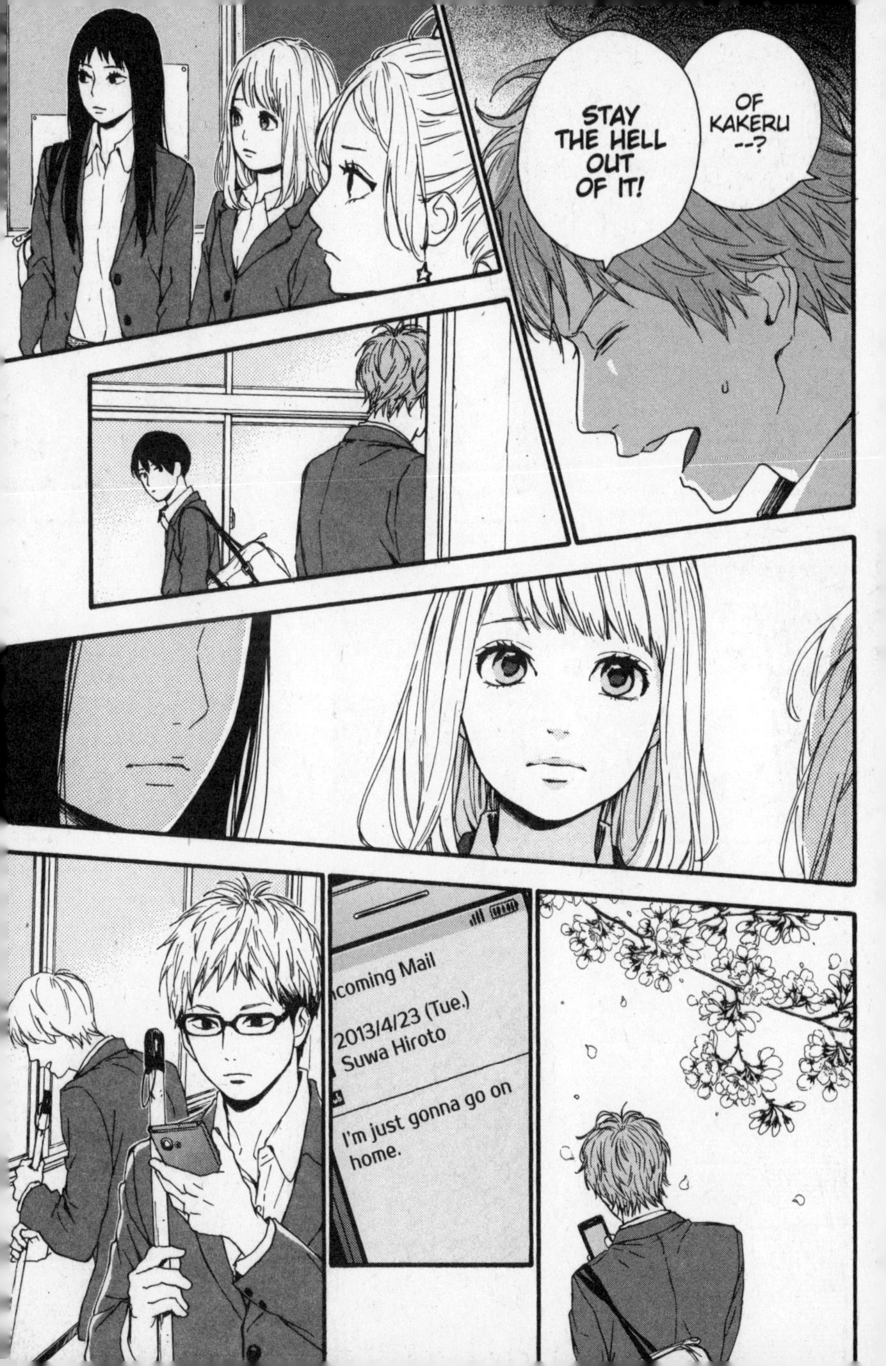
OF KAKERU --?
STAY THE HELL OUT OF IT!
ncoming Mail
2013/4/23 (Tue.)
Suwa Hiroto
I'm just gonna go on home.

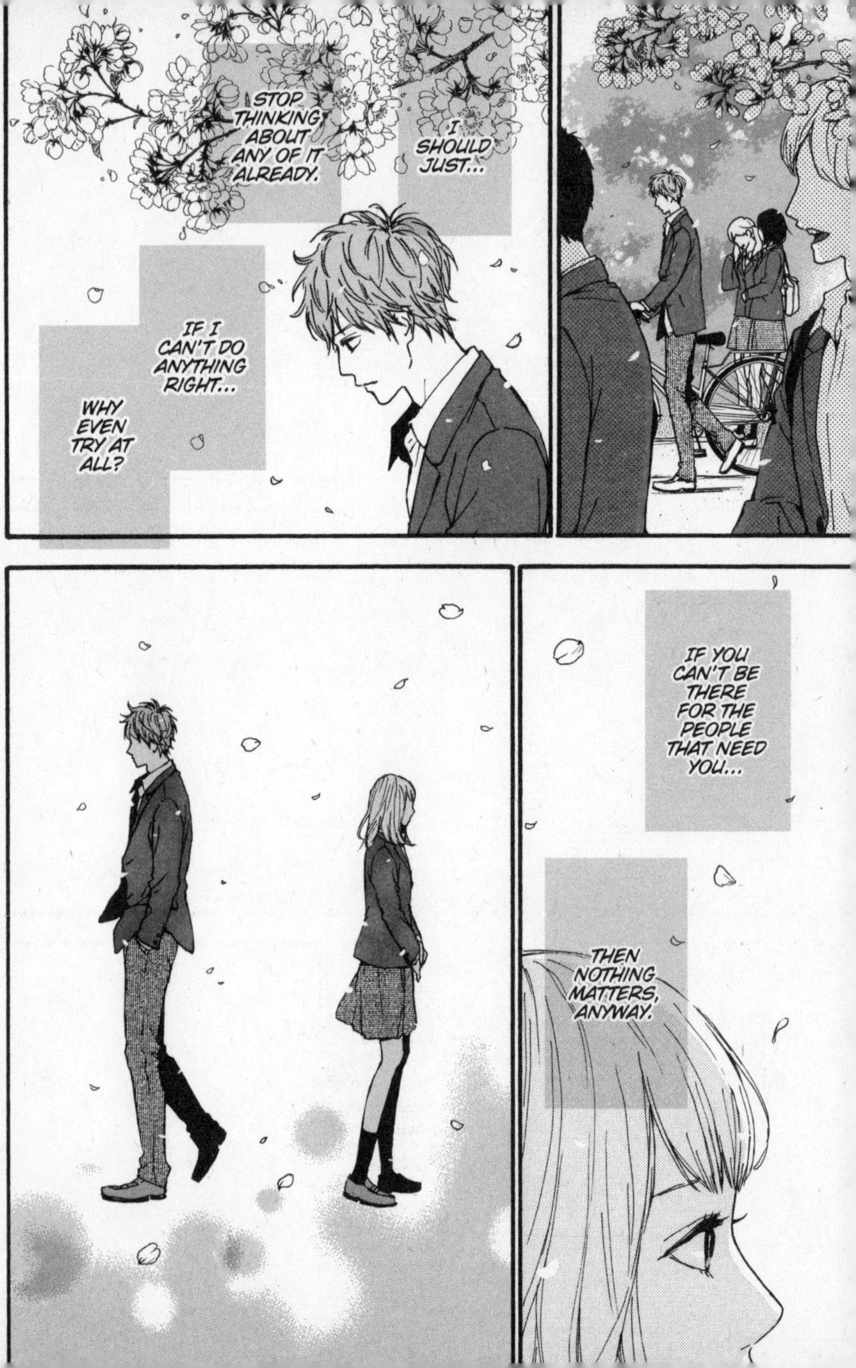
STOP THINKING ABOUT ANY OF IT ALREADY.
I SHOULD JUST...
IF I CAN'T DO ANYTHING RIGHT...
WHY EVEN TRY AT ALL?
IF YOU CAN'T BE THERE FOR THE PEOPLE THAT NEED YOU...
THEN NOTHING MATTERS, ANYWAY.

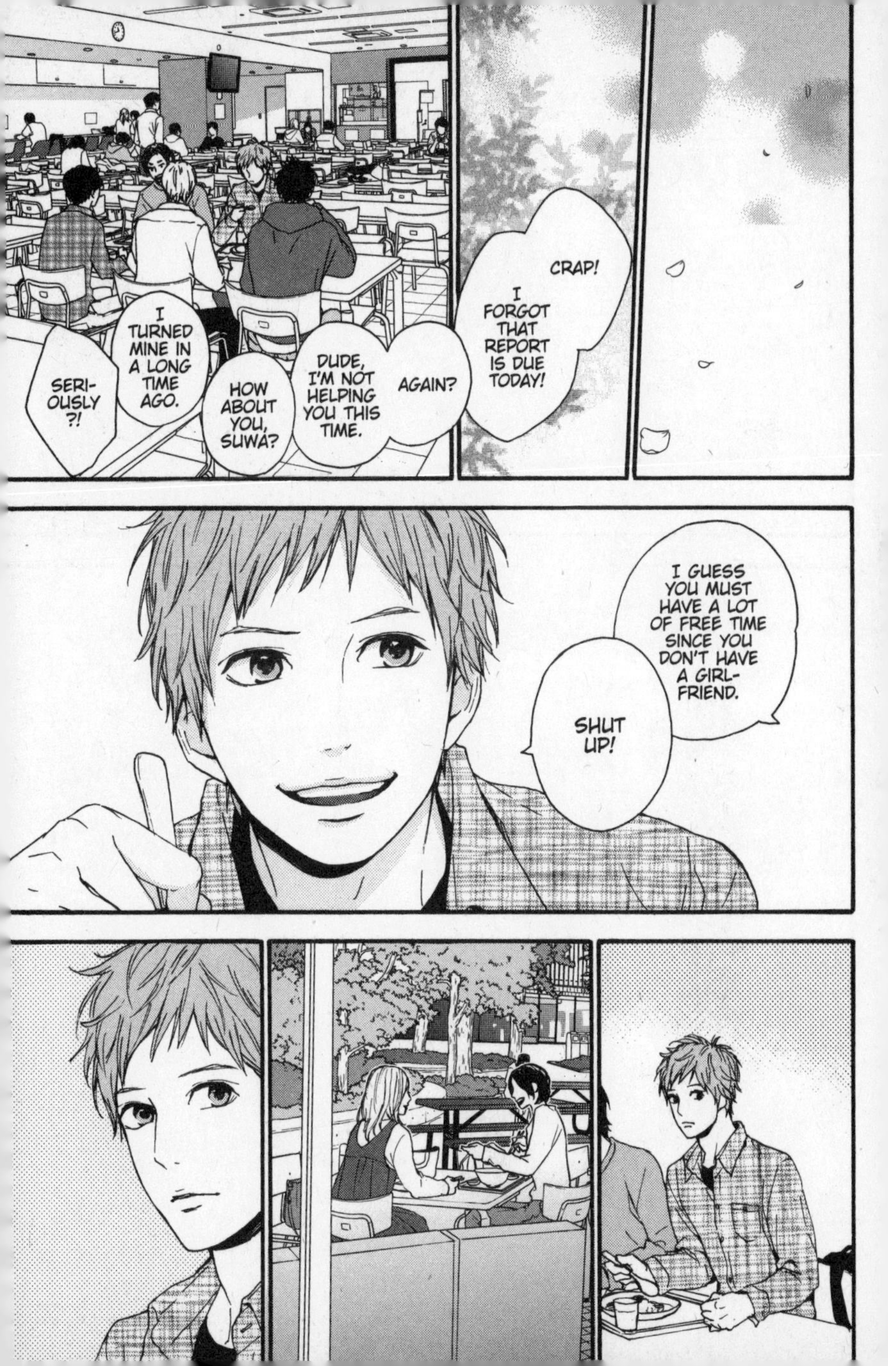
CRAP!
I FORGOT THAT REPORT IS DUE TODAY!
AGAIN?
DUDE, I'M NOT HELPING YOU THIS TIME.
HOW ABOUT YOU, SUWA?
I TURNED MINE IN A LONG TIME AGO.
SERI-OUSLY?!
I GUESS YOU MUST HAVE A LOT OF FREE TIME SINCE YOU DON'T HAVE A GIRL-FRIEND.
SHUT UP!

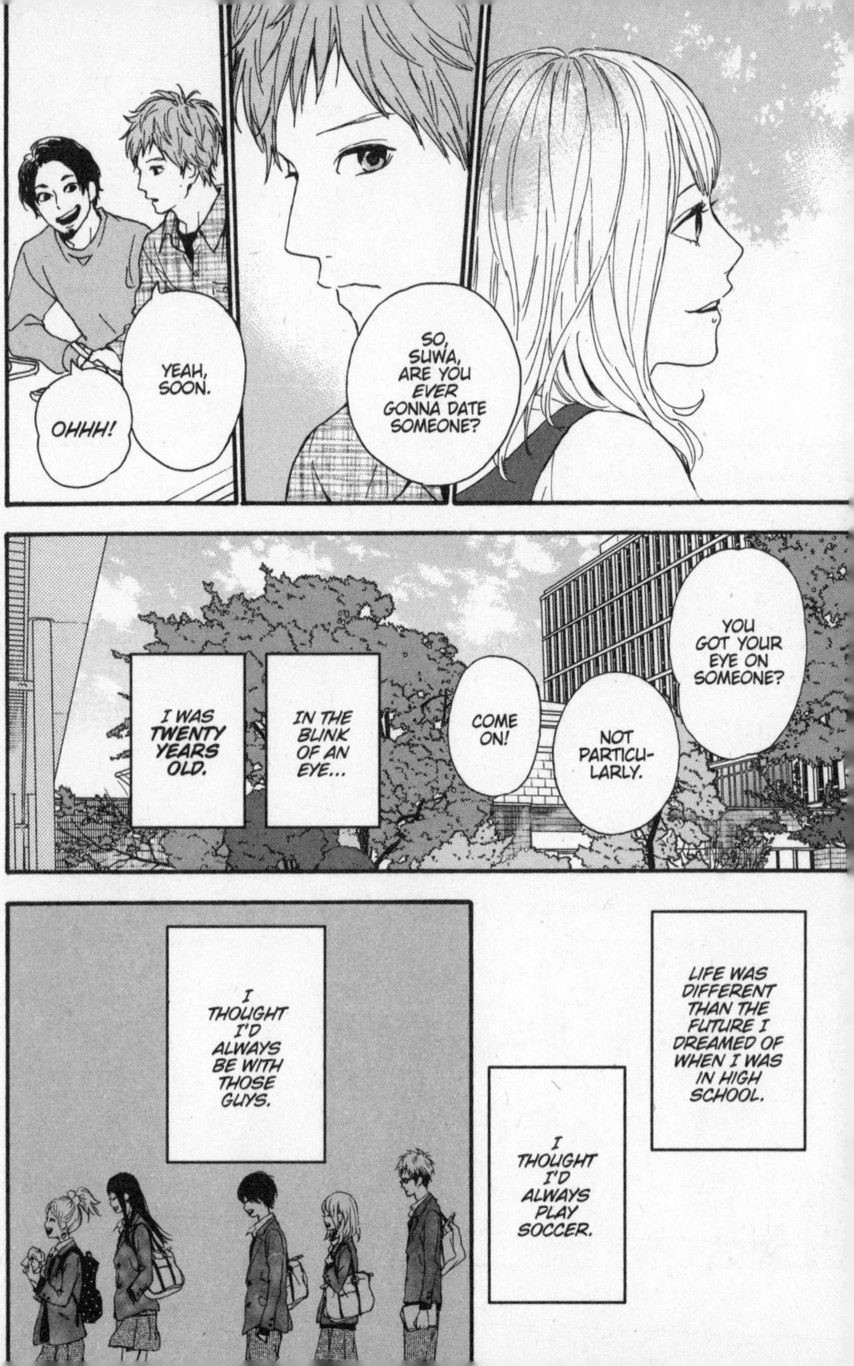
SO, SUWA, ARE YOU EVER GONNA DATE SOMEONE?
YEAH, SOON.
OHHH!
YOU GOT YOUR EYE ON SOMEONE?
NOT PARTICU-LARLY.
COME ON!
IN THE BLINK OF AN EYE...
I WAS TWENTY YEARS OLD.
LIFE WAS DIFFERENT THAN THE FUTURE I DREAMED OF WHEN I WAS IN HIGH SCHOOL.
I THOUGHT I'D ALWAYS PLAY SOCCER.
I THOUGHT I'D ALWAYS BE WITH THOSE GUYS.

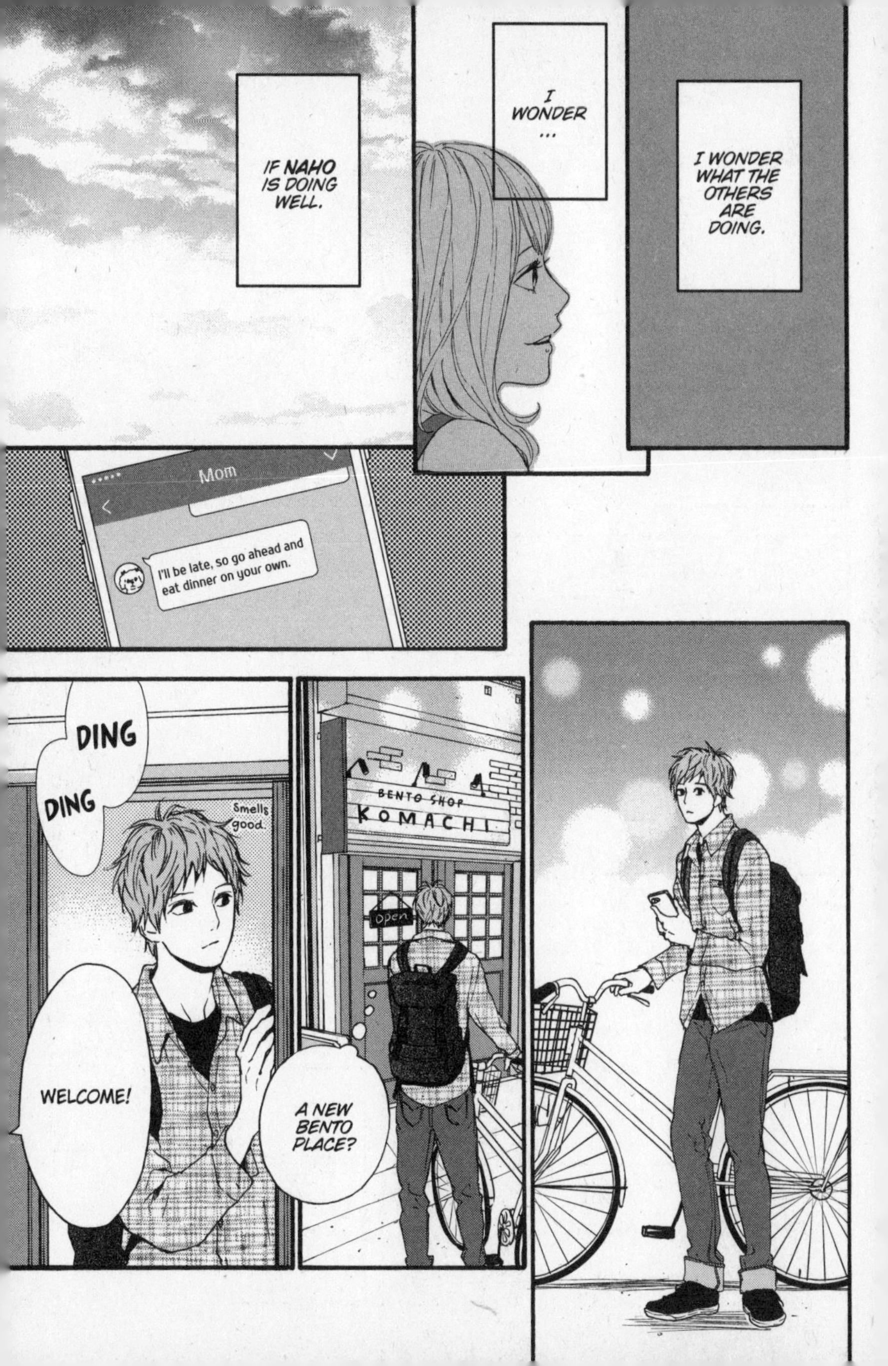
I WONDER WHAT THE OTHERS ARE DOING.
I WONDER ...
IF NAHO IS DOING WELL.
Mom
I'll be late, so go ahead and eat dinner on your own.
BENTO SHOP
KOMACHI
open
A NEW BENTO PLACE?
DING
DING
Smells good.
WELCOME!

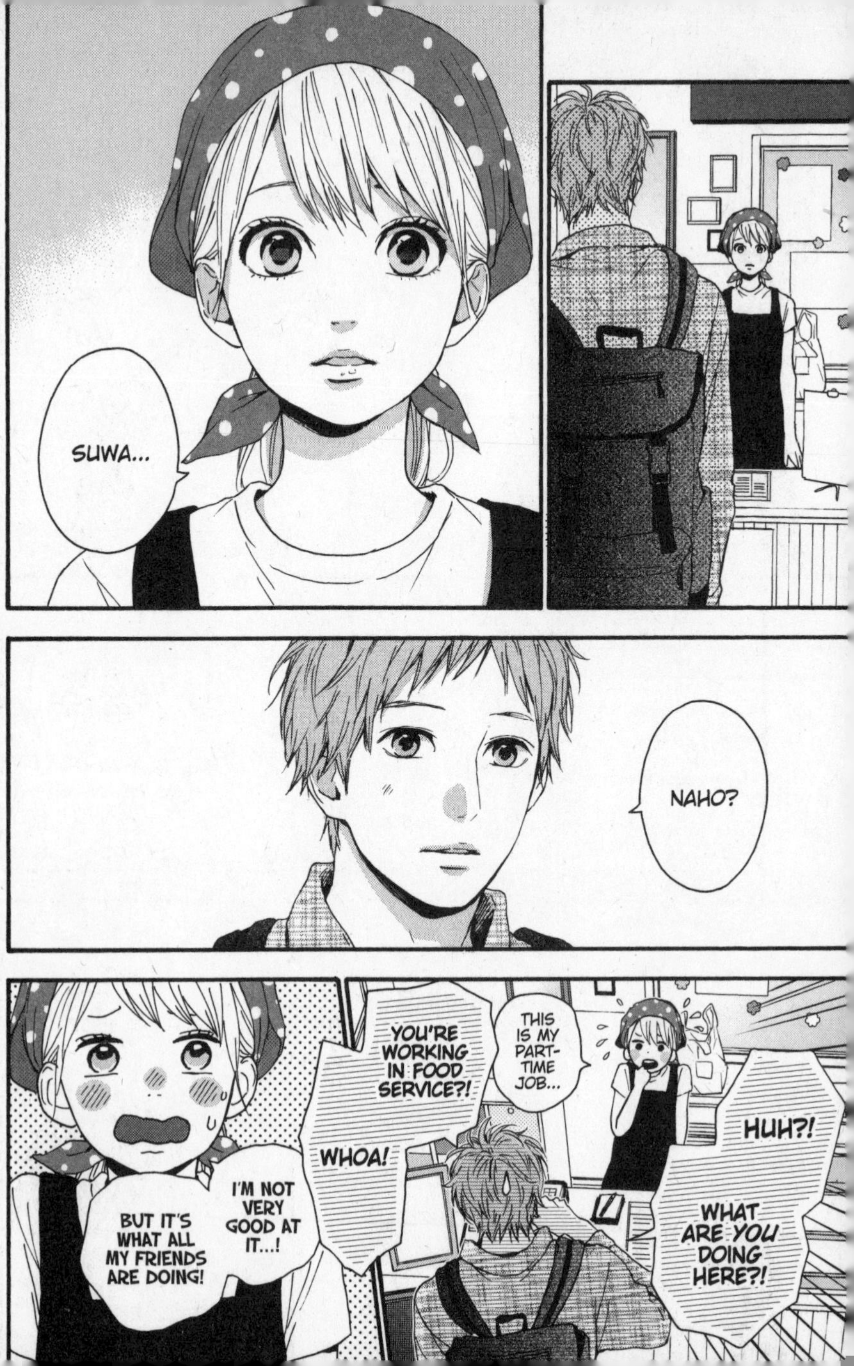
SUWA...
NAHO?
HUH?!
WHAT ARE YOU DOING HERE?!
THIS IS MY PART-TIME JOB...
YOU'RE WORKING IN FOOD SERVICE?!
WHOA!
I'M NOT VERY GOOD AT IT...!
BUT IT'S WHAT ALL MY FRIENDS ARE DOING!

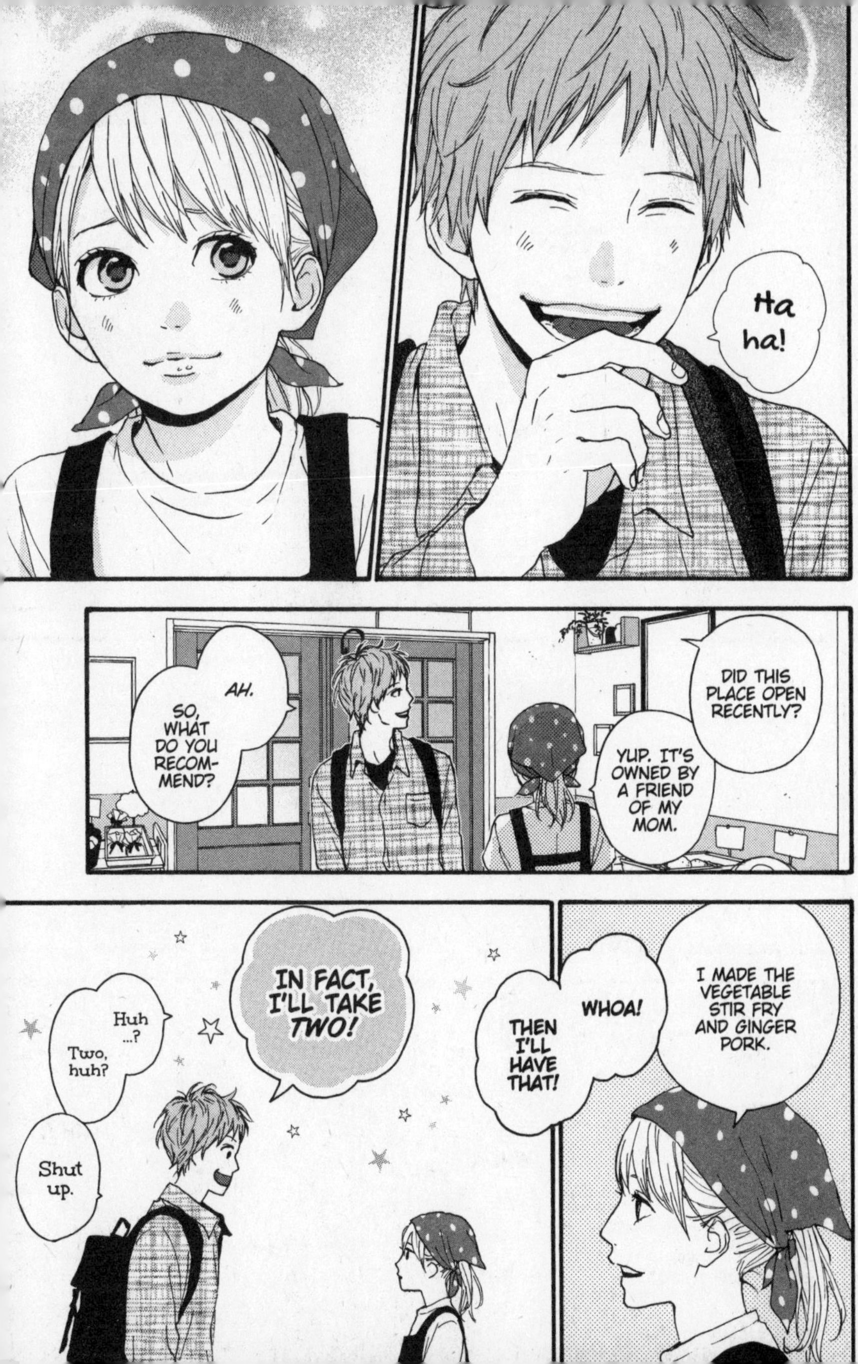
Ha ha!
DID THIS PLACE OPEN RECENTLY?
YUP. IT'S OWNED BY A FRIEND OF MY MOM.
AH. SO, WHAT DO YOU RECOMMEND?
I MADE THE VEGETABLE STIR FRY AND GINGER PORK.
WHOA! THEN I'LL HAVE THAT!
IN FACT, I'LL TAKE *TWO!*
Huh ...? Two, huh?
Shut up.

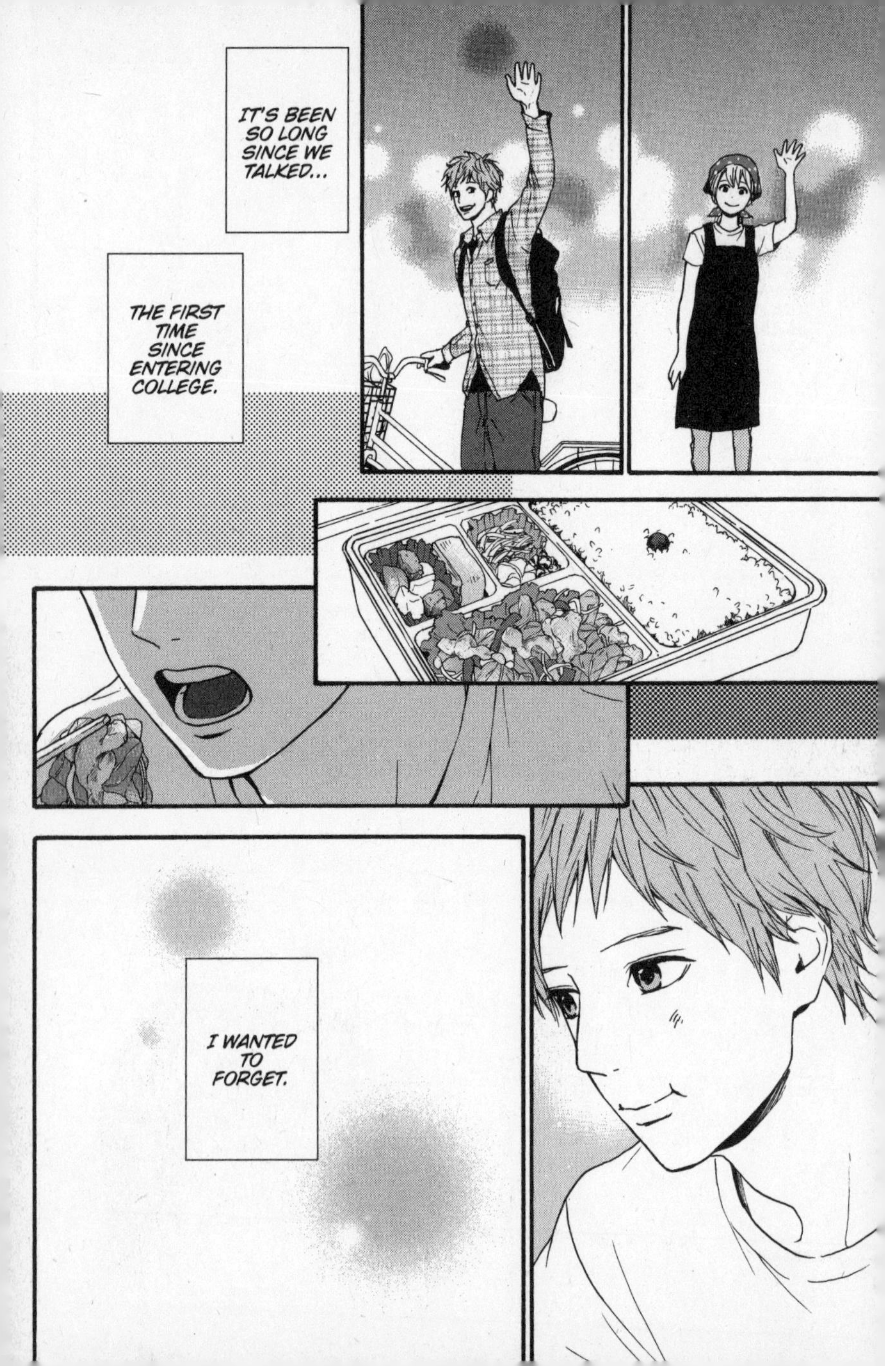
IT'S BEEN SO LONG SINCE WE TALKED...
THE FIRST TIME SINCE ENTERING COLLEGE.
I WANTED TO FORGET.

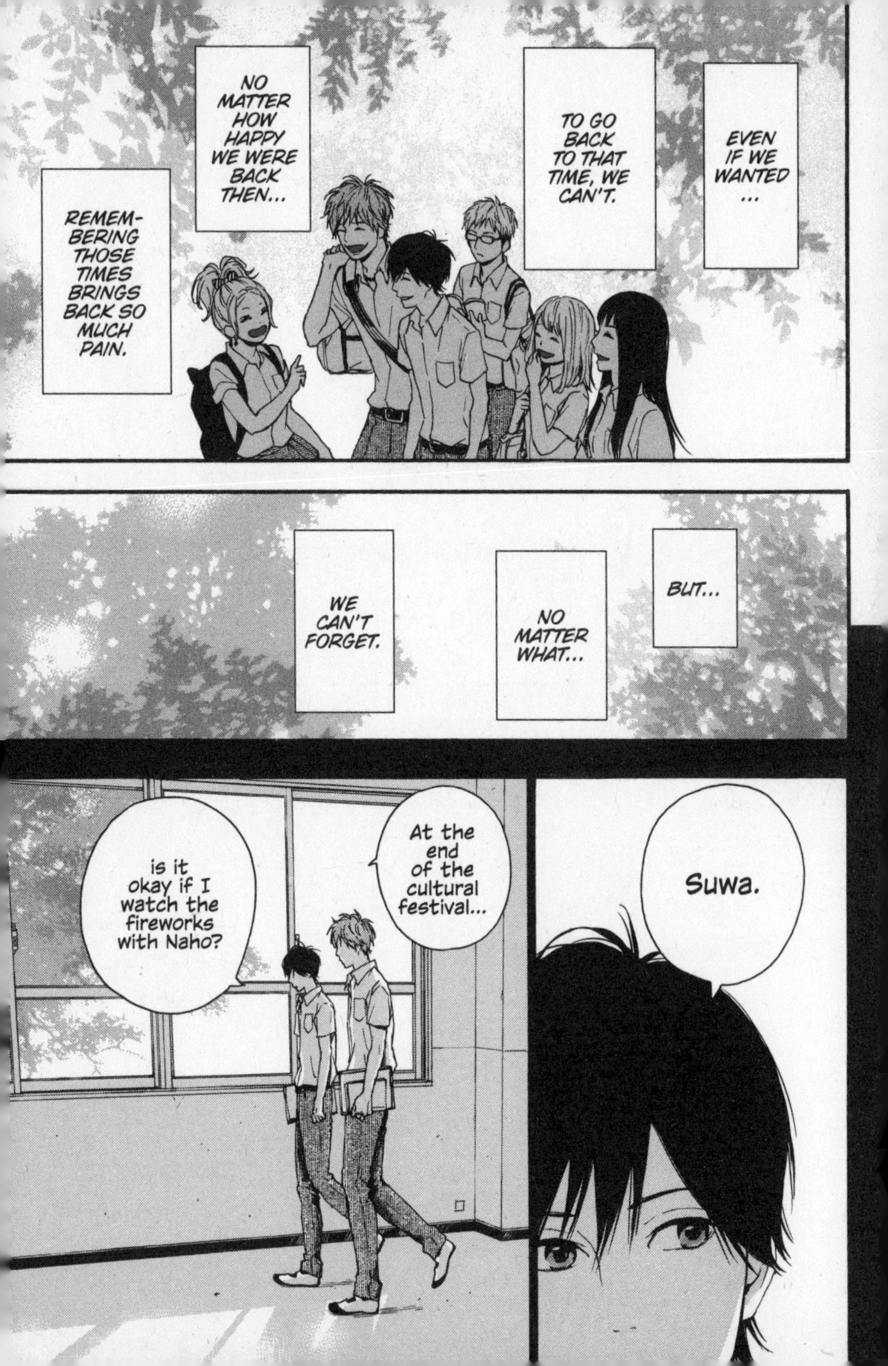
EVEN IF WE WANTED...
TO GO BACK TO THAT TIME, WE CAN'T.
NO MATTER HOW HAPPY WE WERE BACK THEN...
REMEMBERING THOSE TIMES BRINGS BACK SO MUCH PAIN.
BUT...
NO MATTER WHAT...
WE CAN'T FORGET.
Suwa.
At the end of the cultural festival...
is it okay if I watch the fireworks with Naho?

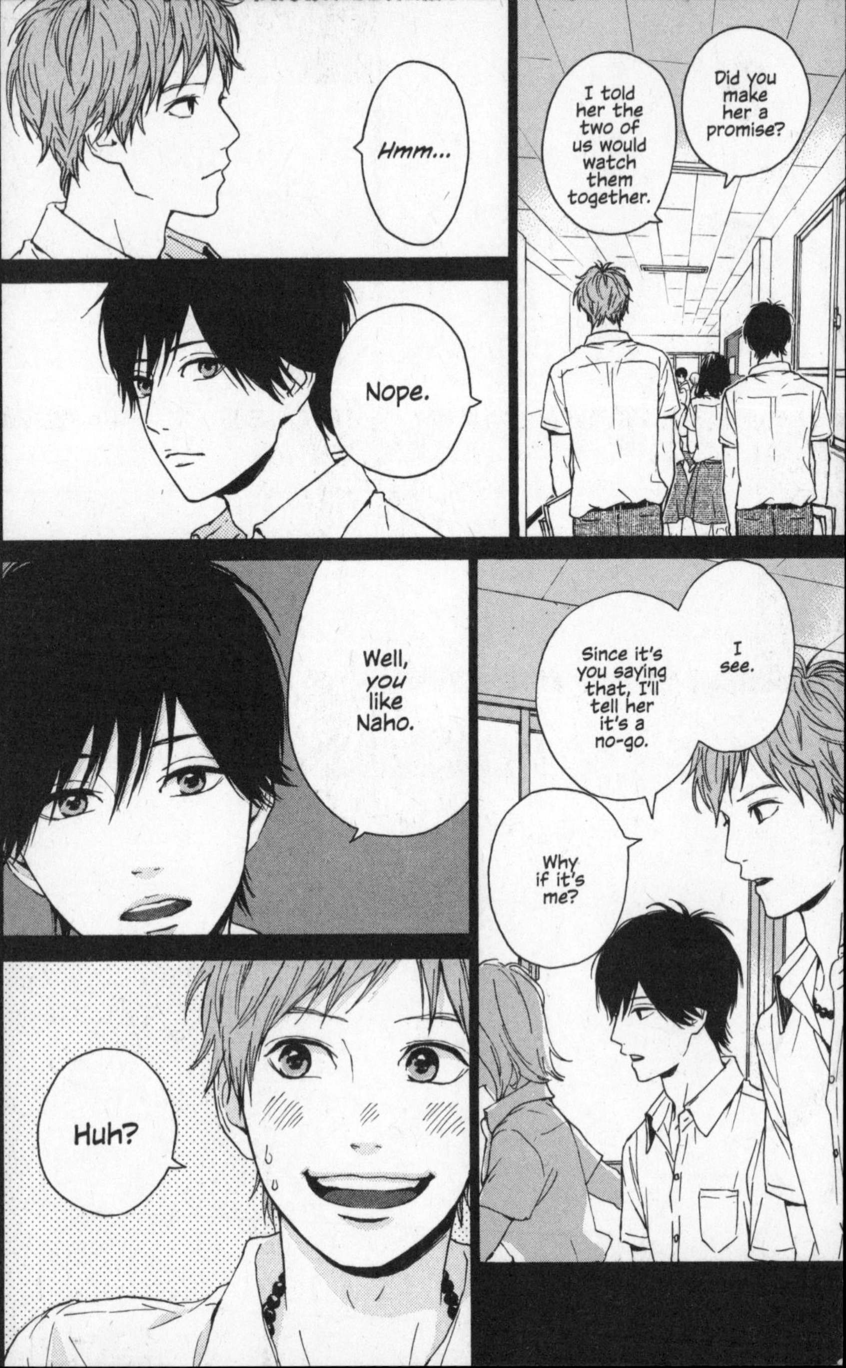
Did you make her a promise?
I told her the two of us would watch them together.
Hmm...
Nope.
I see.
Since it's you saying that, I'll tell her it's a no-go.
Why if it's me?
Well, *you* like Naho.
Huh?

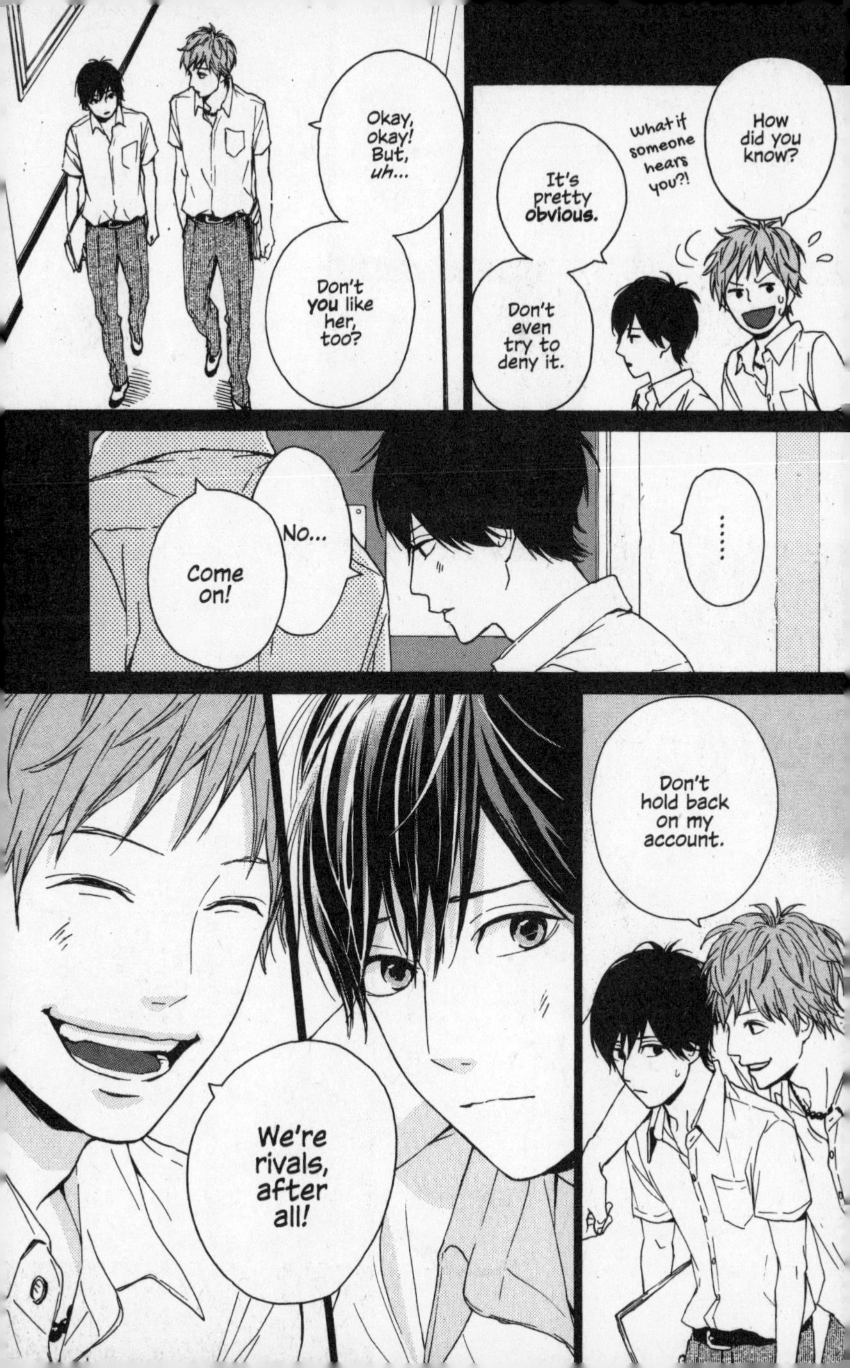
How did you know?
What if someone hears you?!
It's pretty obvious.
Don't even try to deny it.
Okay, okay! But, uh...
Don't you like her, too?
......
No...
Come on!
Don't hold back on my account.
We're rivals, after all!

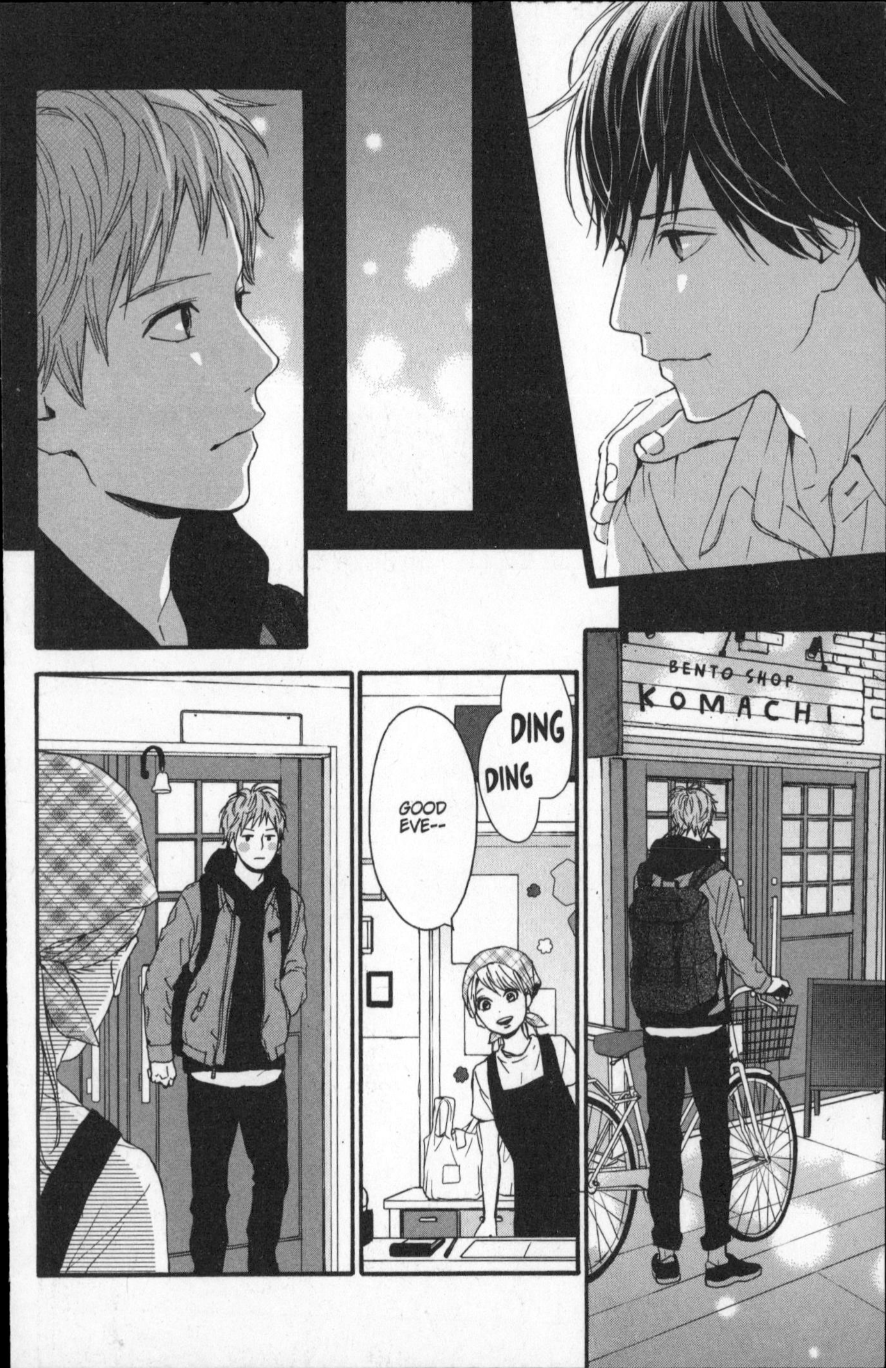
BENTO SHOP
KOMACHI
DING
DING
GOOD EVE--

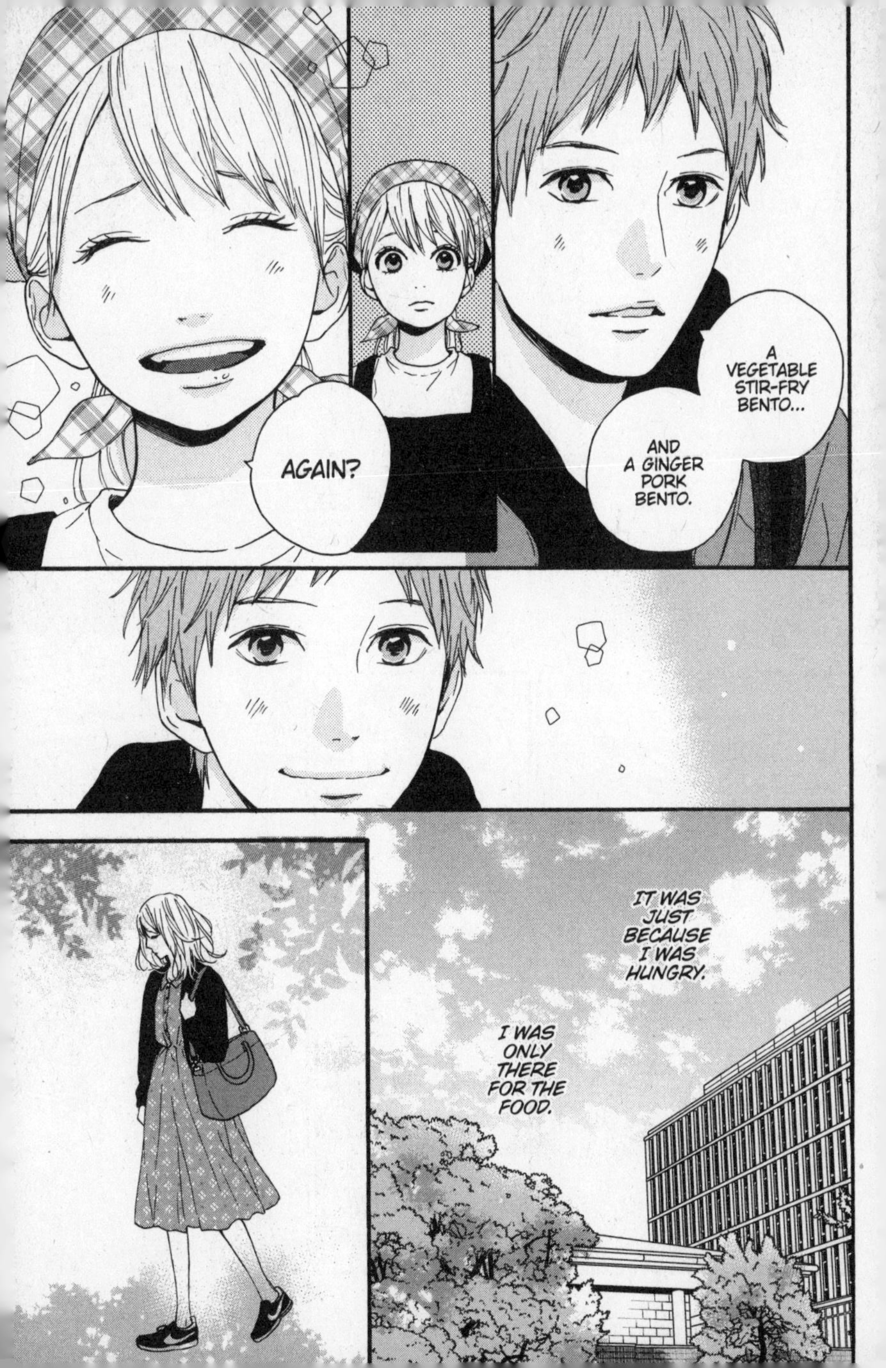
A VEGETABLE STIR-FRY BENTO...
AND A GINGER PORK BENTO.
AGAIN?
IT WAS JUST BECAUSE I WAS HUNGRY.
I WAS ONLY THERE FOR THE FOOD.

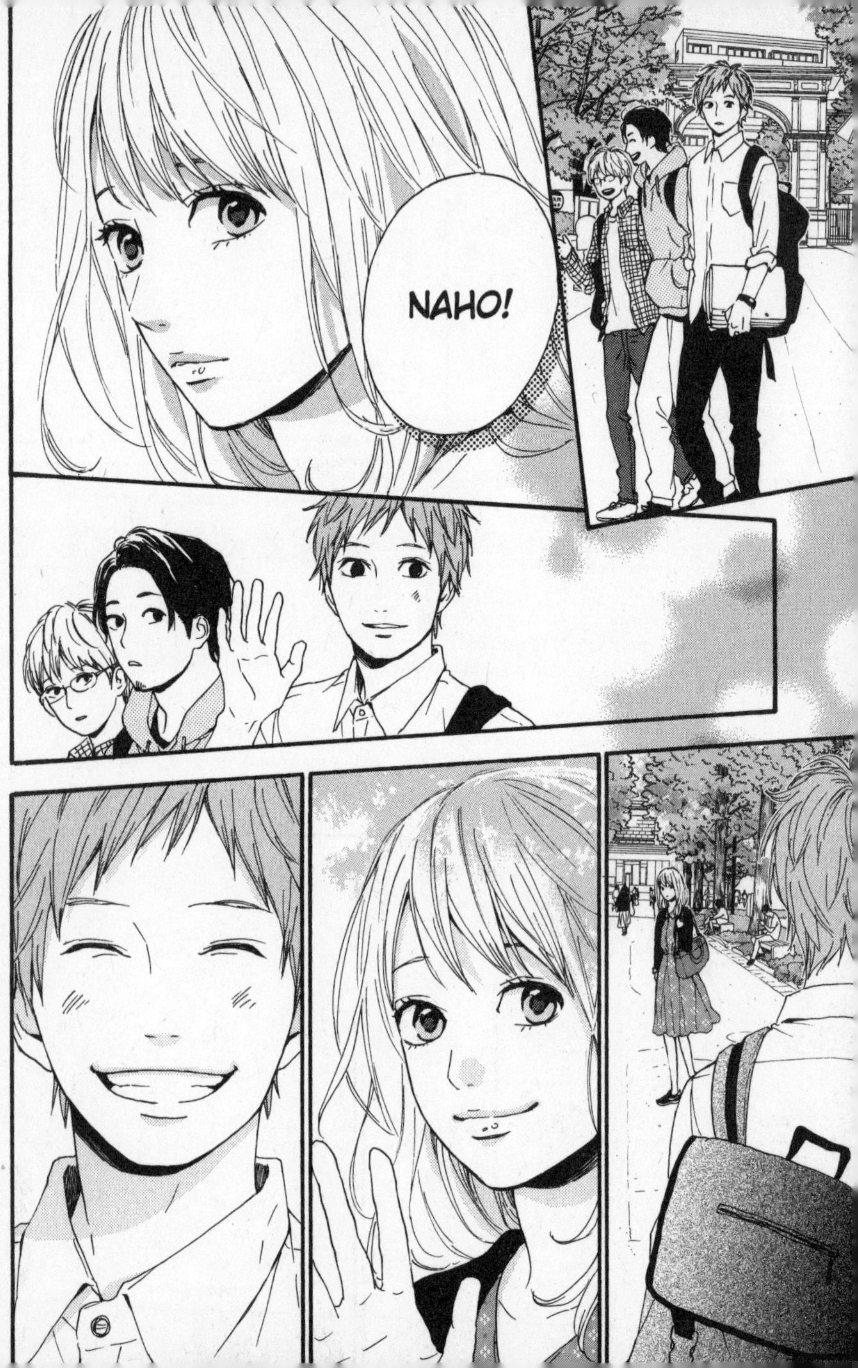
NAHO!

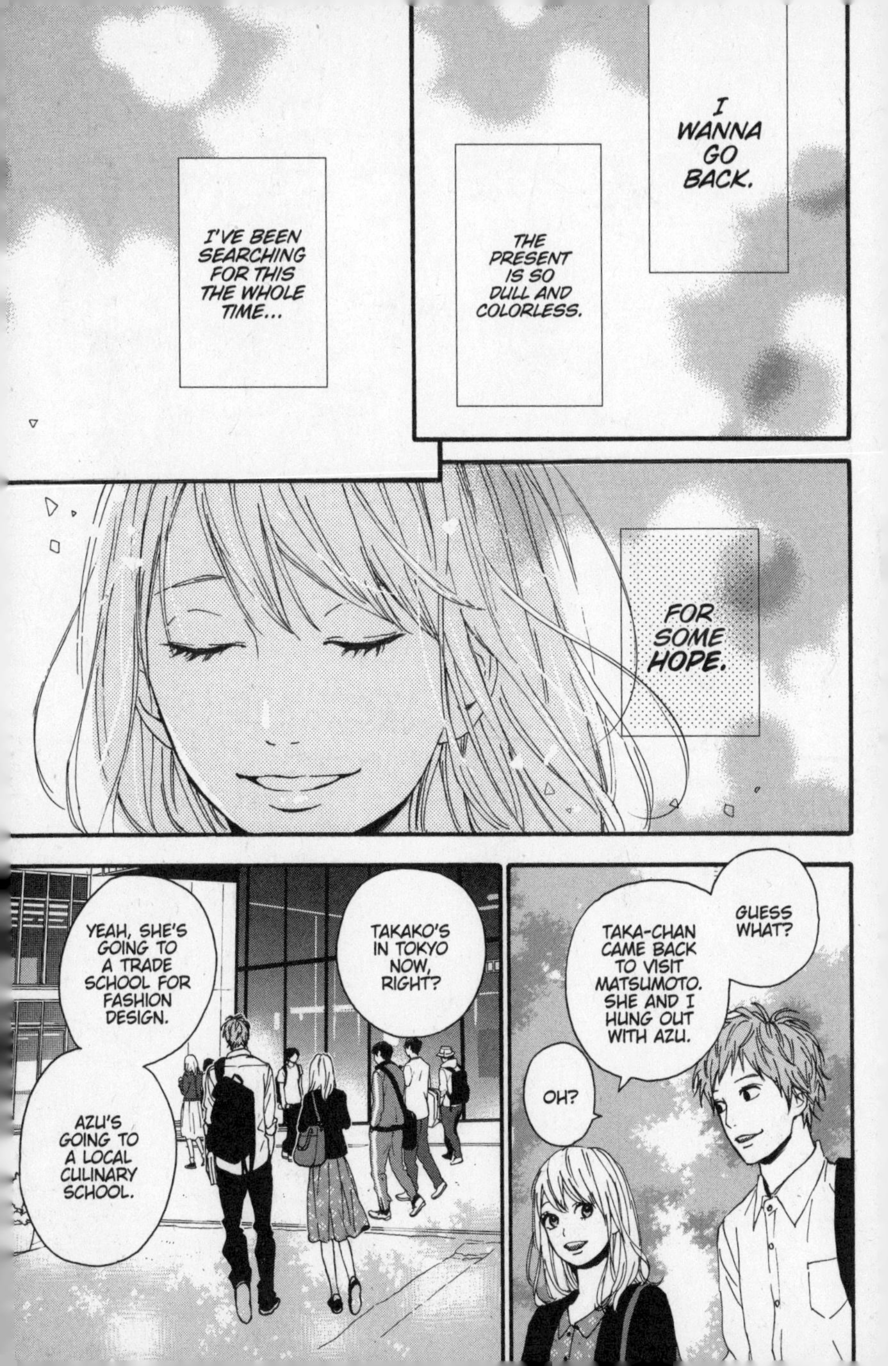
I WANNA GO BACK.
THE PRESENT IS SO DULL AND COLORLESS.
I'VE BEEN SEARCHING FOR THIS THE WHOLE TIME...
FOR SOME HOPE.
GUESS WHAT?
TAKA-CHAN CAME BACK TO VISIT MATSUMOTO. SHE AND I HUNG OUT WITH AZU.
OH?
TAKAKO'S IN TOKYO NOW, RIGHT?
YEAH, SHE'S GOING TO A TRADE SCHOOL FOR FASHION DESIGN.
AZU'S GOING TO A LOCAL CULINARY SCHOOL.

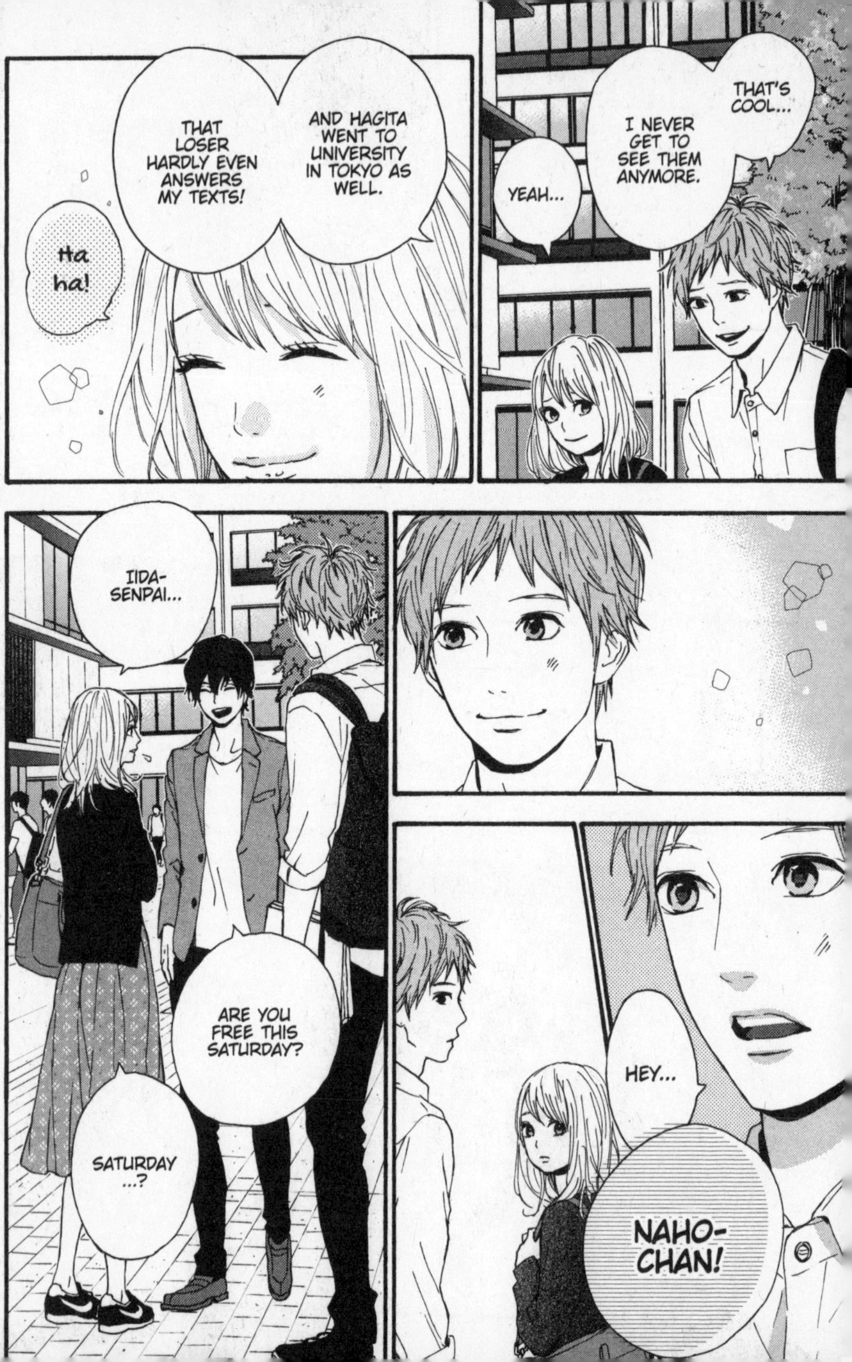
THAT'S COOL...
I NEVER GET TO SEE THEM ANYMORE.
YEAH...
AND HAGITA WENT TO UNIVERSITY IN TOKYO AS WELL.
THAT LOSER HARDLY EVEN ANSWERS MY TEXTS!
Ha ha!
HEY...
NAHO-CHAN!
IIDA-SENPAI...
ARE YOU FREE THIS SATURDAY?
SATURDAY ...?

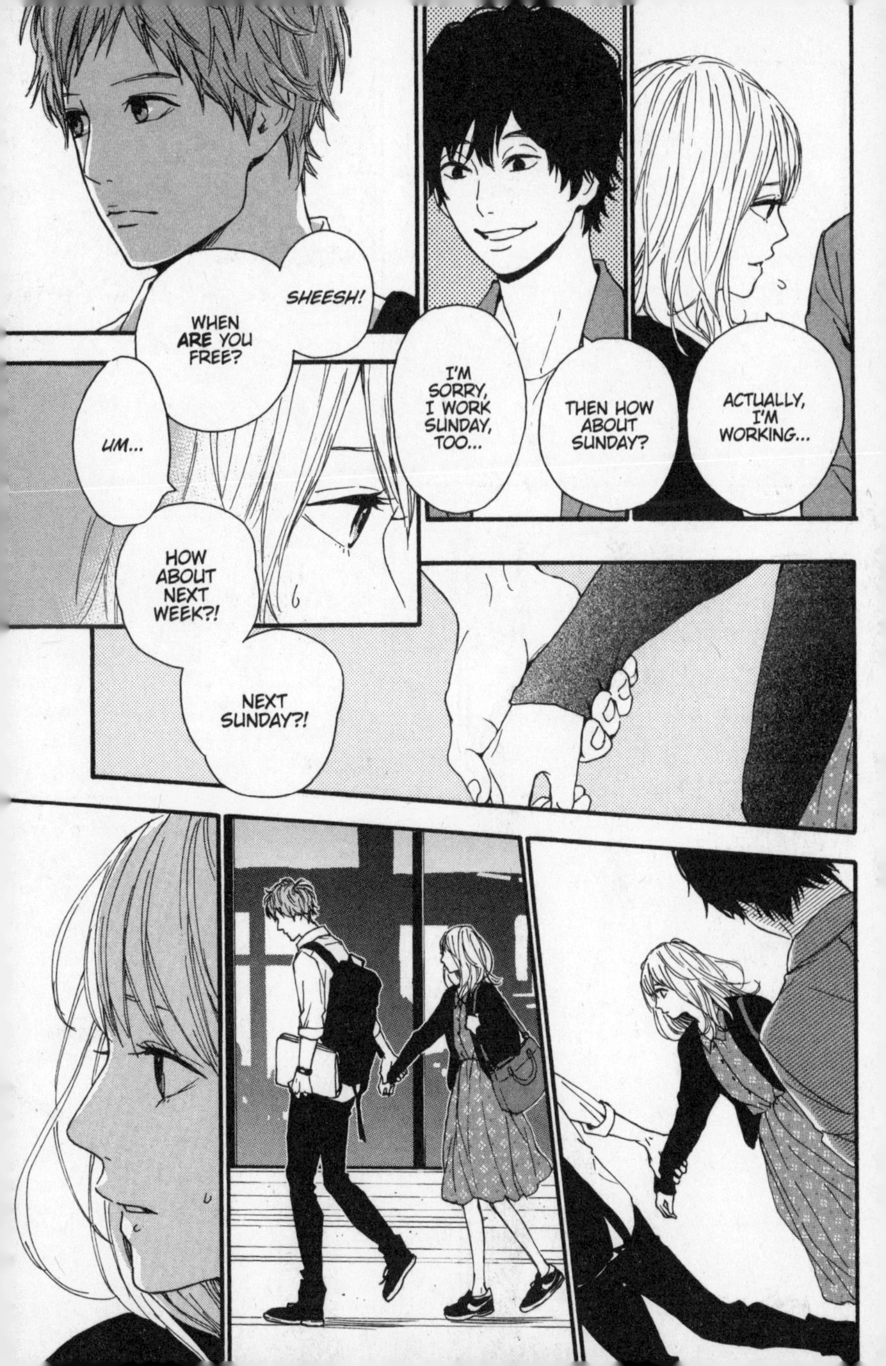
ACTUALLY, I'M WORKING...
THEN HOW ABOUT SUNDAY?
I'M SORRY, I WORK SUNDAY, TOO...
SHEESH!
WHEN ARE YOU FREE?
UM...
HOW ABOUT NEXT WEEK?!
NEXT SUNDAY?!

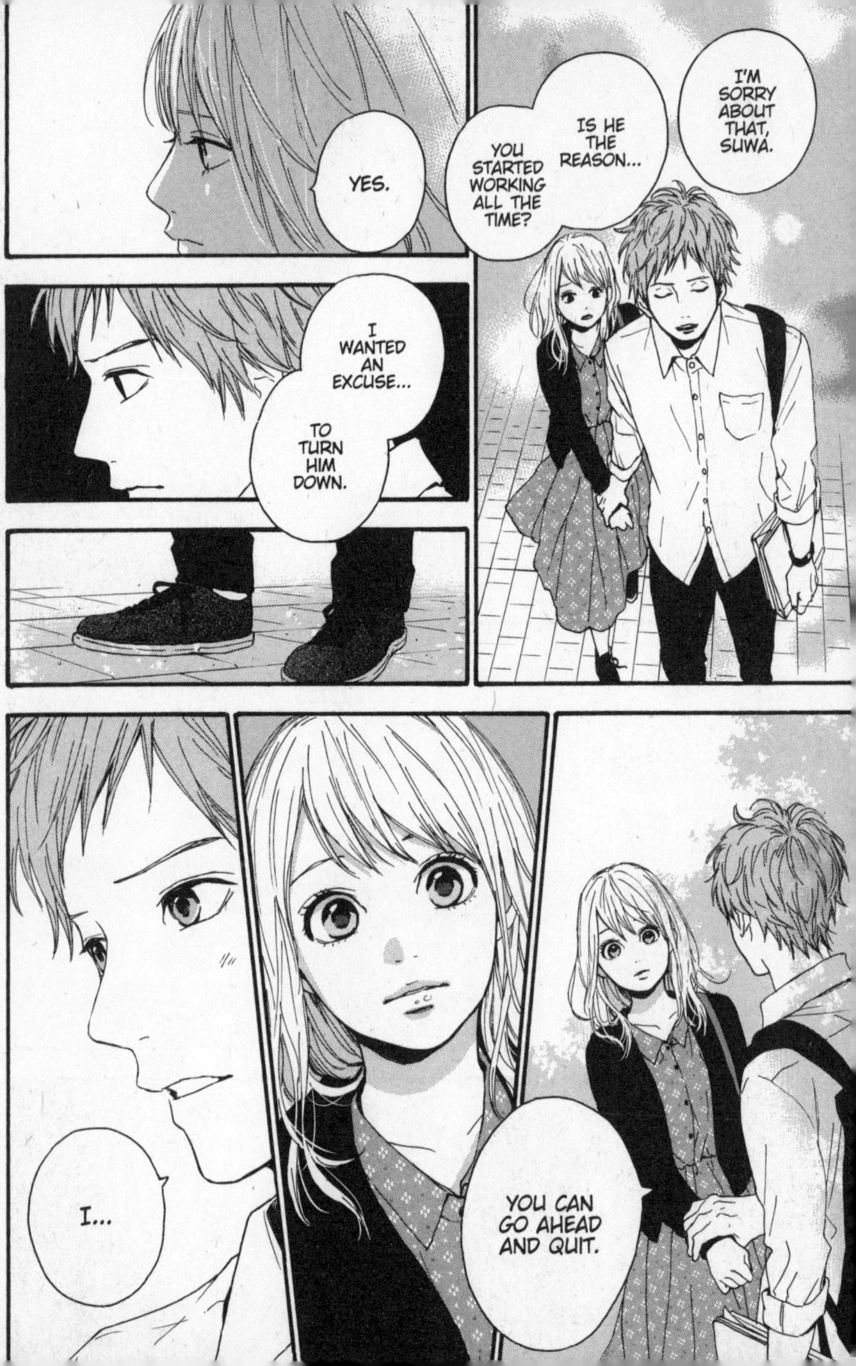
I'M SORRY ABOUT THAT, SUWA.
IS HE THE REASON... YOU STARTED WORKING ALL THE TIME?
YES.
I WANTED AN EXCUSE...
TO TURN HIM DOWN.
YOU CAN GO AHEAD AND QUIT.
I...

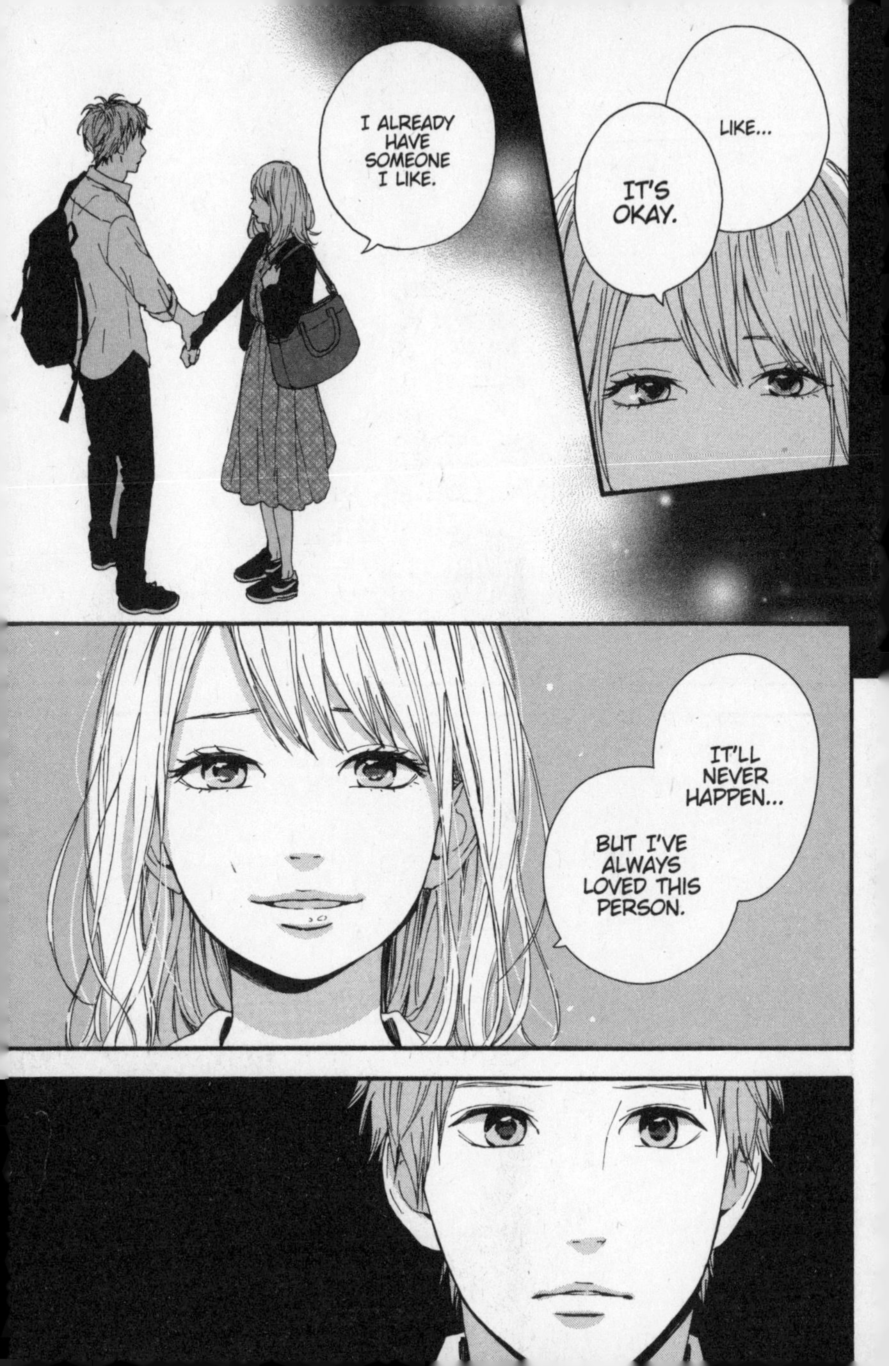
LIKE...
IT'S OKAY.
I ALREADY HAVE SOMEONE I LIKE.
IT'LL NEVER HAPPEN...
BUT I'VE ALWAYS LOVED THIS PERSON.

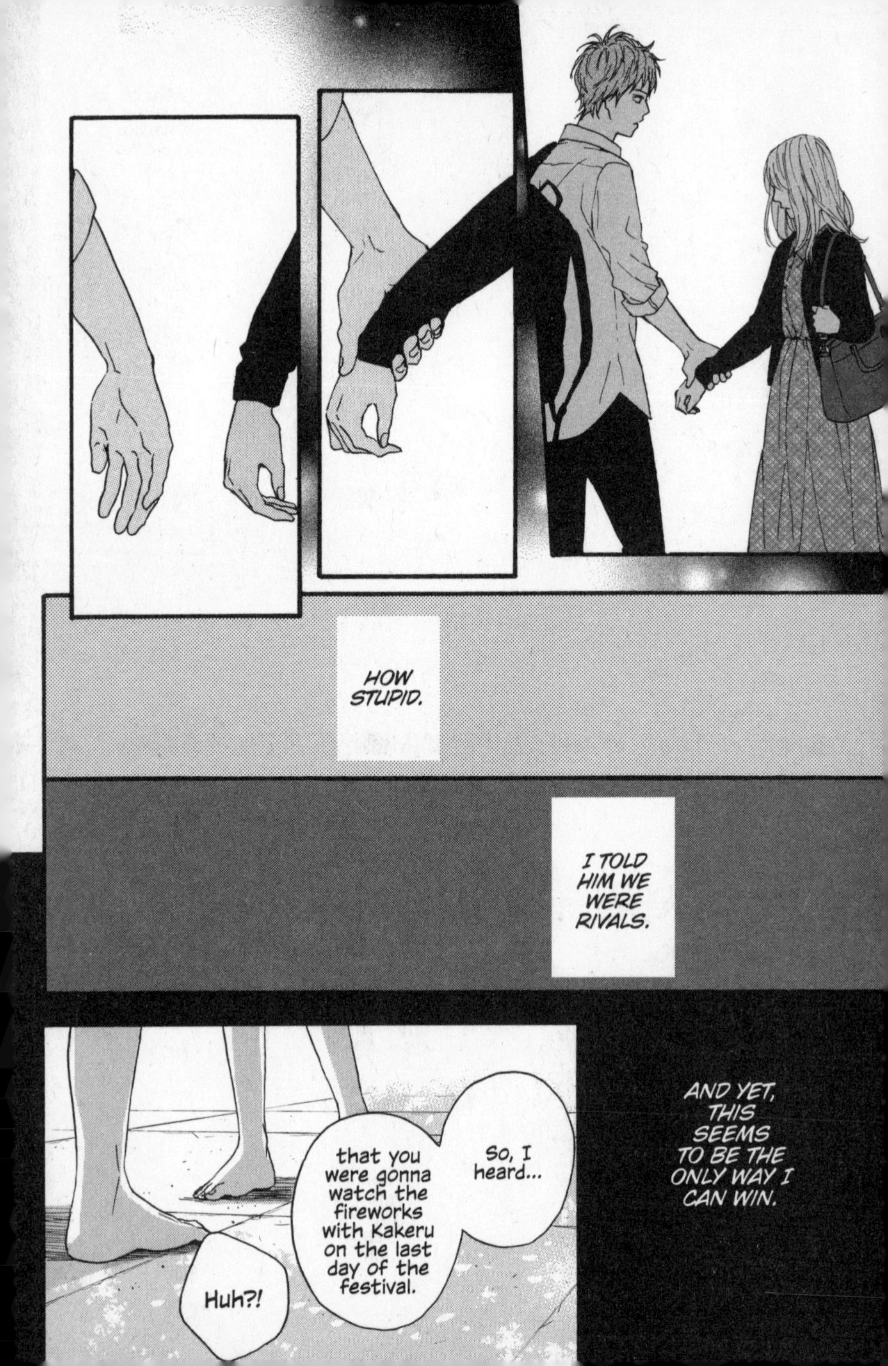
HOW STUPID.
I TOLD HIM WE WERE RIVALS.
AND YET, THIS SEEMS TO BE THE ONLY WAY I CAN WIN.
So, I heard...
that you were gonna watch the fireworks with Kakeru on the last day of the festival.
Huh?!

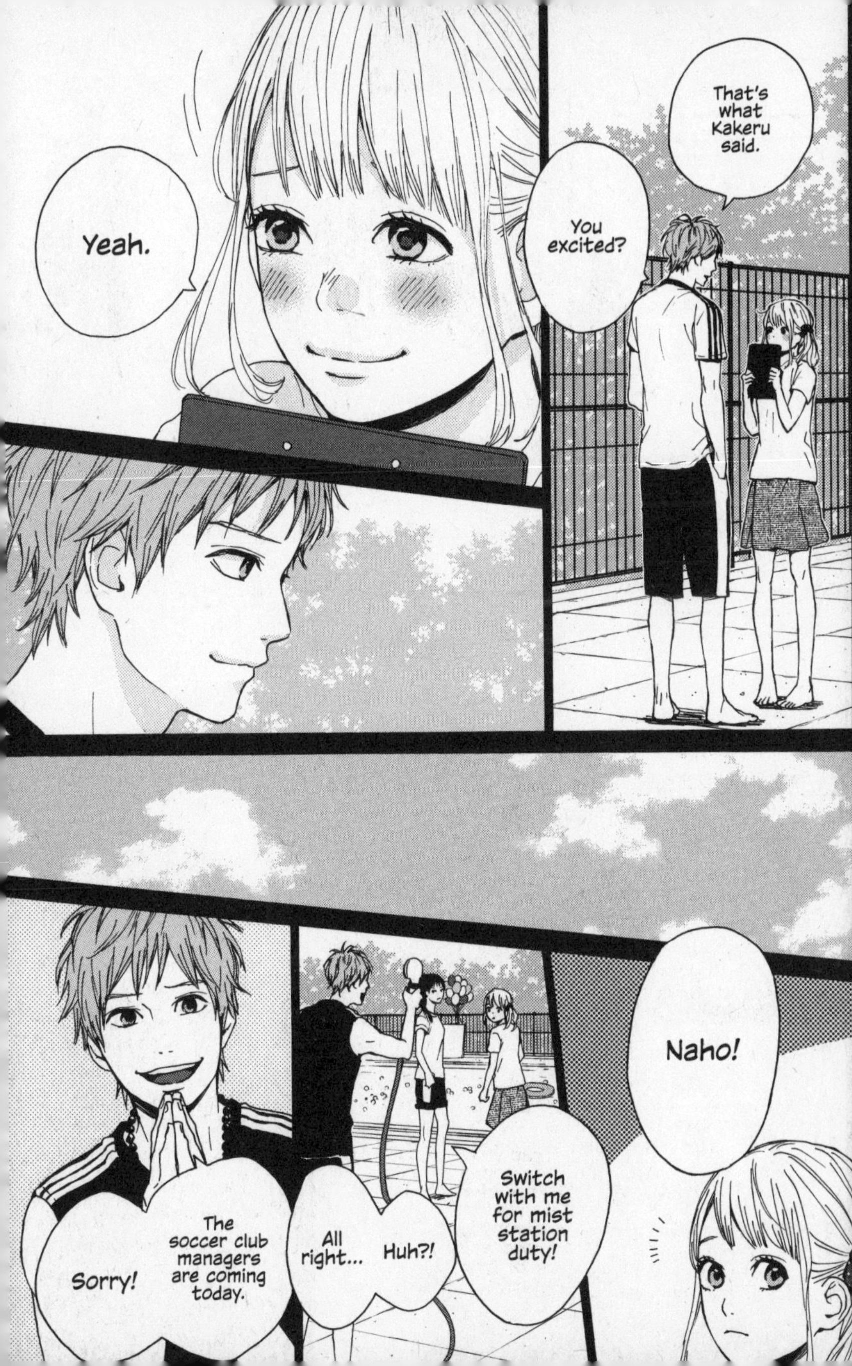
That's what Kakeru said.
You excited?
Yeah.
Naho!
Switch with me for mist station duty!
Huh?!
All right...
The soccer club managers are coming today.
Sorry!

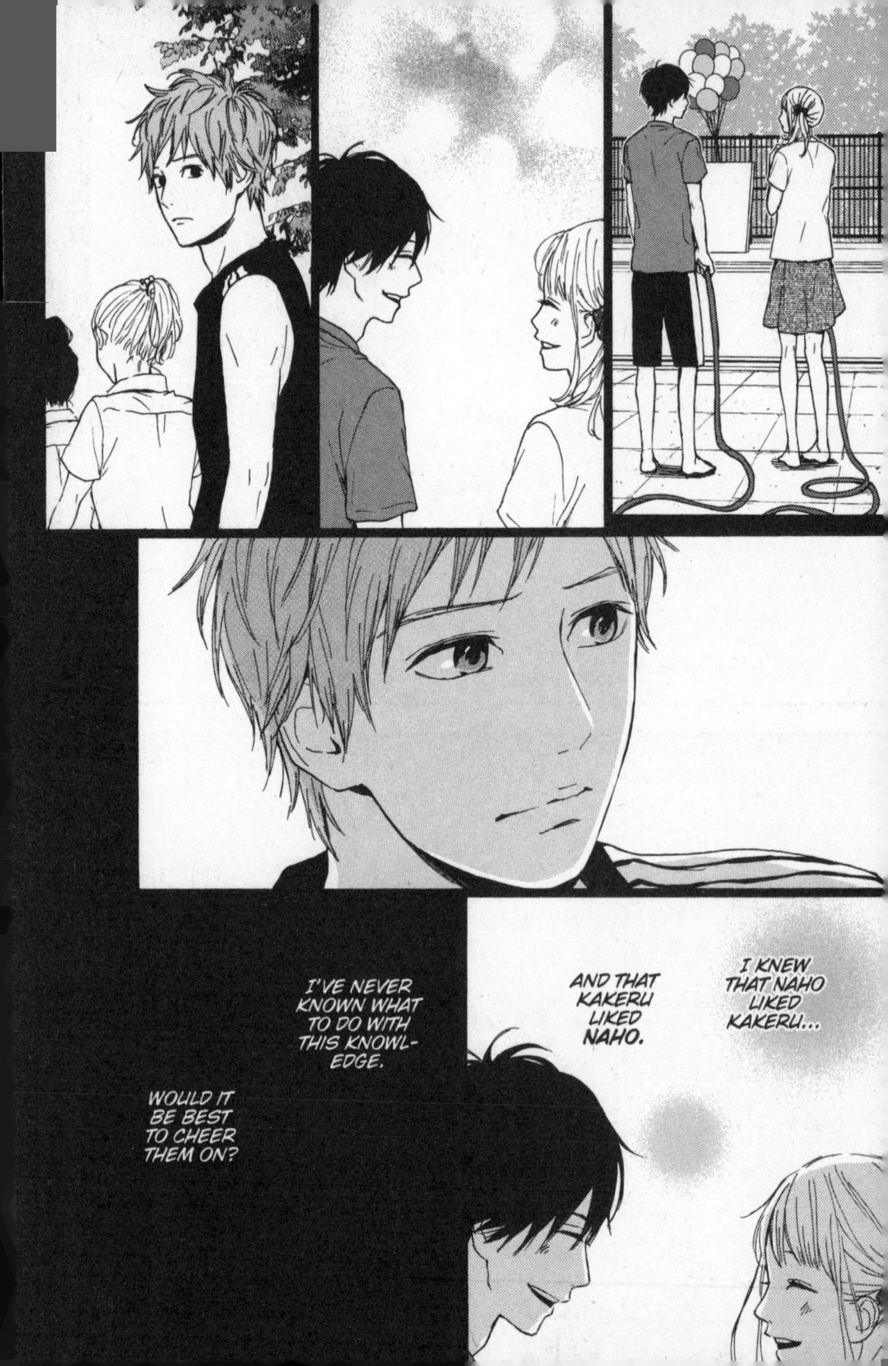
I KNEW THAT NAHO LIKED KAKERU...
AND THAT KAKERU LIKED NAHO.
I'VE NEVER KNOWN WHAT TO DO WITH THIS KNOWL-EDGE.
WOULD IT BE BEST TO CHEER THEM ON?

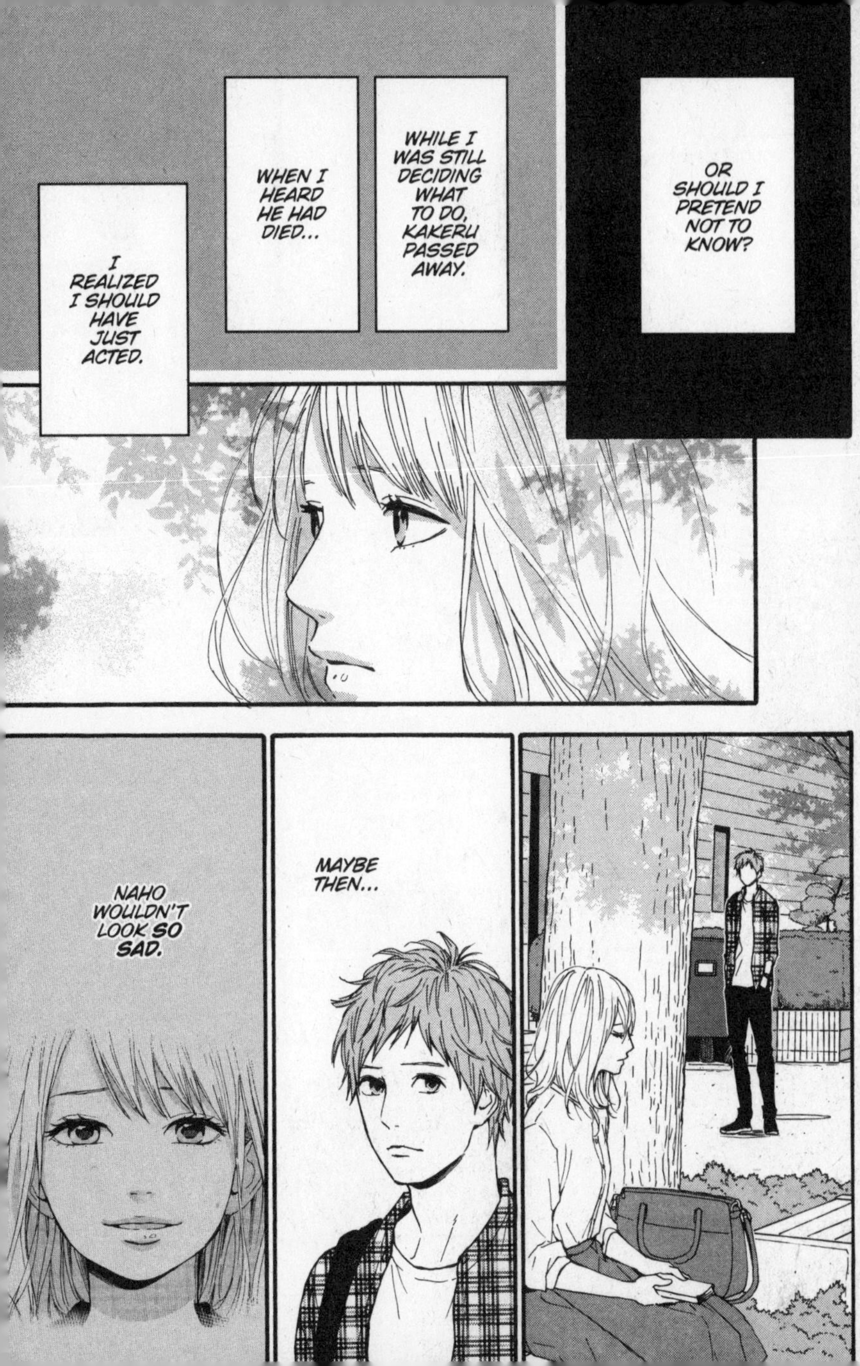

OR SHOULD I PRETEND NOT TO KNOW?
WHILE I WAS STILL DECIDING WHAT TO DO, KAKERU PASSED AWAY.
WHEN I HEARD HE HAD DIED...
I REALIZED I SHOULD HAVE JUST ACTED.
MAYBE THEN...
NAHO WOULDN'T LOOK SO SAD.

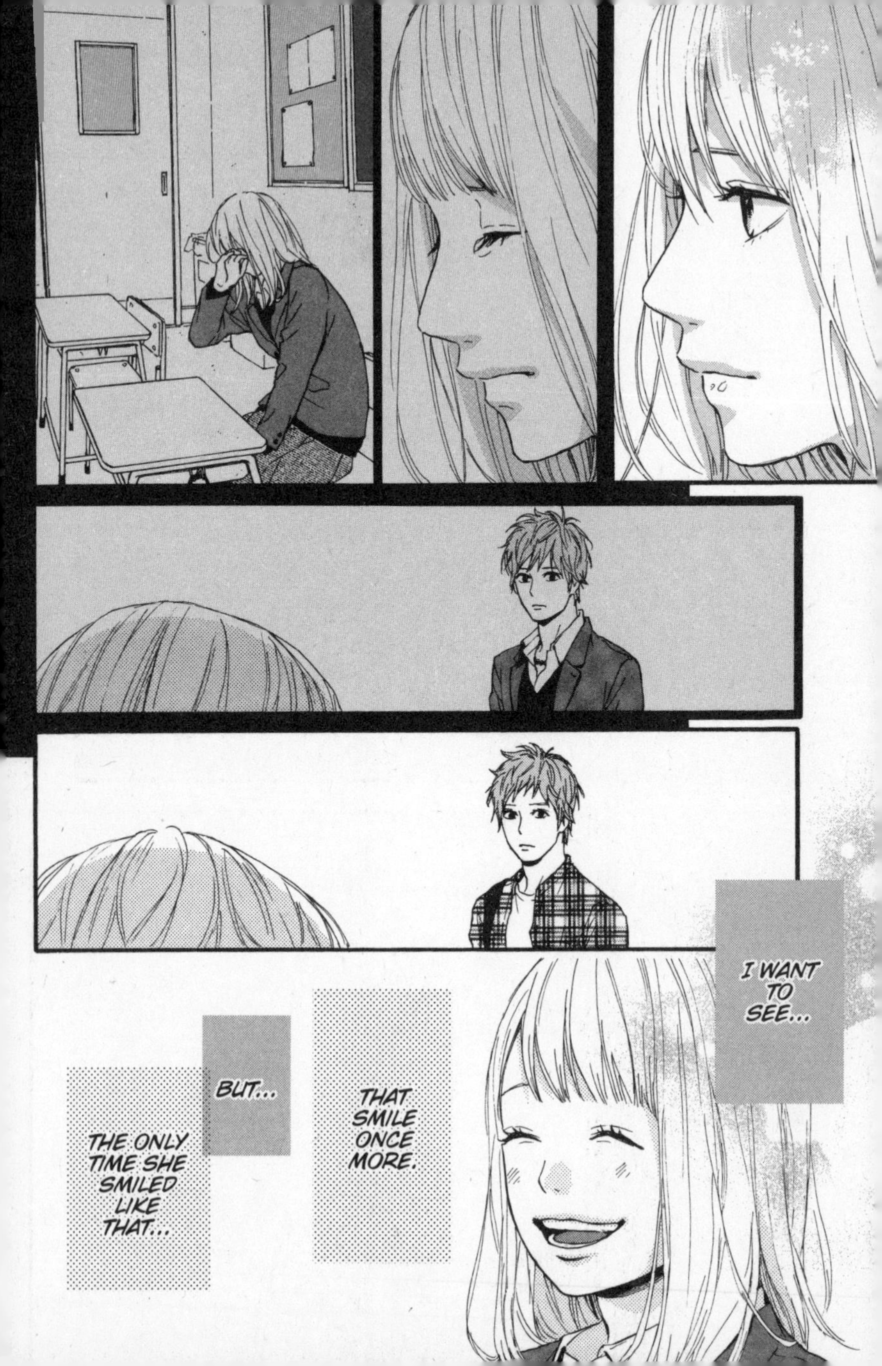

I WANT TO SEE...
THAT SMILE ONCE MORE.
BUT...
THE ONLY TIME SHE SMILED LIKE THAT...

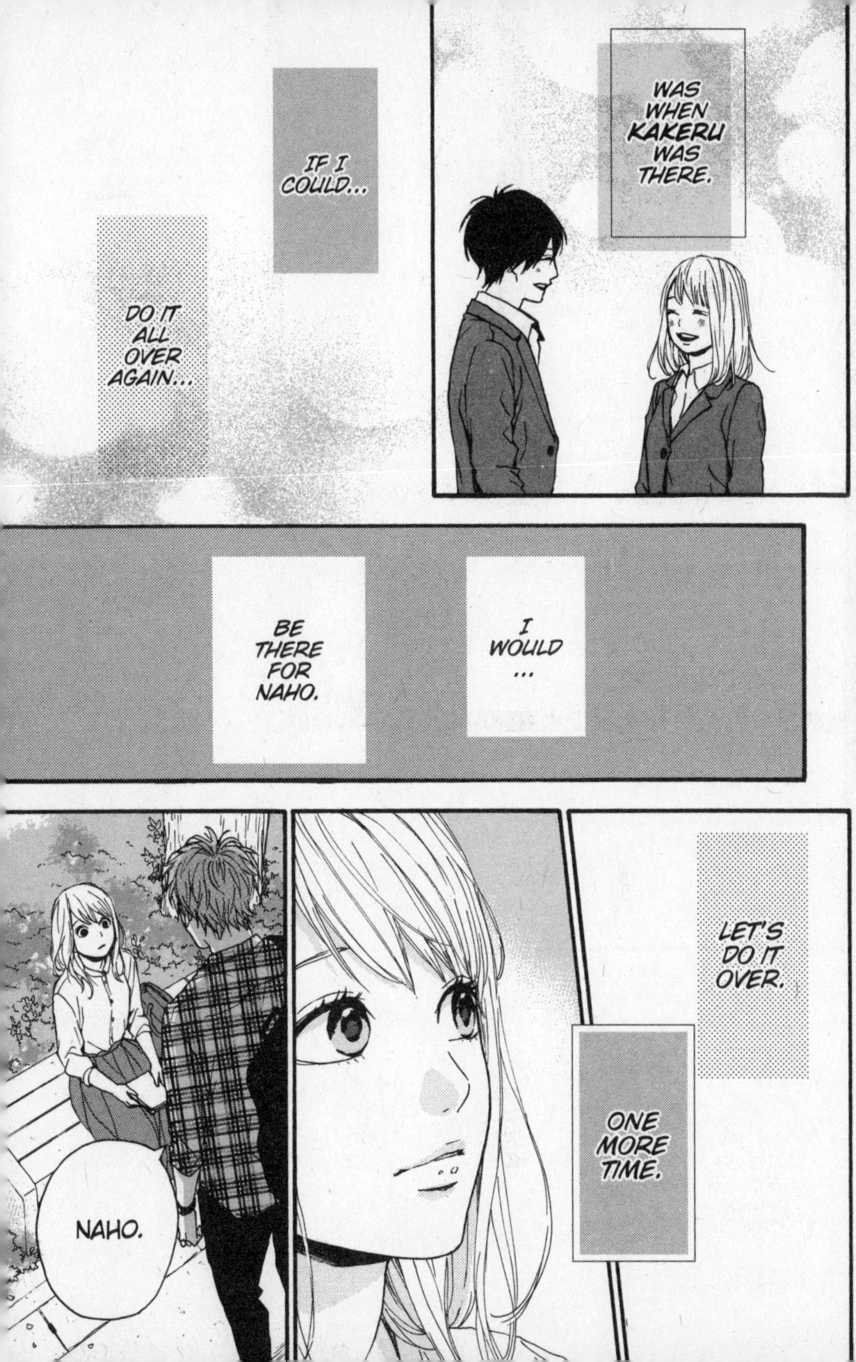
WAS WHEN KAKERU WAS THERE.
IF I COULD...
DO IT ALL OVER AGAIN...
I WOULD ...
BE THERE FOR NAHO.
LET'S DO IT OVER.
ONE MORE TIME.
NAHO.

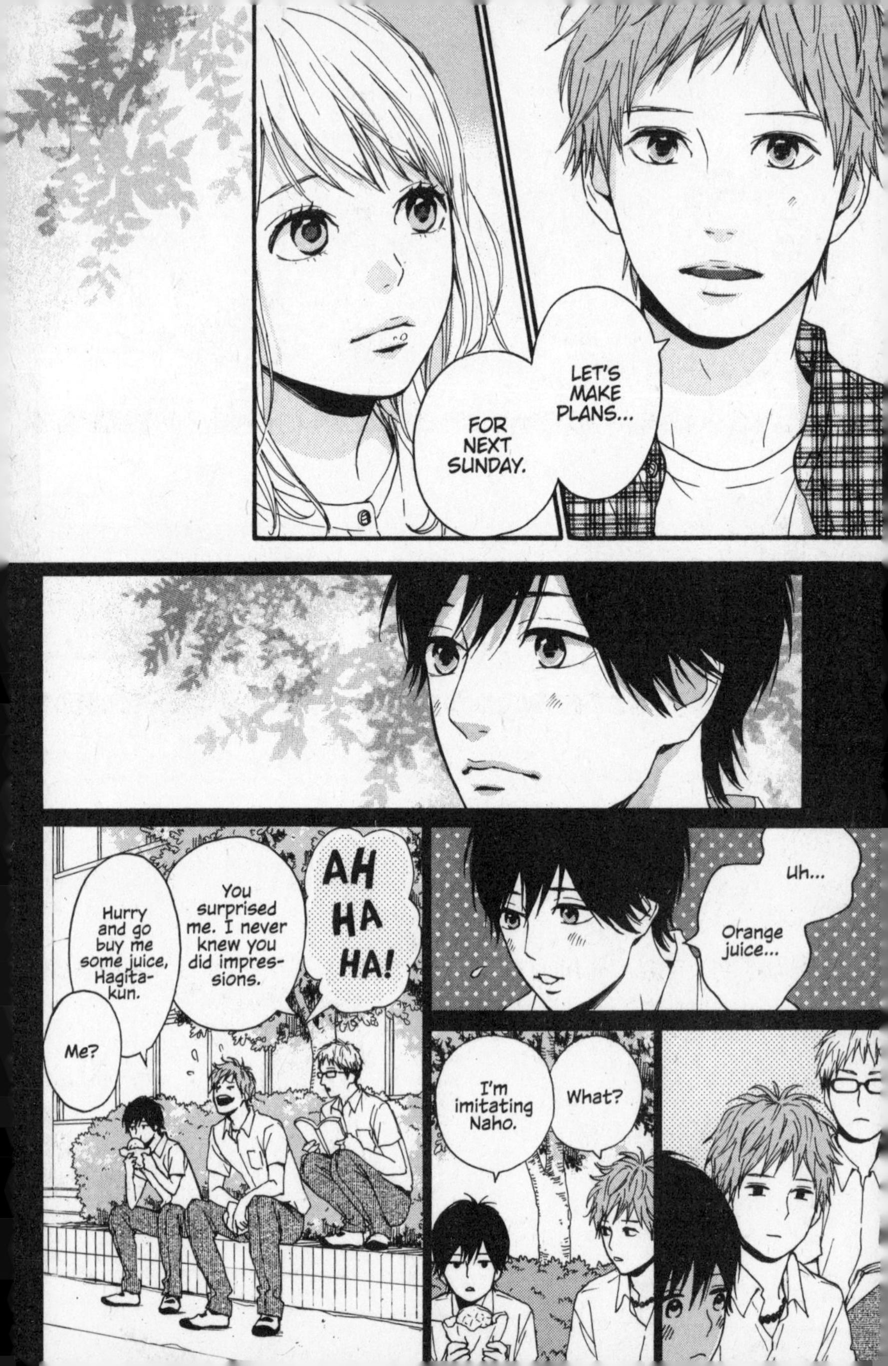

LET'S MAKE PLANS...
FOR NEXT SUNDAY.
Uh...
Orange juice...
What?
I'm imitating Naho.
AH HA HA!
You surprised me. I never knew you did impressions.
Hurry and go buy me some juice, Hagita-kun.
Me?

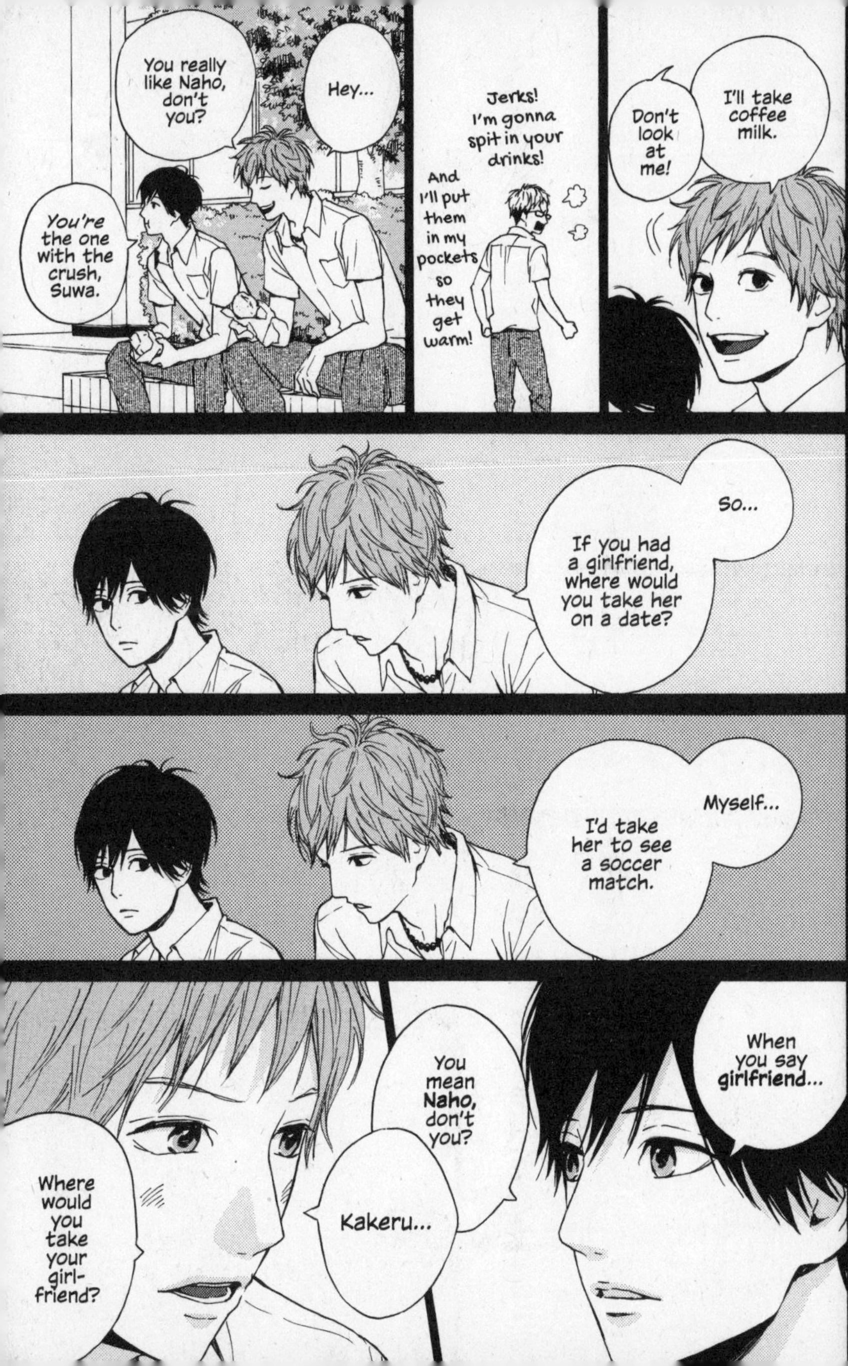
I'll take coffee milk.
Don't look at me!
Jerks! I'm gonna spit in your drinks!
And I'll put them in my pockets so they get warm!
Hey...
You really like Naho, don't you?
You're the one with the crush, Suwa.
So...
If you had a girlfriend, where would you take her on a date?
Myself...
I'd take her to see a soccer match.
When you say girlfriend...
You mean Naho, don't you?
Kakeru...
Where would you take your girl-friend?

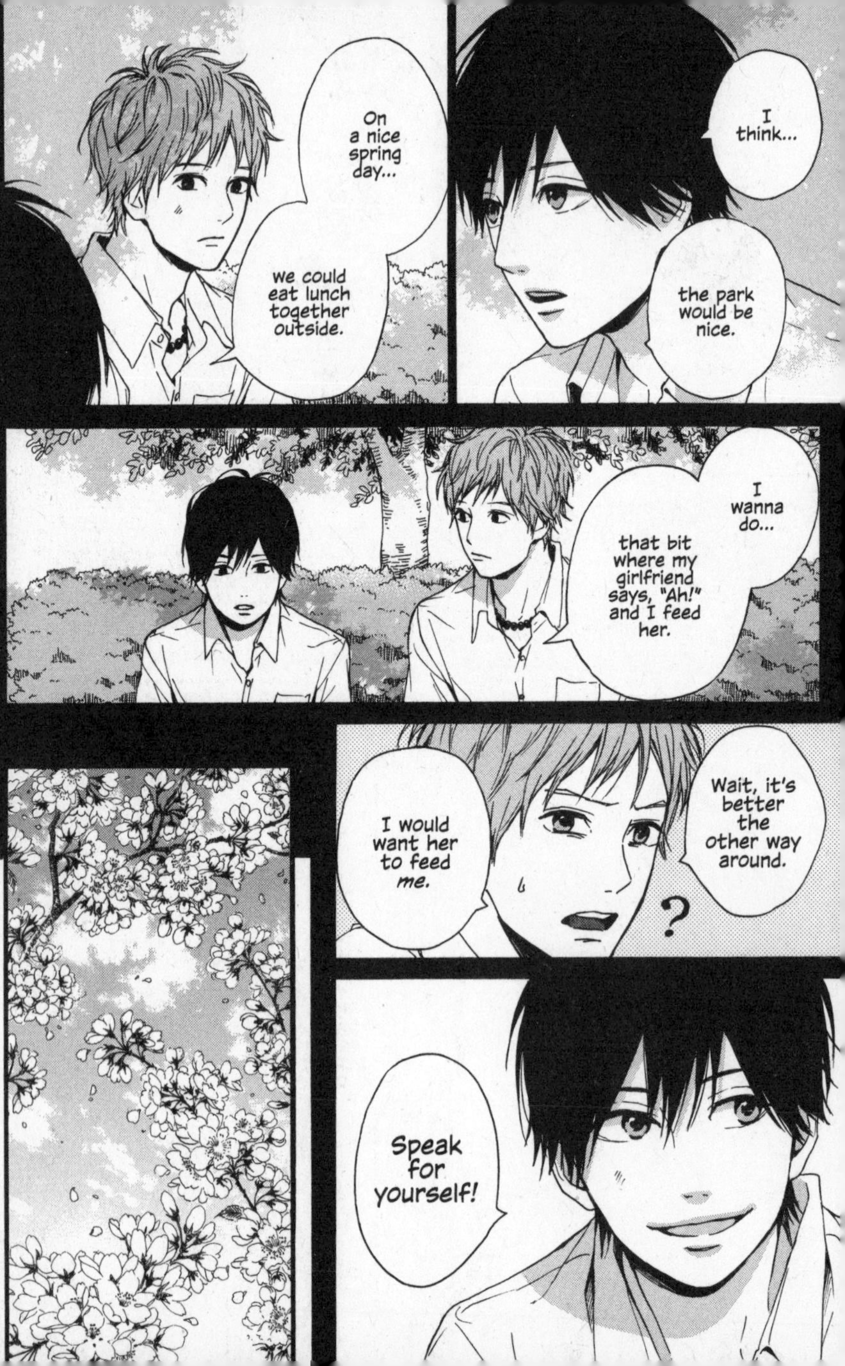
I think...
the park would be nice.
On a nice spring day...
we could eat lunch together outside.
I wanna do...
that bit where my girlfriend says, "Ah!" and I feed her.
Wait, it's better the other way around.
I would want her to feed *me.*
?
Speak for yourself!

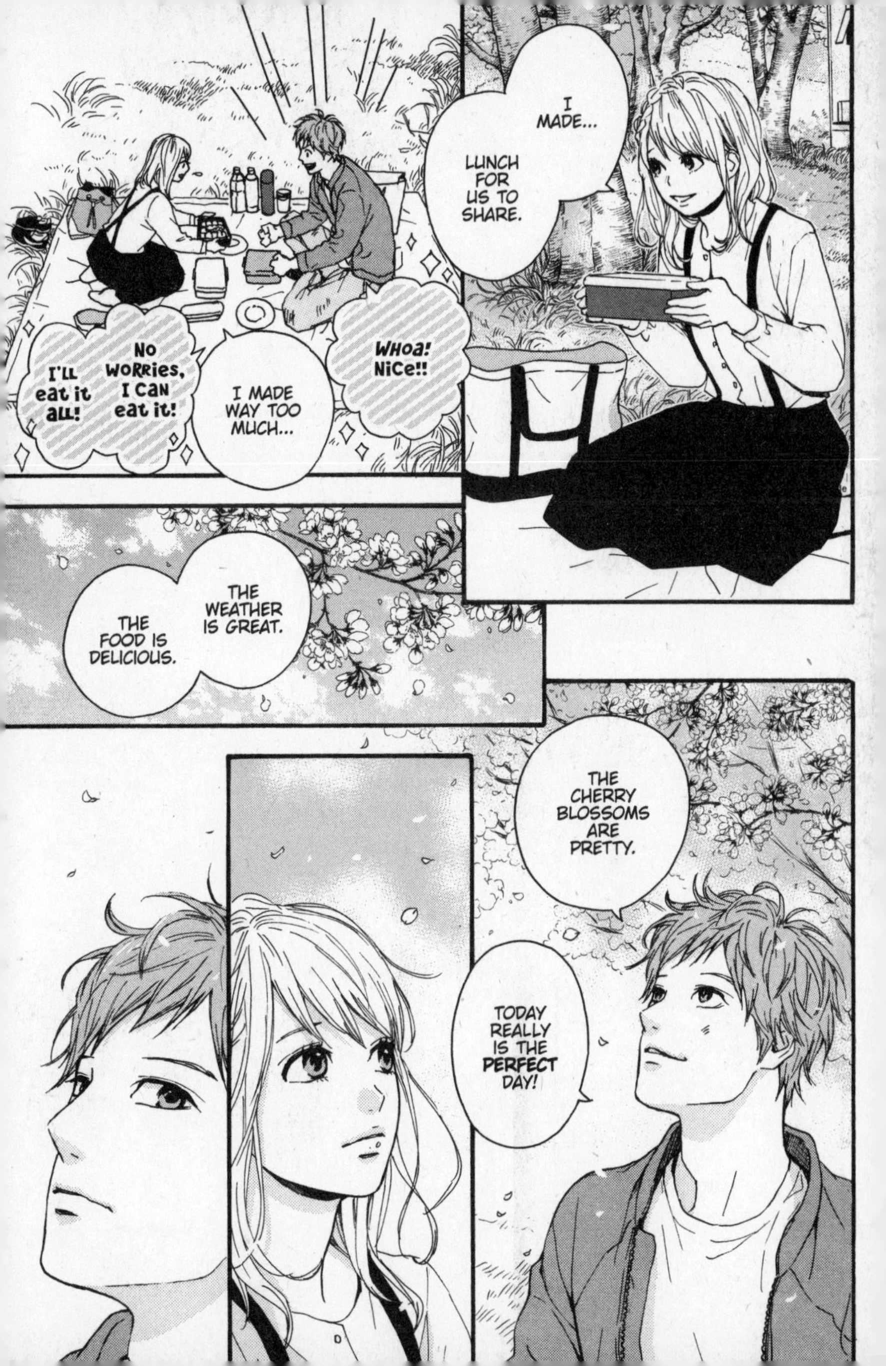
I MADE...
LUNCH FOR US TO SHARE.
WHOA! NICE!!
I MADE WAY TOO MUCH...
NO WORRIES, I CAN EAT IT!
I'LL EAT IT ALL!
THE WEATHER IS GREAT.
THE FOOD IS DELICIOUS.
THE CHERRY BLOSSOMS ARE PRETTY.
TODAY REALLY IS THE PERFECT DAY!

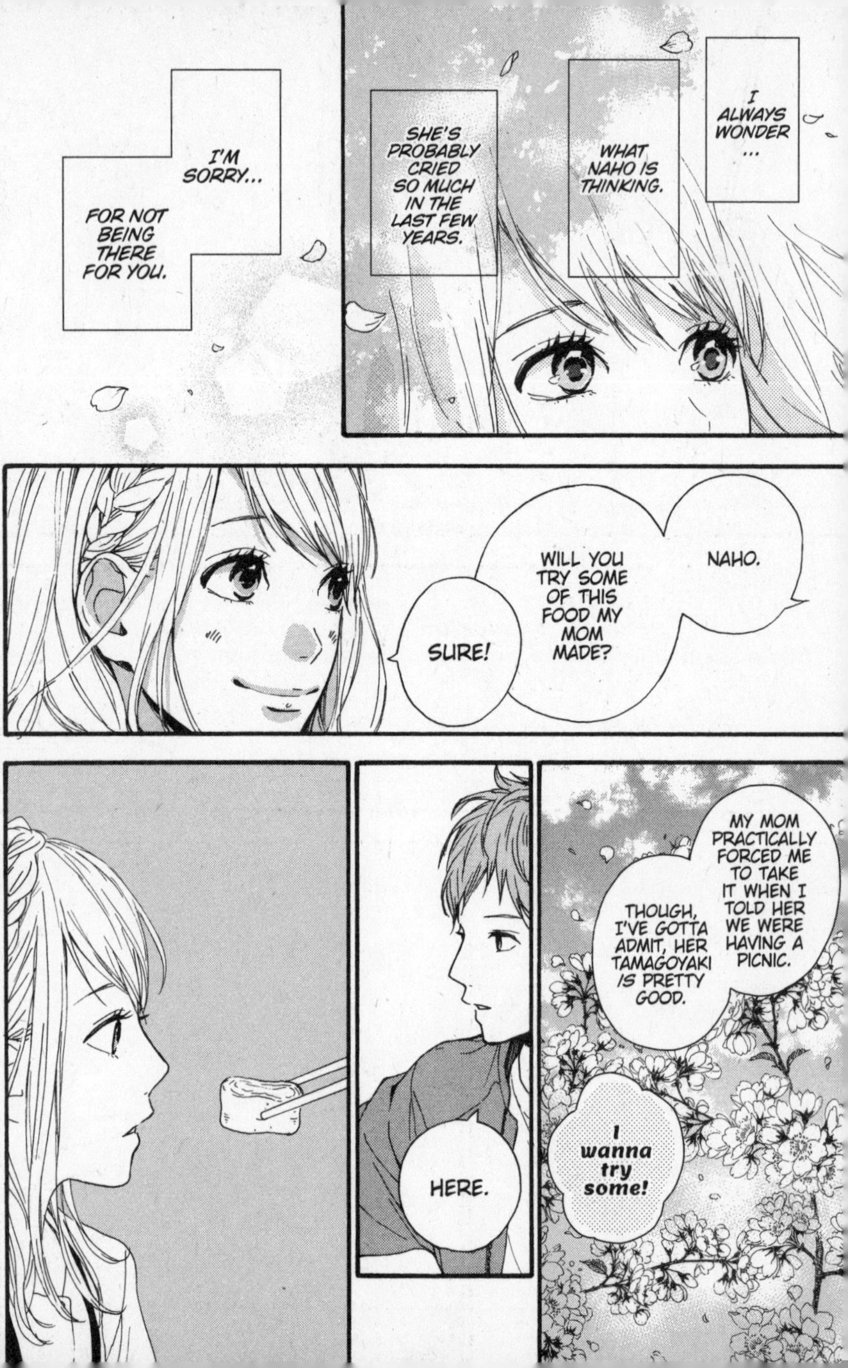
I ALWAYS WONDER ...
WHAT NAHO IS THINKING.
SHE'S PROBABLY CRIED SO MUCH IN THE LAST FEW YEARS.
I'M SORRY...
FOR NOT BEING THERE FOR YOU.
NAHO.
WILL YOU TRY SOME OF THIS FOOD MY MOM MADE?
SURE!
MY MOM PRACTICALLY FORCED ME TO TAKE IT WHEN I TOLD HER WE WERE HAVING A PICNIC.
THOUGH, I'VE GOTTA ADMIT, HER TAMAGOYAKI IS PRETTY GOOD.
I wanna try some!
HERE.

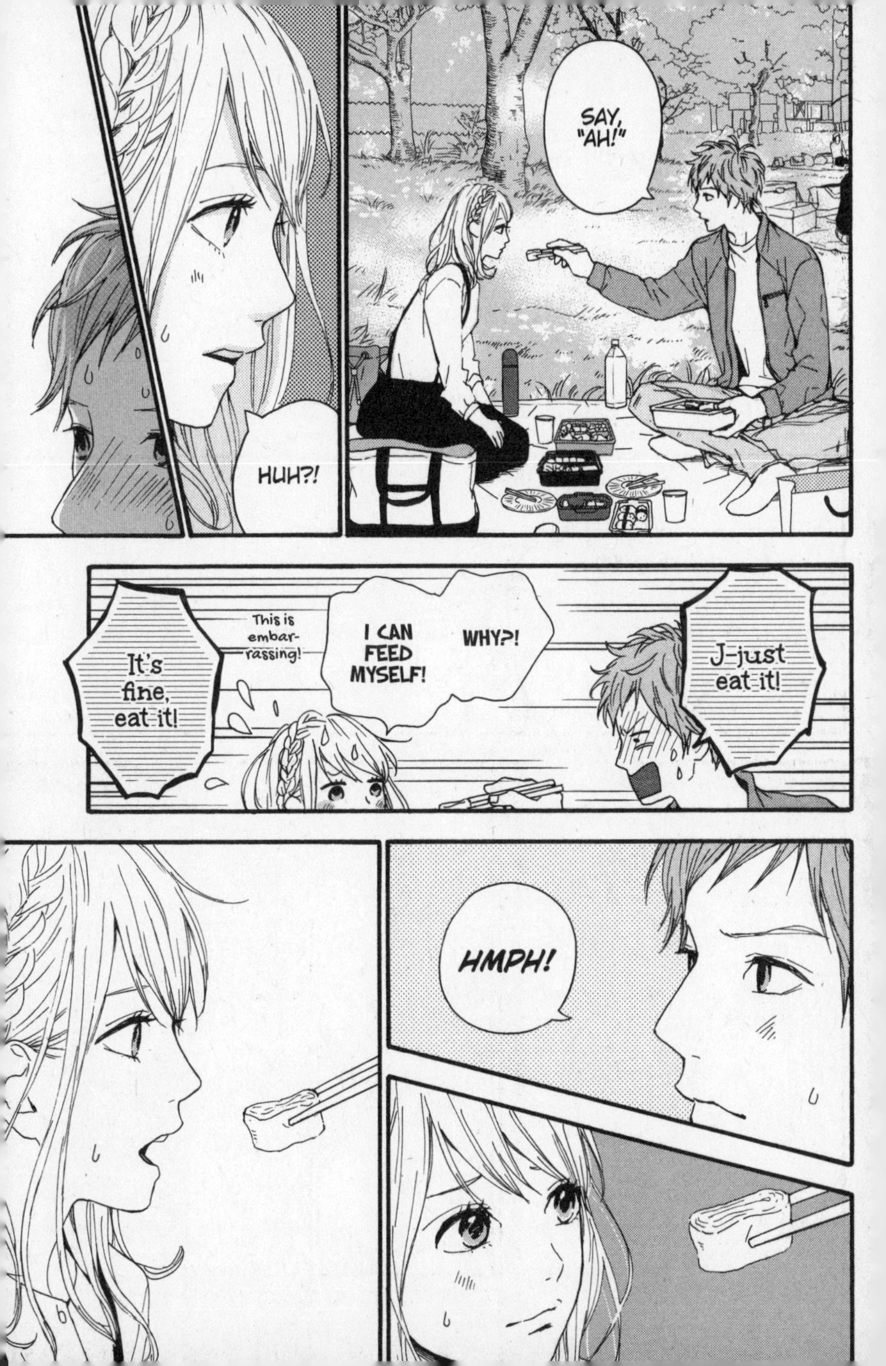
SAY, "AH!"
HUH?!
J-just eat it!
WHY?!
I CAN FEED MYSELF!
This is embarrassing!
It's fine, eat it!
HMPH!

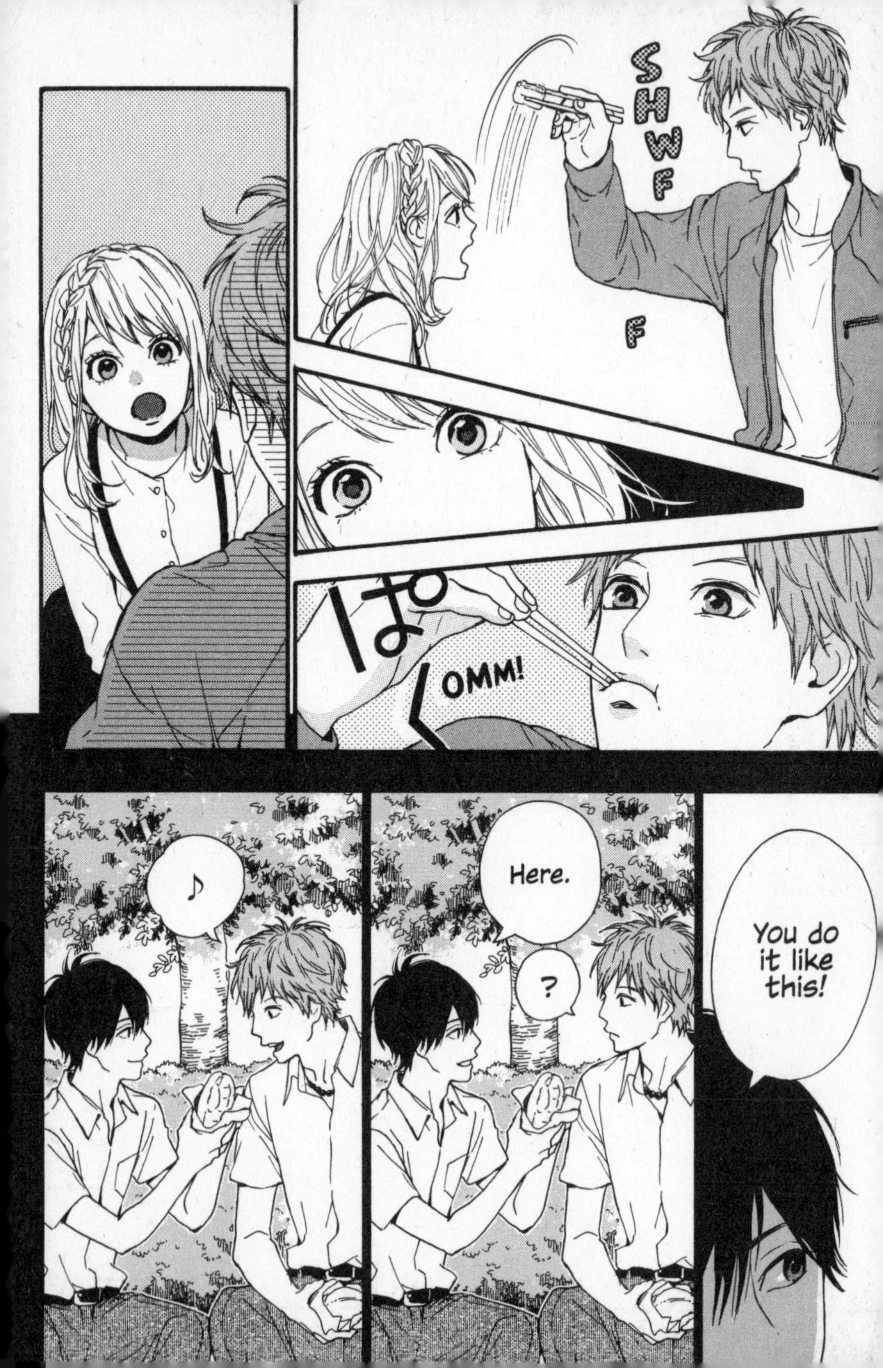
SHWF
F
ぱく
OMM!
You do it like this!
Here.
?
♪

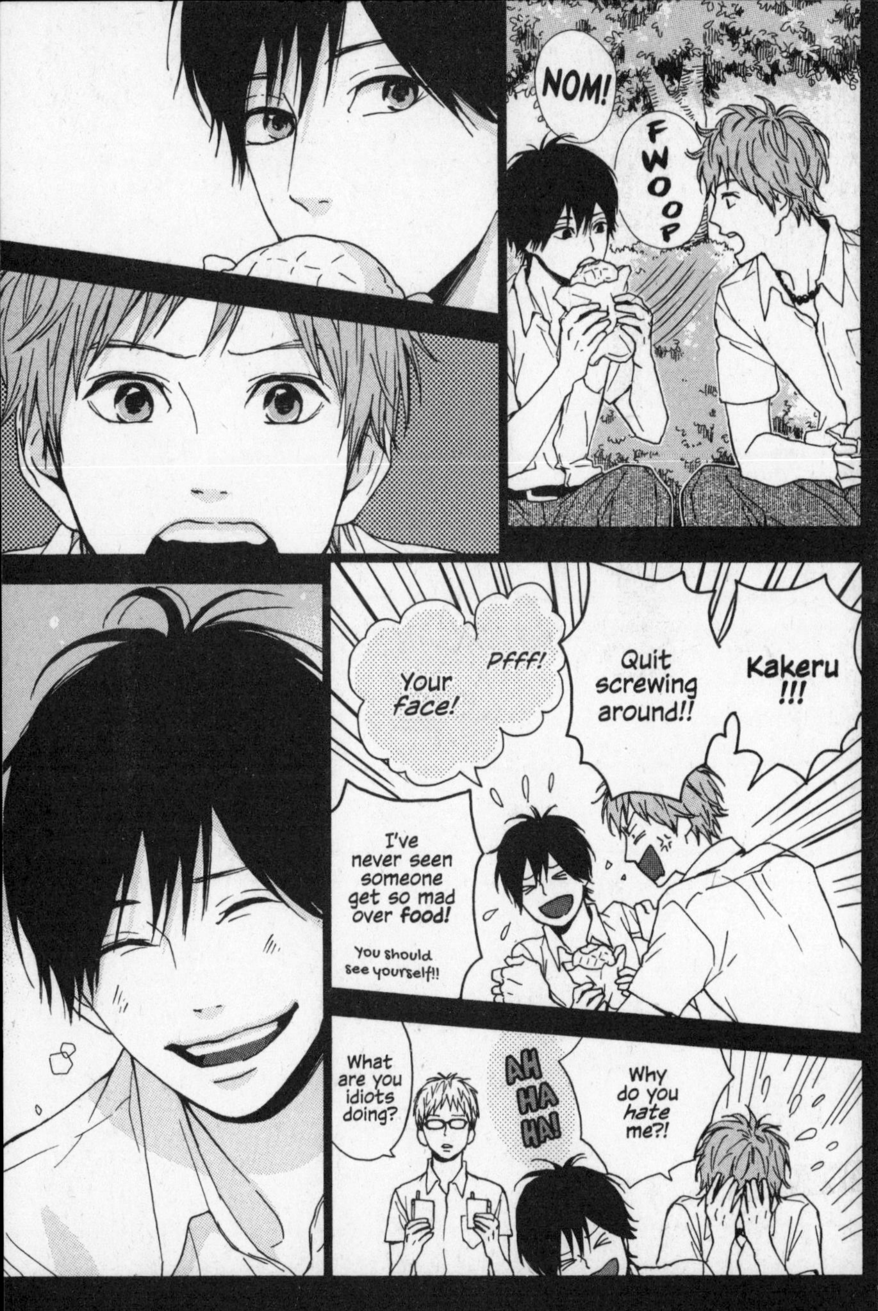
NOM!
FWOOP
Kakeru !!!
Quit screwing around!!
Pfff!
Your face!
I've never seen someone get so mad over food!
You should see yourself!!
Why do you hate me?!
AH HA HA!
What are you idiots doing?

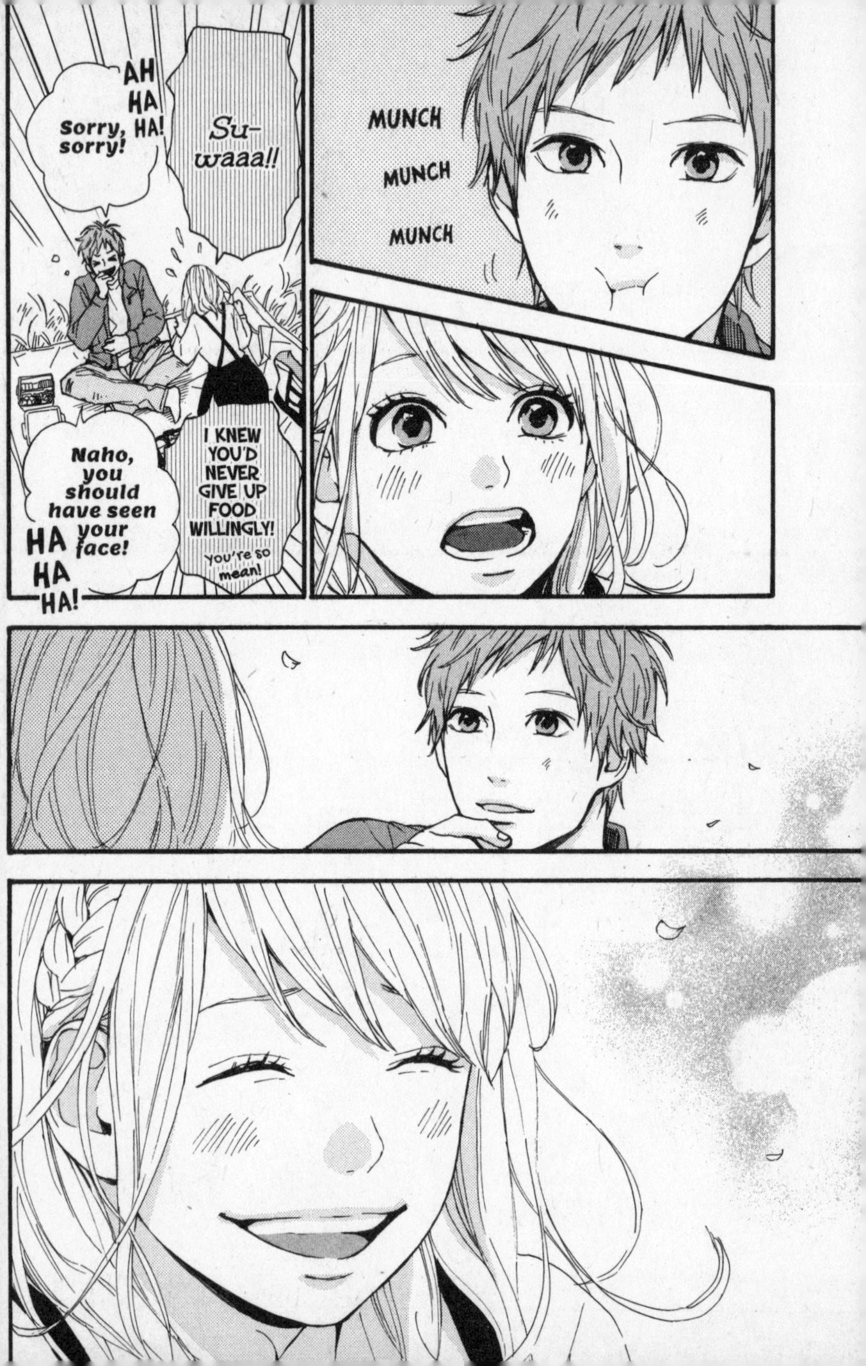

MUNCH
MUNCH
MUNCH
Su-waaa!!
AH HA HA!
Sorry, sorry!
I KNEW YOU'D NEVER GIVE UP FOOD WILLINGLY!
You're so mean!
Naho, you should have seen your face!
HA HA HA!

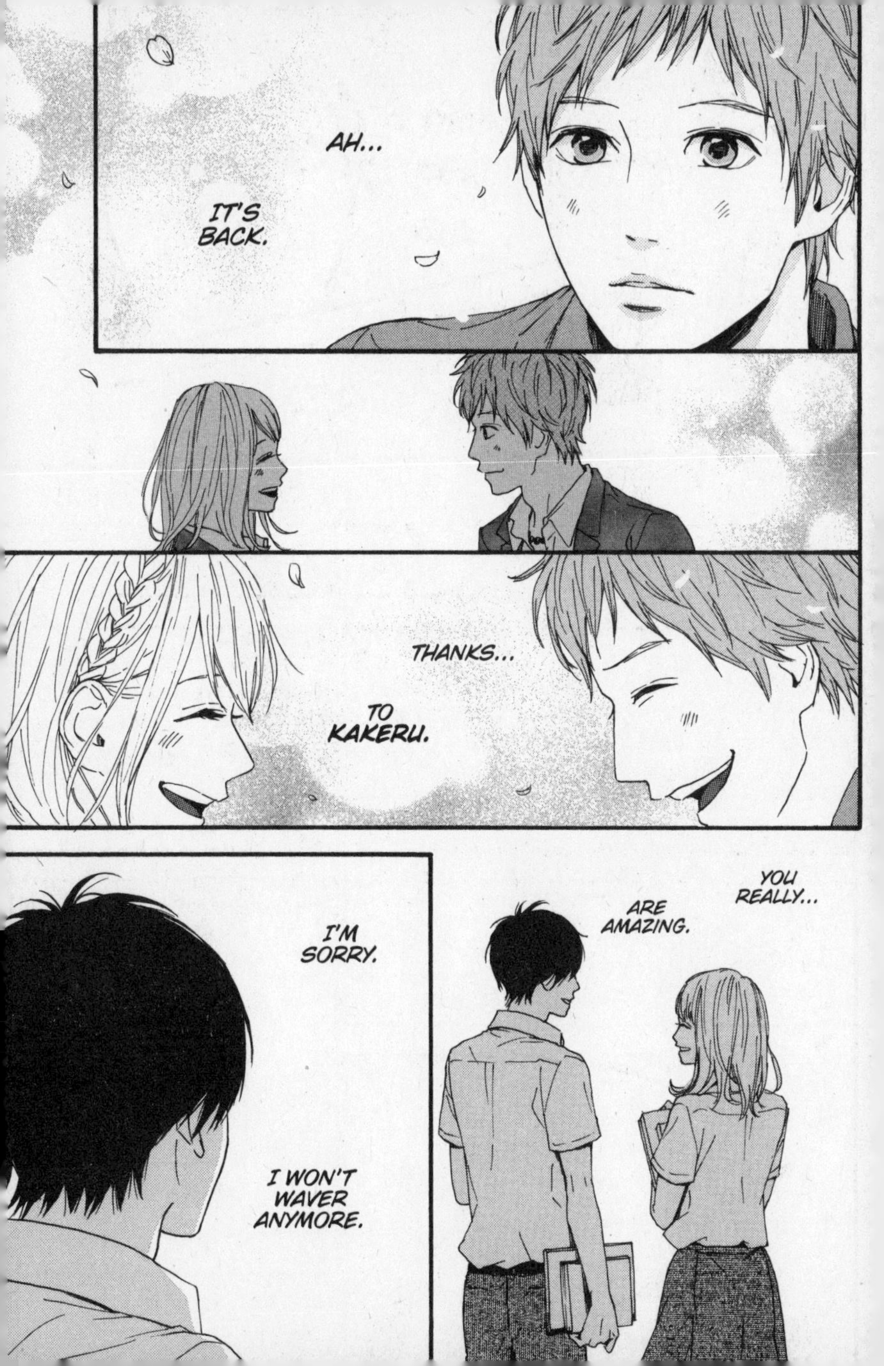
AH...
IT'S BACK.
THANKS...
TO KAKERU.
YOU REALLY...
ARE AMAZING.
I'M SORRY.
I WON'T WAVER ANYMORE.

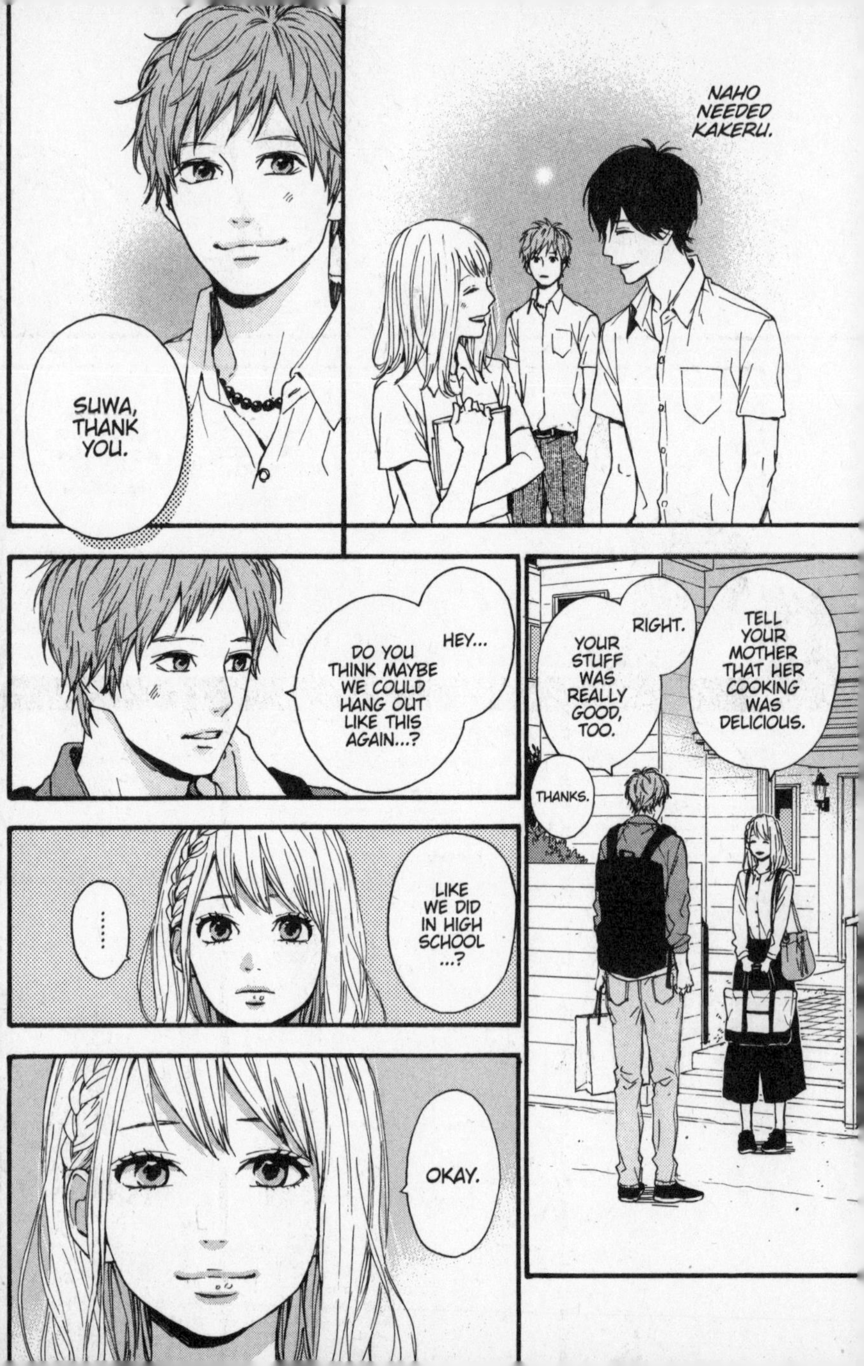
NAHO NEEDED KAKERU.
SUWA, THANK YOU.
TELL YOUR MOTHER THAT HER COOKING WAS DELICIOUS.
RIGHT. YOUR STUFF WAS REALLY GOOD, TOO.
THANKS.
HEY... DO YOU THINK MAYBE WE COULD HANG OUT LIKE THIS AGAIN...?
LIKE WE DID IN HIGH SCHOOL ...?
......
OKAY.

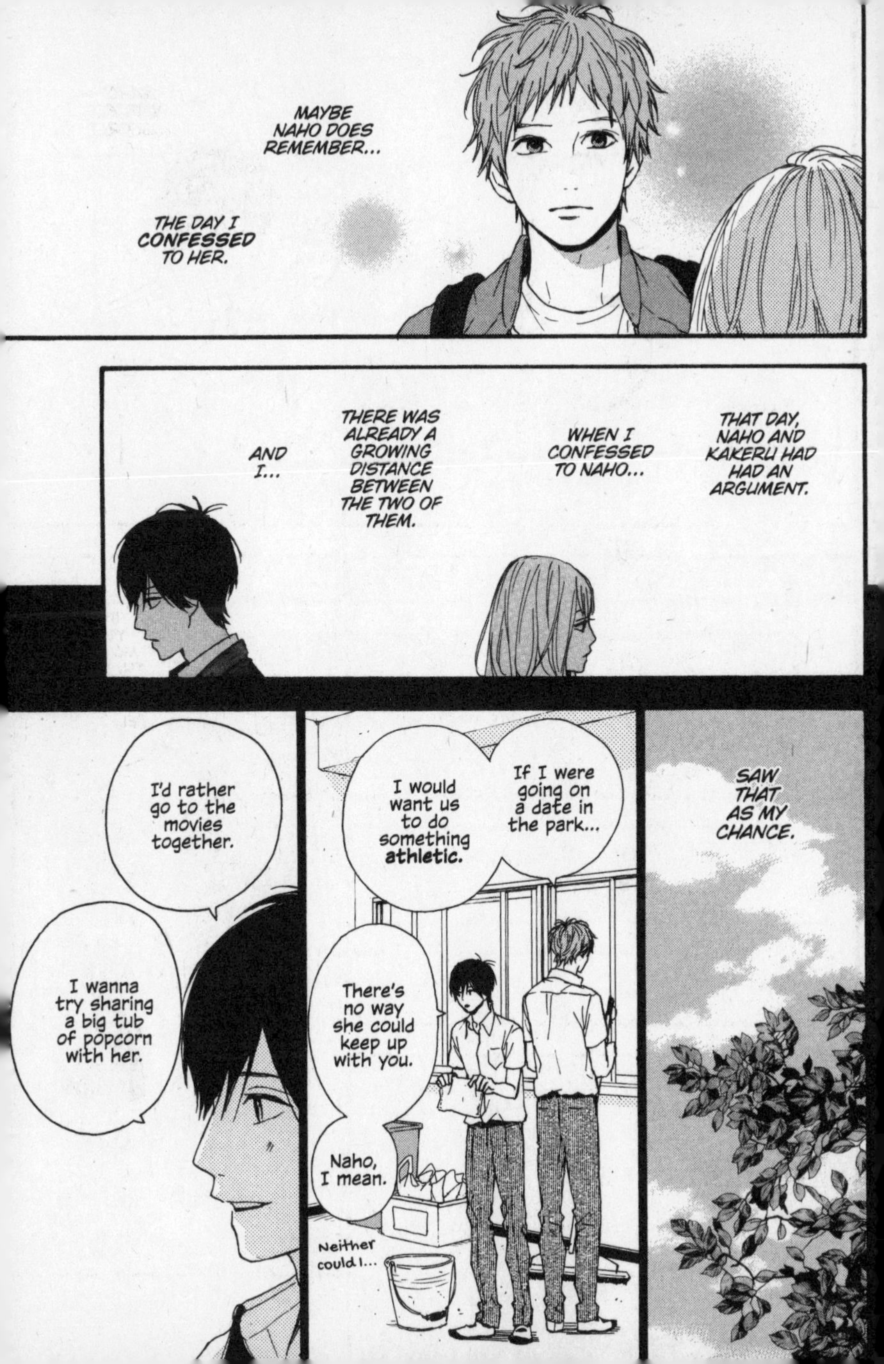
MAYBE NAHO DOES REMEMBER...
THE DAY I CONFESSED TO HER.
THAT DAY, NAHO AND KAKERU HAD HAD AN ARGUMENT.
WHEN I CONFESSED TO NAHO...
THERE WAS ALREADY A GROWING DISTANCE BETWEEN THE TWO OF THEM.
AND I...
SAW THAT AS MY CHANCE.
If I were going on a date in the park...
I would want us to do something **athletic.**
There's no way she could keep up with you.
Naho, I mean.
Neither could I...
I'd rather go to the movies together.
I wanna try sharing a big tub of popcorn with her.

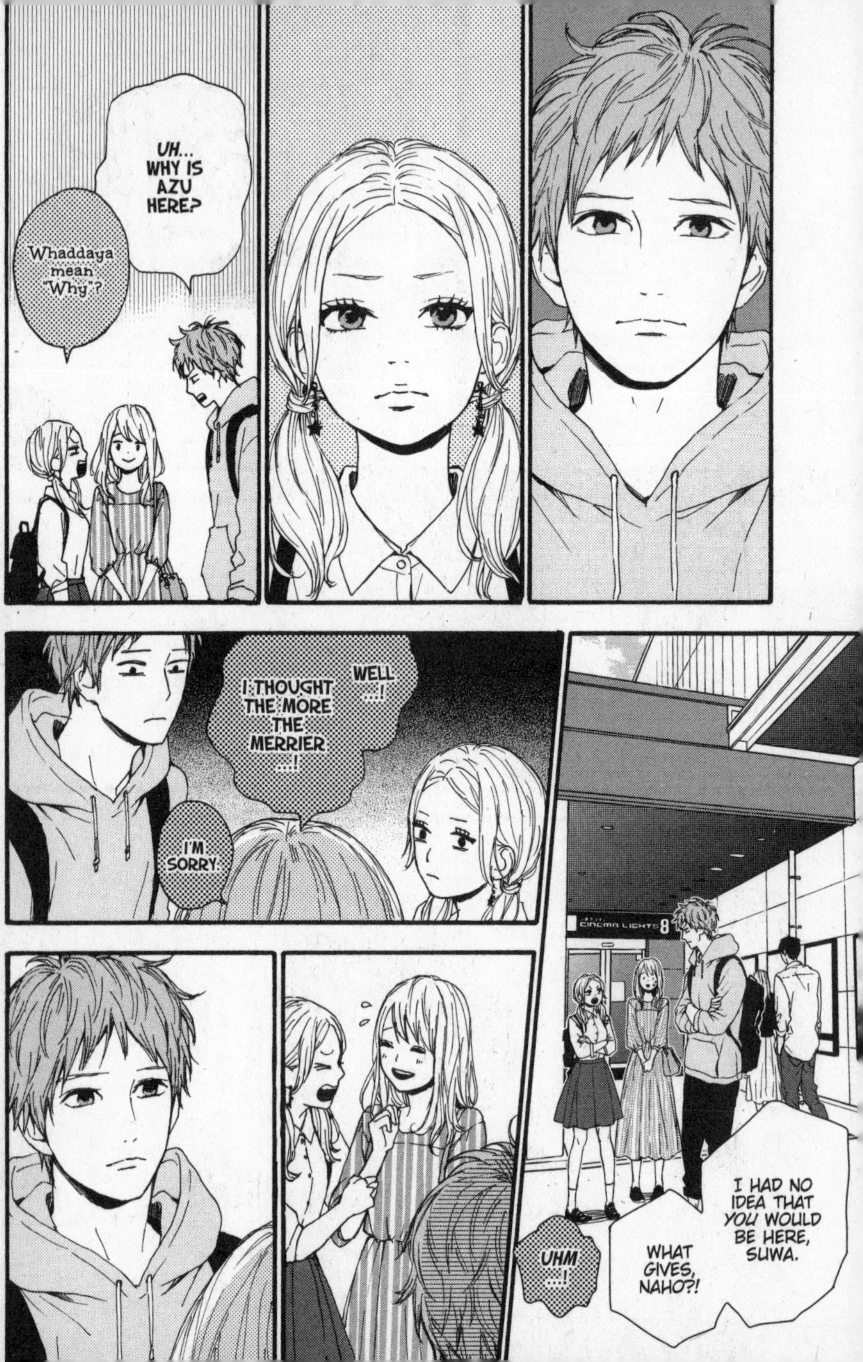
UH... WHY IS AZU HERE?
Whaddaya mean "Why"?
CINEMA LIGHTS 8
I HAD NO IDEA THAT YOU WOULD BE HERE, SUWA.
WHAT GIVES, NAHO?!
UHM ...!
WELL ...!
I THOUGHT THE MORE THE MERRIER ...!
I'M SORRY.

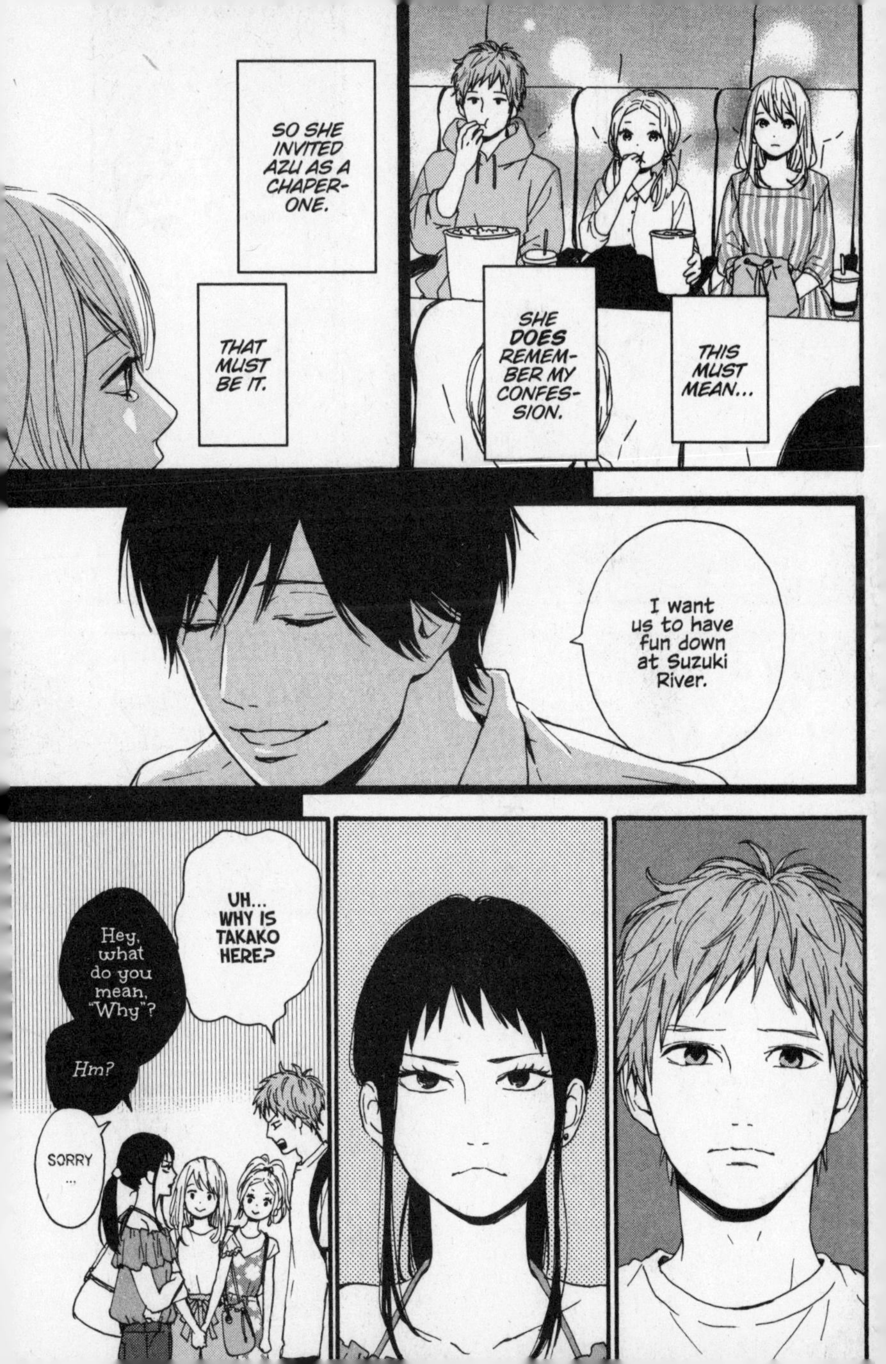
SO SHE INVITED AZU AS A CHAPER-ONE.
THAT MUST BE IT.
THIS MUST MEAN...
SHE DOES REMEMBER MY CONFES-SION.
I want us to have fun down at Suzuki River.
UH... WHY IS TAKAKO HERE?
Hey, what do you mean, "Why"?
Hm?
SORRY ...

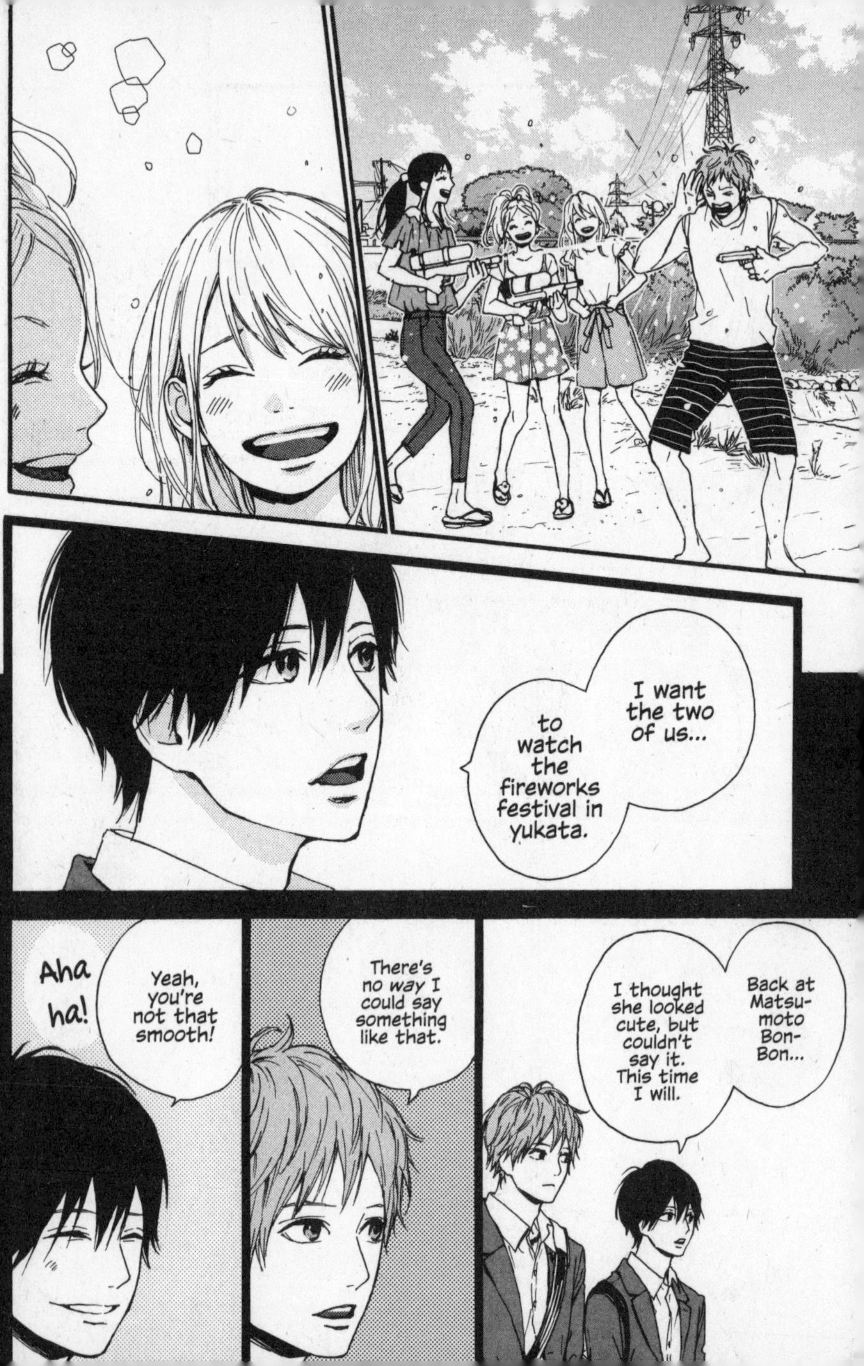
I want the two of us...
to watch the fireworks festival in yukata.
Back at Matsu-moto Bon-Bon...
I thought she looked cute, but couldn't say it. This time I will.
There's no way I could say something like that.
Yeah, you're not that smooth!
Aha ha!

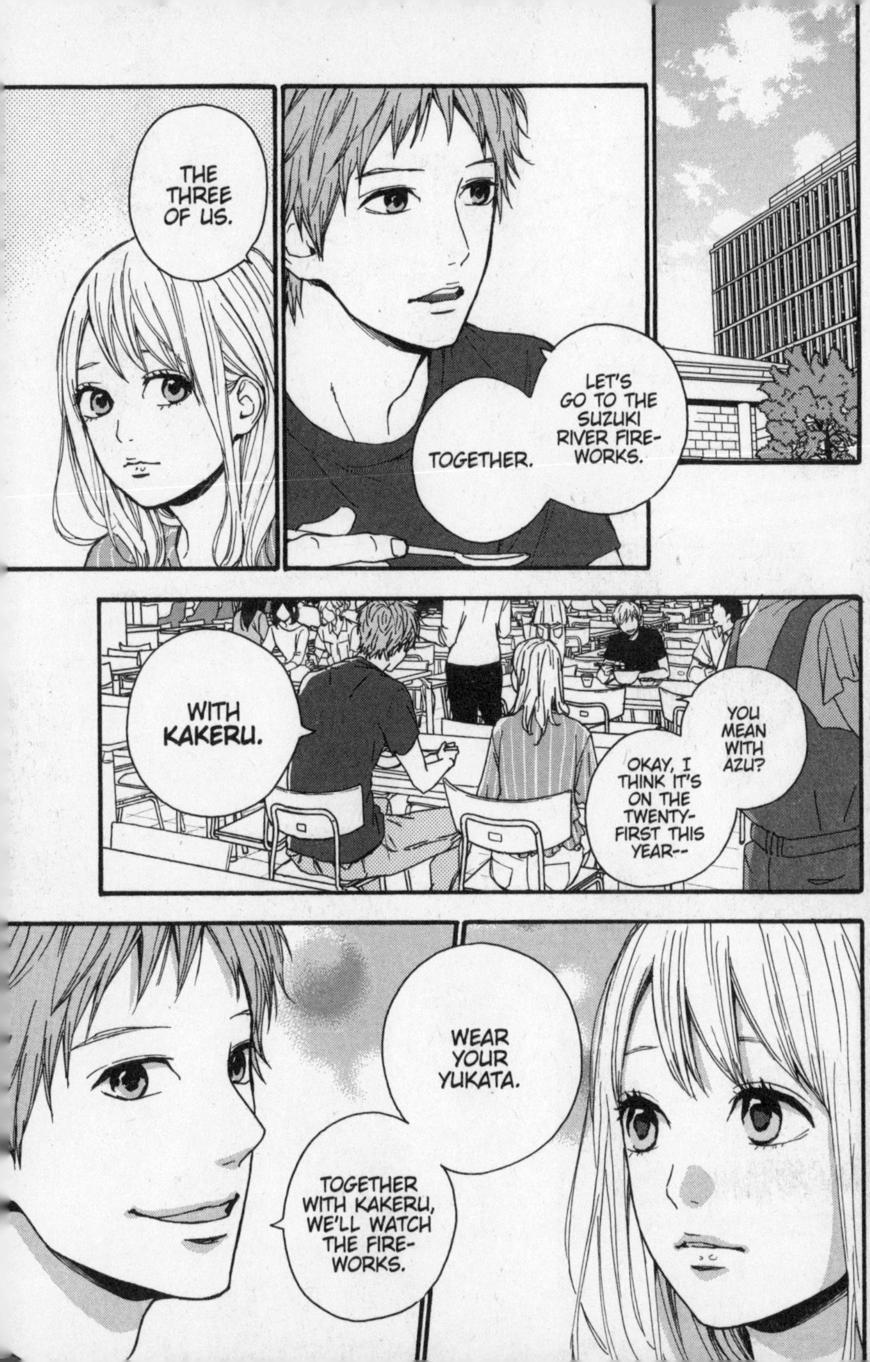
LET'S GO TO THE SUZUKI RIVER FIRE-WORKS.
TOGETHER.
THE THREE OF US.
YOU MEAN WITH AZU?
OKAY, I THINK IT'S ON THE TWENTY-FIRST THIS YEAR--
WITH KAKERU.
WEAR YOUR YUKATA.
TOGETHER WITH KAKERU, WE'LL WATCH THE FIRE-WORKS.

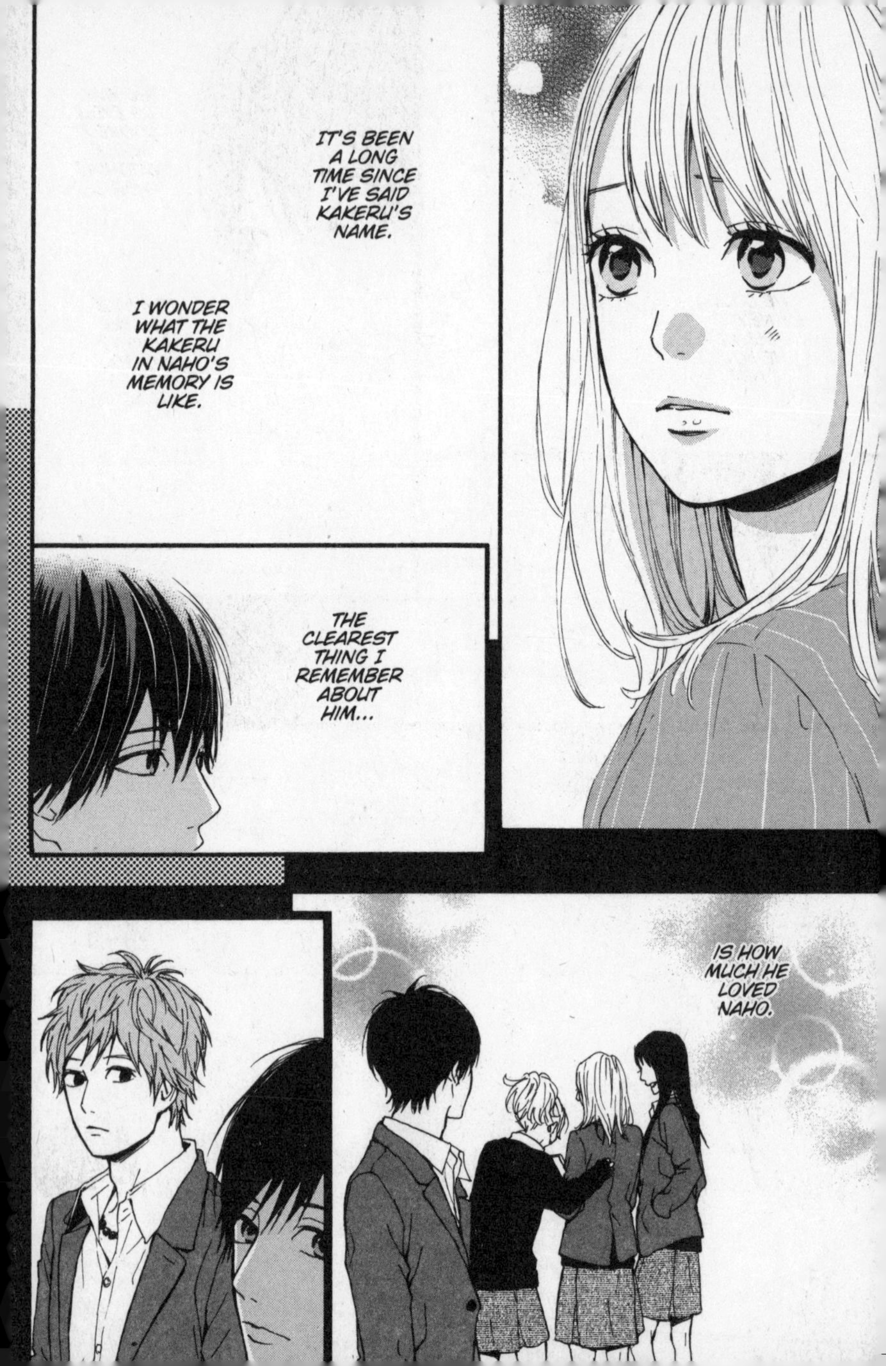
IT'S BEEN A LONG TIME SINCE I'VE SAID KAKERU'S NAME.
I WONDER WHAT THE KAKERU IN NAHO'S MEMORY IS LIKE.
THE CLEAREST THING I REMEMBER ABOUT HIM...
IS HOW MUCH HE LOVED NAHO.

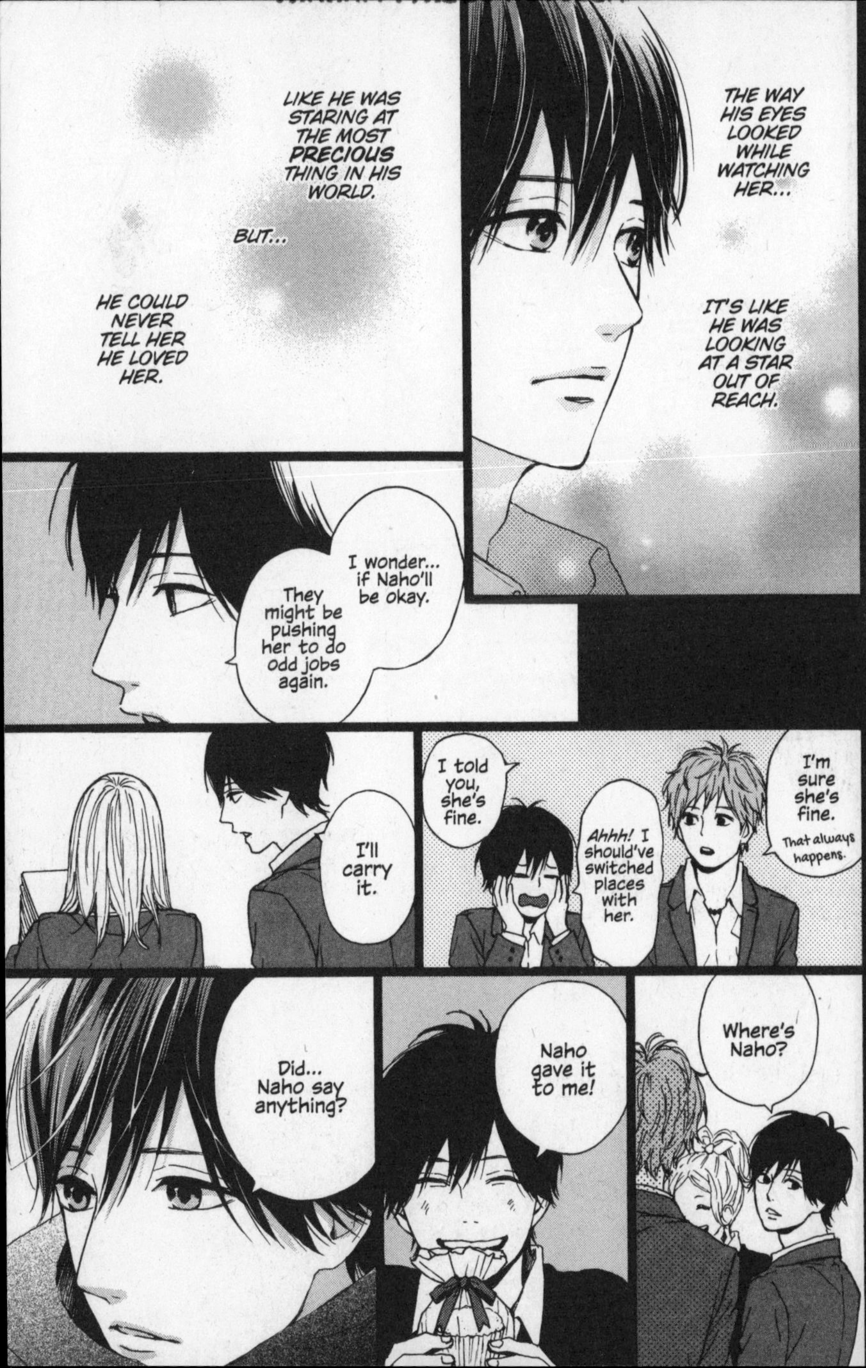
THE WAY HIS EYES LOOKED WHILE WATCHING HER...
IT'S LIKE HE WAS LOOKING AT A STAR OUT OF REACH.
LIKE HE WAS STARING AT THE MOST PRECIOUS THING IN HIS WORLD.
BUT...
HE COULD NEVER TELL HER HE LOVED HER.
I wonder... if Naho'll be okay.
They might be pushing her to do odd jobs again.
I'm sure she's fine.
That always happens.
Ahhh! I should've switched places with her.
I told you, she's fine.
I'll carry it.
Where's Naho?
Naho gave it to me!
Did... Naho say anything?

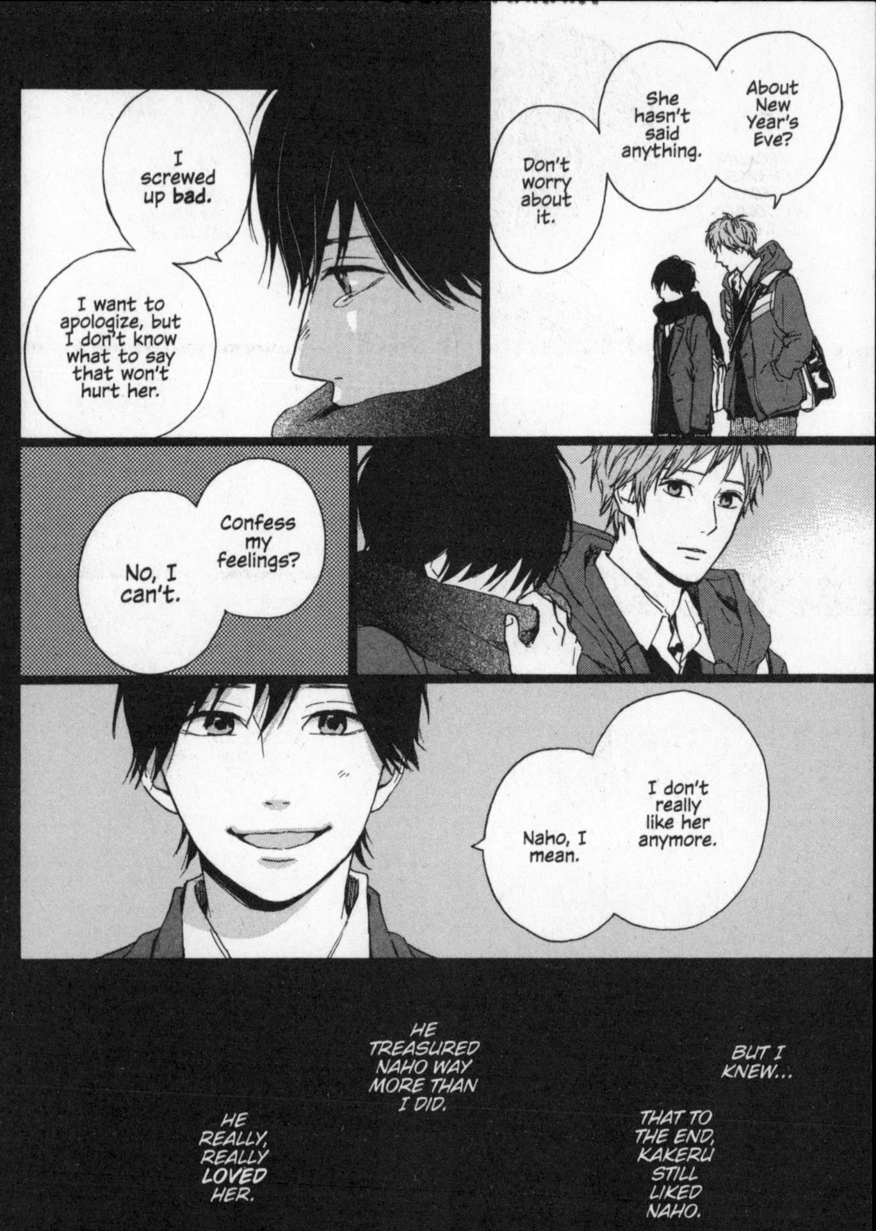
About New Year's Eve?
She hasn't said anything.
Don't worry about it.
I screwed up bad.
I want to apologize, but I don't know what to say that won't hurt her.
Confess my feelings?
No, I can't.
I don't really like her anymore.
Naho, I mean.
BUT I KNEW...
THAT TO THE END, KAKERU STILL LIKED NAHO.
HE TREASURED NAHO WAY MORE THAN I DID.
HE REALLY, REALLY LOVED HER.

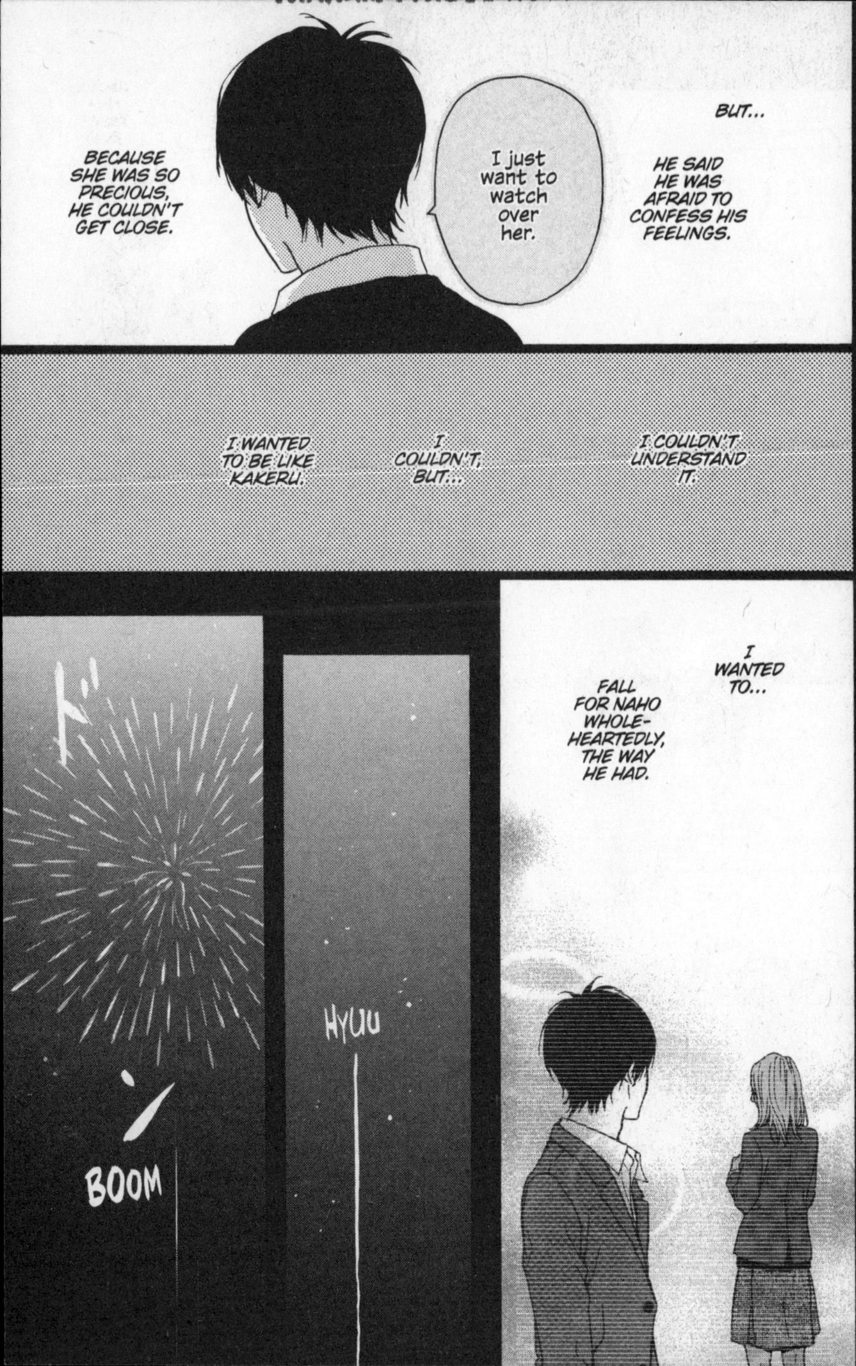
BUT...
HE SAID HE WAS AFRAID TO CONFESS HIS FEELINGS.
I just want to watch over her.
BECAUSE SHE WAS SO PRECIOUS, HE COULDN'T GET CLOSE.
I COULDN'T UNDERSTAND IT.
I COULDN'T, BUT...
I WANTED TO BE LIKE KAKERU.
I WANTED TO...
FALL FOR NAHO WHOLE-HEARTEDLY, THE WAY HE HAD.
HYUU
BOOM

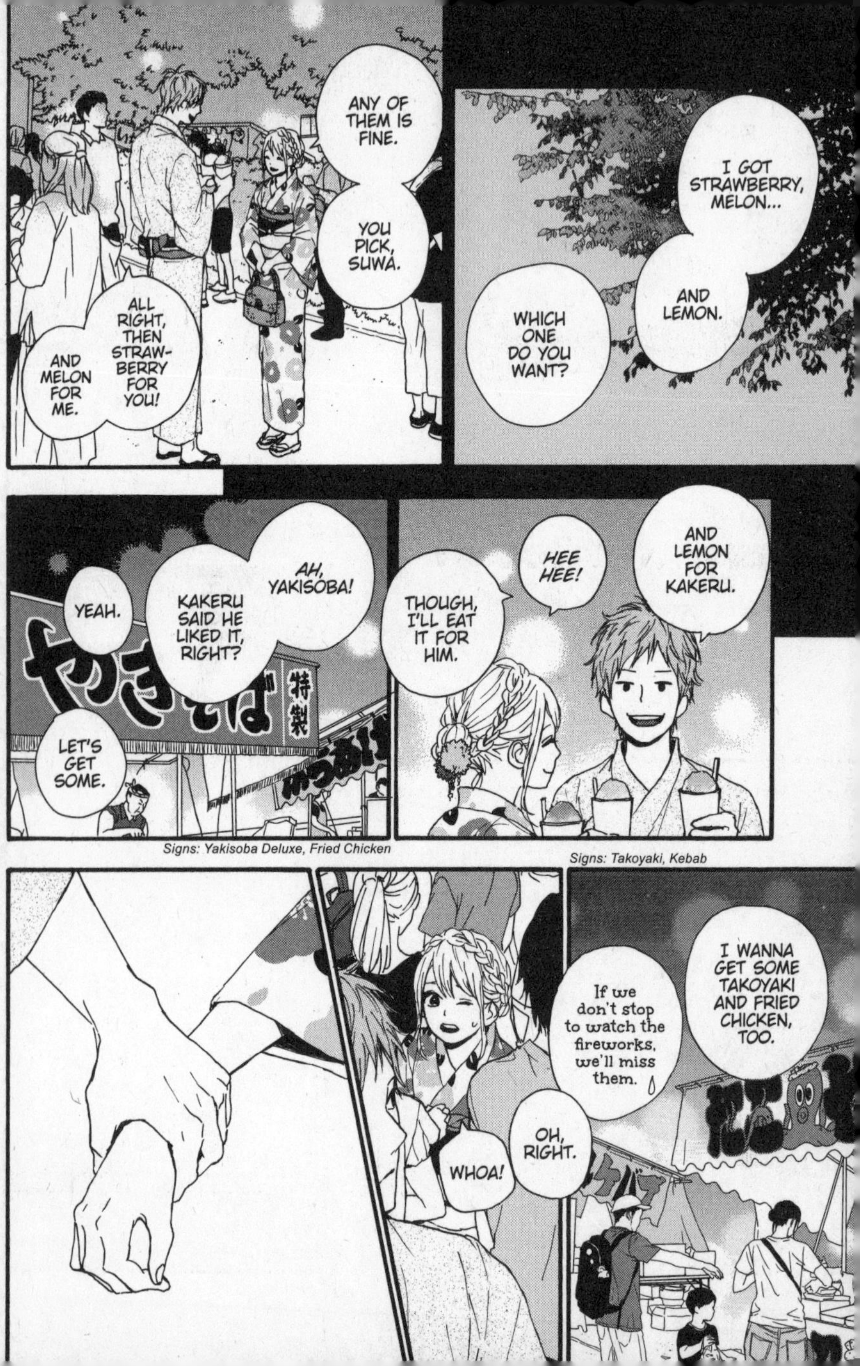
I GOT STRAWBERRY, MELON...
AND LEMON.
WHICH ONE DO YOU WANT?
ANY OF THEM IS FINE.
YOU PICK, SUWA.
ALL RIGHT, THEN STRAWBERRY FOR YOU!
AND MELON FOR ME.
AND LEMON FOR KAKERU.
HEE HEE!
THOUGH, I'LL EAT IT FOR HIM.
AH, YAKISOBA!
KAKERU SAID HE LIKED IT, RIGHT?
YEAH.
LET'S GET SOME.
I WANNA GET SOME TAKOYAKI AND FRIED CHICKEN, TOO.
If we don't stop to watch the fireworks, we'll miss them.
OH, RIGHT.
WHOA!

Signs: Yakisoba Deluxe, Fried Chicken

Signs: Takoyaki, Kebab

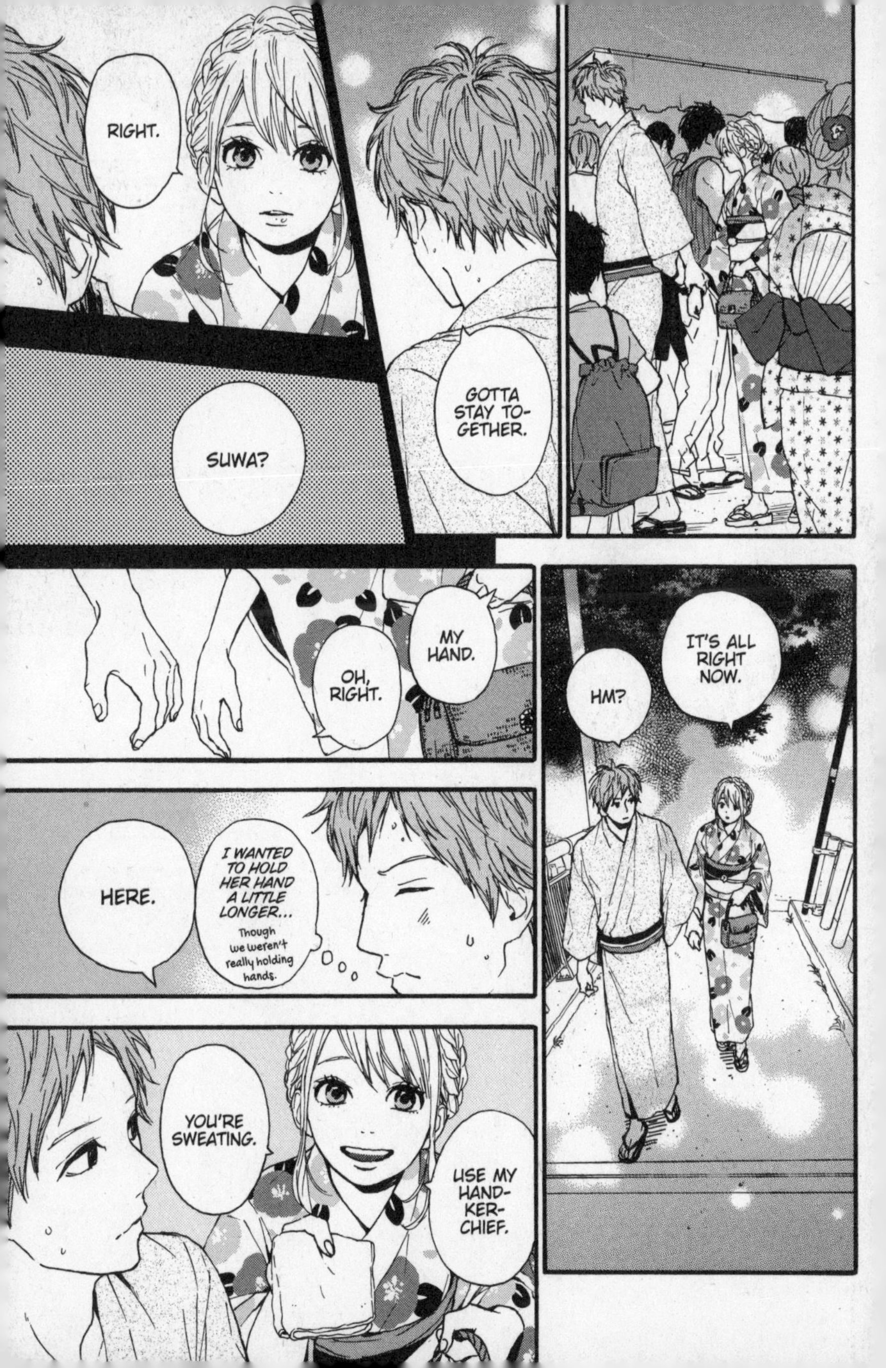
GOTTA STAY TO-GETHER.
RIGHT.
SUWA?
IT'S ALL RIGHT NOW.
HM?
MY HAND.
OH, RIGHT.
I WANTED TO HOLD HER HAND A LITTLE LONGER...
Though we weren't really holding hands.
HERE.
YOU'RE SWEATING.
USE MY HAND-KER-CHIEF.

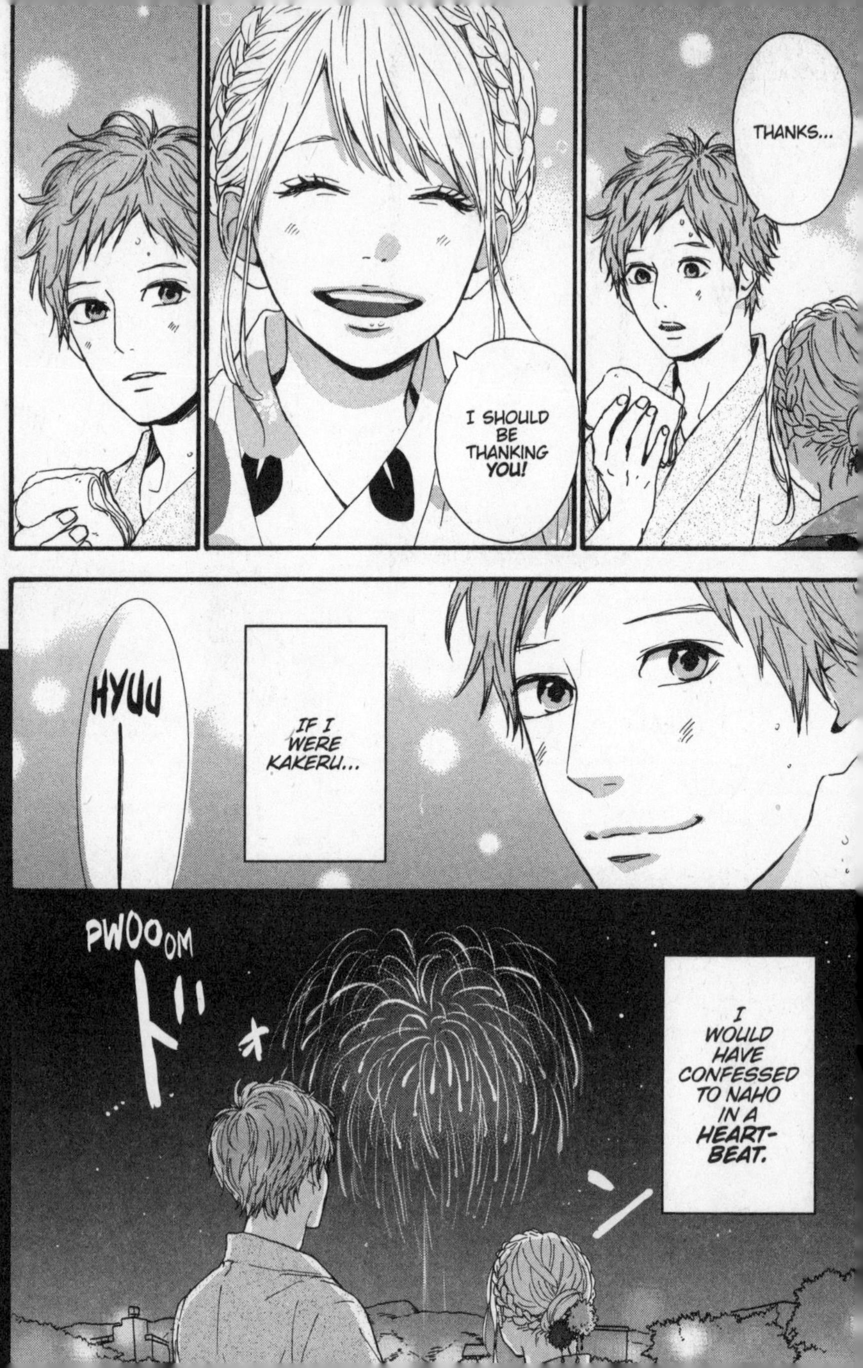
THANKS...
I SHOULD BE THANKING YOU!
IF I WERE KAKERU...
HYUU
PWOOOM
ドーン
I WOULD HAVE CONFESSED TO NAHO IN A HEART-BEAT.

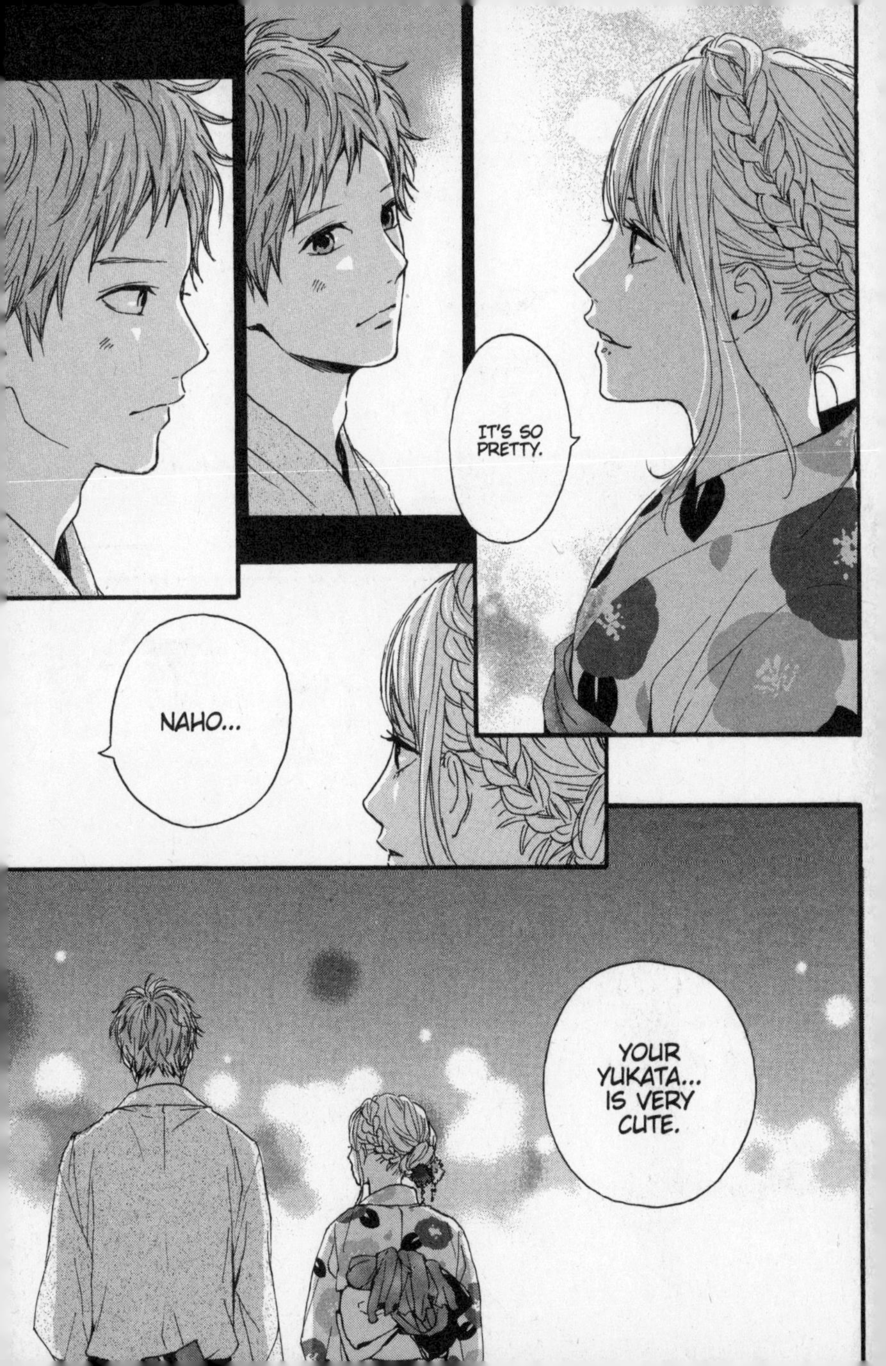
IT'S SO PRETTY.
NAHO...
YOUR YUKATA... IS VERY CUTE.

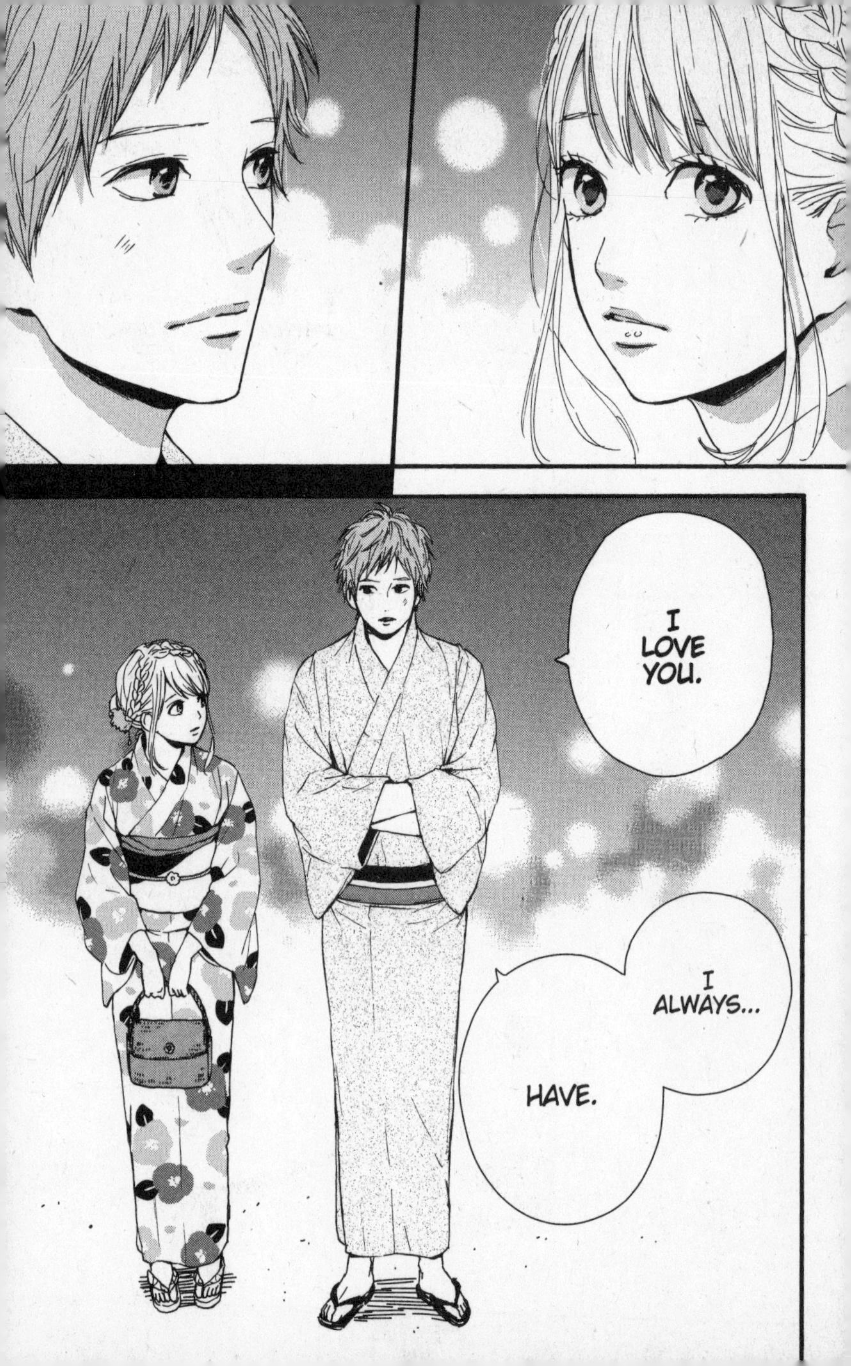
I LOVE YOU.
I ALWAYS...
HAVE.

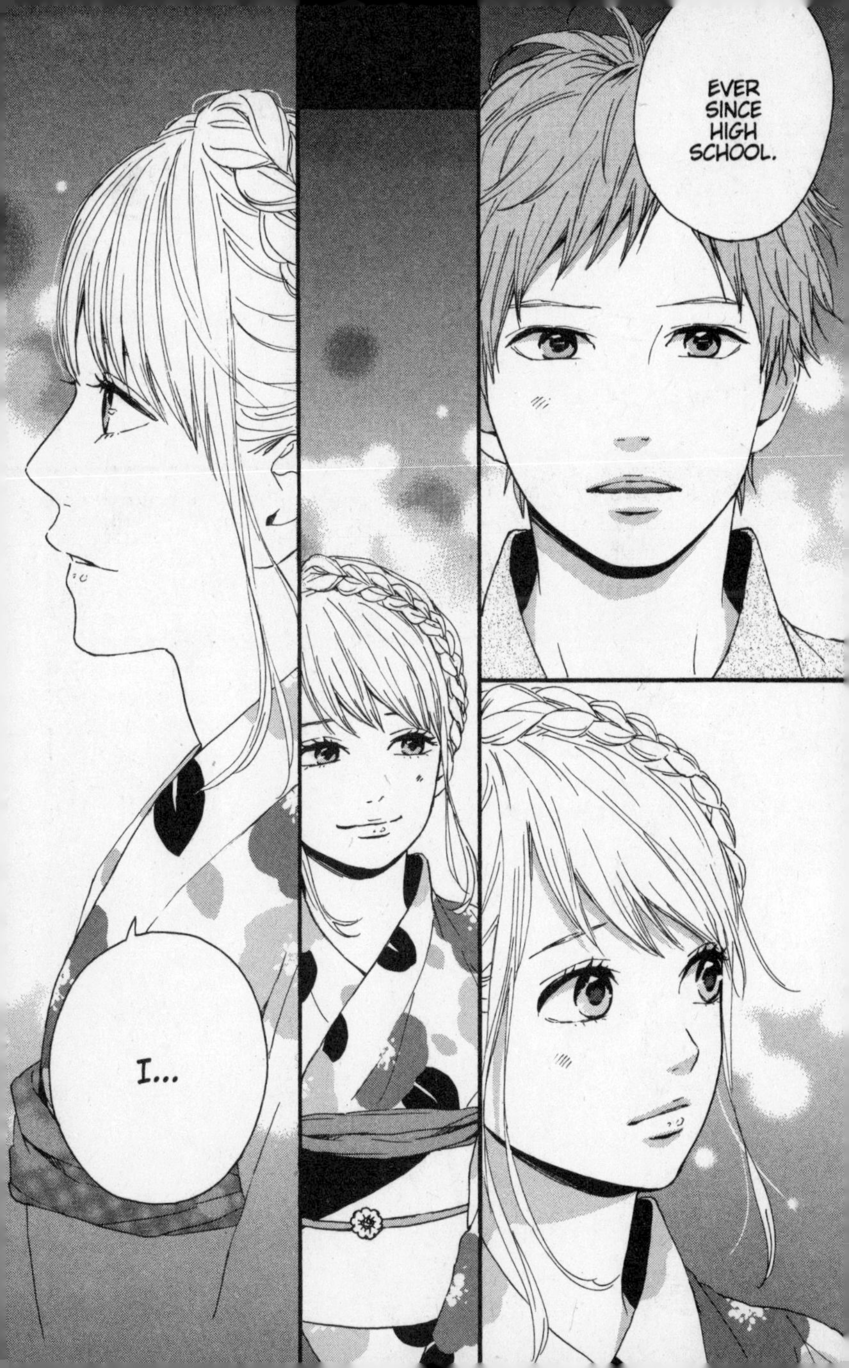
EVER SINCE HIGH SCHOOL.
I...

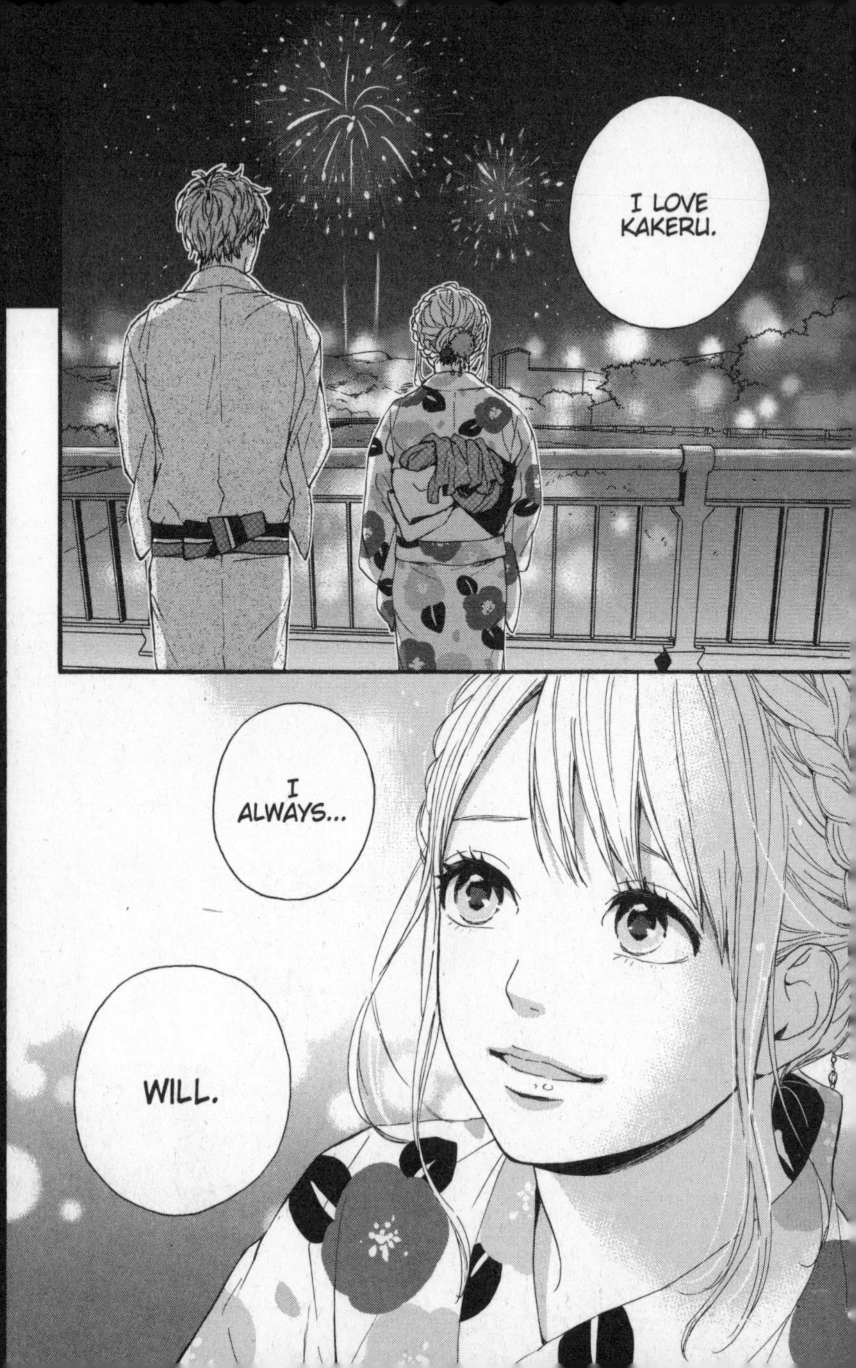
I LOVE KAKERU.
I ALWAYS...
WILL.

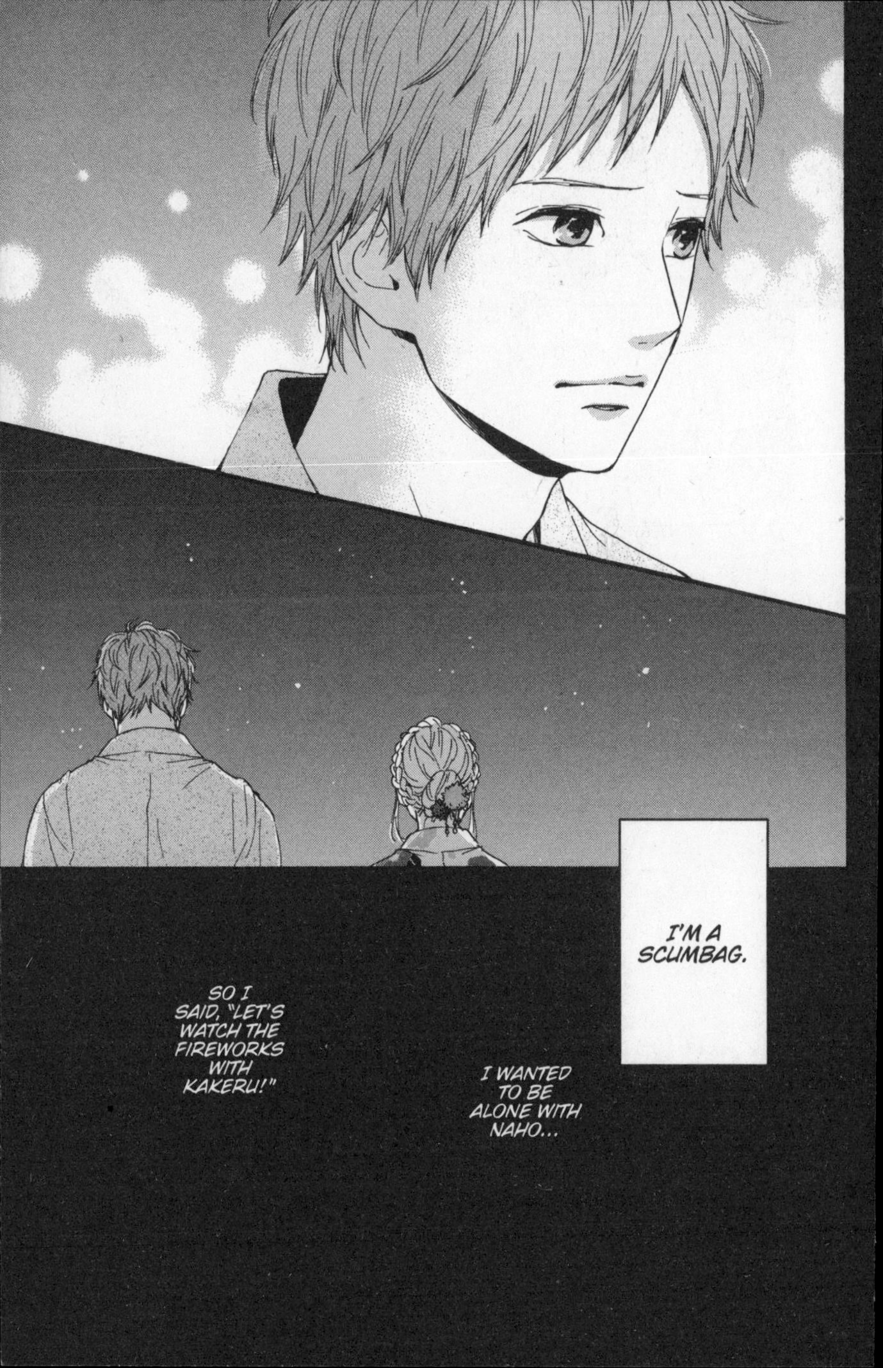
I'M A SCUMBAG.
I WANTED TO BE ALONE WITH NAHO...
SO I SAID, "LET'S WATCH THE FIREWORKS WITH KAKERU!"

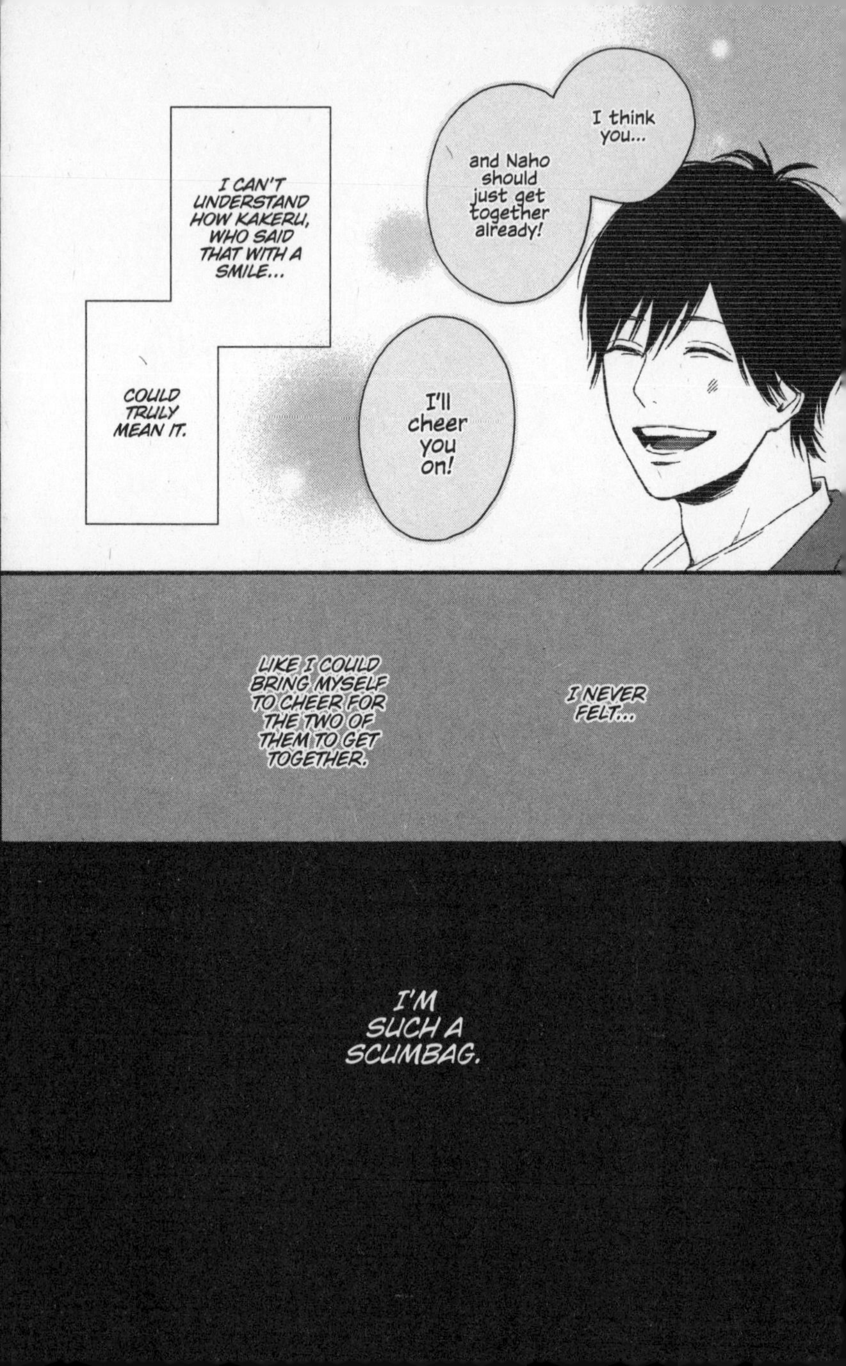
I think you...
and Naho should just get together already!
I'll cheer you on!
I CAN'T UNDERSTAND HOW KAKERU, WHO SAID THAT WITH A SMILE...
COULD TRULY MEAN IT.
I NEVER FELT...
LIKE I COULD BRING MYSELF TO CHEER FOR THE TWO OF THEM TO GET TOGETHER.
I'M SUCH A SCUMBAG.

orange

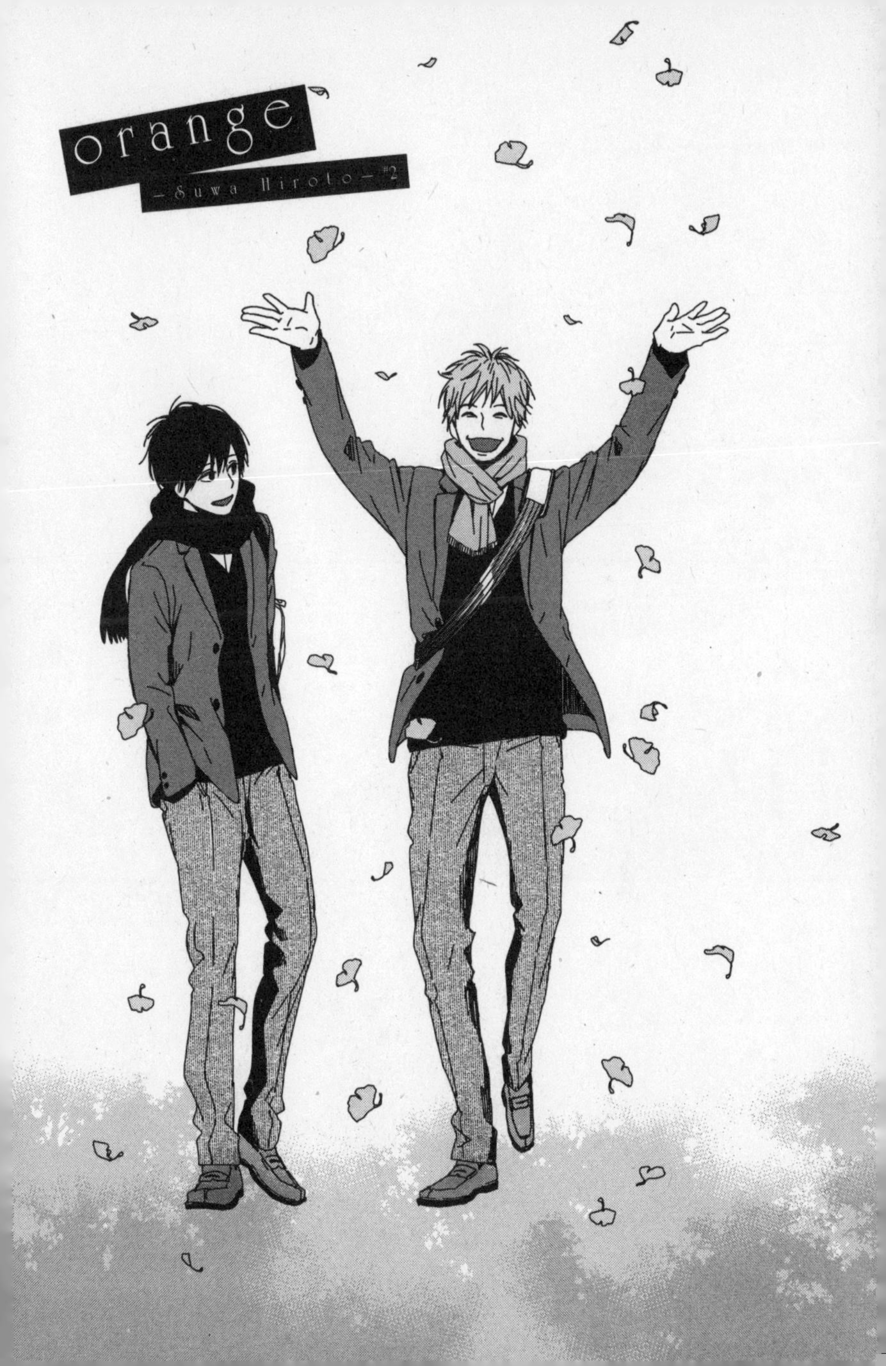
orange
—Suwa Hiroto— #2

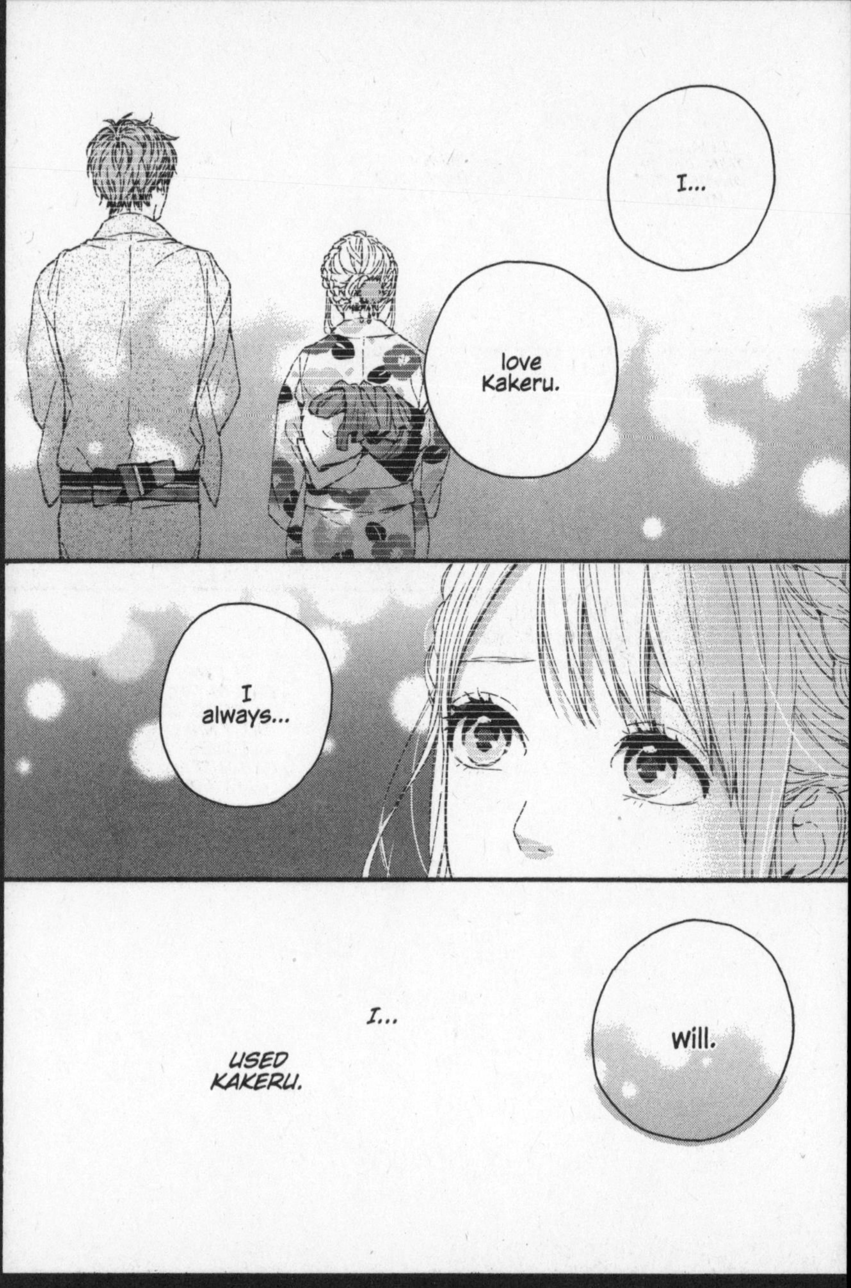
I...
love Kakeru.
I always...
Will.
I...
USED KAKERU.

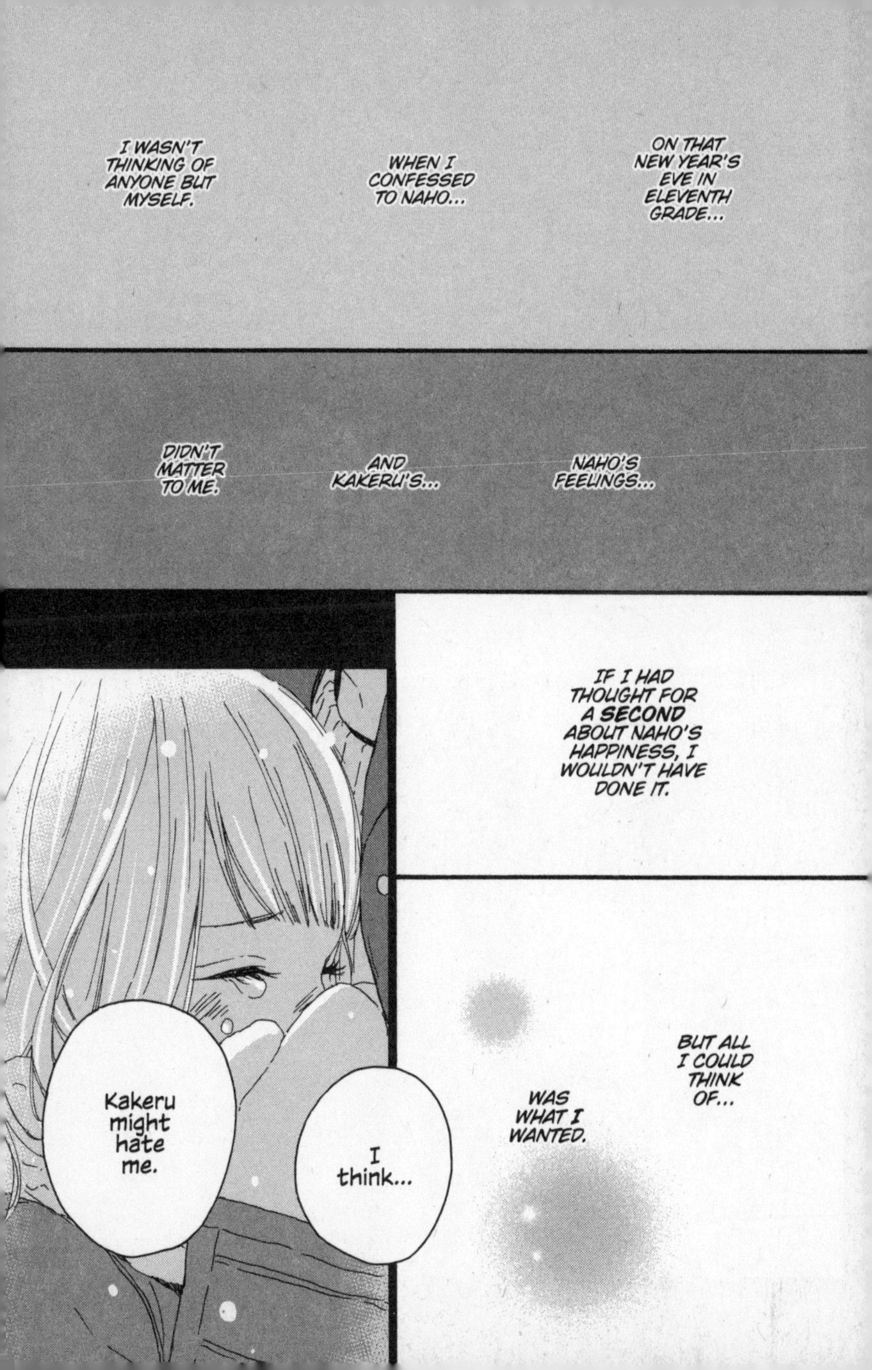
ON THAT NEW YEAR'S EVE IN ELEVENTH GRADE...
WHEN I CONFESSED TO NAHO...
I WASN'T THINKING OF ANYONE BUT MYSELF.
NAHO'S FEELINGS...
AND KAKERU'S...
DIDN'T MATTER TO ME.
IF I HAD THOUGHT FOR A **SECOND** ABOUT NAHO'S HAPPINESS, I WOULDN'T HAVE DONE IT.
BUT ALL I COULD THINK OF...
WAS WHAT I WANTED.
I think...
Kakeru might hate me.

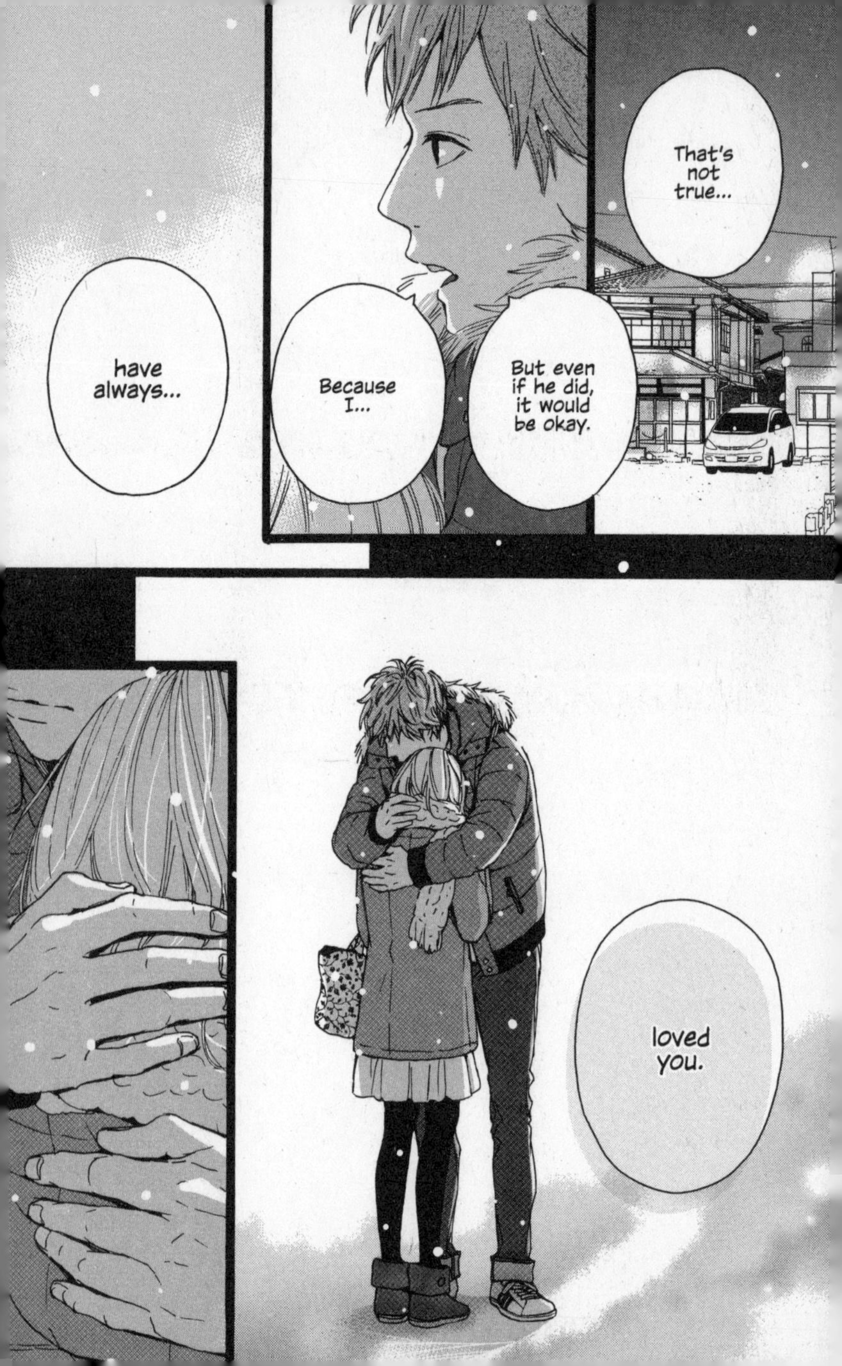
That's not true...
But even if he did, it would be okay.
Because I...
have always...
loved you.

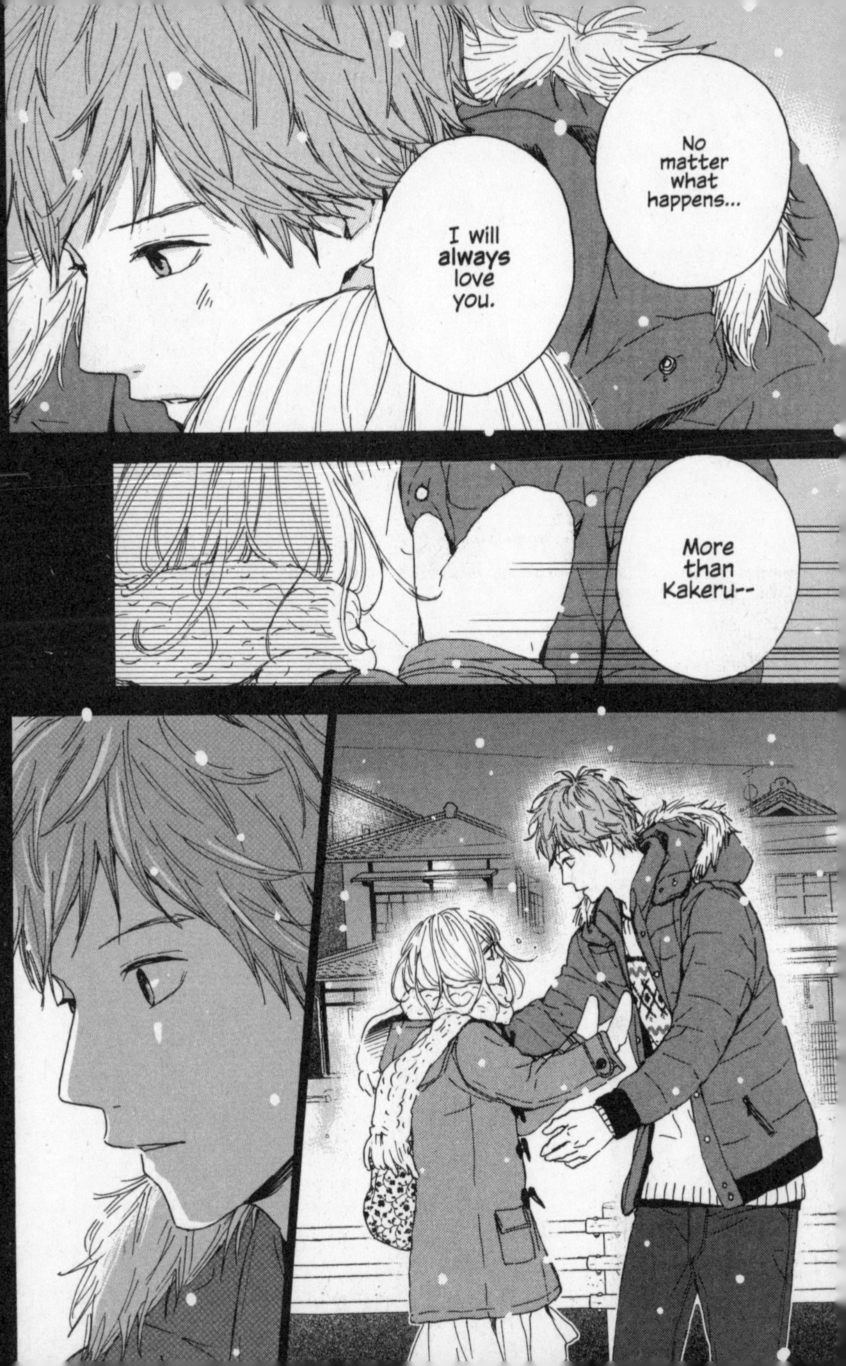
No matter what happens...
I will always love you.
More than Kakeru--

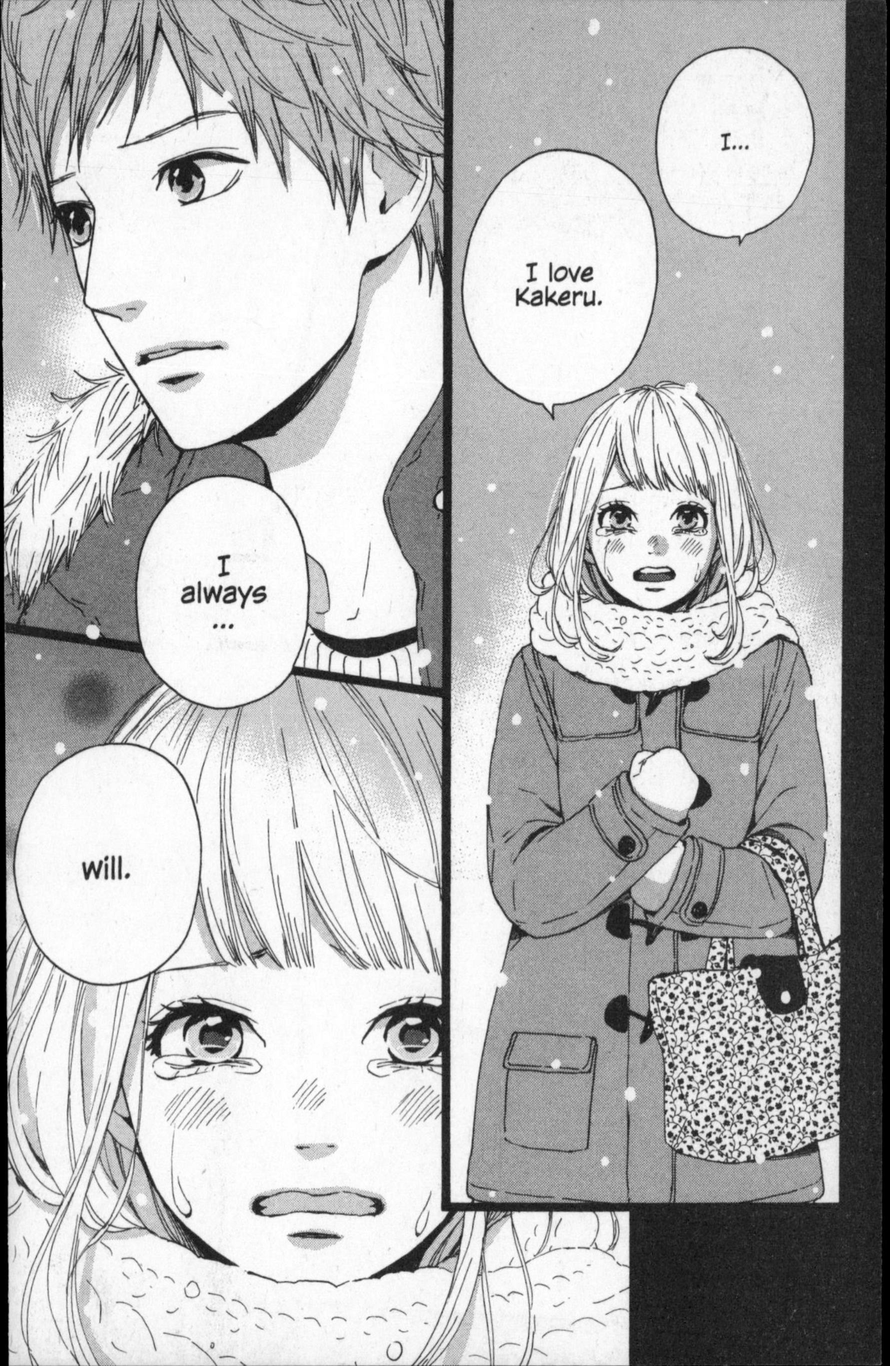
I...
I love Kakeru.
I always ...
will.

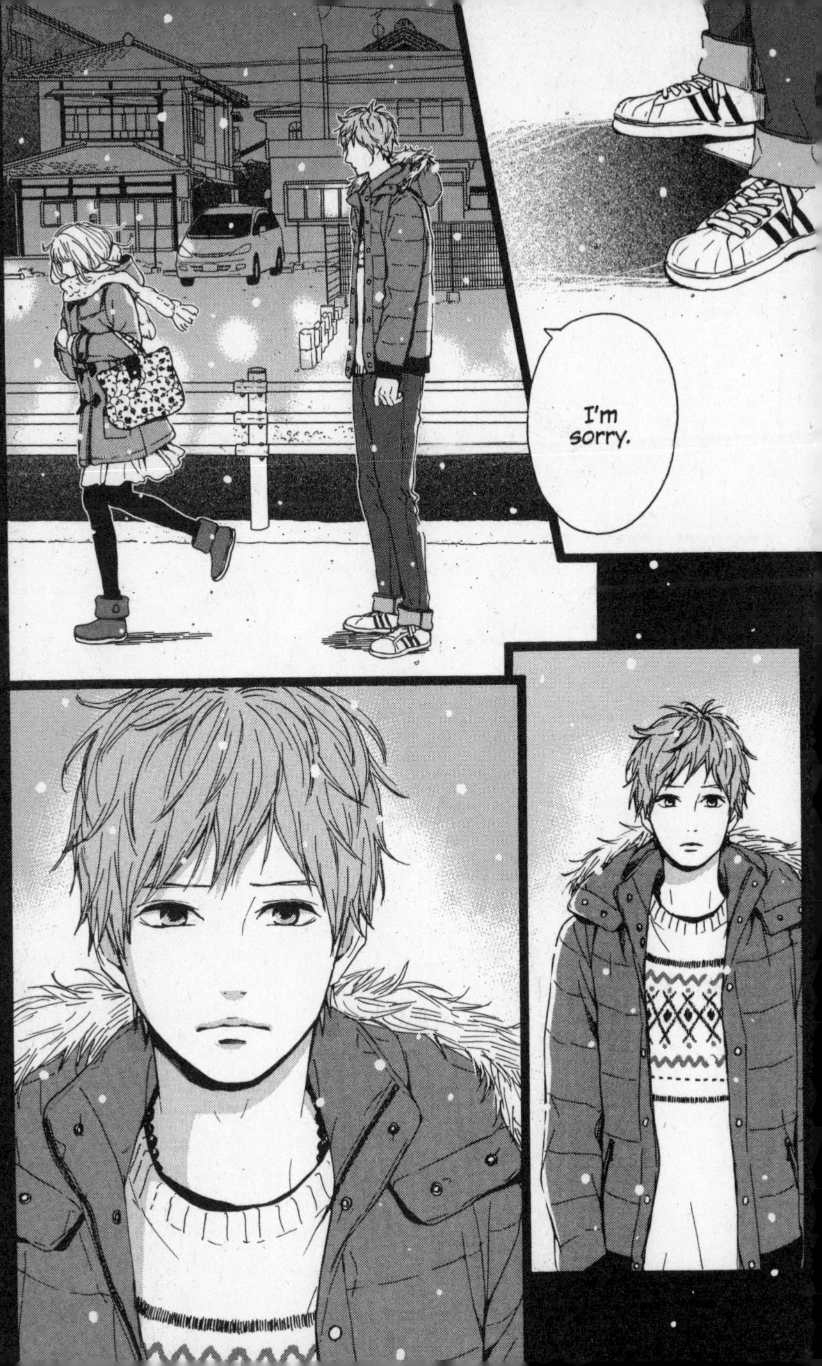
I'm sorry.

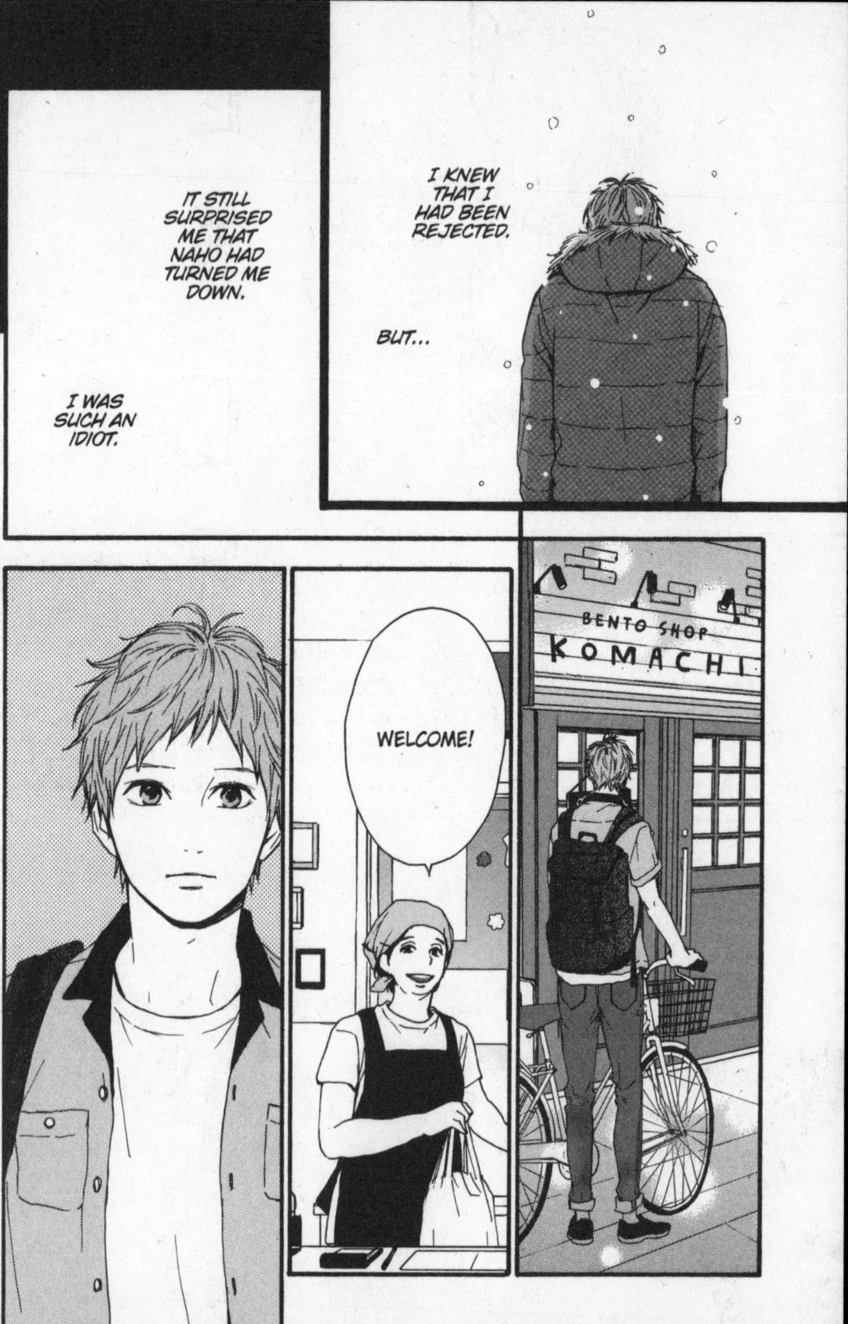
I KNEW THAT I HAD BEEN REJECTED.
BUT...
IT STILL SURPRISED ME THAT NAHO HAD TURNED ME DOWN.
I WAS SUCH AN IDIOT.
BENTO SHOP KOMACHI
WELCOME!

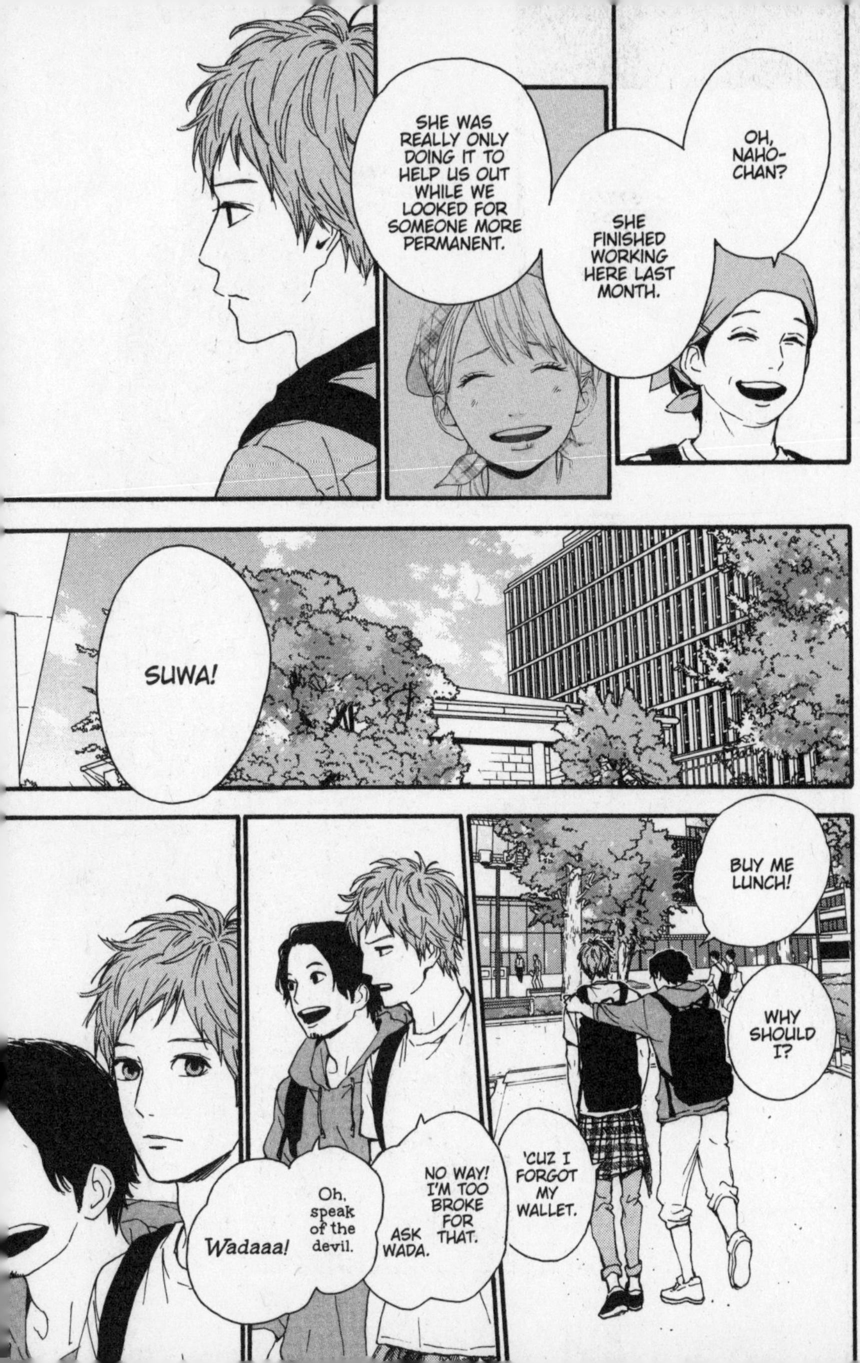
OH, NAHO-CHAN?
SHE FINISHED WORKING HERE LAST MONTH.
SHE WAS REALLY ONLY DOING IT TO HELP US OUT WHILE WE LOOKED FOR SOMEONE MORE PERMANENT.
SUWA!
BUY ME LUNCH!
WHY SHOULD I?
'CUZ I FORGOT MY WALLET.
NO WAY! I'M TOO BROKE FOR THAT.
ASK WADA.
Oh, speak of the devil.
Wadaaa!

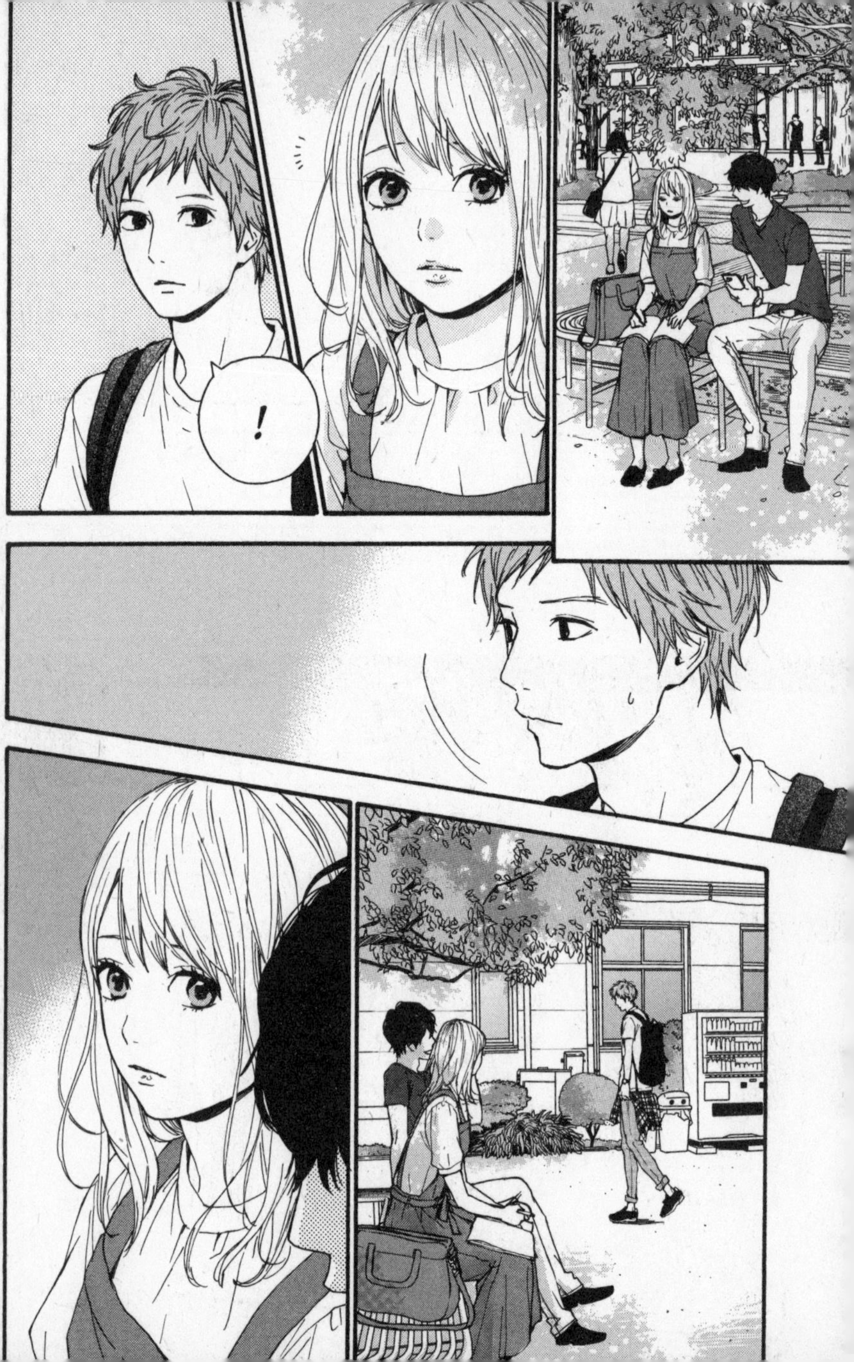
!

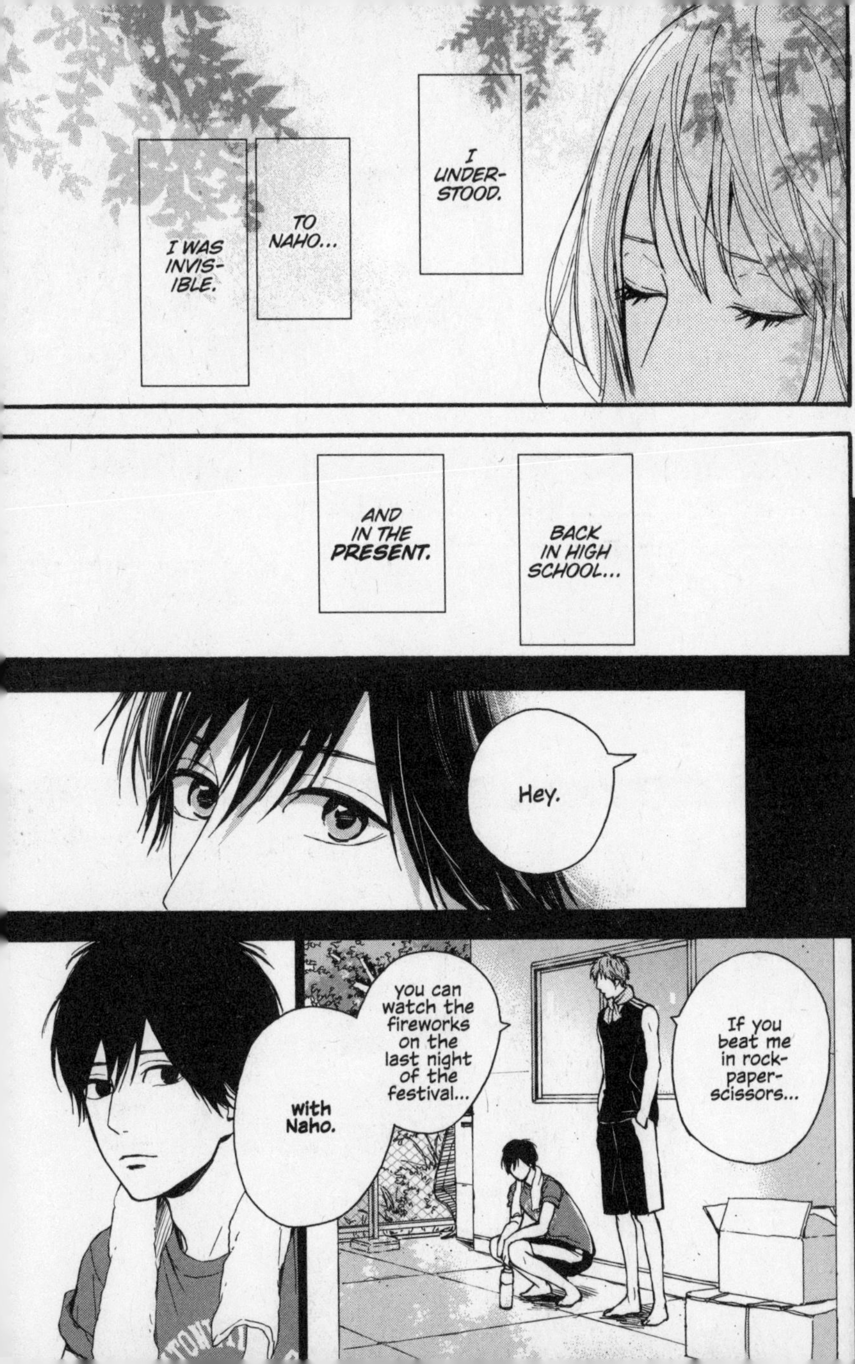
I UNDERSTOOD.
TO NAHO...
I WAS INVISIBLE.
BACK IN HIGH SCHOOL...
AND IN THE PRESENT.
Hey.
If you beat me in rock-paper-scissors...
you can watch the fireworks on the last night of the festival...
with Naho.

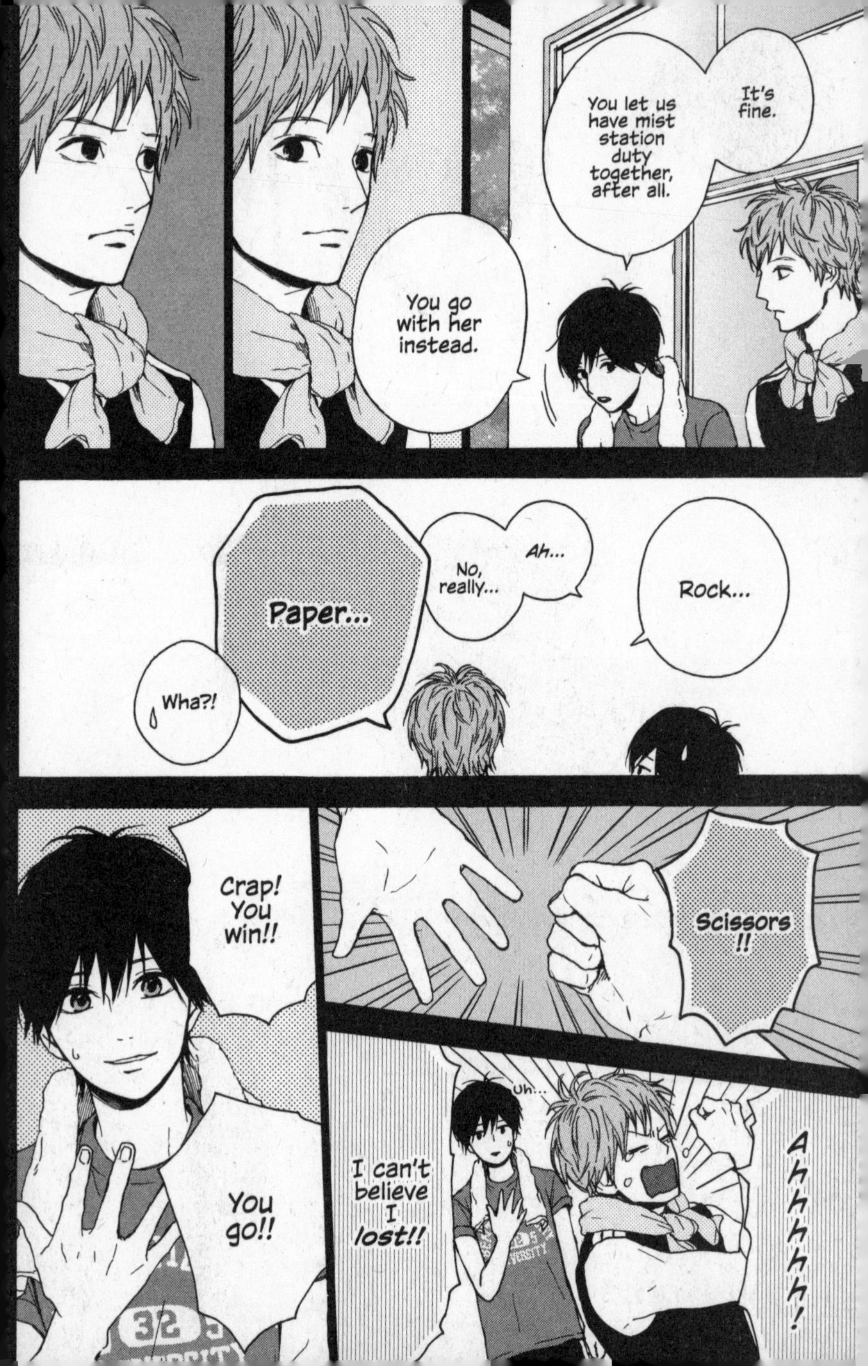
It's fine.
You let us have mist station duty together, after all.
You go with her instead.
Rock...
Ah...
No, really...
Paper...
Wha?!
Scissors!!
Ahhhhh!
Uh...
I can't believe I lost!!
Crap! You win!!
You go!!

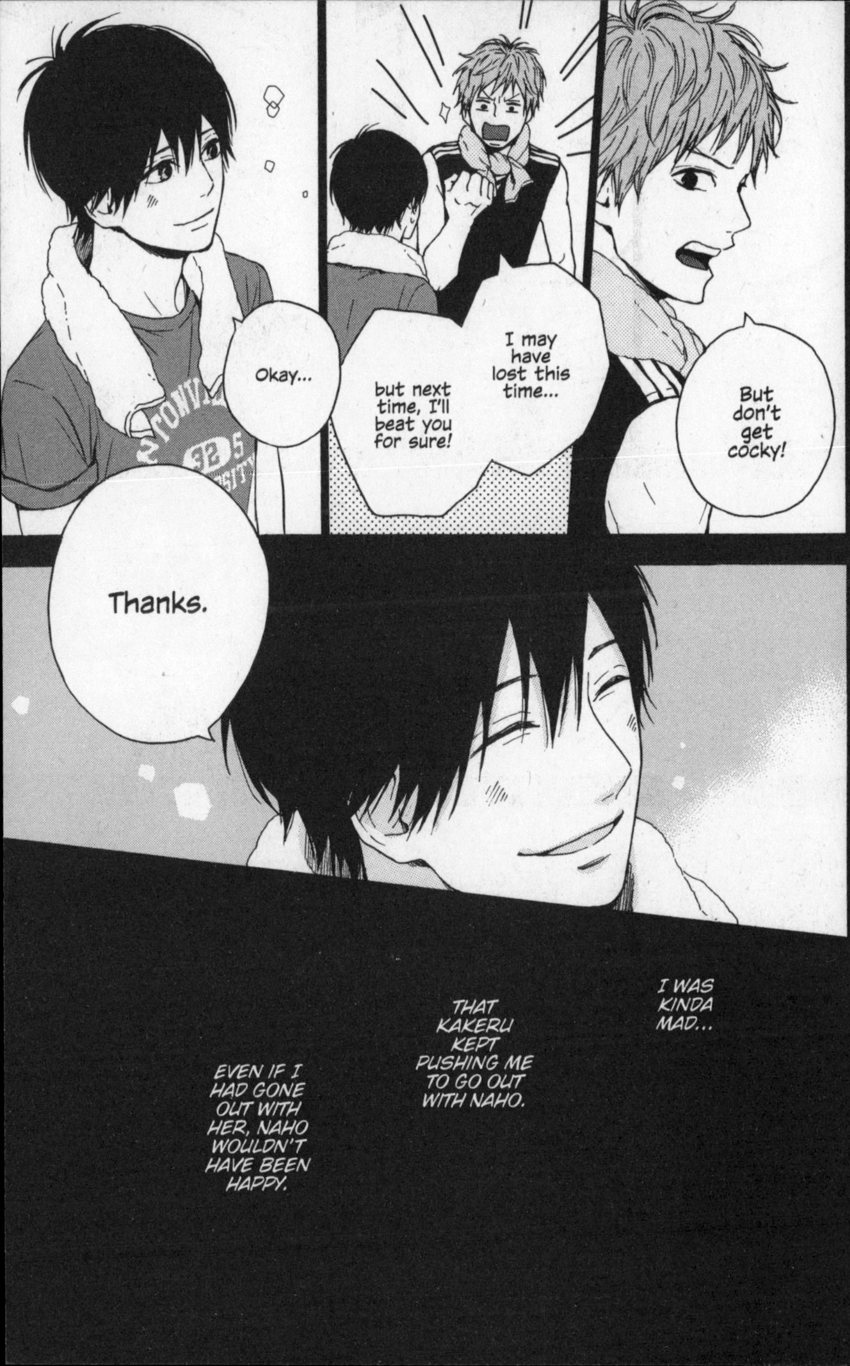
But don't get cocky!
I may have lost this time...
but next time, I'll beat you for sure!
Okay...
Thanks.
I WAS KINDA MAD...
THAT KAKERU KEPT PUSHING ME TO GO OUT WITH NAHO.
EVEN IF I HAD GONE OUT WITH HER, NAHO WOULDN'T HAVE BEEN HAPPY.

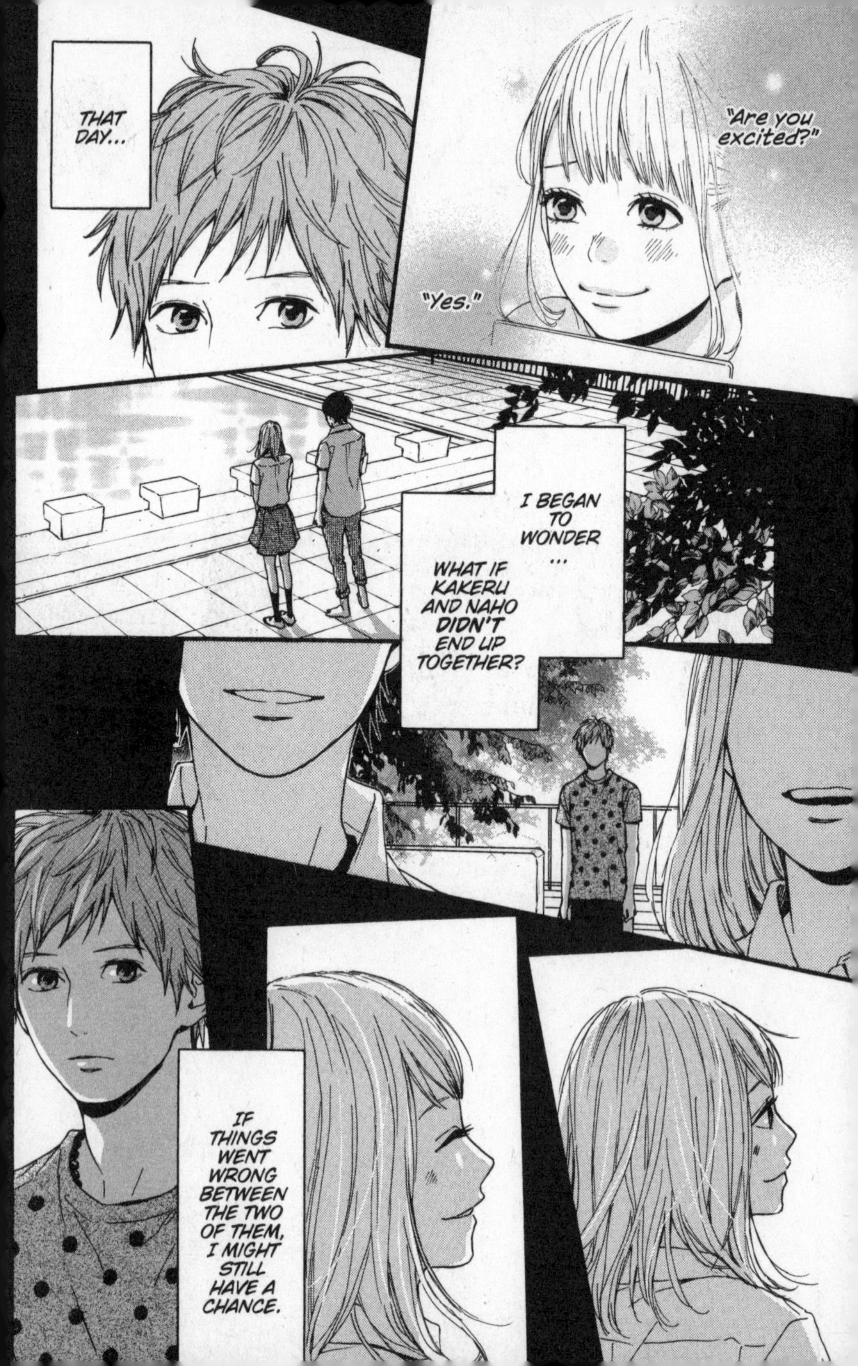
"Are you excited?"
"Yes."
THAT DAY...
I BEGAN TO WONDER ...
WHAT IF KAKERU AND NAHO DIDN'T END UP TOGETHER?
IF THINGS WENT WRONG BETWEEN THE TWO OF THEM, I MIGHT STILL HAVE A CHANCE.

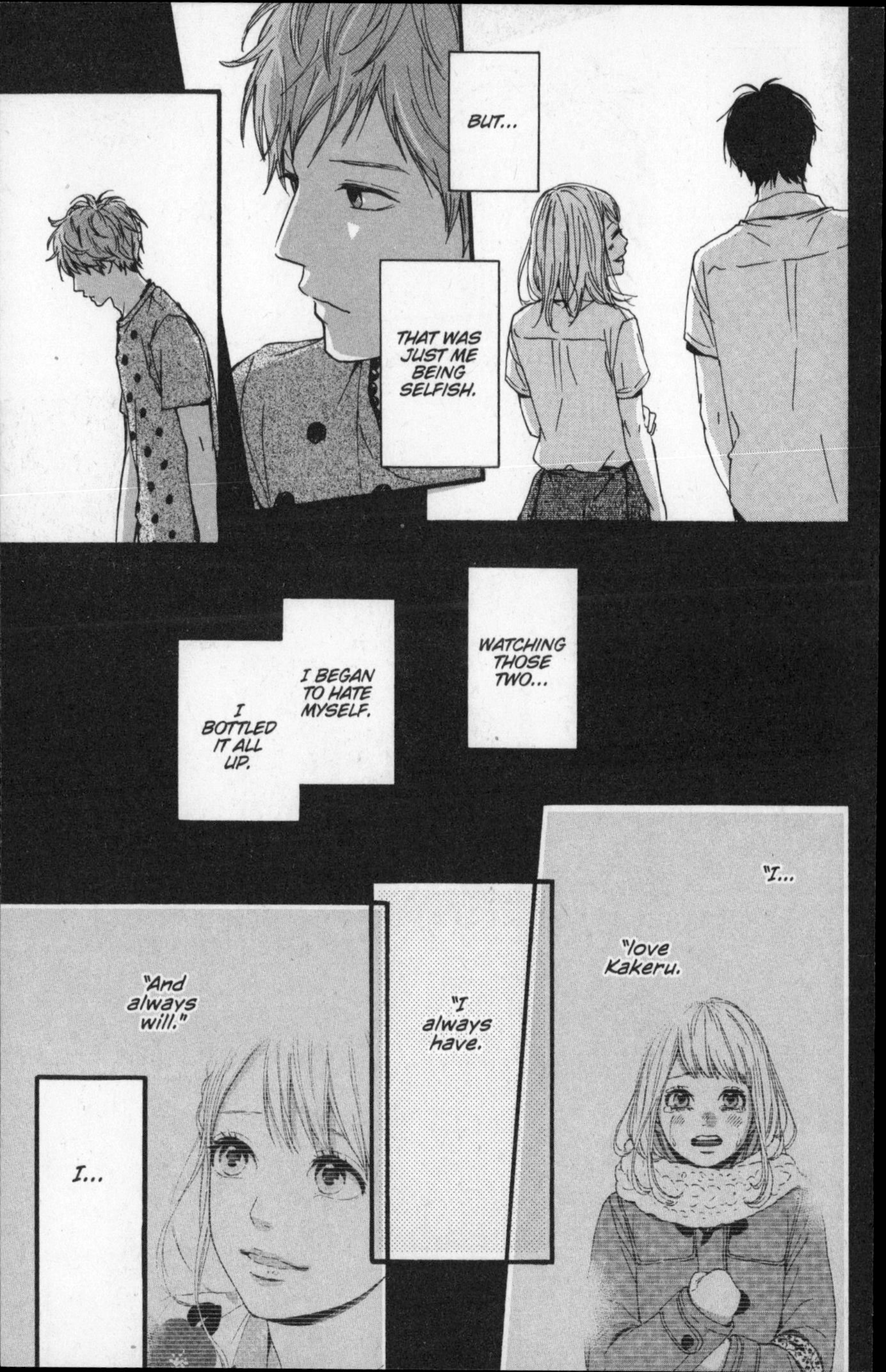
BUT...
THAT WAS JUST ME BEING SELFISH.
WATCHING THOSE TWO...
I BEGAN TO HATE MYSELF.
I BOTTLED IT ALL UP.
"I...
"love Kakeru.
"I always have.
"And always will."
I...

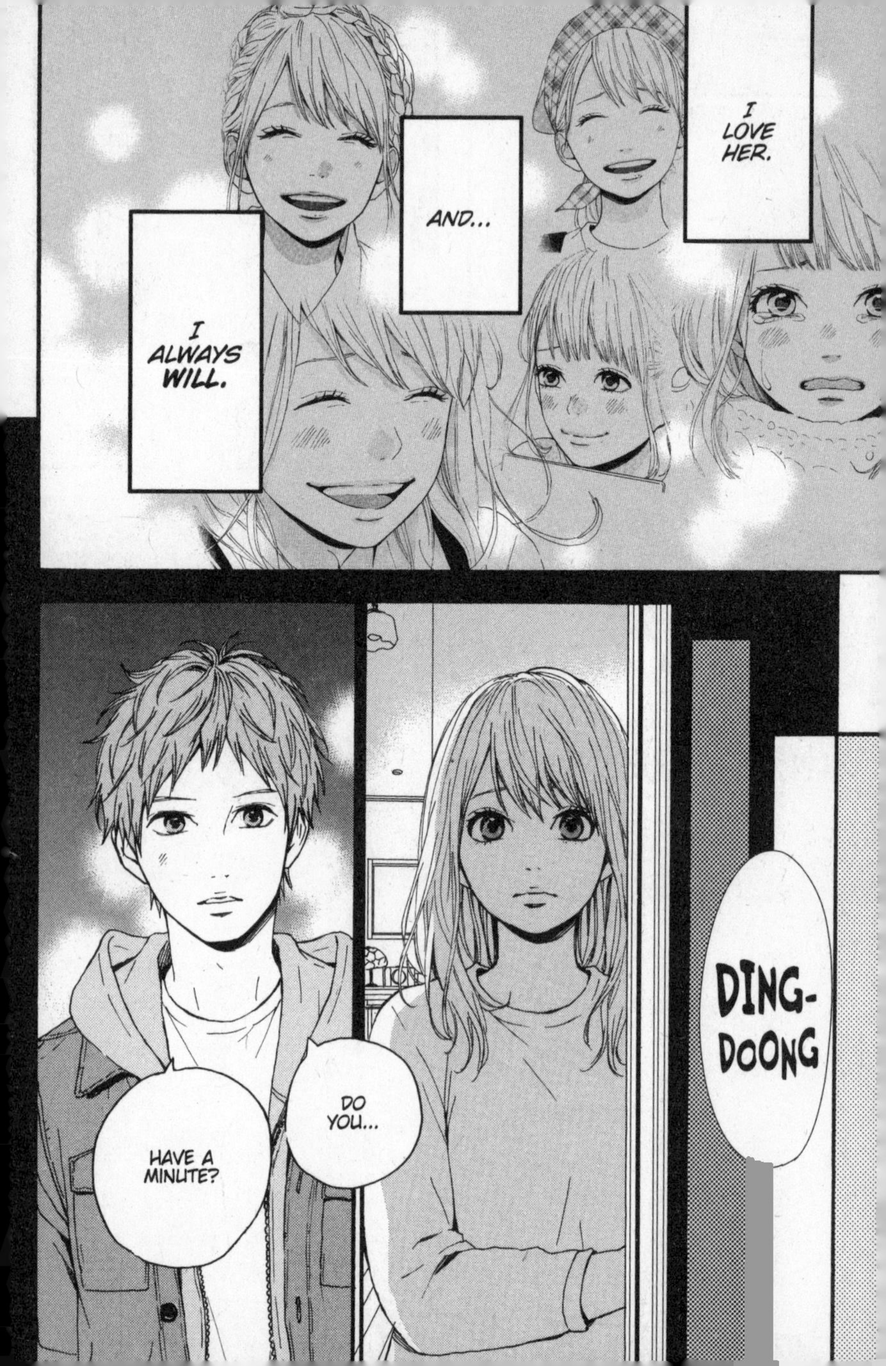
I LOVE HER.
AND...
I ALWAYS WILL.
DING-DOONG
DO YOU...
HAVE A MINUTE?

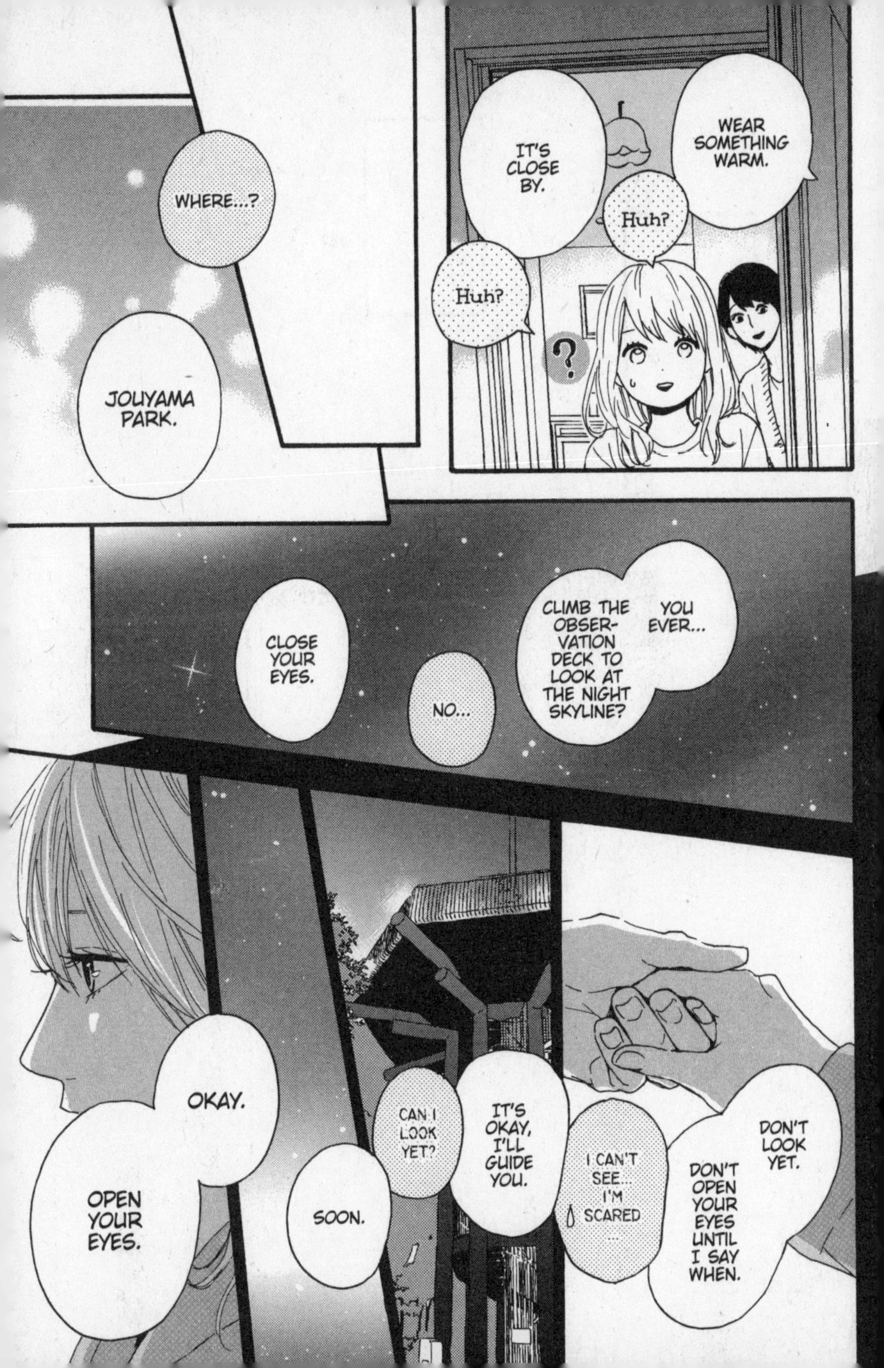
WEAR SOMETHING WARM.
IT'S CLOSE BY.
Huh?
Huh?
WHERE...?
JOUYAMA PARK.
YOU EVER... CLIMB THE OBSERVATION DECK TO LOOK AT THE NIGHT SKYLINE?
NO...
CLOSE YOUR EYES.
DON'T LOOK YET.
DON'T OPEN YOUR EYES UNTIL I SAY WHEN.
I CAN'T SEE... I'M SCARED...
IT'S OKAY, I'LL GUIDE YOU.
CAN I LOOK YET?
SOON.
OKAY.
OPEN YOUR EYES.

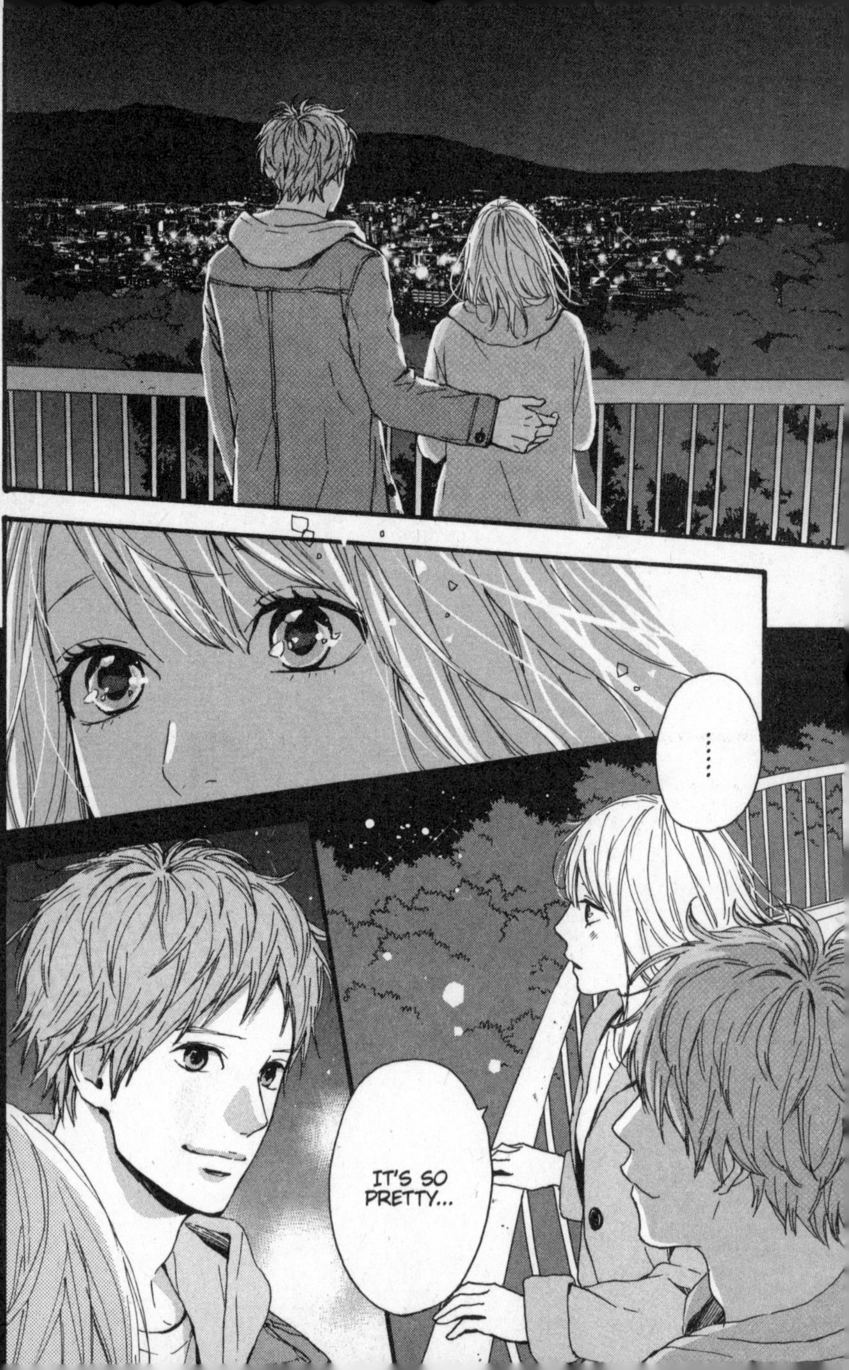
......
IT'S SO PRETTY...

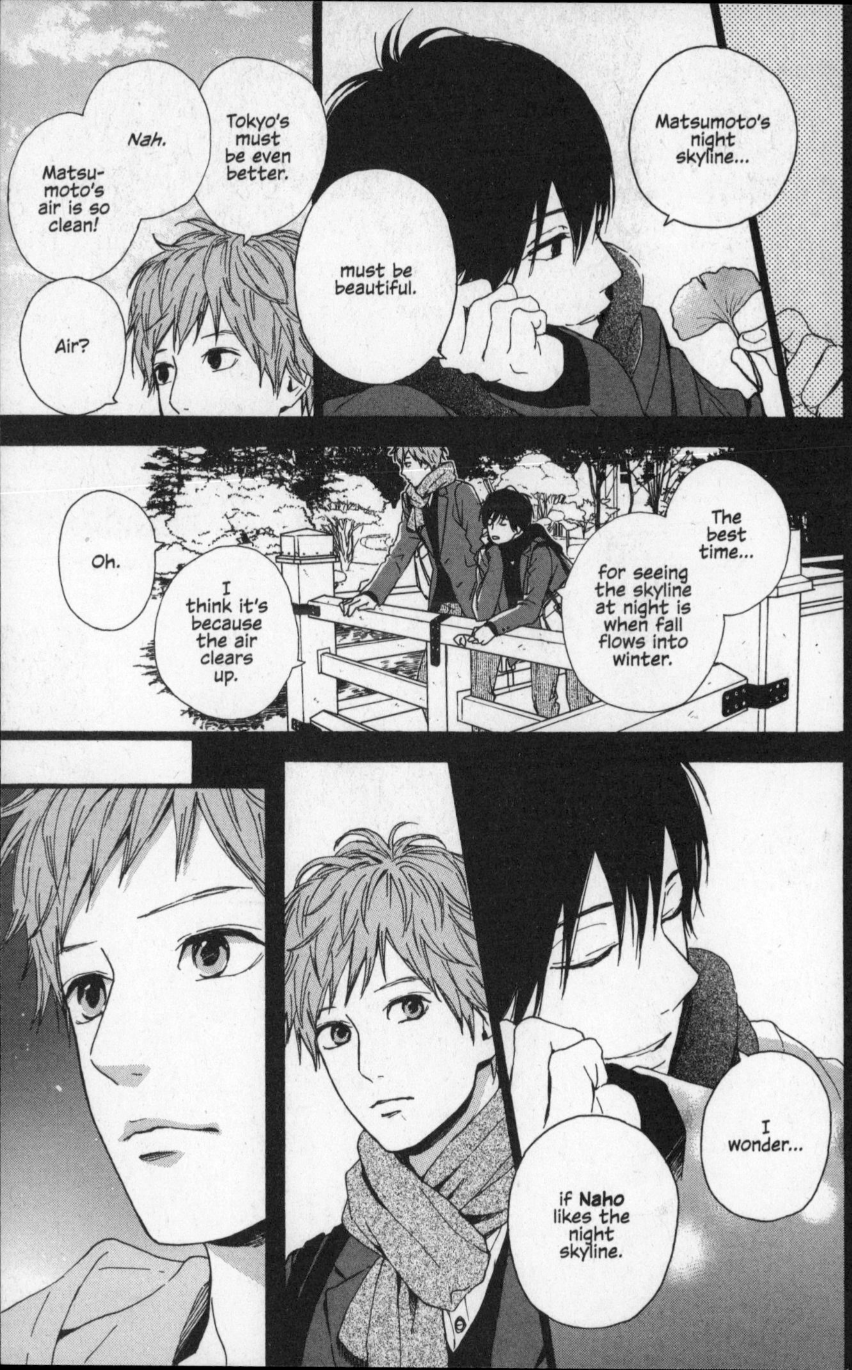
Matsumoto's night skyline...
must be beautiful.
Tokyo's must be even better.
Nah.
Matsumoto's air is so clean!
Air?
The best time...
for seeing the skyline at night is when fall flows into winter.
I think it's because the air clears up.
Oh.
I wonder...
if Naho likes the night skyline.

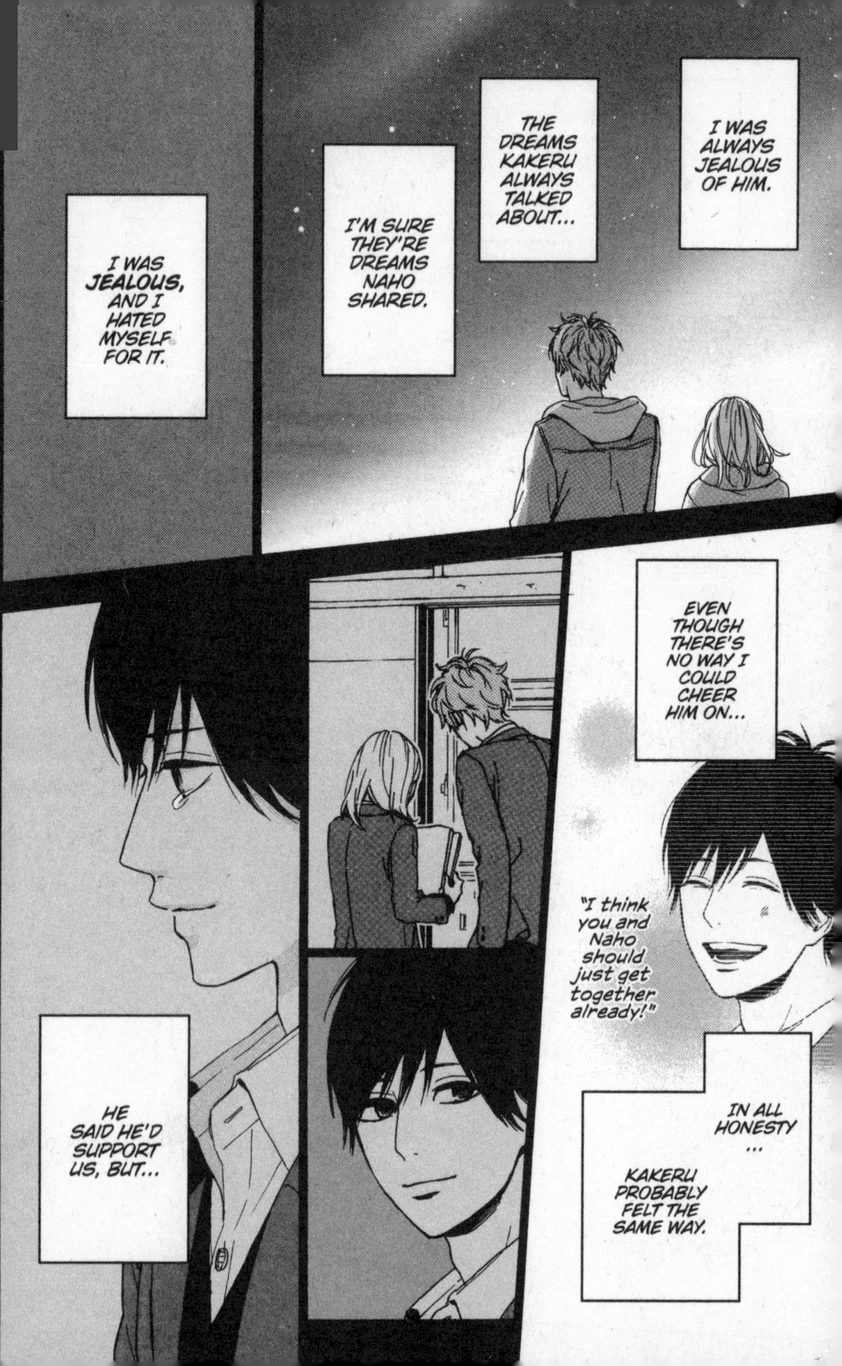
I WAS ALWAYS JEALOUS OF HIM.
THE DREAMS KAKERU ALWAYS TALKED ABOUT...
I'M SURE THEY'RE DREAMS NAHO SHARED.
I WAS JEALOUS, AND I HATED MYSELF FOR IT.
EVEN THOUGH THERE'S NO WAY I COULD CHEER HIM ON...
"I think you and Naho should just get together already!"
IN ALL HONESTY ...
KAKERU PROBABLY FELT THE SAME WAY.
HE SAID HE'D SUPPORT US, BUT...

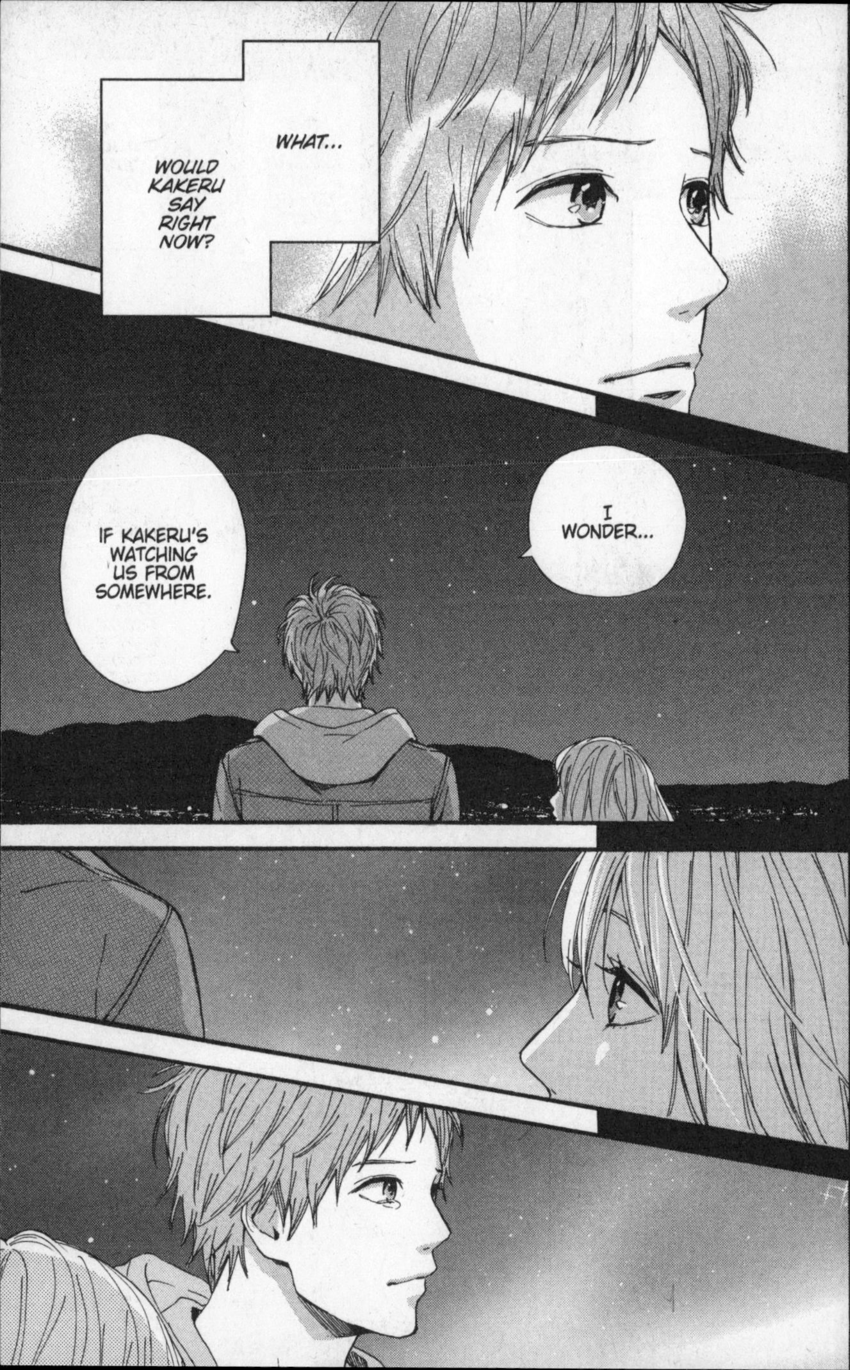
WHAT...
WOULD KAKERU SAY RIGHT NOW?
I WONDER...
IF KAKERU'S WATCHING US FROM SOMEWHERE.

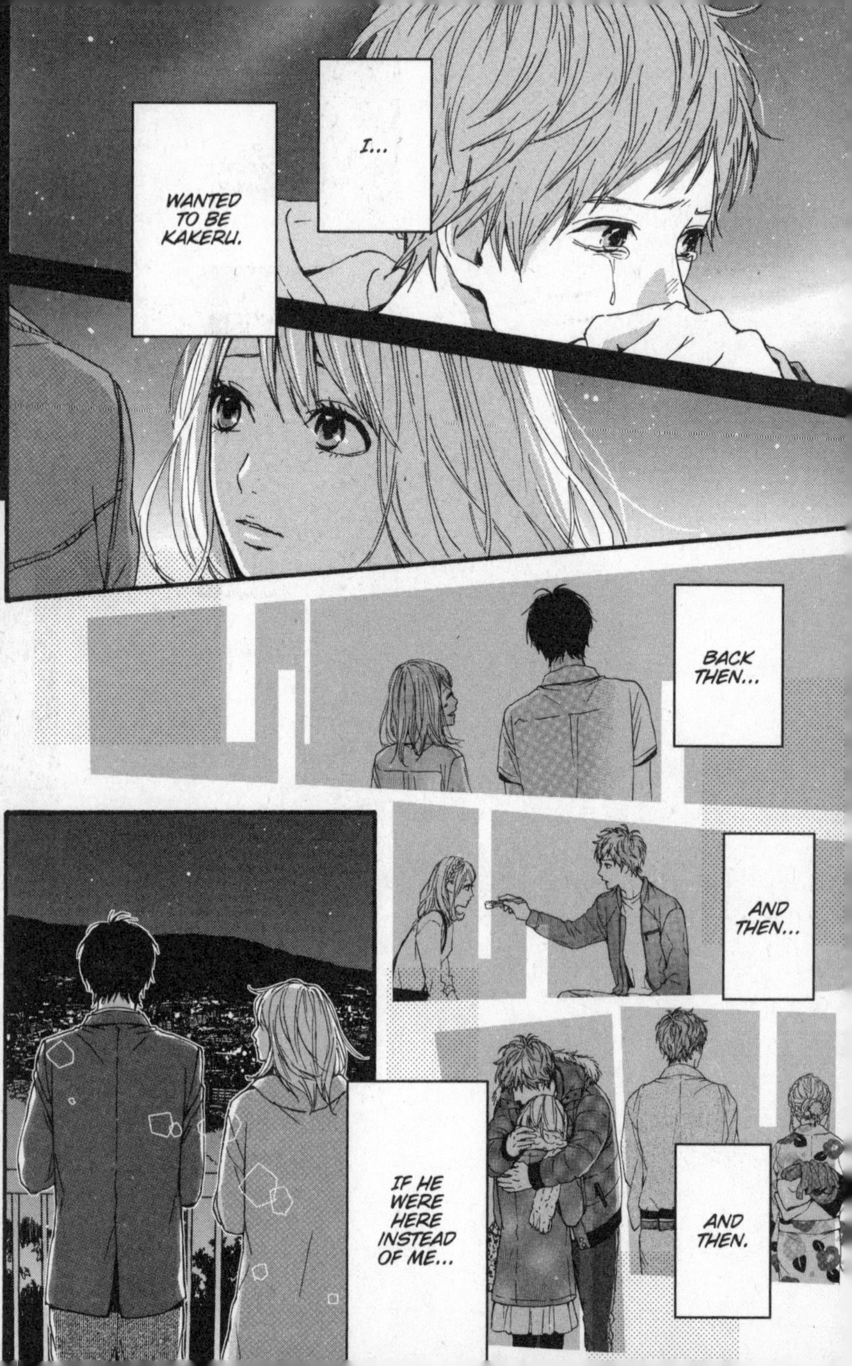
I...
WANTED TO BE KAKERU.
BACK THEN...
AND THEN...
AND THEN.
IF HE WERE HERE INSTEAD OF ME...

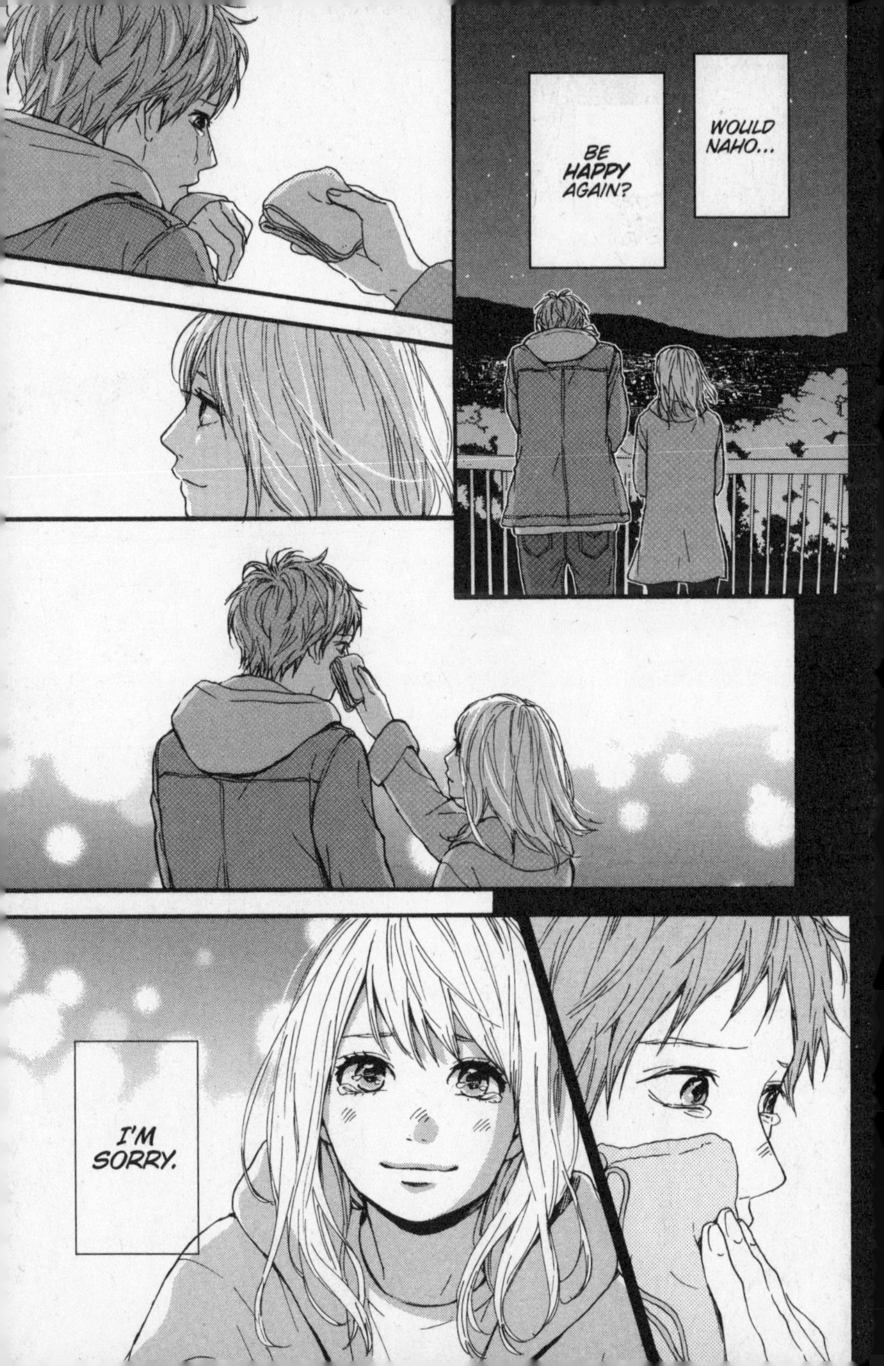
WOULD NAHO...
BE HAPPY AGAIN?
I'M SORRY.

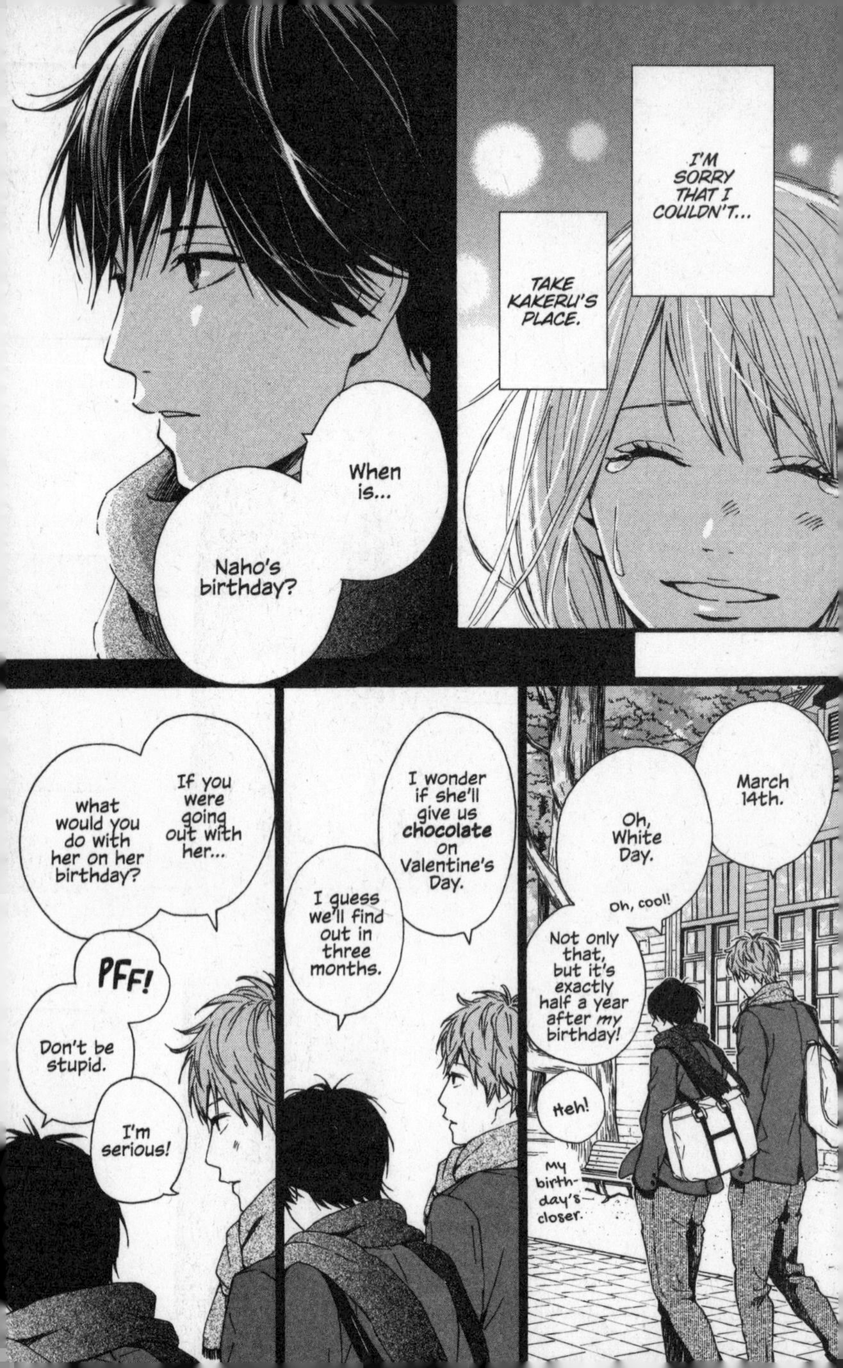
I'M SORRY THAT I COULDN'T...
TAKE KAKERU'S PLACE.
When is...
Naho's birthday?
March 14th.
Oh, White Day.
Oh, cool!
Not only that, but it's exactly half a year after *my* birthday!
Heh!
My birth-day's closer.
I wonder if she'll give us **chocolate** on Valentine's Day.
I guess we'll find out in three months.
If you were going out with her...
what would you do with her on her birthday?
PFF!
Don't be stupid.
I'm serious!

What about you, Suwa?
......
We would go bowling, then to karaoke, then to eat yakiniku...
And I would give her a hundred roses!
PFFF!
Don't laugh!
That sounds like a wrap party!
Well, you've certainly got lots of ideas...
you're funny!
Why do you make it sound like an insult?!
Like that bit about dressing up as Santa and throwing gifts from the window on Christmas! Another great plan!
Okay, drop it!
So, what would you do, Kakeru?!
Hmm...
Well, for her birthday...
a surprise would be good...
but I can't think of anything.

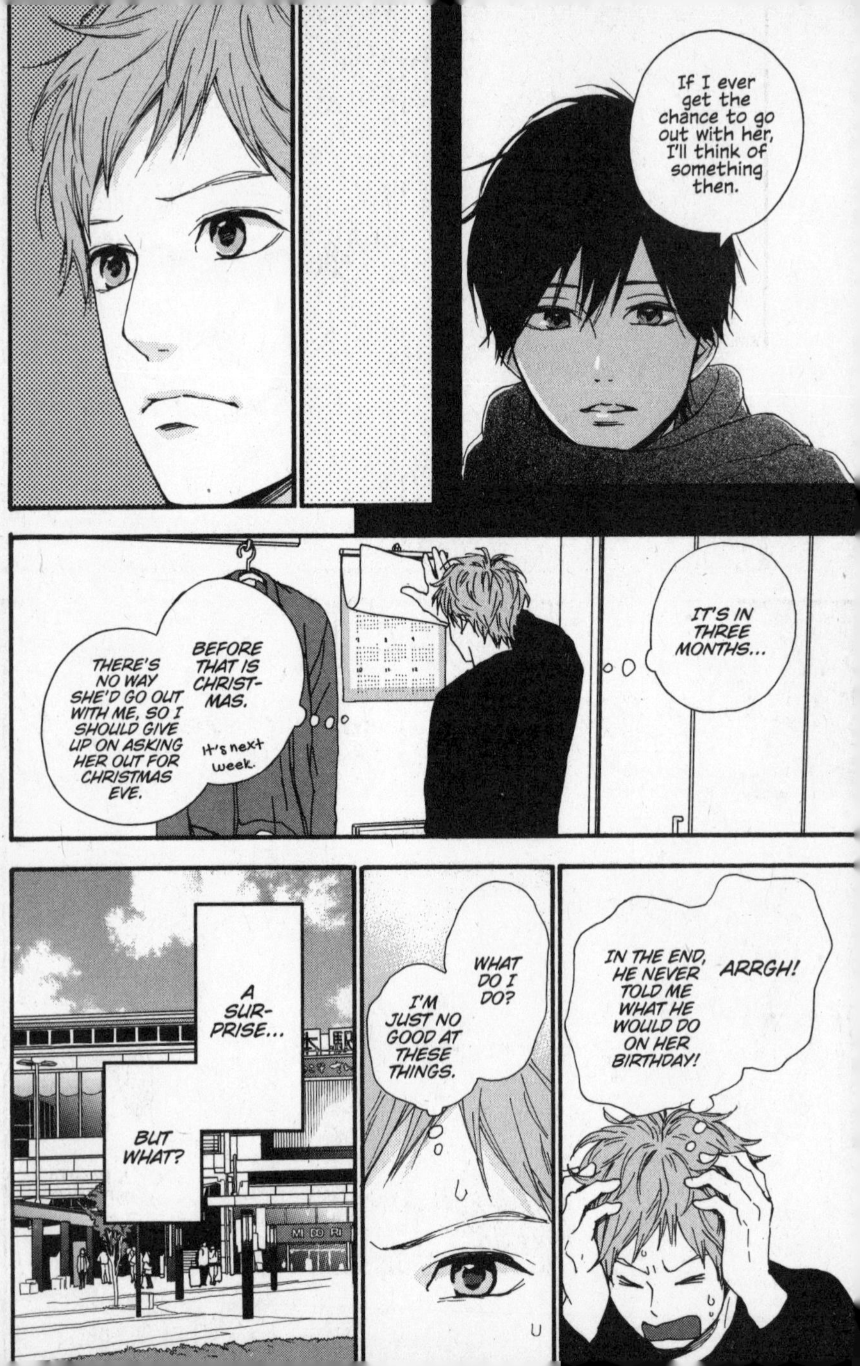
If I ever get the chance to go out with her, I'll think of something then.
IT'S IN THREE MONTHS...
BEFORE THAT IS CHRIST-MAS.
It's next week.
THERE'S NO WAY SHE'D GO OUT WITH ME, SO I SHOULD GIVE UP ON ASKING HER OUT FOR CHRISTMAS EVE.
ARRGH!
IN THE END, HE NEVER TOLD ME WHAT HE WOULD DO ON HER BIRTHDAY!
WHAT DO I DO?
I'M JUST NO GOOD AT THESE THINGS.
A SUR-PRISE...
BUT WHAT?

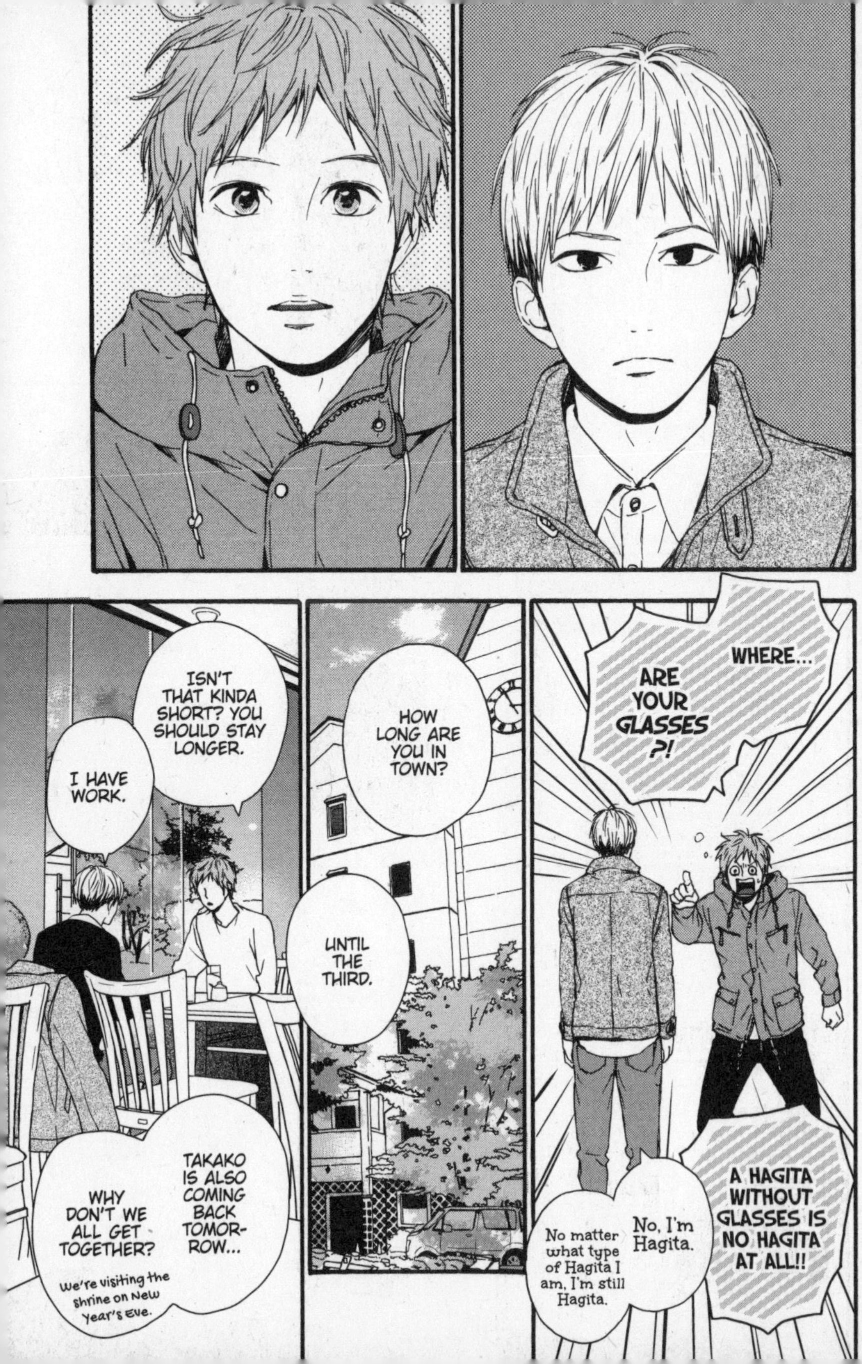
WHERE... ARE YOUR GLASSES ?!
A HAGITA WITHOUT GLASSES IS NO HAGITA AT ALL!!
No, I'm Hagita.
No matter what type of Hagita I am, I'm still Hagita.
HOW LONG ARE YOU IN TOWN?
UNTIL THE THIRD.
ISN'T THAT KINDA SHORT? YOU SHOULD STAY LONGER.
I HAVE WORK.
TAKAKO IS ALSO COMING BACK TOMOR-ROW...
WHY DON'T WE ALL GET TOGETHER?
We're visiting the shrine on New Year's Eve.

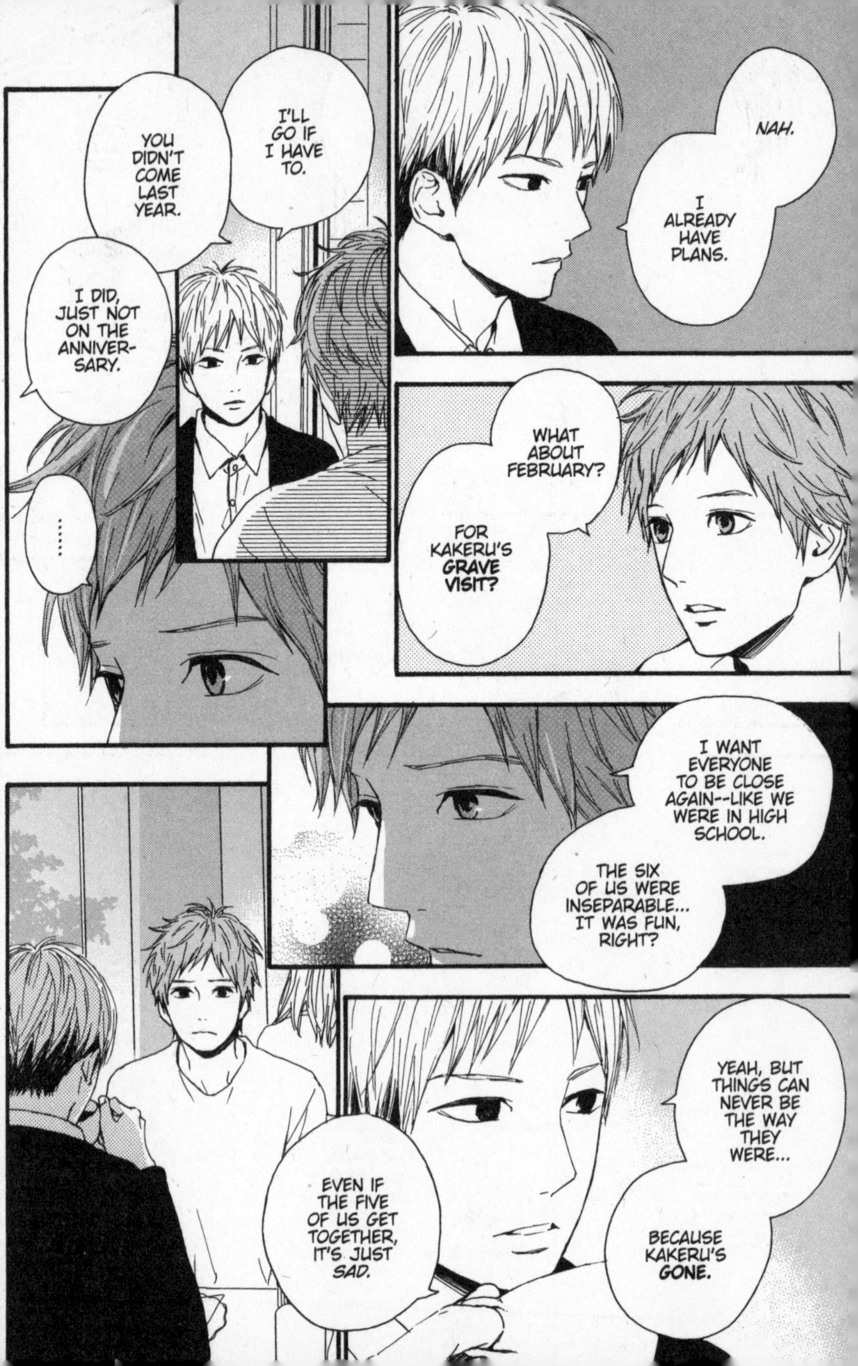
NAH.
I ALREADY HAVE PLANS.
WHAT ABOUT FEBRUARY?
FOR KAKERU'S **GRAVE VISIT?**
I'LL GO IF I HAVE TO.
YOU DIDN'T COME LAST YEAR.
I DID, JUST NOT ON THE ANNIVERSARY.
......
I WANT EVERYONE TO BE CLOSE AGAIN--LIKE WE WERE IN HIGH SCHOOL.
THE SIX OF US WERE INSEPARABLE... IT WAS FUN, RIGHT?
YEAH, BUT THINGS CAN NEVER BE THE WAY THEY WERE...
BECAUSE KAKERU'S **GONE.**
EVEN IF THE FIVE OF US GET TOGETHER, IT'S JUST *SAD.*

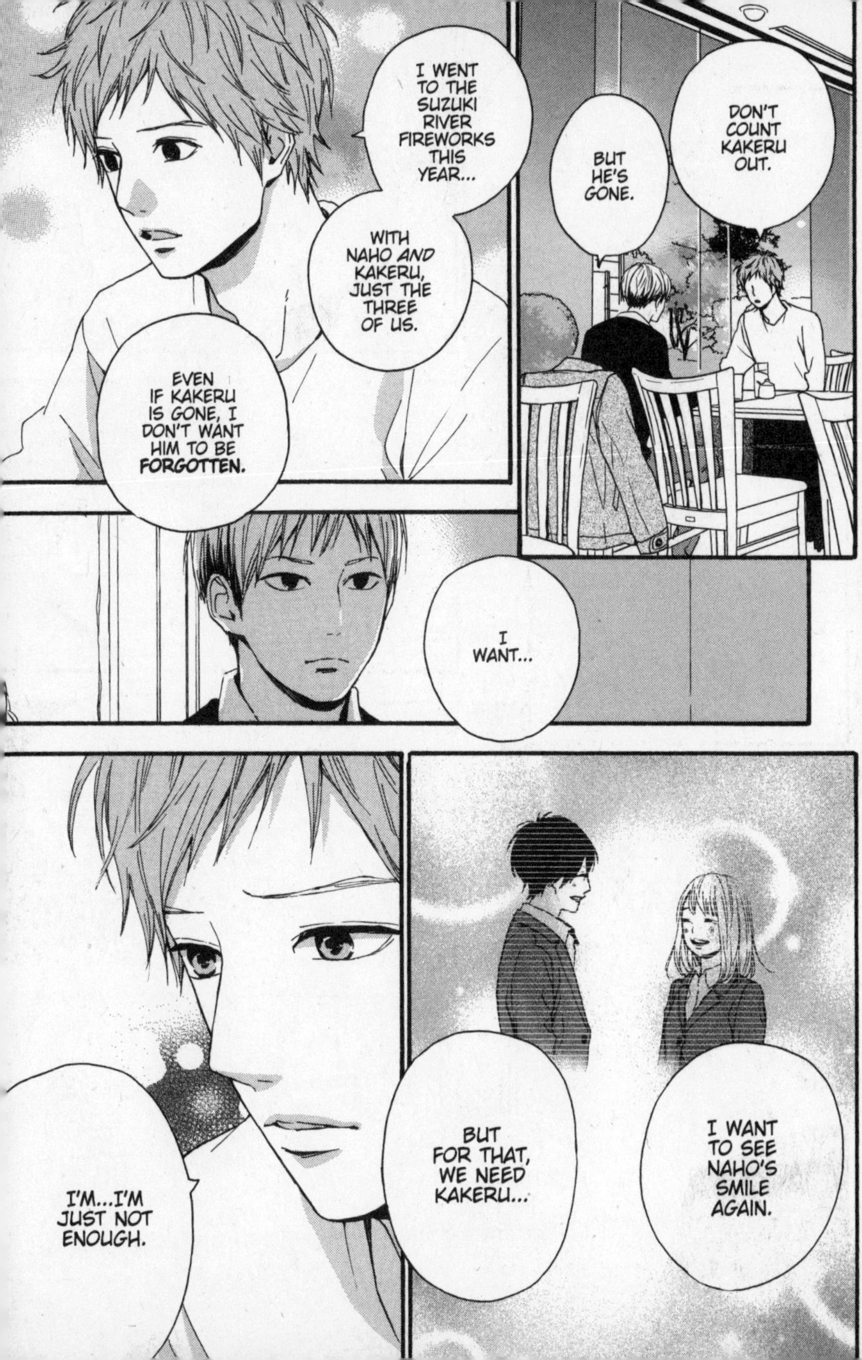
DON'T COUNT KAKERU OUT.
BUT HE'S GONE.
I WENT TO THE SUZUKI RIVER FIREWORKS THIS YEAR...
WITH NAHO AND KAKERU, JUST THE THREE OF US.
EVEN IF KAKERU IS GONE, I DON'T WANT HIM TO BE FORGOTTEN.
I WANT...
I WANT TO SEE NAHO'S SMILE AGAIN.
BUT FOR THAT, WE NEED KAKERU...
I'M...I'M JUST NOT ENOUGH.

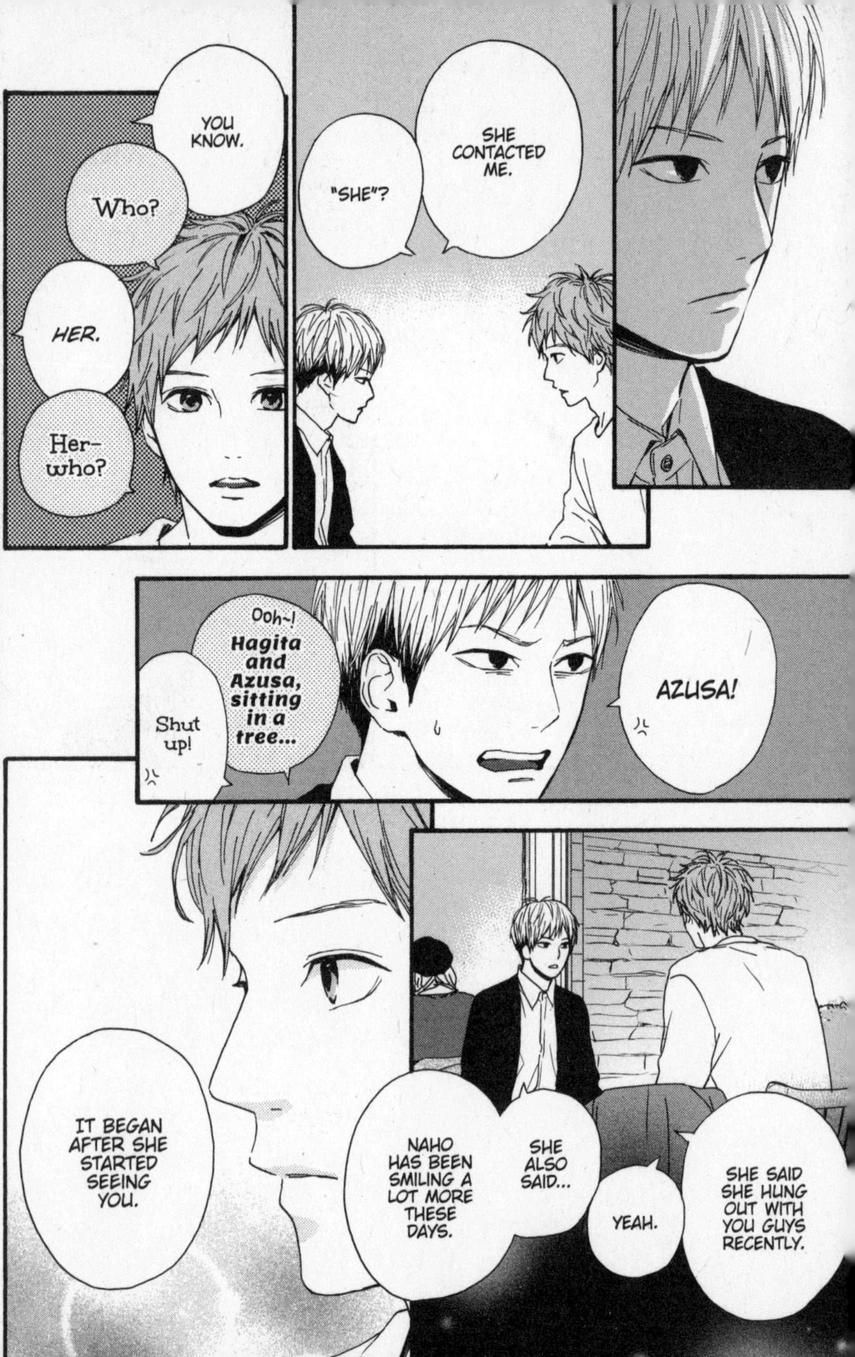
SHE CONTACTED ME.
"SHE"?
YOU KNOW.
Who?
HER.
Her—who?
AZUSA!
Ooh~! Hagita and Azusa, sitting in a tree...
Shut up!
SHE SAID SHE HUNG OUT WITH YOU GUYS RECENTLY.
YEAH.
SHE ALSO SAID...
NAHO HAS BEEN SMILING A LOT MORE THESE DAYS.
IT BEGAN AFTER SHE STARTED SEEING YOU.

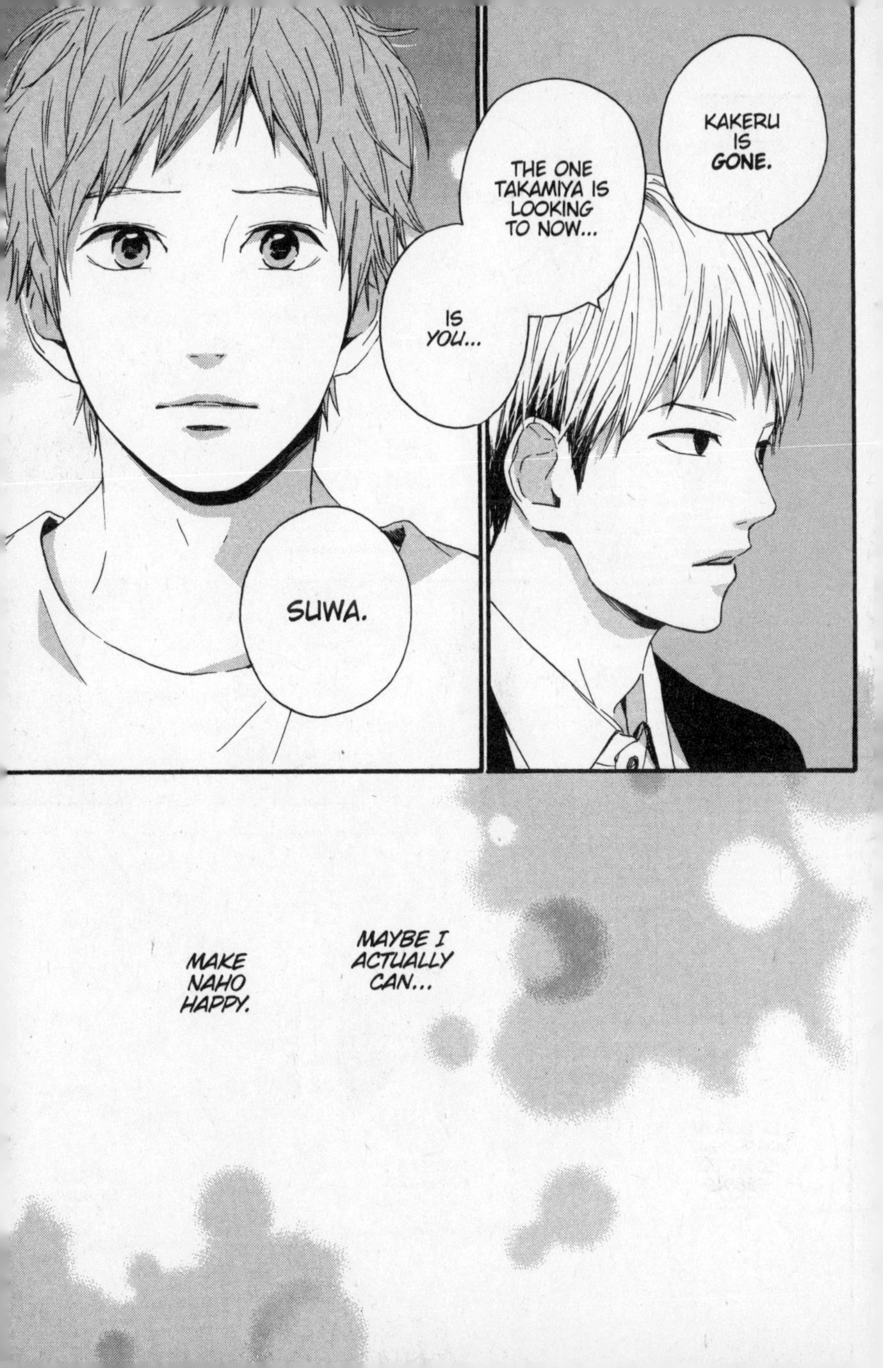

KAKERU IS GONE.
THE ONE TAKAMIYA IS LOOKING TO NOW...
IS YOU...
SUWA.
MAYBE I ACTUALLY CAN...
MAKE NAHO HAPPY.

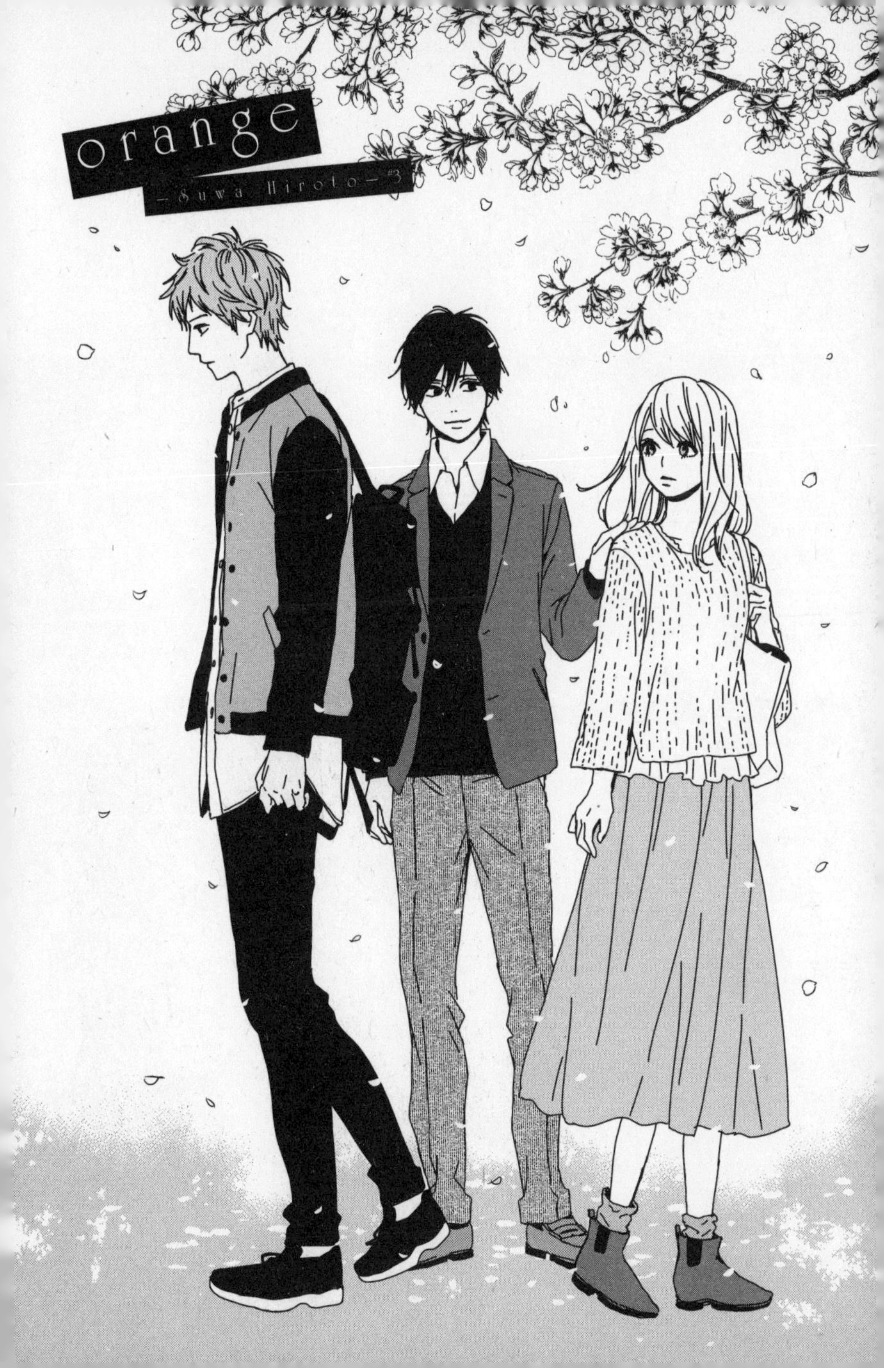
orange
—Suwa Hiroto—#3

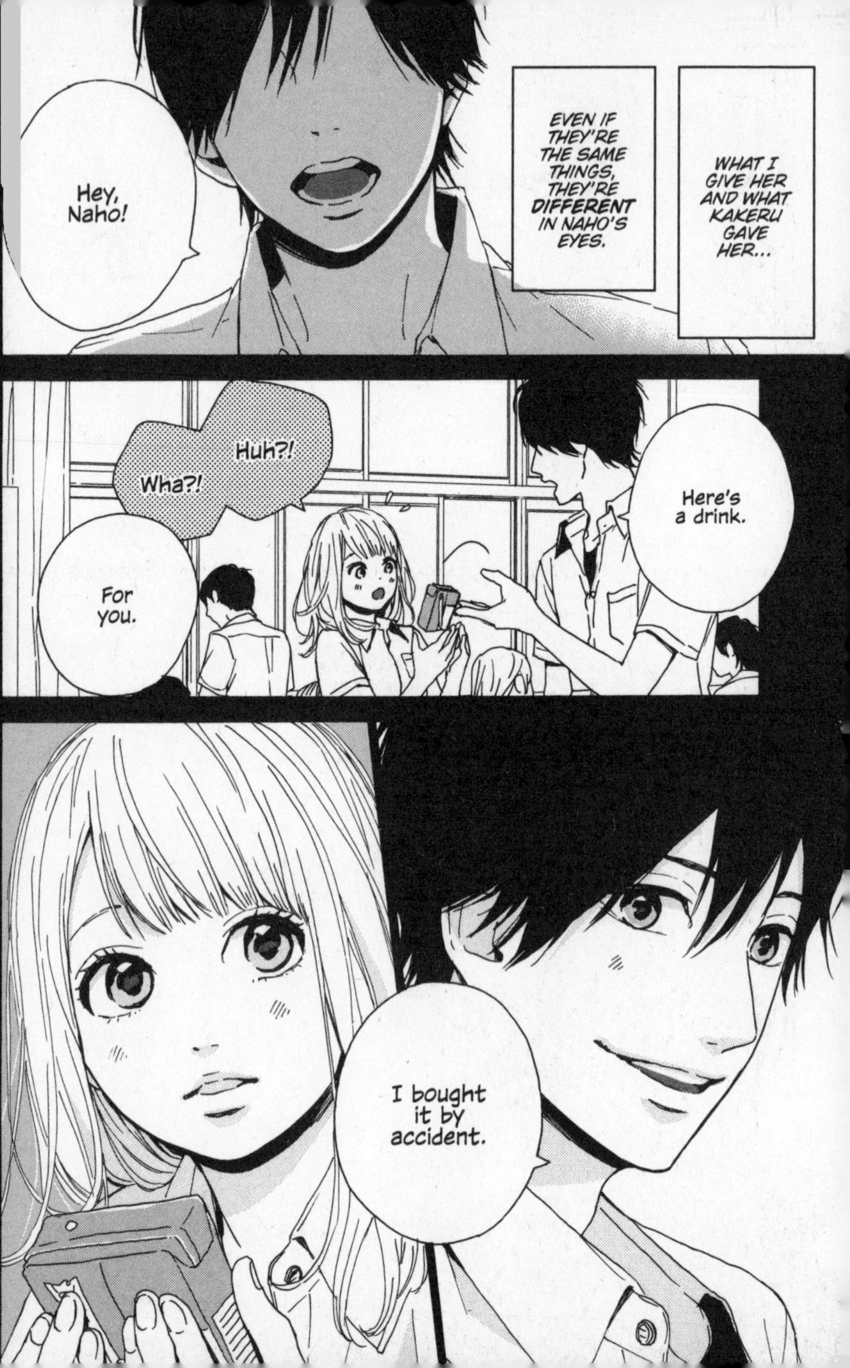
WHAT I GIVE HER AND WHAT KAKERU GAVE HER...
EVEN IF THEY'RE THE SAME THINGS, THEY'RE **DIFFERENT** IN NAHO'S EYES.
Hey, Naho!
Here's a drink.
Huh?!
Wha?!
For you.
I bought it by accident.

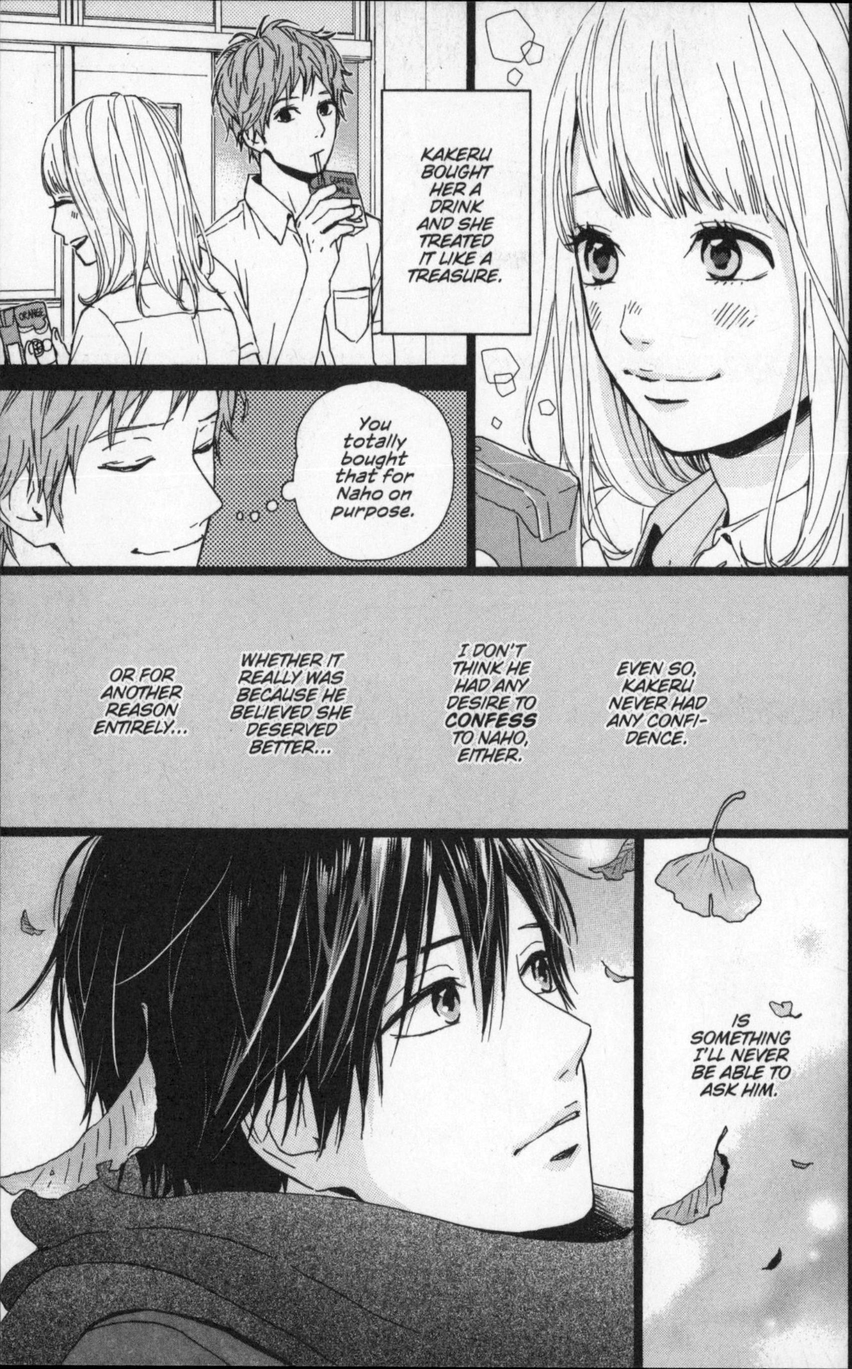
KAKERU BOUGHT HER A DRINK AND SHE TREATED IT LIKE A TREASURE.
ORANGE
You totally bought that for Naho on purpose.
EVEN SO, KAKERU NEVER HAD ANY CONFIDENCE.
I DON'T THINK HE HAD ANY DESIRE TO **CONFESS** TO NAHO, EITHER.
WHETHER IT REALLY WAS BECAUSE HE BELIEVED SHE DESERVED BETTER...
OR FOR ANOTHER REASON ENTIRELY...
IS SOMETHING I'LL NEVER BE ABLE TO ASK HIM.

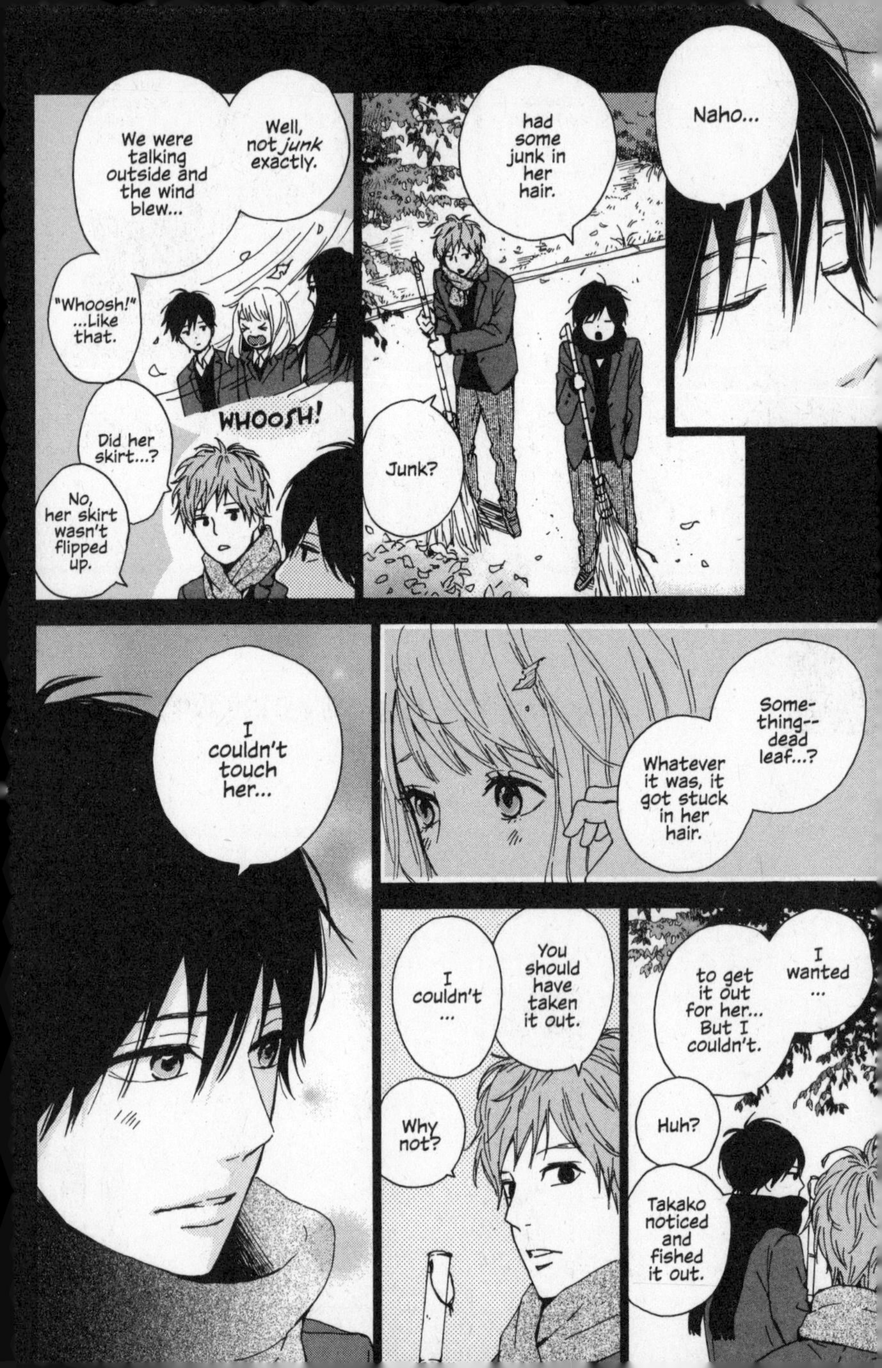

Naho...
had some junk in her hair.
Junk?
Well, not *junk* exactly.
We were talking outside and the wind blew...
"Whoosh!" ...Like that.
WHOOSH!
Did her skirt...?
No, her skirt wasn't flipped up.
Something-- dead leaf...?
Whatever it was, it got stuck in her hair.
I wanted ...
to get it out for her... But I couldn't.
Huh?
Takako noticed and fished it out.
You should have taken it out.
I couldn't ...
Why not?
I couldn't touch her...

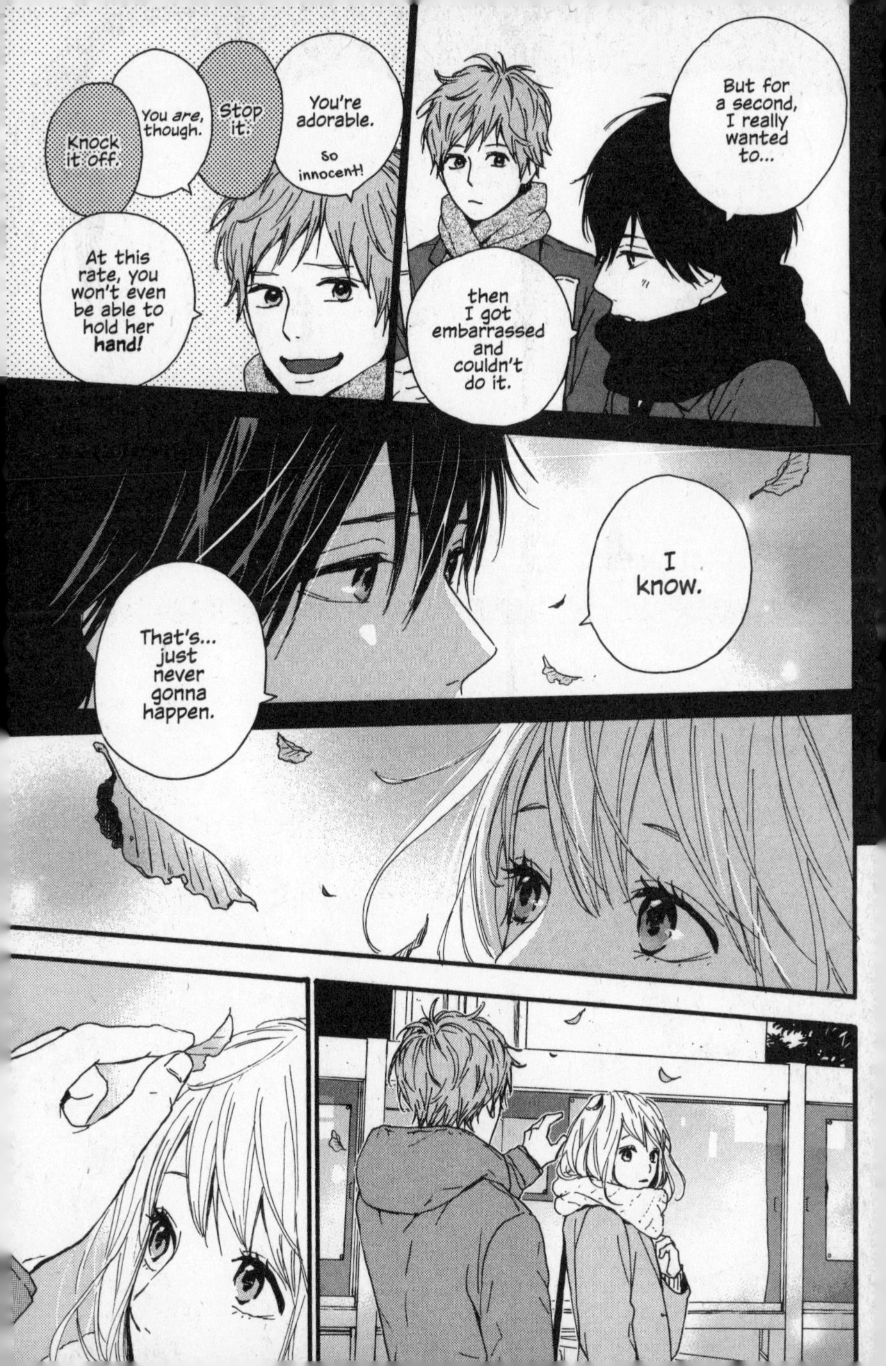
But for a second, I really wanted to...
then I got embarrassed and couldn't do it.
You're adorable.
So innocent!
Stop it.
You are, though.
Knock it off.
At this rate, you won't even be able to hold her **hand!**
I know.
That's... just never gonna happen.

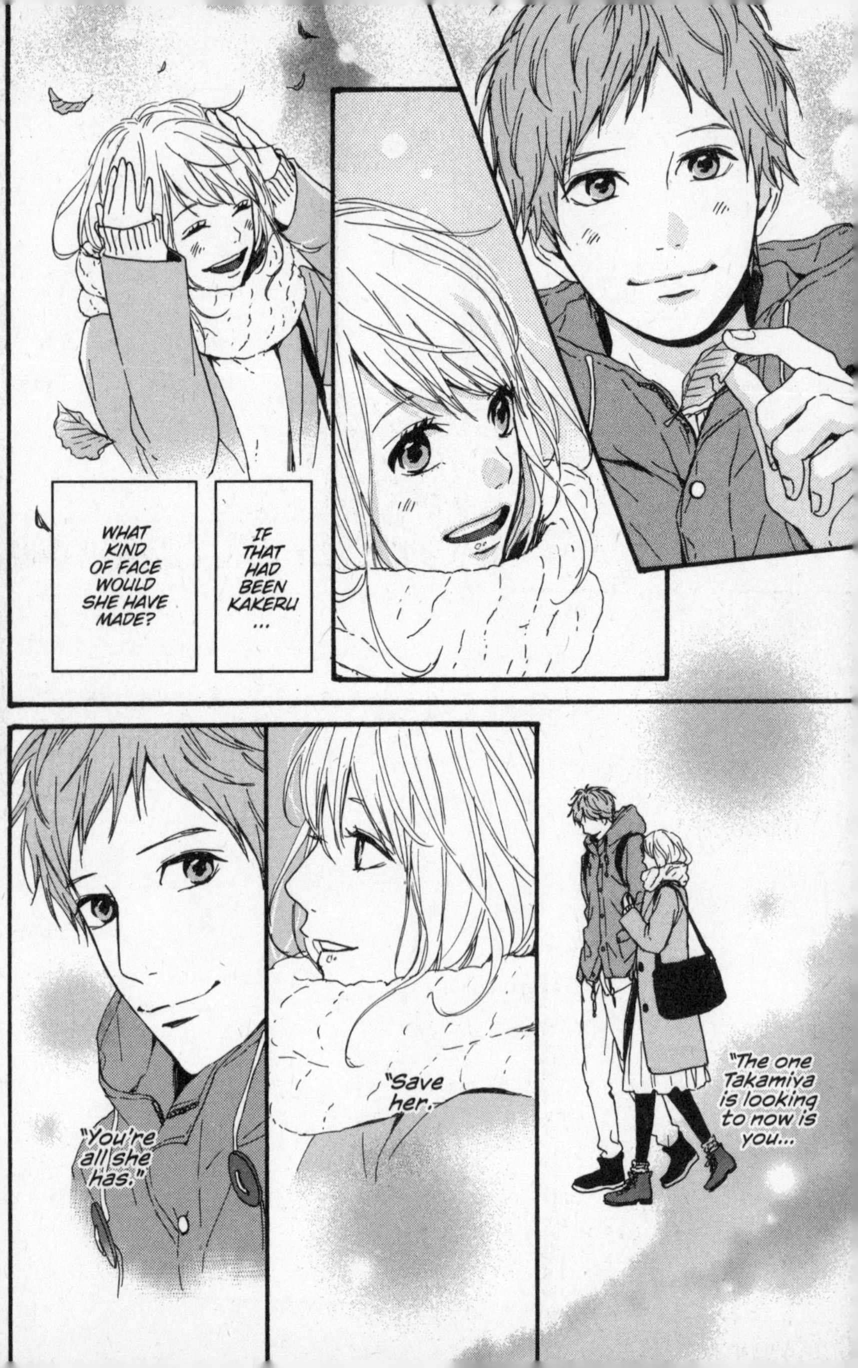
IF THAT HAD BEEN KAKERU ...
WHAT KIND OF FACE WOULD SHE HAVE MADE?
"The one Takamiya is looking to now is you...
"Save her.
"You're all she has."

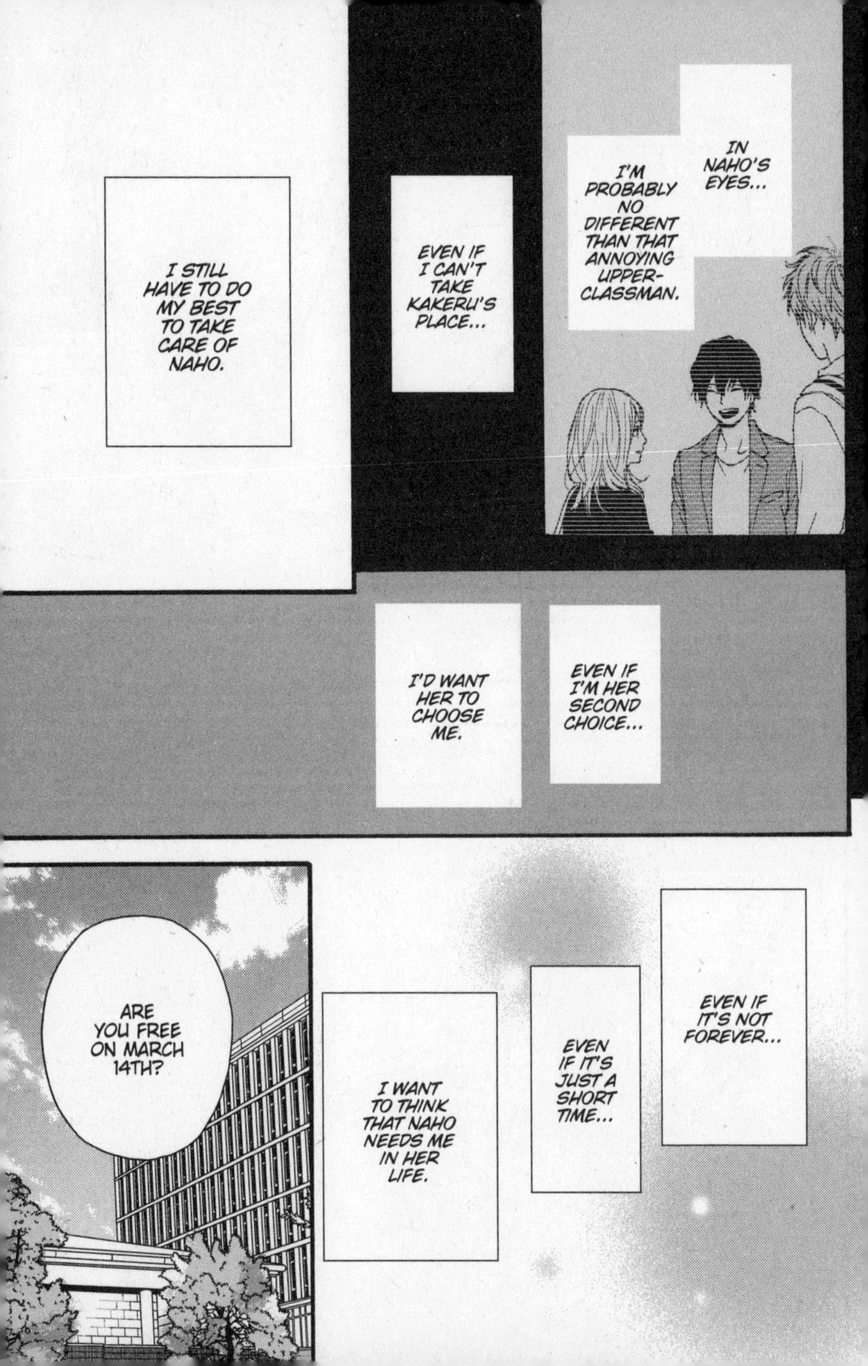
IN NAHO'S EYES...
I'M PROBABLY NO DIFFERENT THAN THAT ANNOYING UPPER-CLASSMAN.
EVEN IF I CAN'T TAKE KAKERU'S PLACE...
I STILL HAVE TO DO MY BEST TO TAKE CARE OF NAHO.
EVEN IF I'M HER SECOND CHOICE...
I'D WANT HER TO CHOOSE ME.
EVEN IF IT'S NOT FOREVER...
EVEN IF IT'S JUST A SHORT TIME...
I WANT TO THINK THAT NAHO NEEDS ME IN HER LIFE.
ARE YOU FREE ON MARCH 14TH?

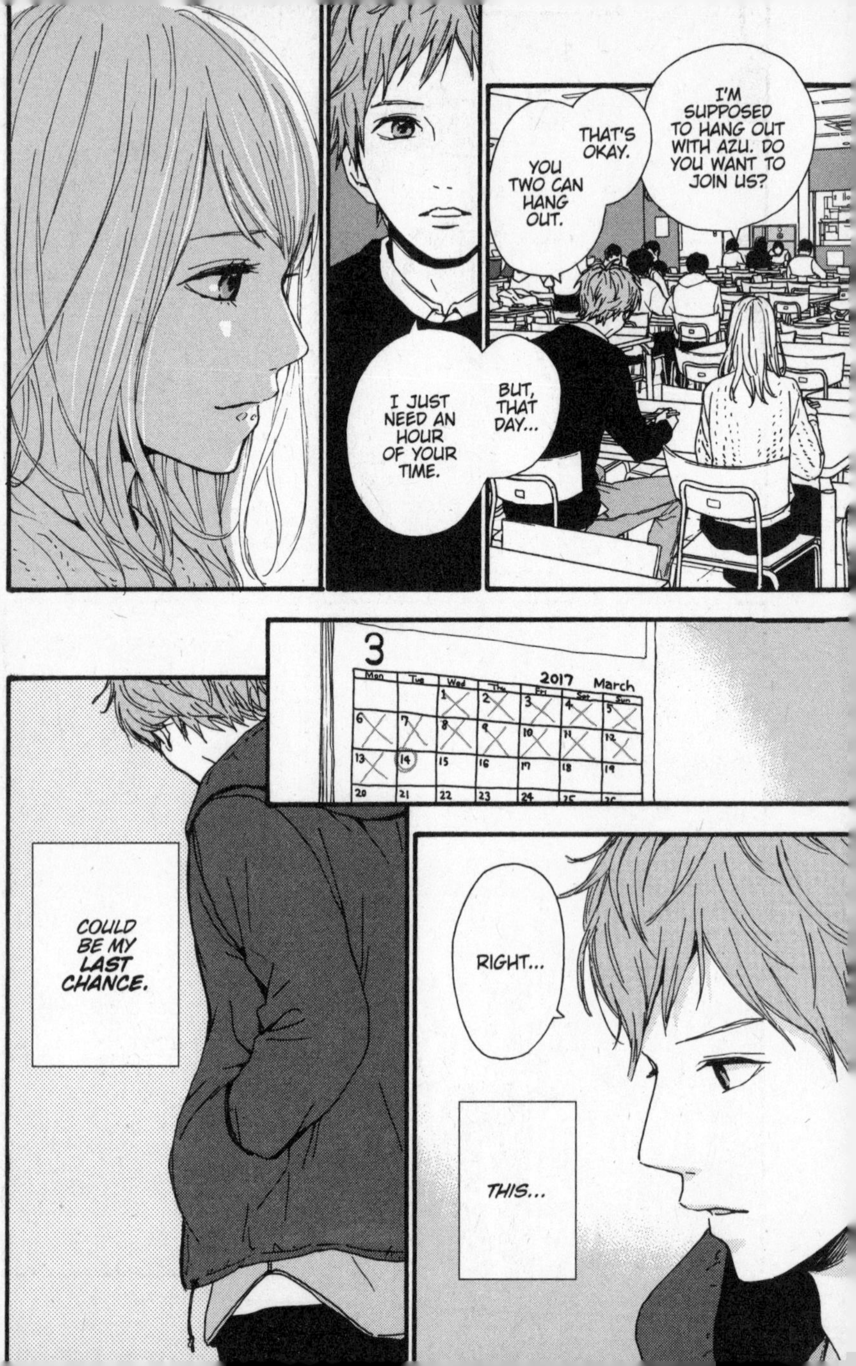
I'M SUPPOSED TO HANG OUT WITH AZU. DO YOU WANT TO JOIN US?
THAT'S OKAY.
YOU TWO CAN HANG OUT.
BUT, THAT DAY...
I JUST NEED AN HOUR OF YOUR TIME.
3
2017 March
RIGHT...
THIS...
COULD BE MY LAST CHANCE.

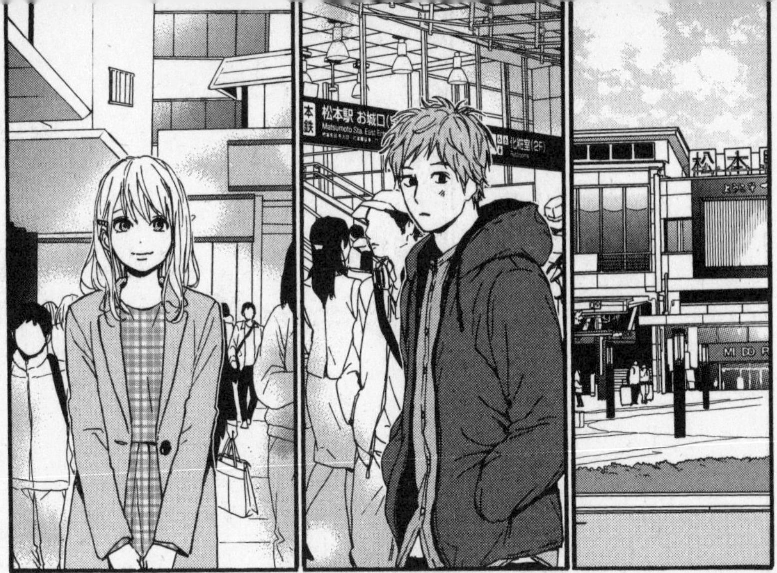
松本駅 お城口

Sign: Matsumoto Station

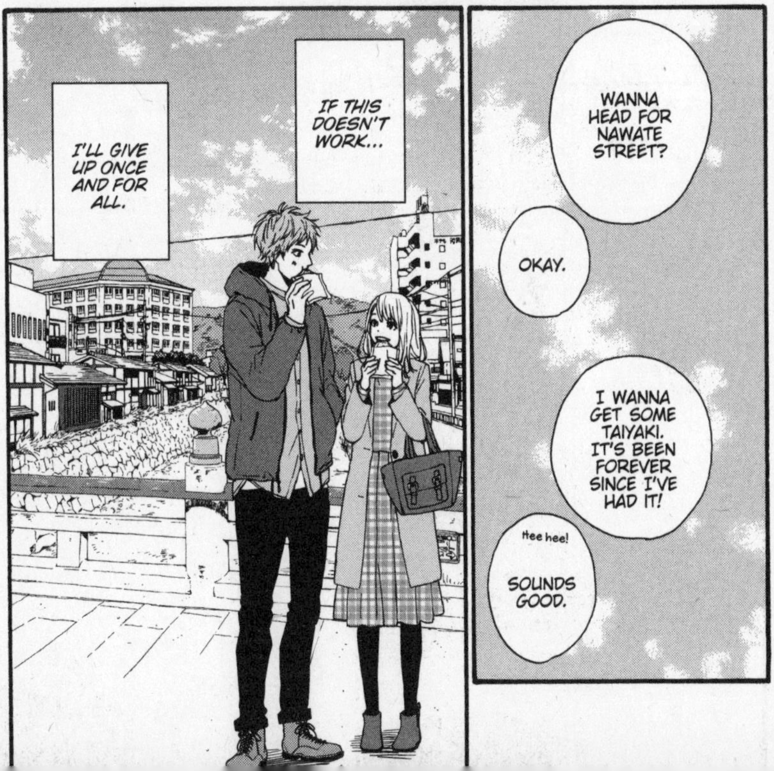
WANNA HEAD FOR NAWATE STREET?
OKAY.
I WANNA GET SOME TAIYAKI. IT'S BEEN FOREVER SINCE I'VE HAD IT!
Hee hee!
SOUNDS GOOD.
IF THIS DOESN'T WORK...
I'LL GIVE UP ONCE AND FOR ALL.

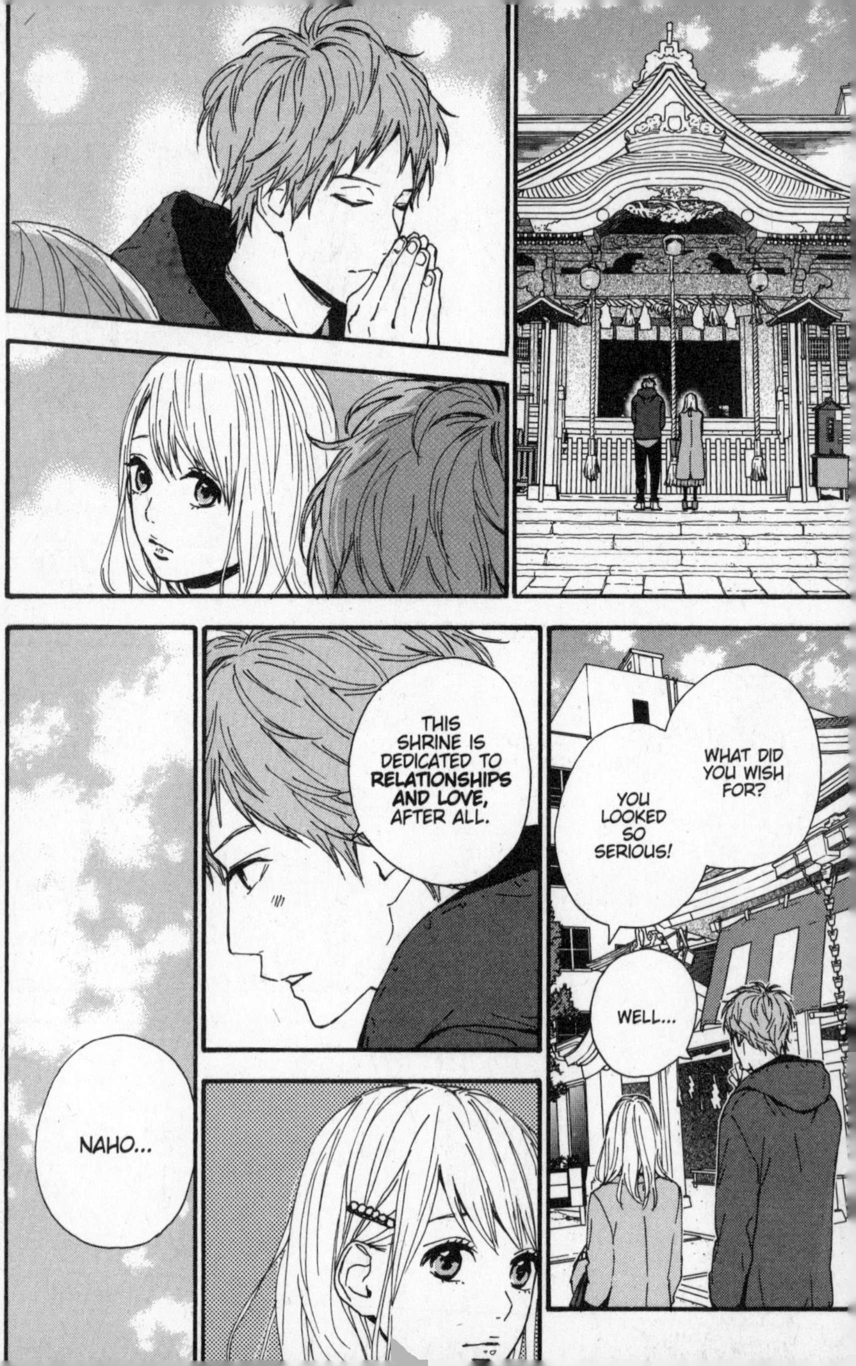
WHAT DID YOU WISH FOR?
YOU LOOKED SO SERIOUS!
WELL...
THIS SHRINE IS DEDICATED TO **RELATIONSHIPS AND LOVE**, AFTER ALL.
NAHO...

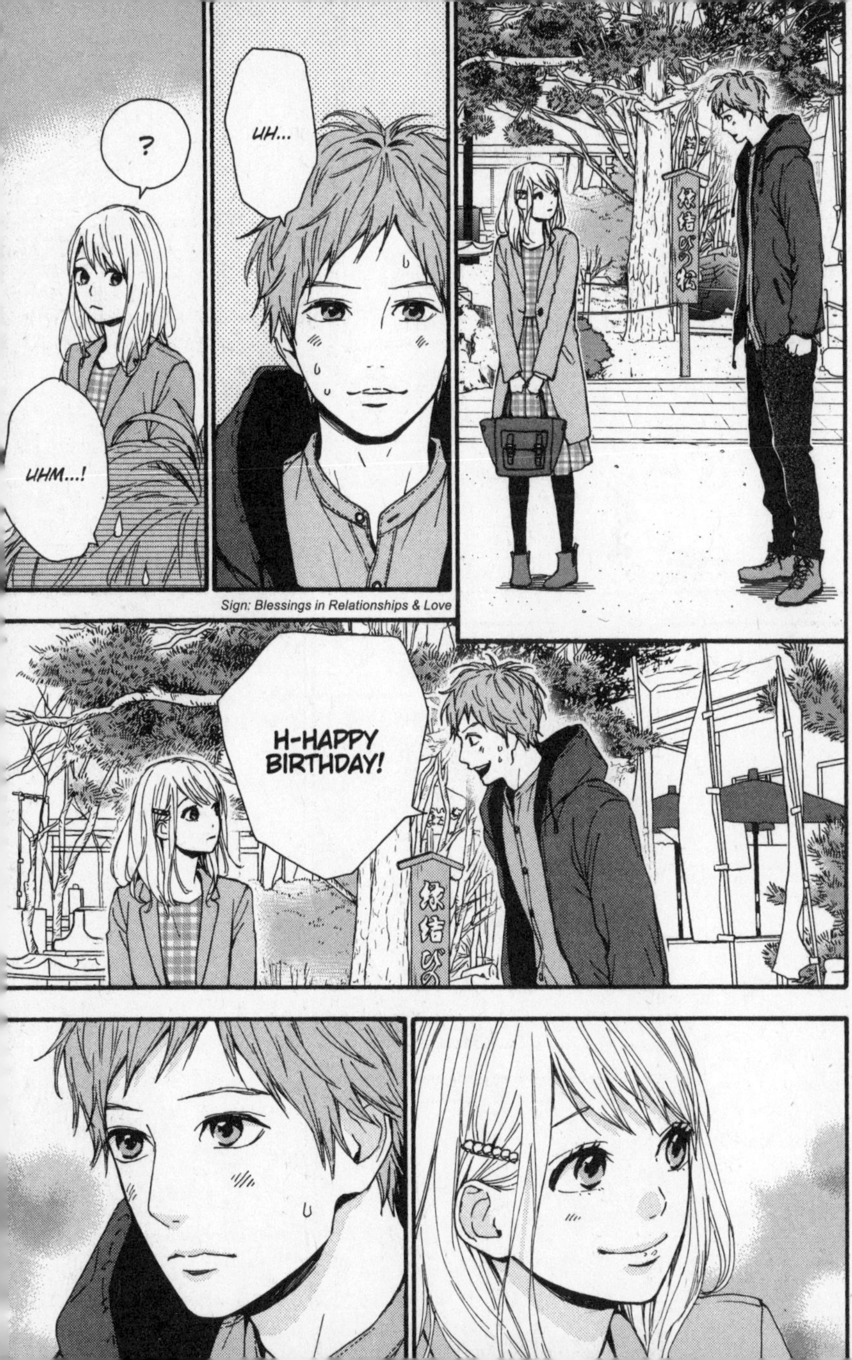
UH...
?
UHM...!
Sign: Blessings in Relationships & Love
H-HAPPY BIRTHDAY!

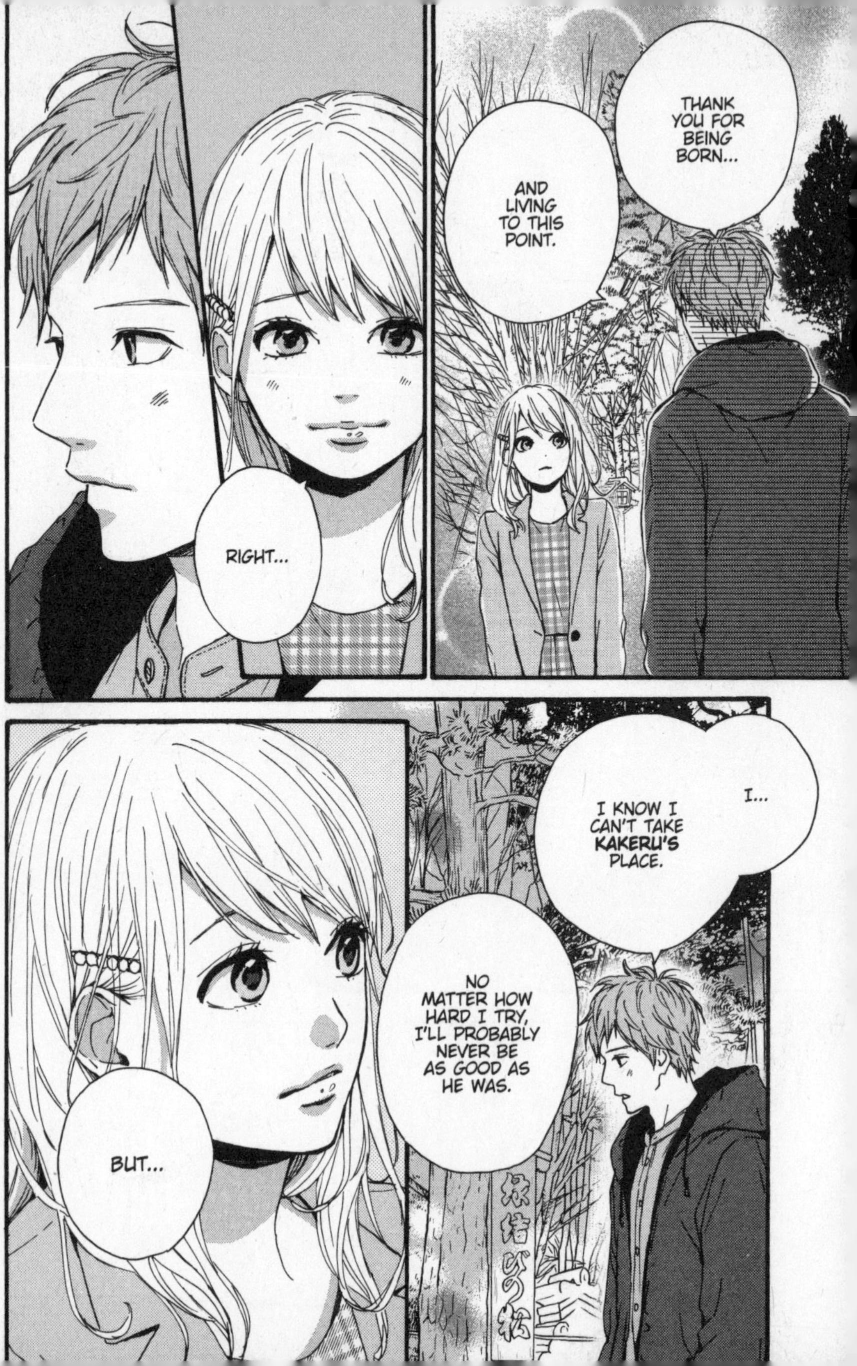

THANK YOU FOR BEING BORN...
AND LIVING TO THIS POINT.
RIGHT...
I...
I KNOW I CAN'T TAKE KAKERU'S PLACE.
NO MATTER HOW HARD I TRY, I'LL PROBABLY NEVER BE AS GOOD AS HE WAS.
縁結びの松
BUT...

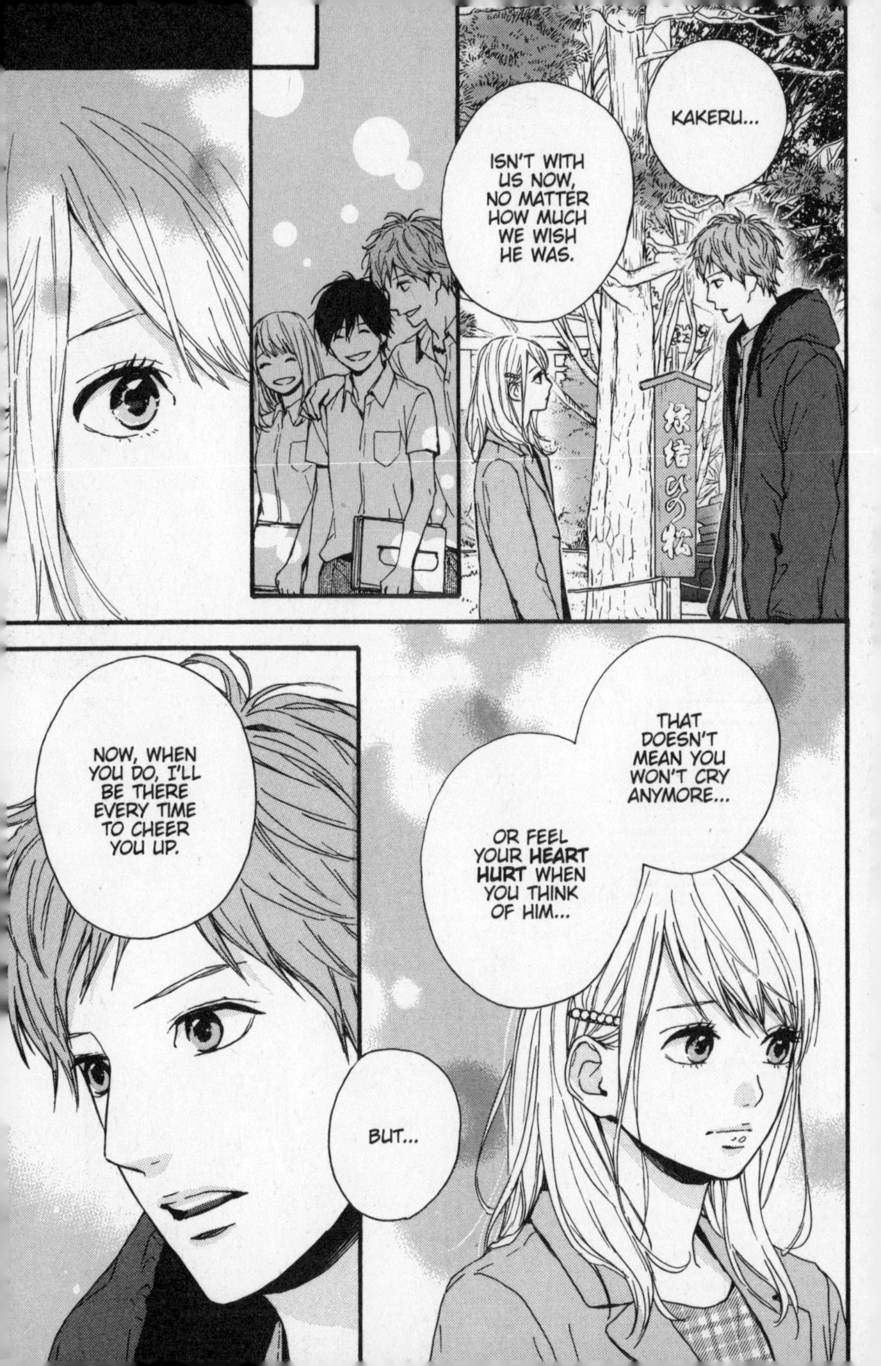
KAKERU...
ISN'T WITH US NOW, NO MATTER HOW MUCH WE WISH HE WAS.
THAT DOESN'T MEAN YOU WON'T CRY ANYMORE...
OR FEEL YOUR **HEART HURT** WHEN YOU THINK OF HIM...
BUT...
NOW, WHEN YOU DO, I'LL BE THERE EVERY TIME TO CHEER YOU UP.

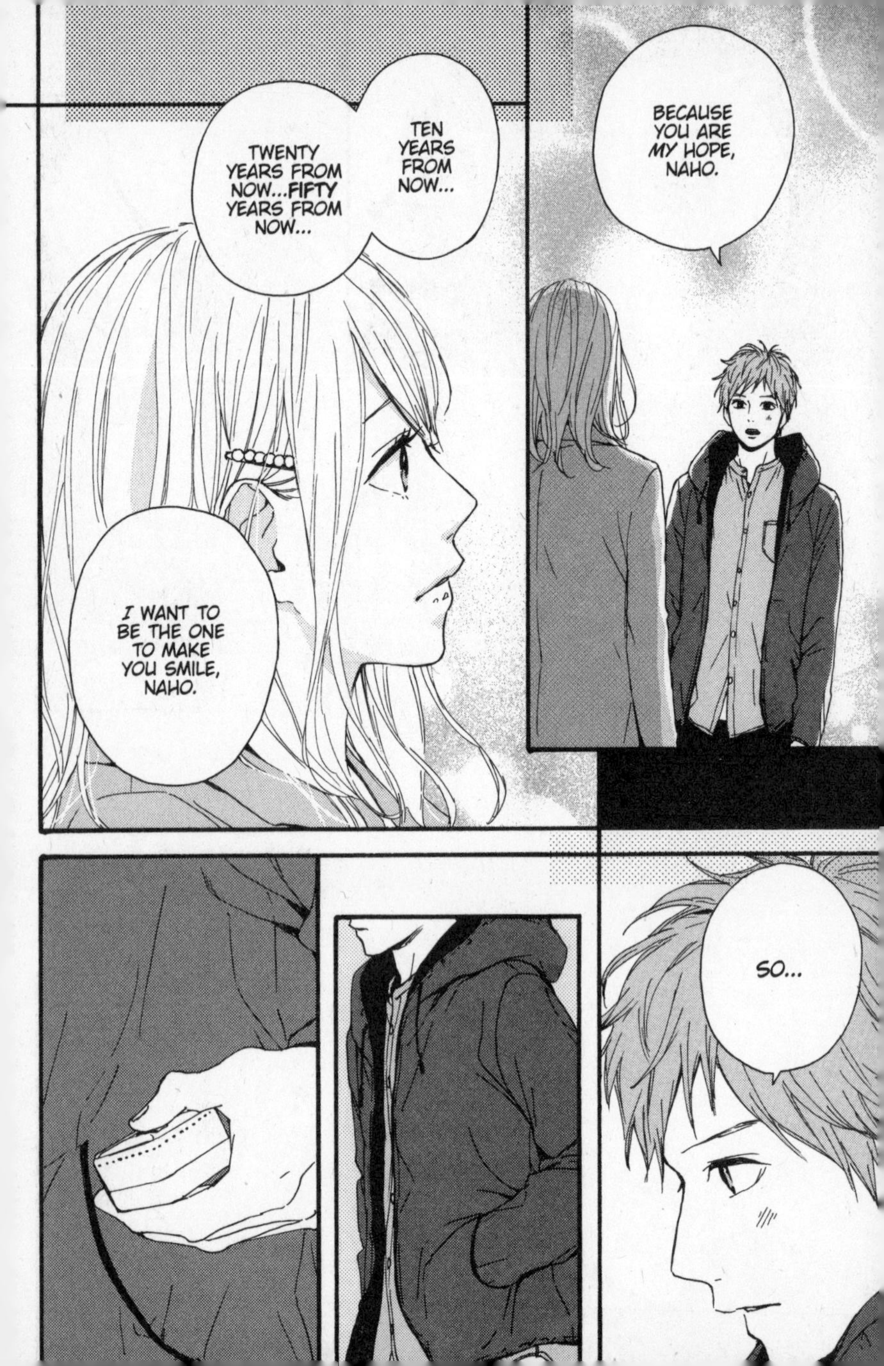
BECAUSE YOU ARE MY HOPE, NAHO.
TEN YEARS FROM NOW...
TWENTY YEARS FROM NOW...FIFTY YEARS FROM NOW...
I WANT TO BE THE ONE TO MAKE YOU SMILE, NAHO.
SO...

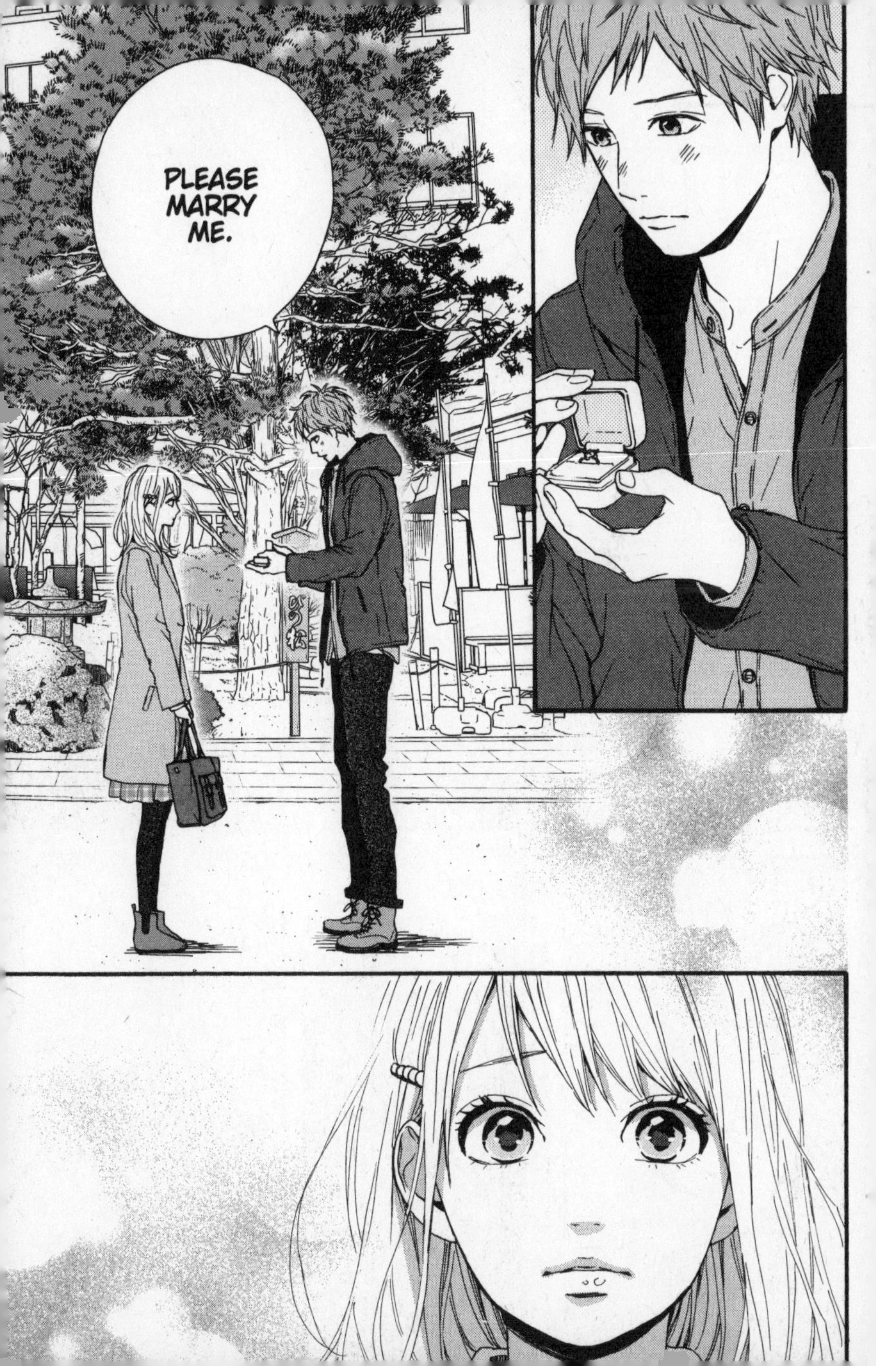
PLEASE MARRY ME.

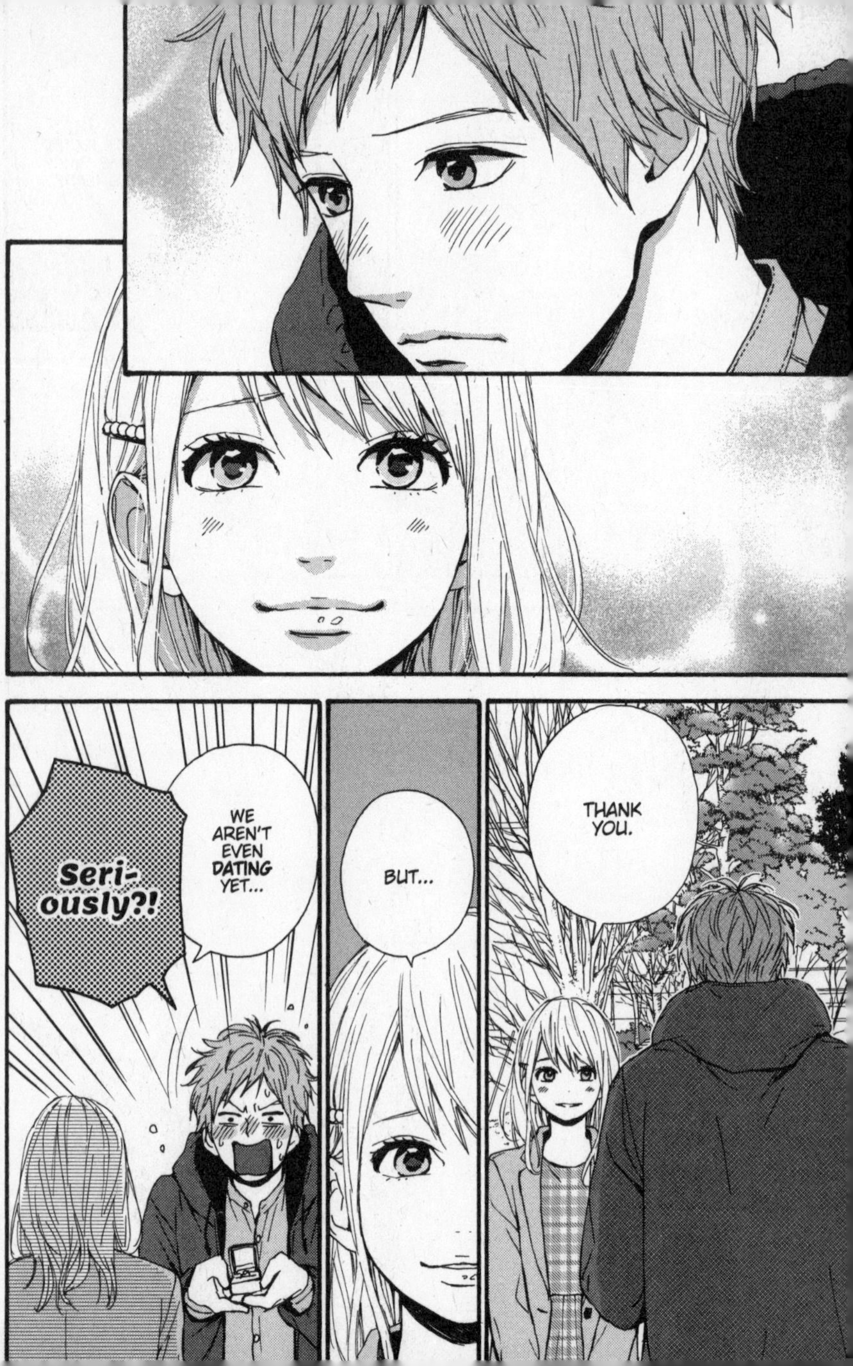
THANK YOU.
BUT...
WE AREN'T EVEN DATING YET...
Seri-ously?!

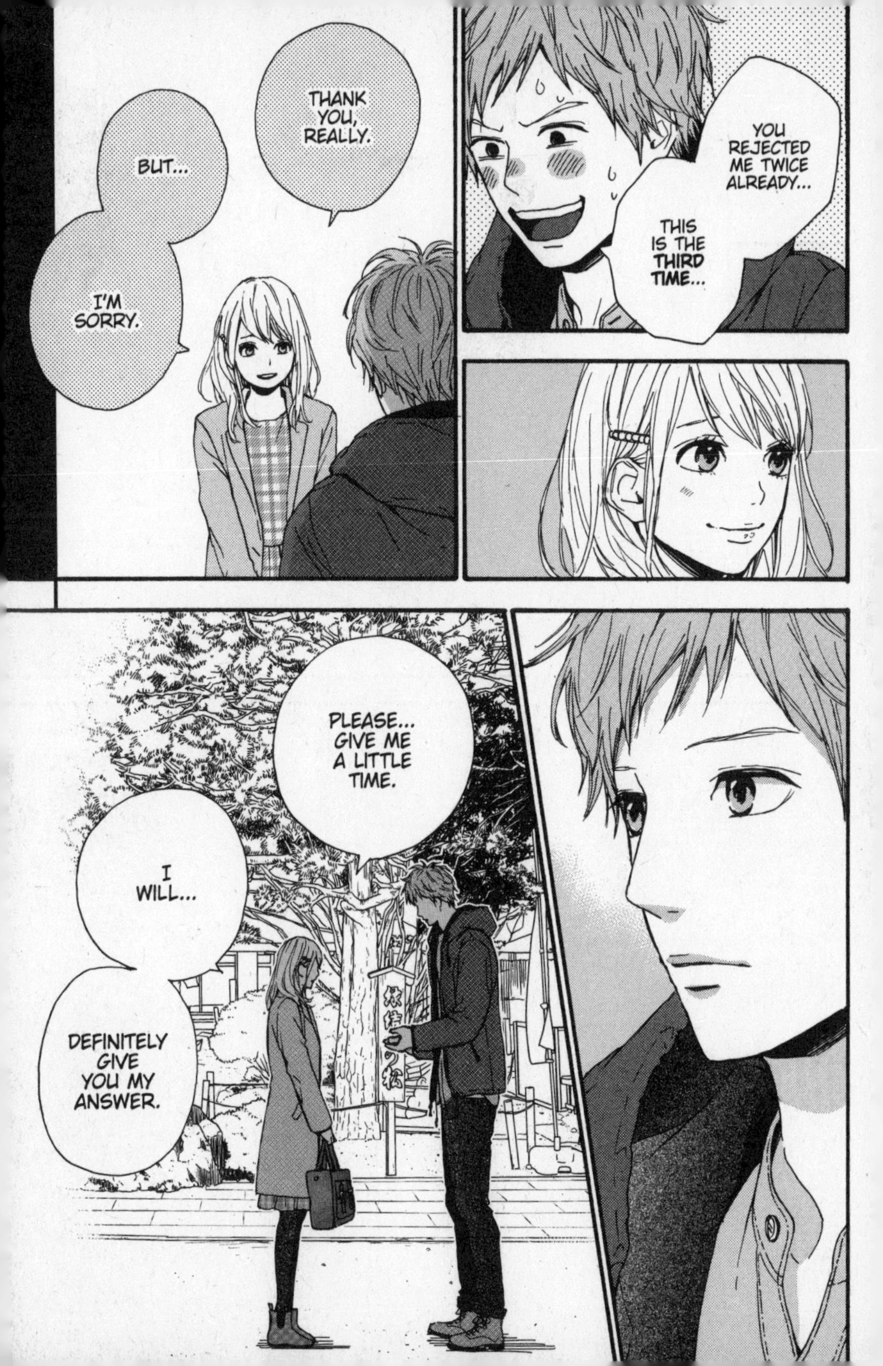
YOU REJECTED ME TWICE ALREADY...
THIS IS THE THIRD TIME...
THANK YOU, REALLY.
BUT...
I'M SORRY.
PLEASE... GIVE ME A LITTLE TIME.
I WILL...
DEFINITELY GIVE YOU MY ANSWER.

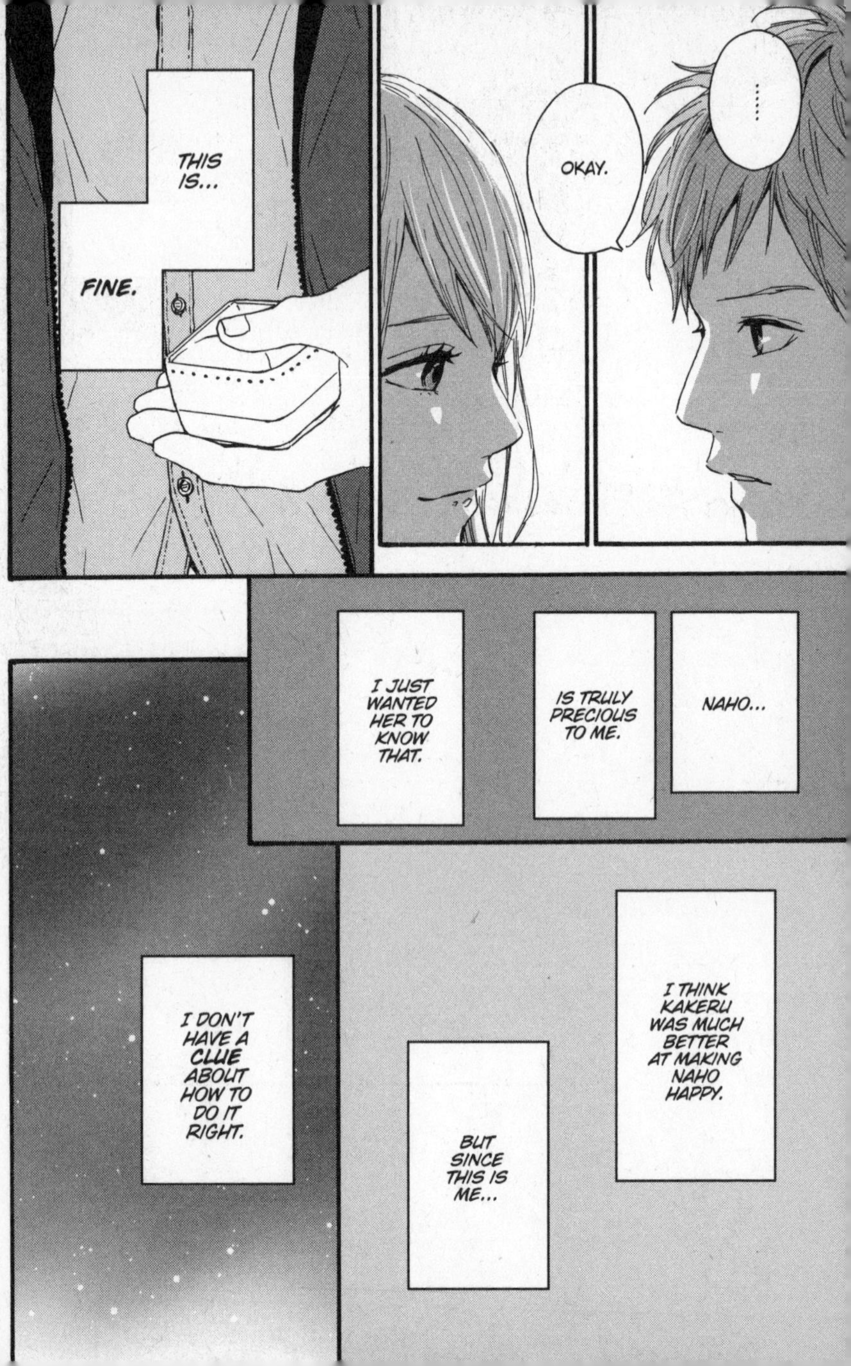
......
OKAY.
THIS IS...
FINE.
NAHO...
IS TRULY PRECIOUS TO ME.
I JUST WANTED HER TO KNOW THAT.
I THINK KAKERU WAS MUCH BETTER AT MAKING NAHO HAPPY.
BUT SINCE THIS IS ME...
I DON'T HAVE A CLUE ABOUT HOW TO DO IT RIGHT.

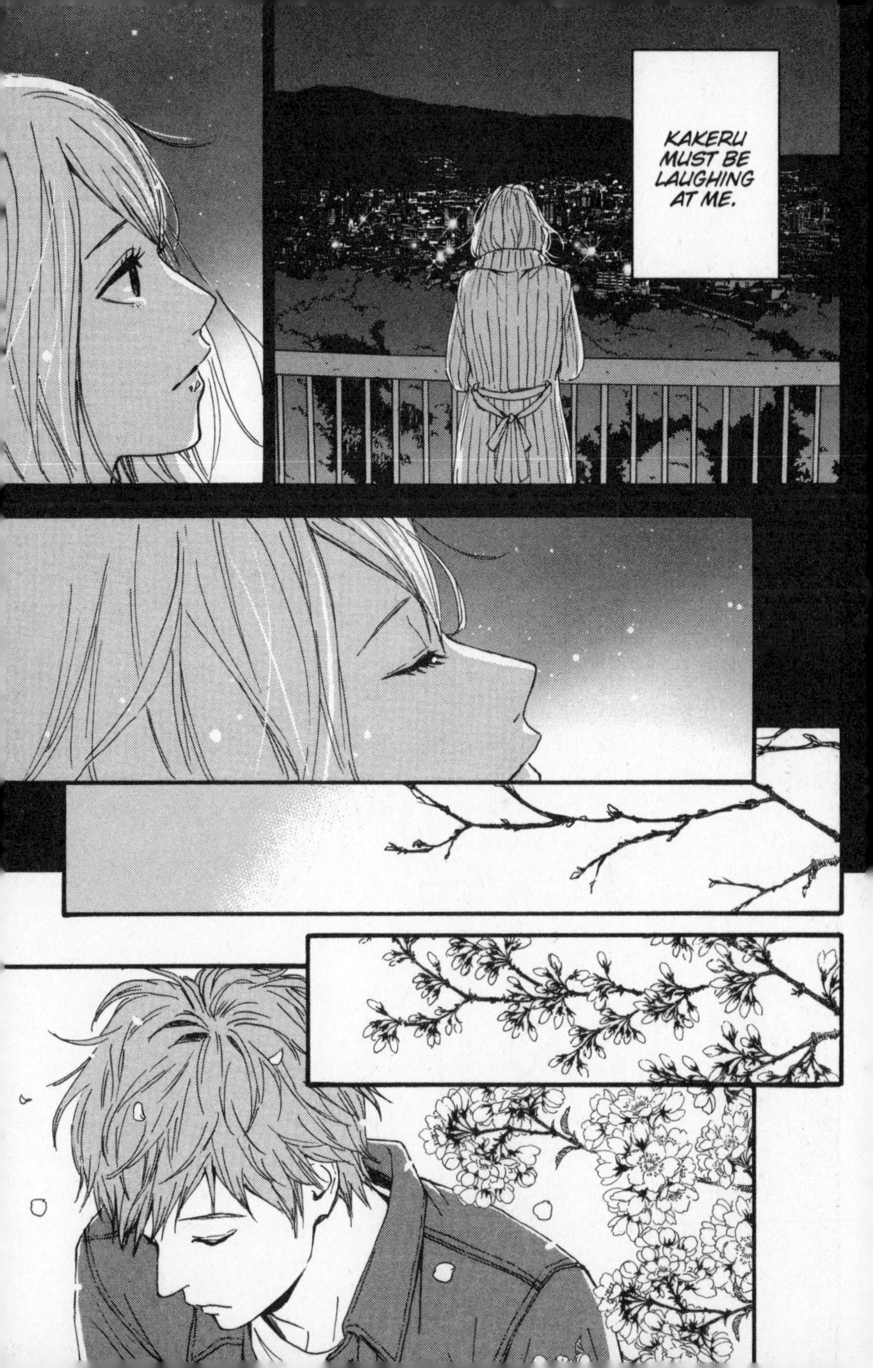
KAKERU MUST BE LAUGHING AT ME.

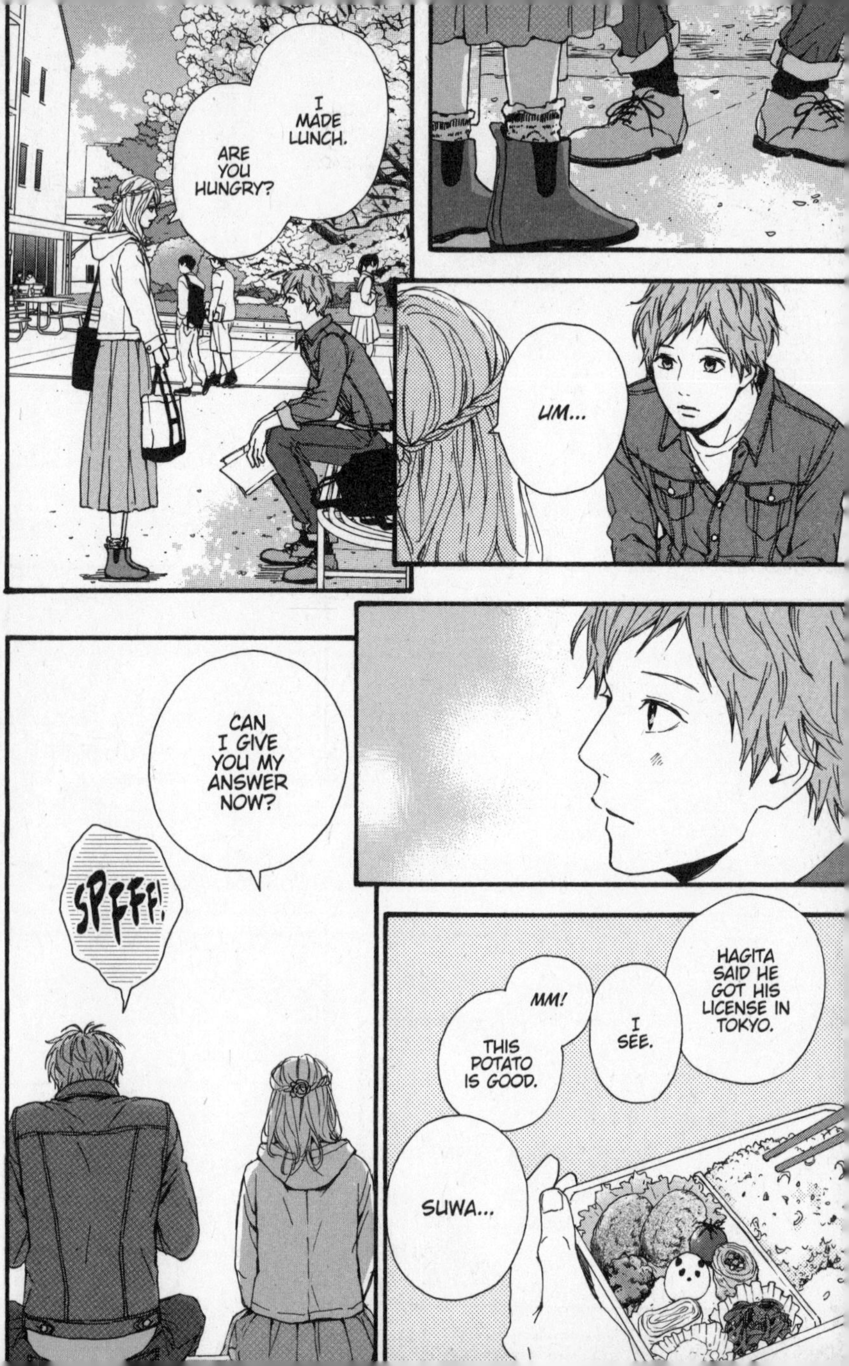
I MADE LUNCH.
ARE YOU HUNGRY?
UM...
HAGITA SAID HE GOT HIS LICENSE IN TOKYO.
I SEE.
MM! THIS POTATO IS GOOD.
SUWA...
CAN I GIVE YOU MY ANSWER NOW?
SPFFF!

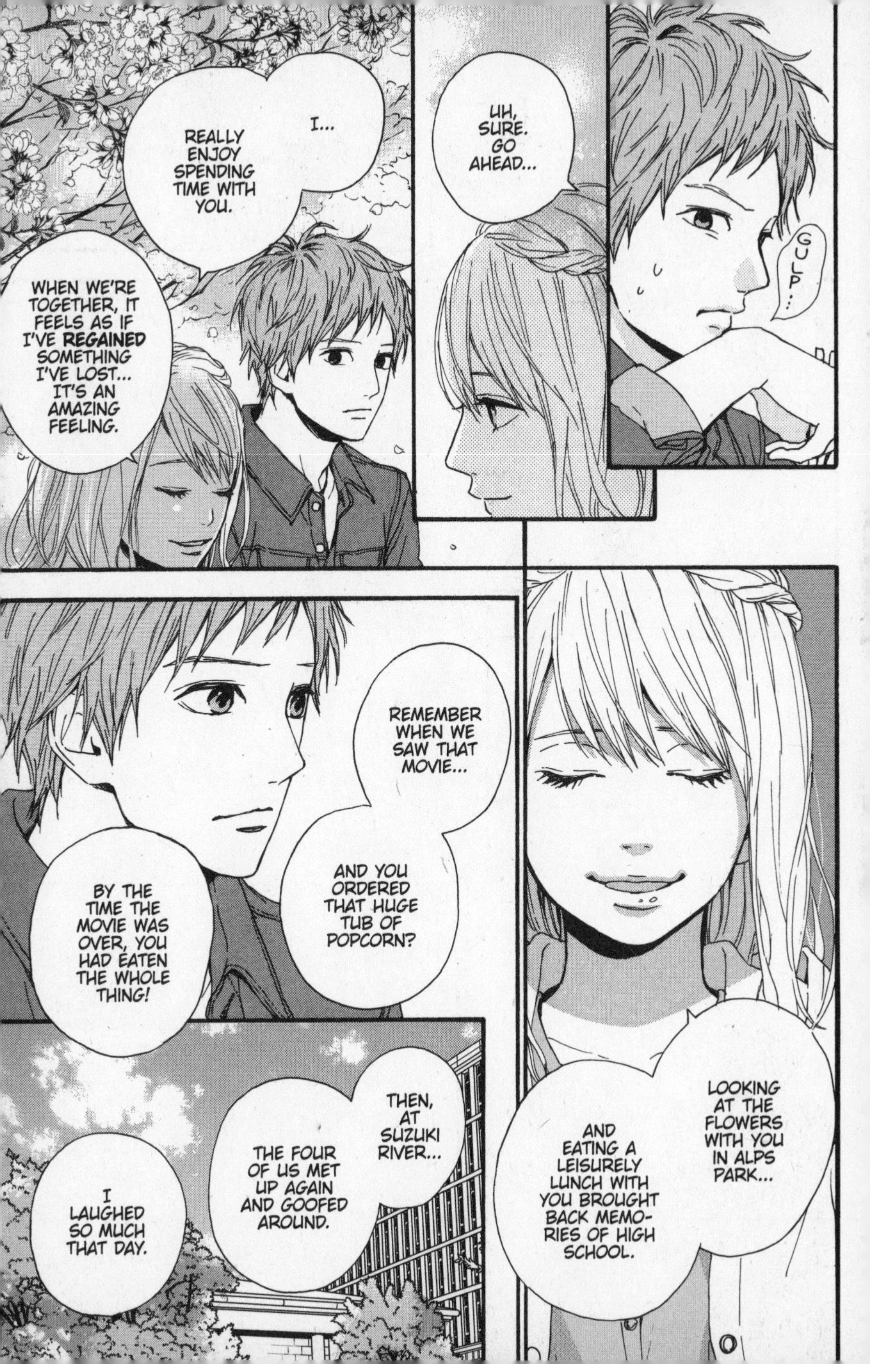
GULP...
UH, SURE. GO AHEAD...
I...
REALLY ENJOY SPENDING TIME WITH YOU.
WHEN WE'RE TOGETHER, IT FEELS AS IF I'VE **REGAINED** SOMETHING I'VE LOST... IT'S AN AMAZING FEELING.
LOOKING AT THE FLOWERS WITH YOU IN ALPS PARK...
AND EATING A LEISURELY LUNCH WITH YOU BROUGHT BACK MEMO-RIES OF HIGH SCHOOL.
REMEMBER WHEN WE SAW THAT MOVIE...
AND YOU ORDERED THAT HUGE TUB OF POPCORN?
BY THE TIME THE MOVIE WAS OVER, YOU HAD EATEN THE WHOLE THING!
THEN, AT SUZUKI RIVER...
THE FOUR OF US MET UP AGAIN AND GOOFED AROUND.
I LAUGHED SO MUCH THAT DAY.

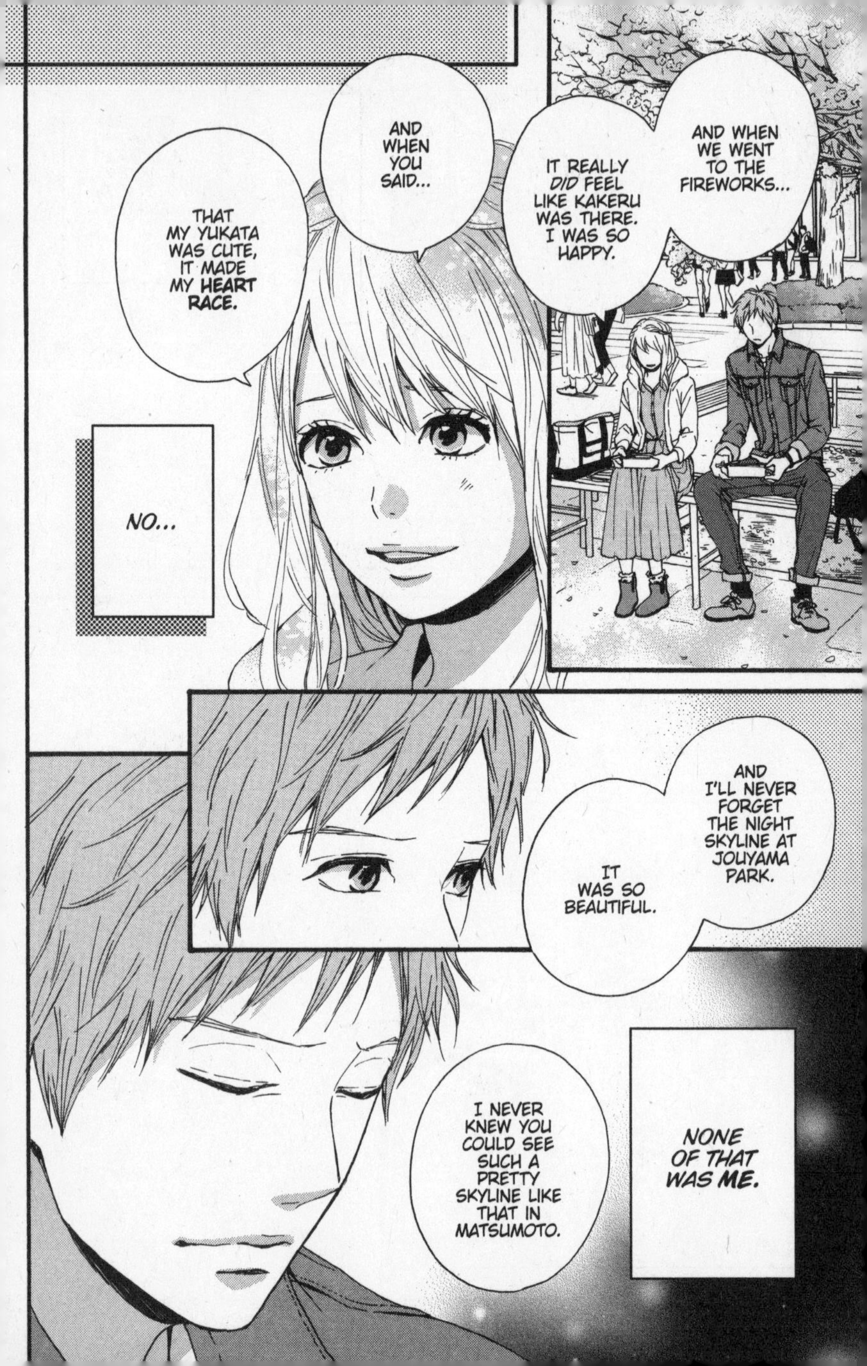
AND WHEN WE WENT TO THE FIREWORKS...
IT REALLY DID FEEL LIKE KAKERU WAS THERE. I WAS SO HAPPY.
AND WHEN YOU SAID...
THAT MY YUKATA WAS CUTE, IT MADE MY HEART RACE.
NO...
AND I'LL NEVER FORGET THE NIGHT SKYLINE AT JOUYAMA PARK.
IT WAS SO BEAUTIFUL.
I NEVER KNEW YOU COULD SEE SUCH A PRETTY SKYLINE LIKE THAT IN MATSUMOTO.
NONE OF THAT WAS ME.

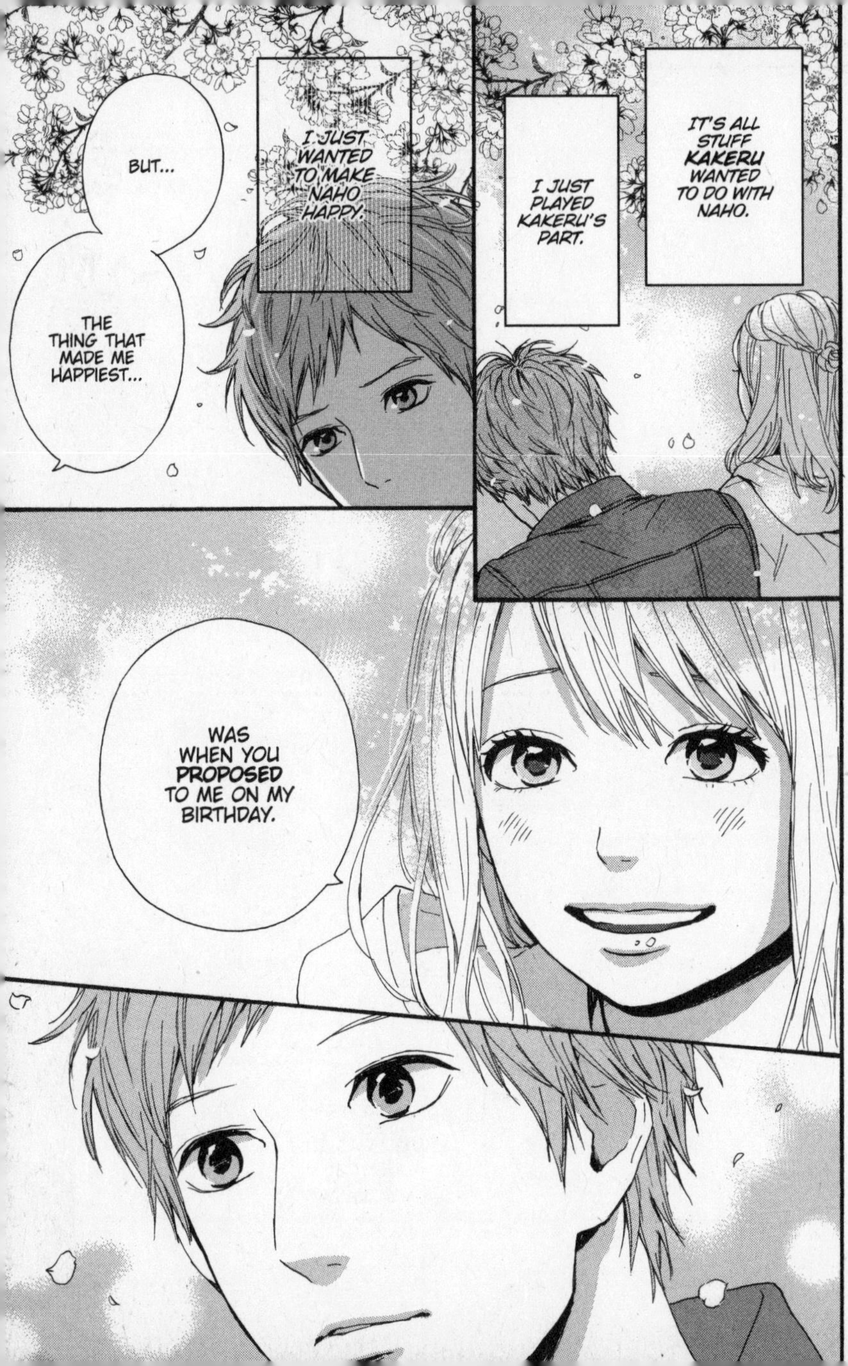
IT'S ALL STUFF KAKERU WANTED TO DO WITH NAHO.
I JUST PLAYED KAKERU'S PART.
I JUST WANTED TO MAKE NAHO HAPPY.
BUT...
THE THING THAT MADE ME HAPPIEST...
WAS WHEN YOU PROPOSED TO ME ON MY BIRTHDAY.

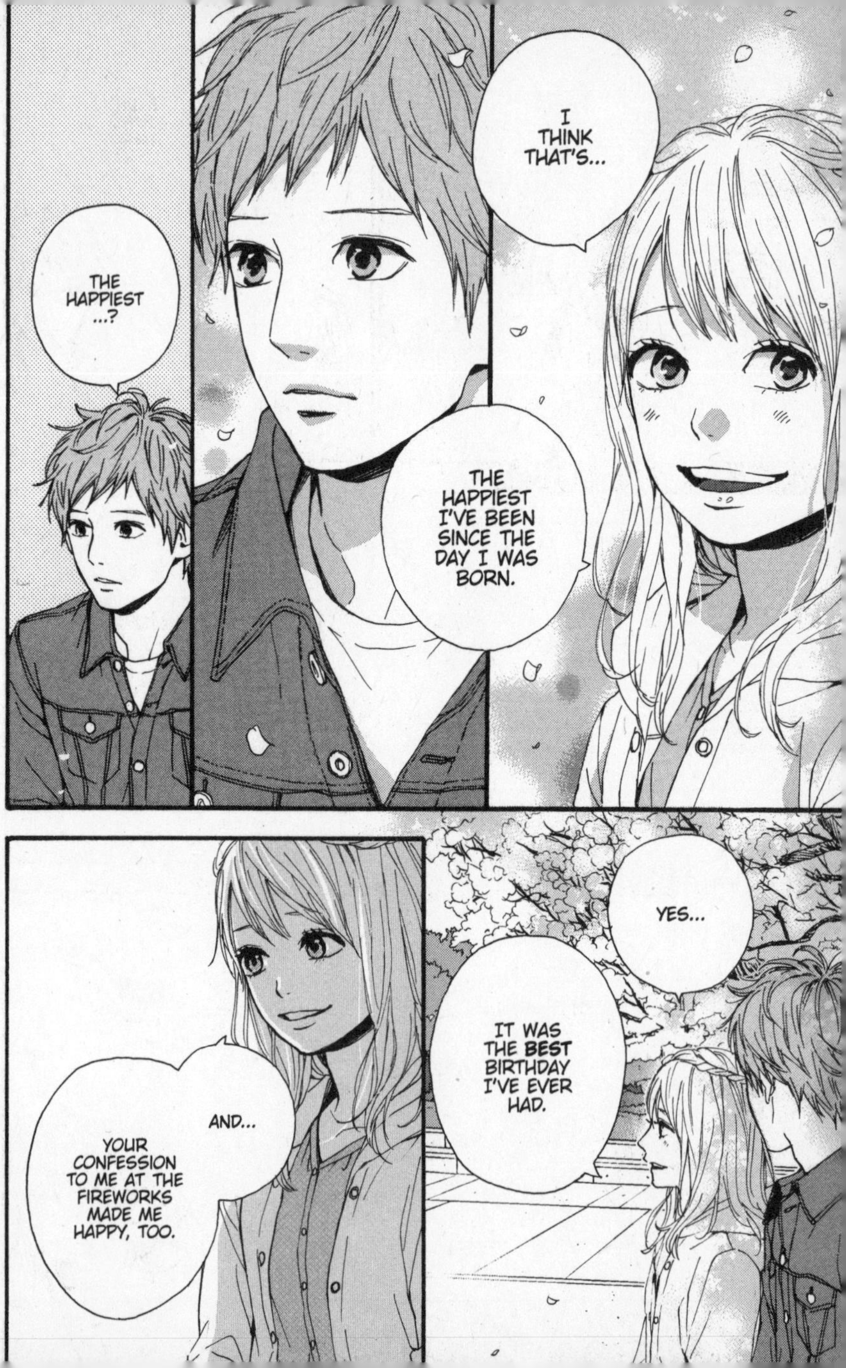
I THINK THAT'S...
THE HAPPIEST I'VE BEEN SINCE THE DAY I WAS BORN.
THE HAPPIEST ...?
YES...
IT WAS THE BEST BIRTHDAY I'VE EVER HAD.
AND...
YOUR CONFESSION TO ME AT THE FIREWORKS MADE ME HAPPY, TOO.

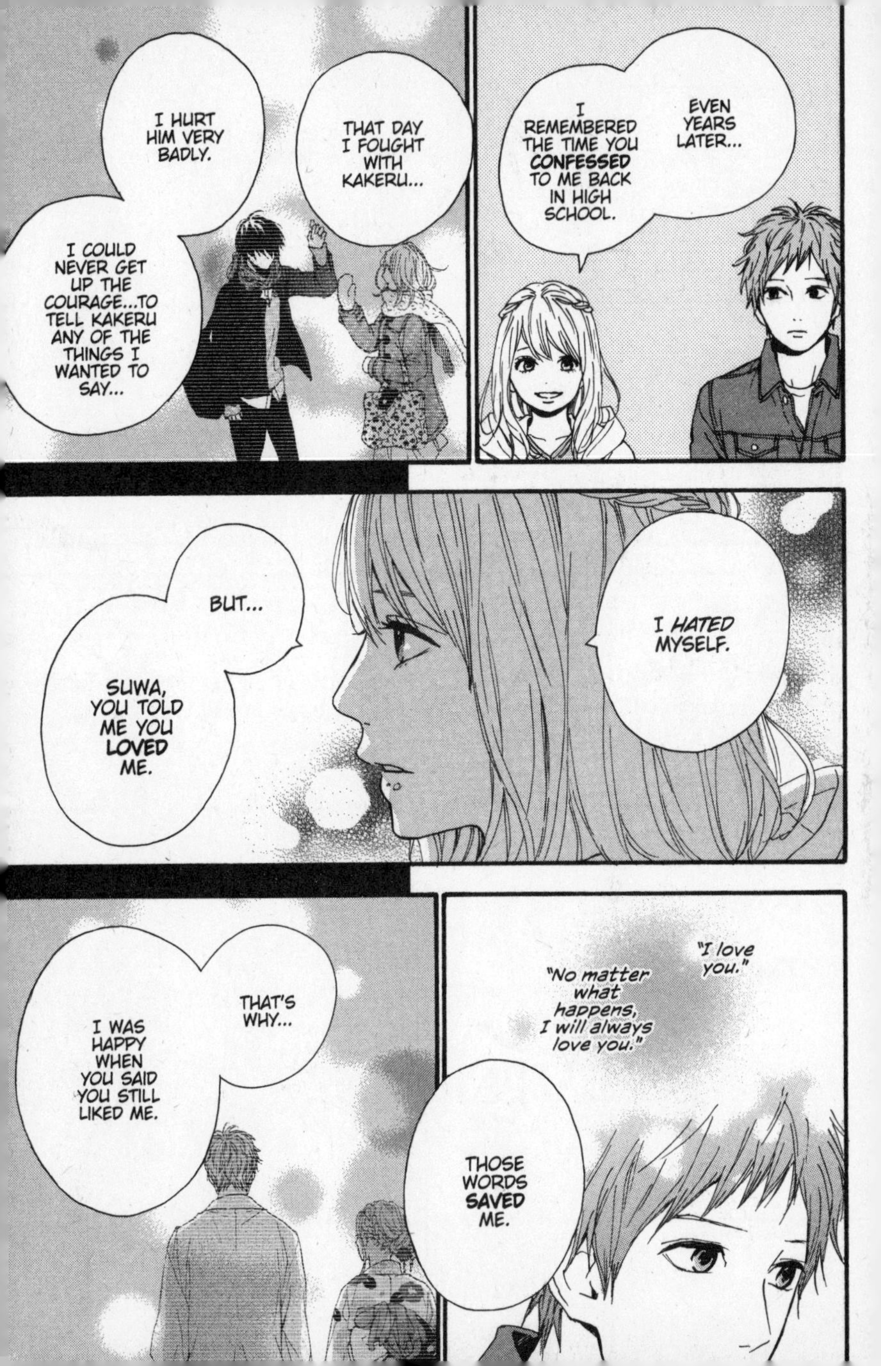
EVEN YEARS LATER...
I REMEMBERED THE TIME YOU CONFESSED TO ME BACK IN HIGH SCHOOL.
THAT DAY I FOUGHT WITH KAKERU...
I HURT HIM VERY BADLY.
I COULD NEVER GET UP THE COURAGE...TO TELL KAKERU ANY OF THE THINGS I WANTED TO SAY...
I HATED MYSELF.
BUT...
SUWA, YOU TOLD ME YOU LOVED ME.
"I love you."
"No matter what happens, I will always love you."
THOSE WORDS SAVED ME.
THAT'S WHY...
I WAS HAPPY WHEN YOU SAID YOU STILL LIKED ME.

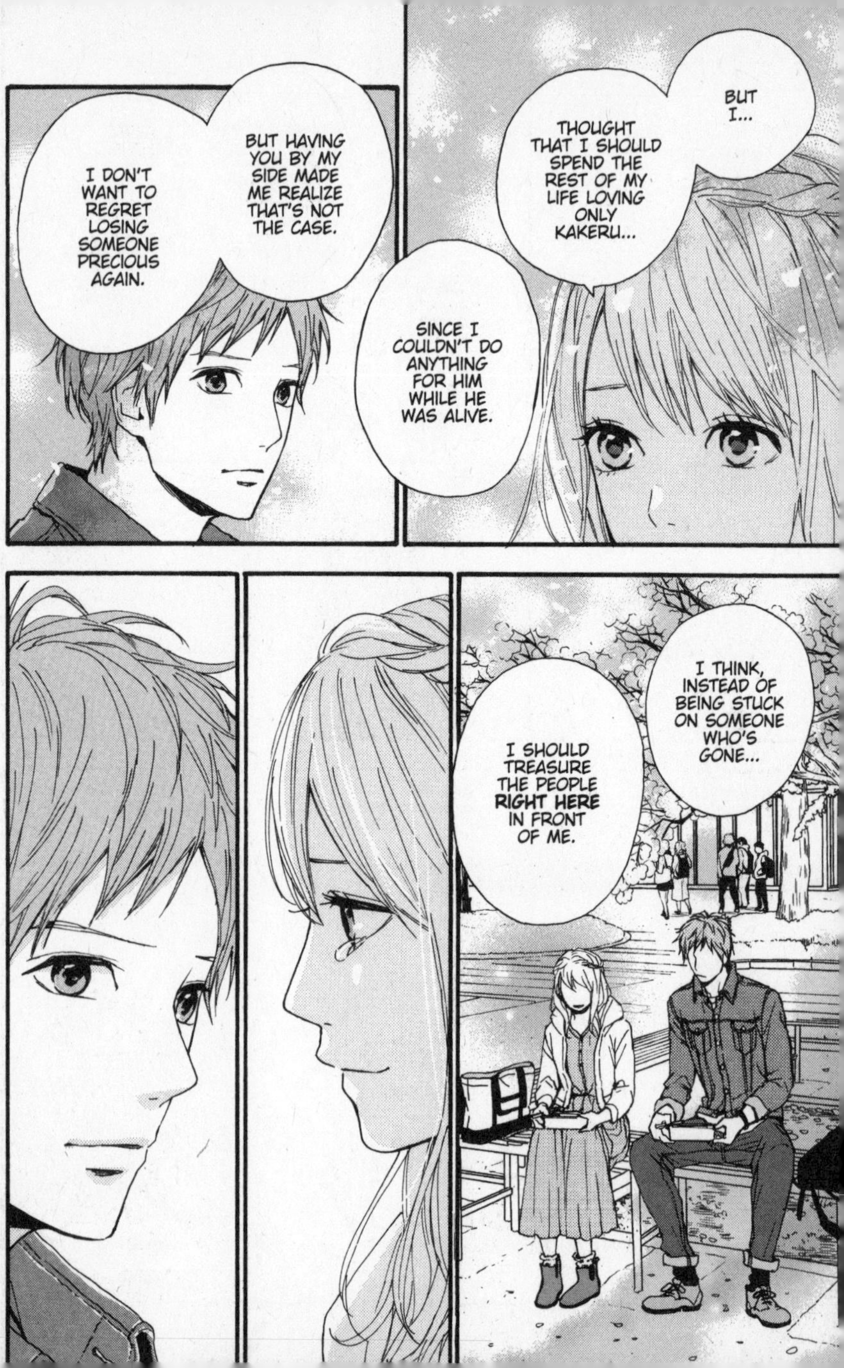
BUT I...
THOUGHT THAT I SHOULD SPEND THE REST OF MY LIFE LOVING ONLY KAKERU...
SINCE I COULDN'T DO ANYTHING FOR HIM WHILE HE WAS ALIVE.
BUT HAVING YOU BY MY SIDE MADE ME REALIZE THAT'S NOT THE CASE.
I DON'T WANT TO REGRET LOSING SOMEONE PRECIOUS AGAIN.
I THINK, INSTEAD OF BEING STUCK ON SOMEONE WHO'S GONE...
I SHOULD TREASURE THE PEOPLE RIGHT HERE IN FRONT OF ME.

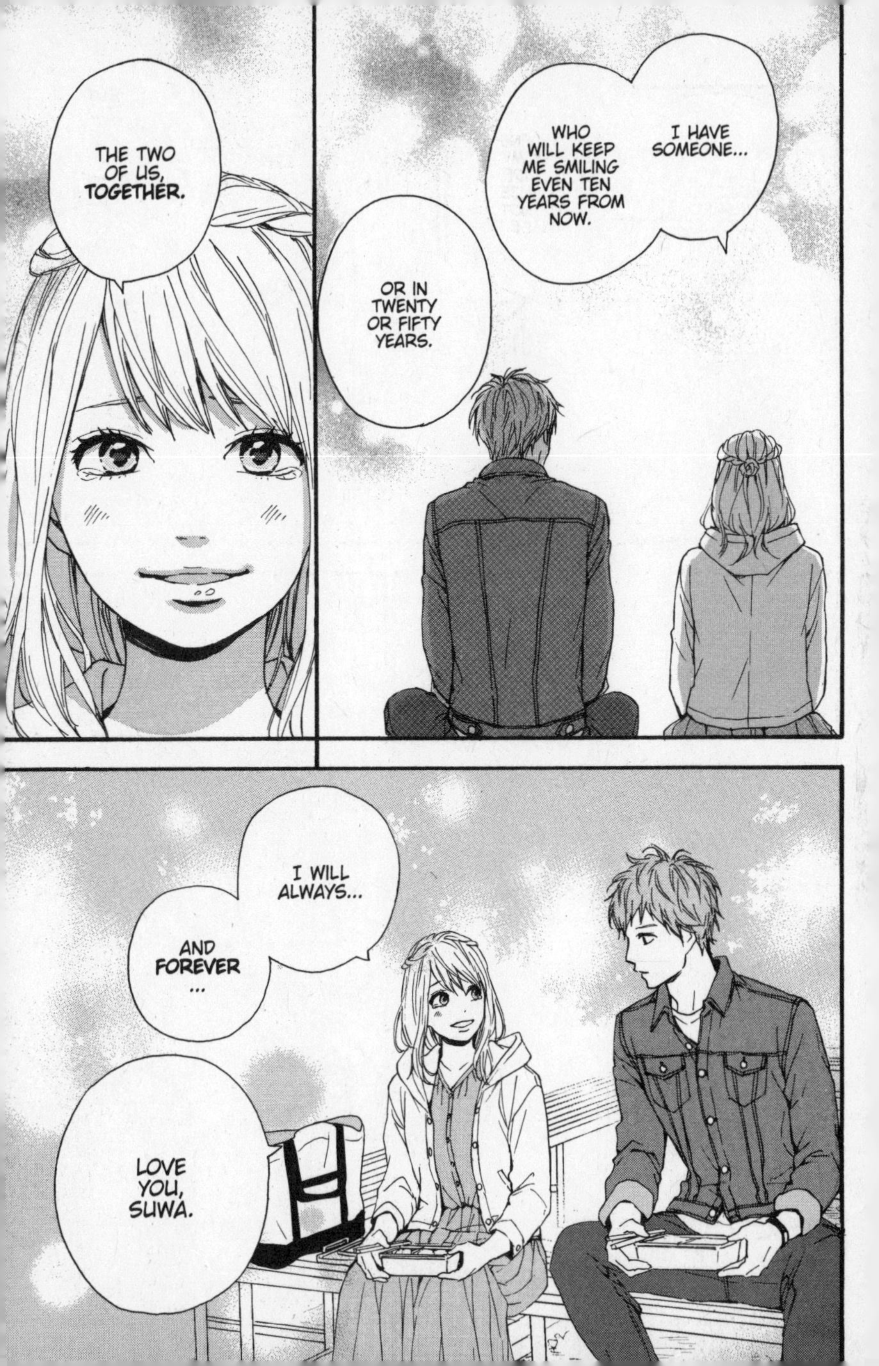
I HAVE SOMEONE...
WHO WILL KEEP ME SMILING EVEN TEN YEARS FROM NOW.
OR IN TWENTY OR FIFTY YEARS.
THE TWO OF US, TOGETHER.
I WILL ALWAYS...
AND FOREVER ...
LOVE YOU, SUWA.

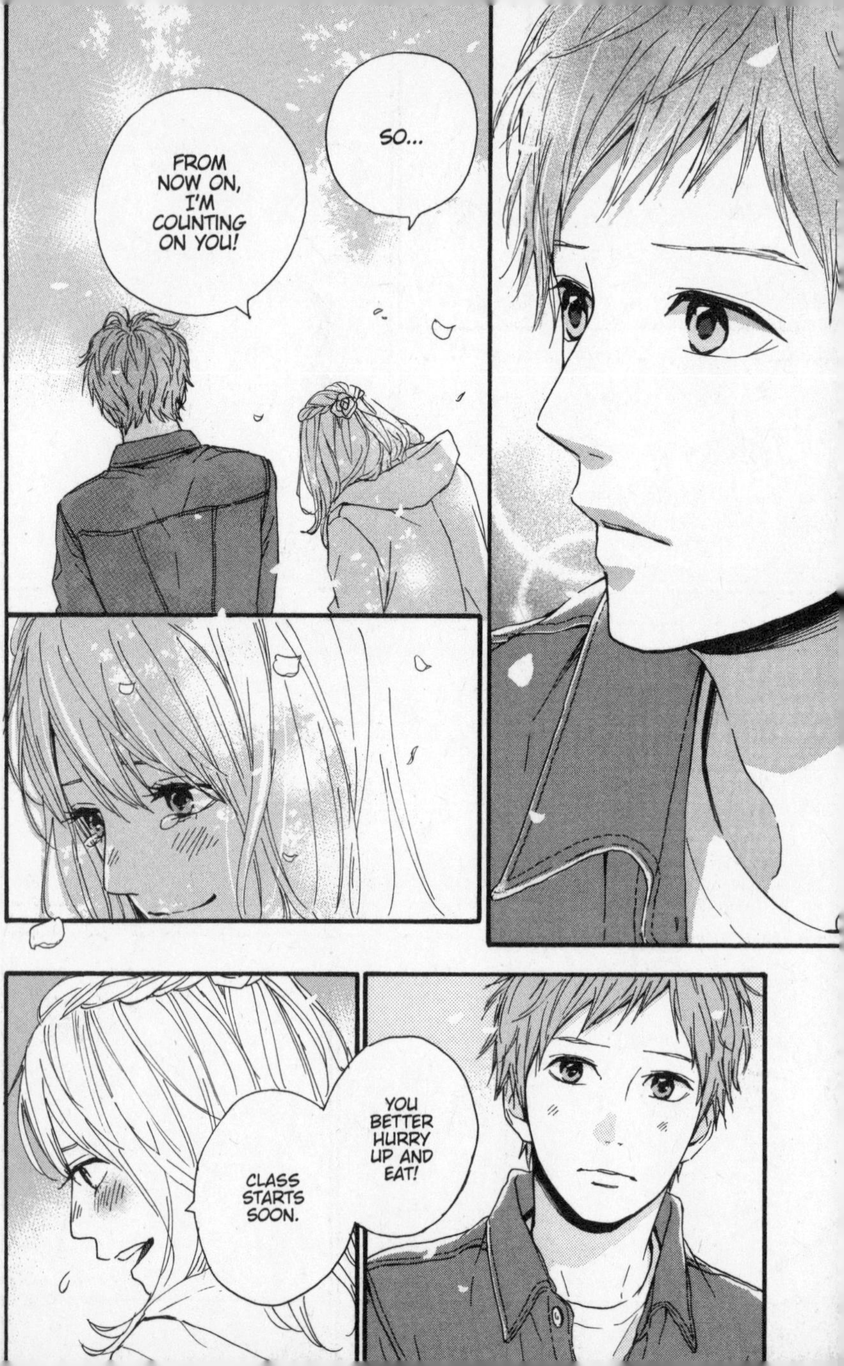
SO...
FROM NOW ON, I'M COUNTING ON YOU!
YOU BETTER HURRY UP AND EAT!
CLASS STARTS SOON.

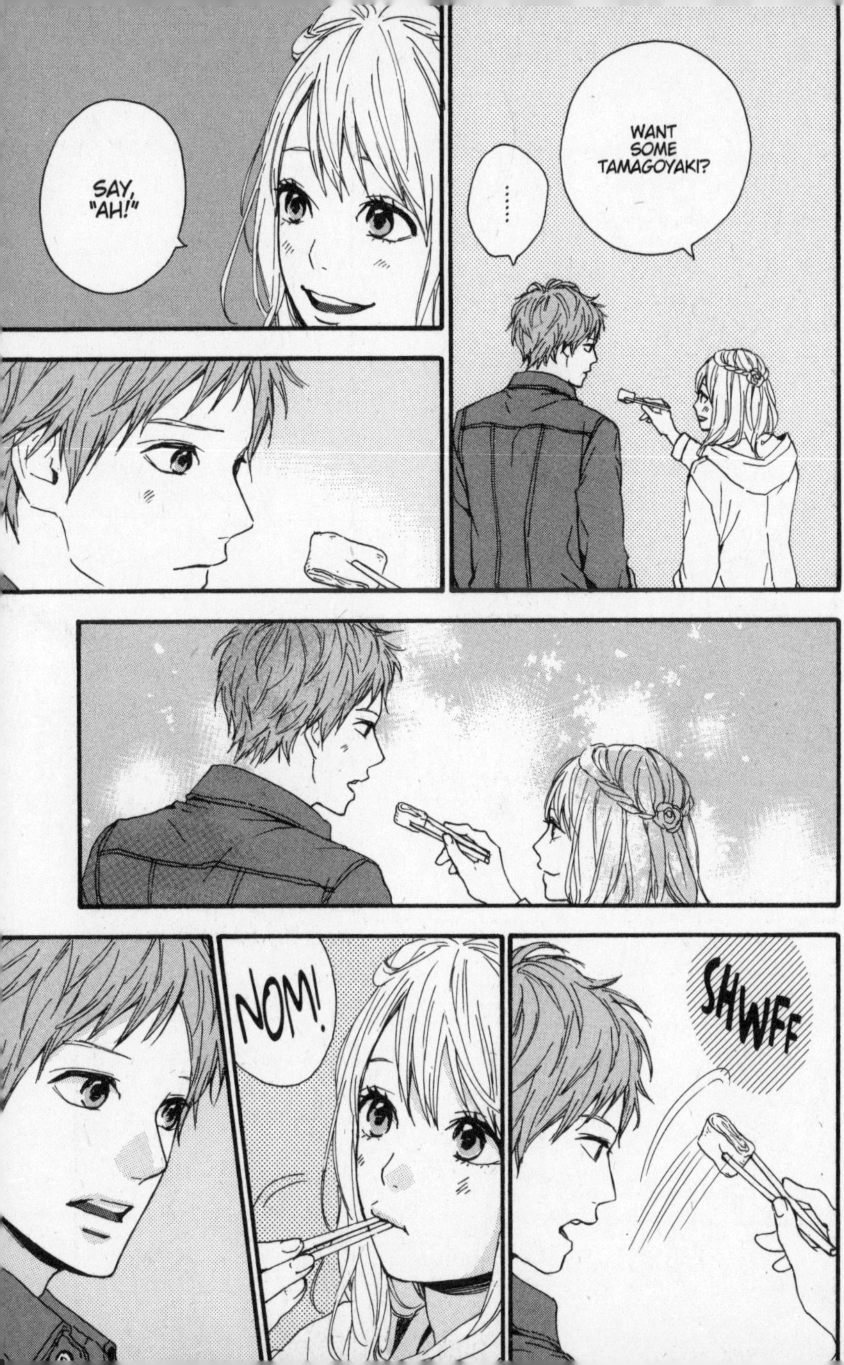
WANT SOME TAMAGOYAKI?
......
SAY, "AH!"
SHWFF
NOM!

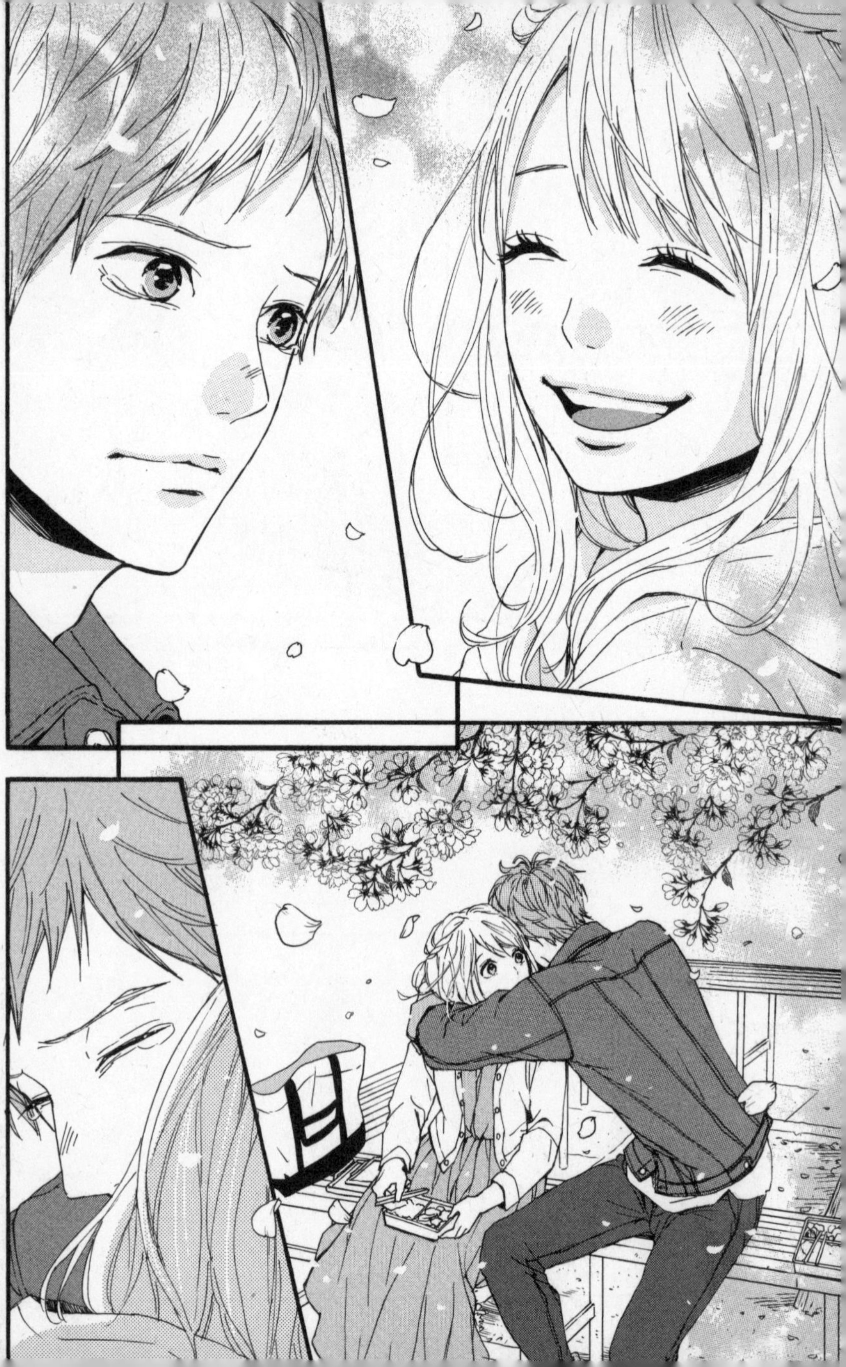

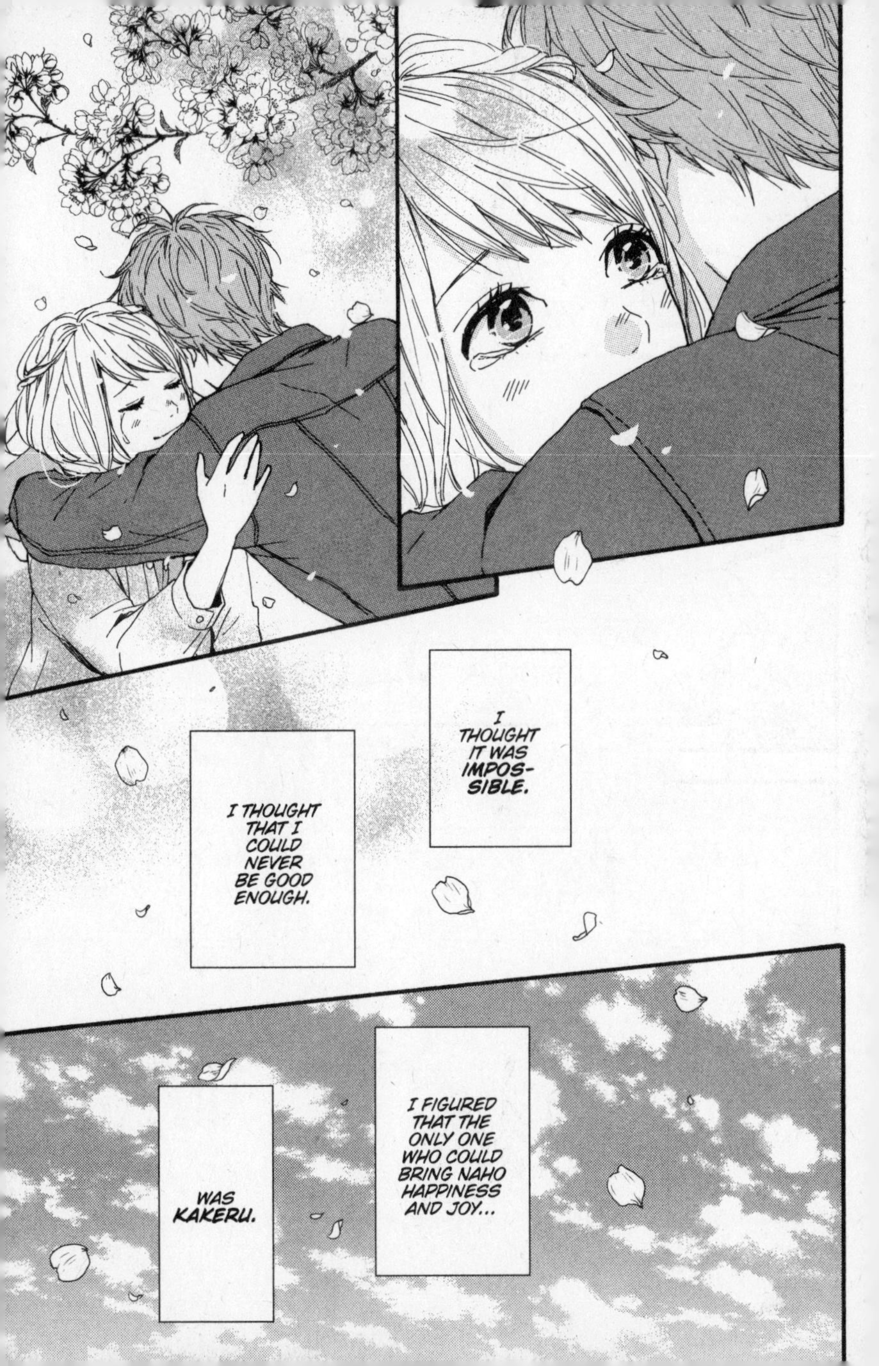
I THOUGHT IT WAS IMPOSSIBLE.
I THOUGHT THAT I COULD NEVER BE GOOD ENOUGH.
I FIGURED THAT THE ONLY ONE WHO COULD BRING NAHO HAPPINESS AND JOY...
WAS KAKERU.

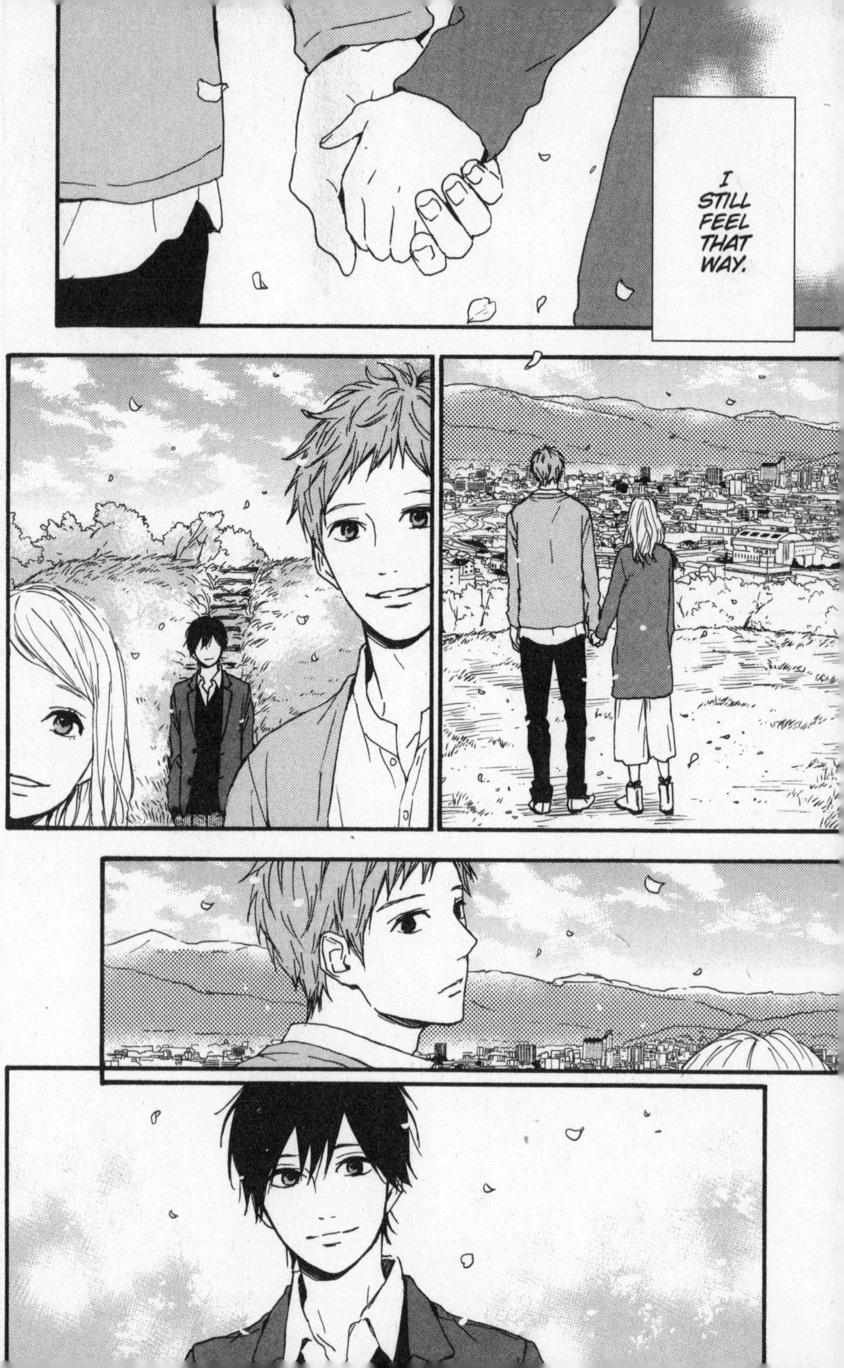
I STILL FEEL THAT WAY.

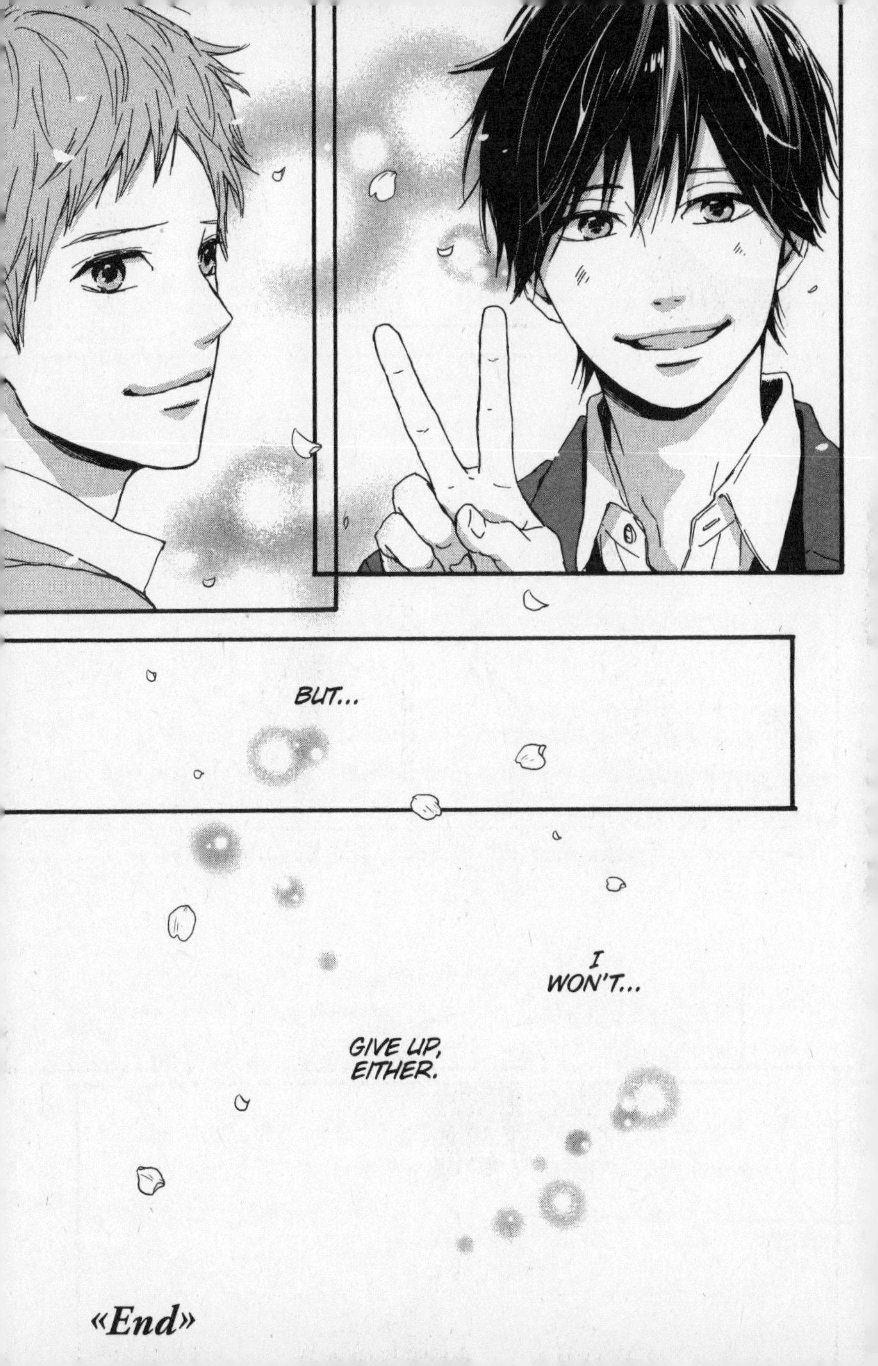
BUT...
I WON'T...
GIVE UP, EITHER.
«End»

To everyone who has picked up volume 6...

Hello, Takano here!

It's been a while. How are you?

I'm so happy that we could meet once more, now that you've picked up Volume 6, which follows the conclusion of Volume 5.

The "future" in the title orange -future- comes from the song "Mirai" (future) that the band Kobukuro wrote for the live-action film. Listening to the song "Mirai," I thought about trying to write a story with Suwa as the protagonist. orange -future- originally appeared as a sequel anime theatrical film to the orange anime adaptation, but back when the first chapter of orange was being serialized, this was the story I originally envisioned as the final chapter.

After everyone saved Kakeru from the accident (and his suicide), I didn't feel like showing that the future had just suddenly changed.

"If someone has been hurt, I want to pick up the pieces and help them."

I wanted to use this work to express that just a few words and sentiments such as this won't suddenly make someone okay. Mending a deeply broken heart takes time.

I wanted to put some time between the conclusion of the series and when I would draw a special chapter showing what happened ten years in the future.

(I was tempted to actually wait ten years...)

Changing the protagonist from Naho to Suwa meant that I could now draw the future I had been imagining.

I think many people have probably asked, "What am I living for?"

I think maybe hearing people express their gratitude helps you appreciate your own existence and worth. No matter what, if you pick up something someone dropped and return it to them, or return something they lost, they'll say, "Thank you."

When people express their gratitude, they may want to say, "You being here saved me," but saying something like that is difficult. But I think that "Thank you" shares a similar meaning.

"Thank you" = "Because you were here, I was saved."

So whenever someone says, "Thank you," please interpret the meaning in this way.

And, if someone does help you, please say, "Thank you." No matter what it was, those helpers in this world are precious, indeed.

I am grateful for everyone I have met through orange.

Thank you very much.

Ichigo Takano

Let's meet again in Volume 7!　高野苺

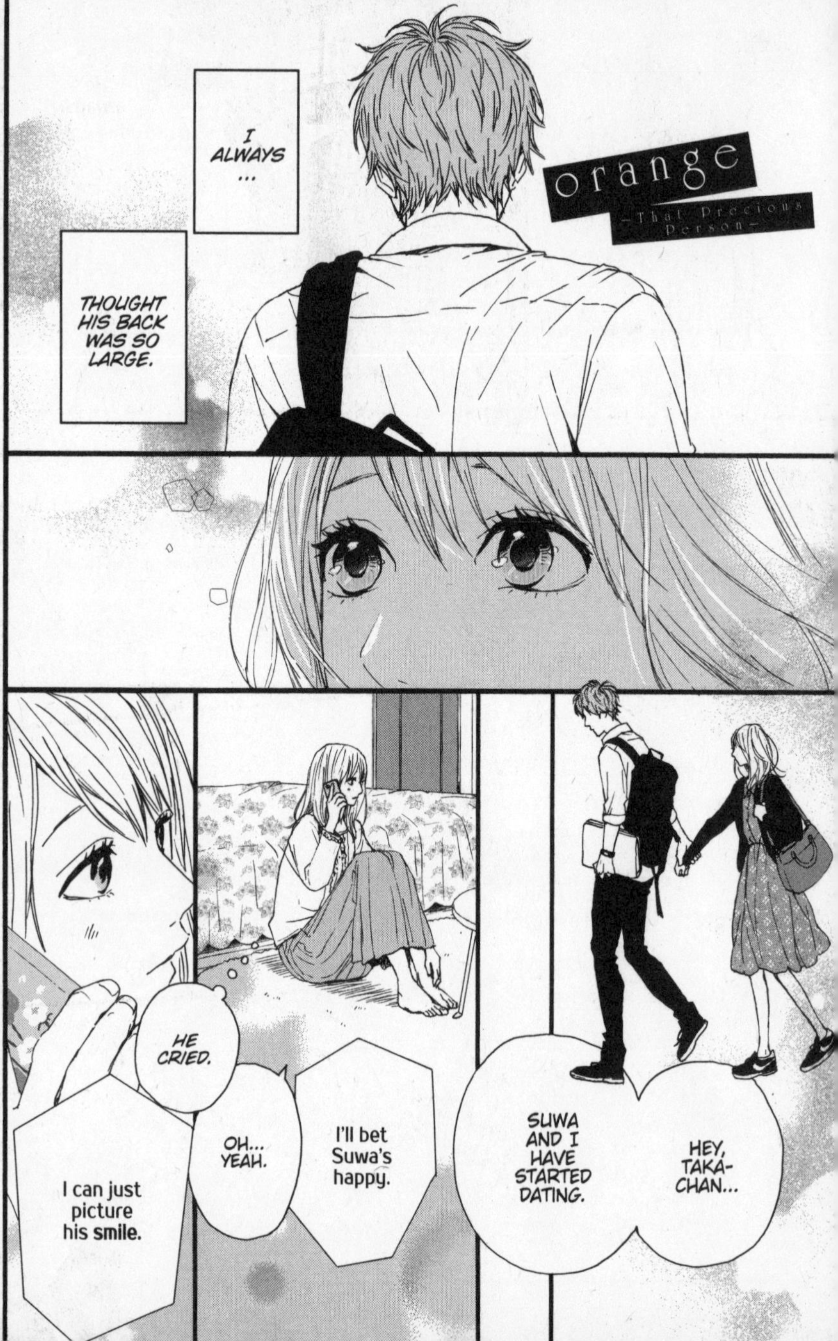
orange
-That Precious Person-
I ALWAYS ...
THOUGHT HIS BACK WAS SO LARGE.
HEY, TAKA-CHAN...
SUWA AND I HAVE STARTED DATING.
I'll bet Suwa's happy.
OH... YEAH.
HE CRIED.
I can just picture his smile.